A SAILOR ON THE SEAS OF FOREVER

A hole opened up in the middle of the room, floating about four feet in the air. A cloaked figure stepped through the hole into the suite.

Shifter looked up into black orbs with no pupils, and for a minute he thought that what towered over him was some new hunter employed by the Darkling.

Then it came to him who it was who had rescued him from the collapsing lair of the Roschach.

The Boatman. The angel of death. The Flying Dutchman.

The end of the world was at hand . . .

Again.

* * *

"Reminiscent of Roger Zelazny's and Tim Powers's best work. . . . Delivers enough excitement for any reader."
—Michael A. Stackpole, author of Once a Hero

"A haunting nightmare. . . . An edge-of-your-seat race against evil across multiple Earths. Nobody writes better contemporary fantasy than Richard A. Knaak, and DUTCHMAN is his best book yet."
**—Robert J. Sawyer, author of
The Terminal Experiment**

"A fascinating glimpse at a world very much like ours, but one even more dangerous and mysterious."
—John Stith, author of Redshift Rendezvous

RICHARD A. KNAAK

DUTCHMAN

ASPECT®

WARNER BOOKS

A Time Warner Company

WARNER BOOKS EDITION

Copyright © 1996 by Richard A. Knaak
All rights reserved.

Aspect® is a registered trademark of Warner Books, Inc.

Cover design by Don Puckey
Cover illustration by Keith Birdsong

Warner Books, Inc.
1271 Avenue of the Americas
New York, NY 10020

Visit our web site at
http://pathfinder.com/twep

Ⓦ A Time Warner Company

Printed in the United States of America

First Printing: August, 1996

10 9 8 7 6 5 4 3 2

DUTCHMAN

1. ABOARD THE *DESPAIR*

He could almost hear the waves lapping against the sides of the ship. The sound was an illusion, but whether the product of his mind or some trick of the vessel itself, he could not say. It was long past the time when he could fully trust his own senses.

Ahead lay a great expanse of nothing. It was much like the nothing that lurked behind them . . . or below them . . . or above them. Only a few lost fragments of matter, rare sights, gave the ship anything to pinpoint on . . . as if there were a reason to bother pinpointing on anything in this place.

The floorboards of the deck creaked with age. He could only guess at how long the vessel had been sailing. The vast, ghostly three-master that he had dubbed *Despair* had been riding the unseen waves of this prison, this emptiness, in one form or another for far longer than he had been captain.

The vines and moss she wore like a shroud remained unchanged, even though countless generations of the plants should have grown and shriveled to dust. The wooden planks that made up her long, brown body should have rotted long before. However, like all else involving the ominous vessel, the creaking planks and the ageless vines were nothing more than dressing. They only hinted at, not revealed, the truth.

Oh, he knew that her appearance was due strictly to his own mind, that she had worn another shape when first he had been cast aboard her, but the sense of age was very real no matter what her form. Perhaps she had even been here since the Beginning, reshaping herself to the thoughts of other prisoners like him. Perhaps she would still be here even in the End.

He was very afraid that he would be here then, too. If there had been others before him, they had found an escape, something that seemed would elude him forever. Likely, the thing that carried him through the nothingness would evermore wear its present form and he would be its captain.

The sails strained as if a fearsome wind filled them, but in truth there was not even a breeze. Another illusion. Sometimes he imagined that the entire ship and perhaps this entire hell was an illusion of his creation. Unfortunately, he knew very well that his prison was all too real.

His eyes drifted to the empty crow's nest. Like most of the vessel, it was empty. He was a captain without a crew. After a few blinks, he shifted his gaze to the wheel, where his sole companion turned it this way and that despite the fact that the ship alone determined their course.

He was noticed. "Orders, captain?"

The voice was perfect, a true seaman's voice. Philo cocked his head and met his captain's gaze with one eye. He had the head of a parrot, but this caused him no discomfort. Philo was as good and able a first mate as any captain could have wanted, even if he was merely an animatron, a thing of metal and gears found on one long-dead world.

He was perhaps the only reason why even a shadow of Dutchman's sanity remained.

Even after all this time, Dutchman wondered what the animatron saw when he looked at him. Did Philo see the tall, gaunt figure, pale and clean-shaven, with a visage best described as weathered? Did he see the loose gray and black hair seeking to escape the broad-rimmed hat or the gray cloak covering the equally gray clothing underneath? Most important, Dutchman wondered if the artificial orbs of his first mate noted what little life remained within the physical shell or how haunted the black, pupilless eyes of the captain were. Did he see that the weathered skin was but a mask covering an emptiness even wider than the nothingness through which the *Despair* sailed?

The parrot continued to await orders. Dutchman shook his head, not wanting to go through the pretense of changing course. The ship would go where it wanted, regardless of his desires. Sometimes he gave orders simply to have something to do. There was so little to occupy himself with. He had little paper and so kept a personal log in his head. The diary, however, was worthwhile only on those rare occasions when he landed. After all, what could he say about this place that he had not said a thousand times before?

Dutchman thought briefly about going below, but found little reason for doing so. He could not sleep, only rest. He did not eat—not here, anyway. The only thing he could do was drink . . . and he had nothing worth drinking. There was a barrel of water, an ever-overflowing barrel, down in the hold. Dutchman hated the barrel, feeling somehow that its offer of plenty was a mockery to his existence. He wanted just one bottle of something stronger, something that would allow him to forget, for even a moment, why he was here.

It was impossible to forget, though. The voices would never let him. They were a constant reminder of what he had done and would do again. A cold fear stirred in his heart. He tried to bury the memories, but that too was impossible. He could not forget that he had murdered a thousand worlds.

The ship creaked and the billowing sails shifted form, a sure sign that they were altering course. Lines changed and the rudder moved of its own accord. Dutchman, his heart suddenly racing, glanced at his first mate, who shrugged as well as any living creature could have. There was nothing they could do. After all this time . . . if time had any definition here . . . the captain knew what was coming next. It was always the same.

"Something bad coming," Philo called. He was programmed to respond to situations in a variety of ways, a result of Dutchman's work, but he seemed, at some point, to have developed a sense of understatement. This made him almost human in the eyes of his captain.

At first the sounds came as buzzing. Like a million million insects swarming the deck, they surrounded him. Sheer reflex made him strike out even though he knew he could neither touch nor silence the voices. The buzzes quickly became whispers, incomprehensible at first, but growing more understandable with each breath he took. There were so many voices. He sometimes believed he was hearing all the people who had ever been or ever would be.

Sooner than he would have desired, Dutchman could understand every word, even though they all spoke at once. He could hear every one of them, speaking of both the trivial and the vital. It brought what he considered selfish tears to his eyes. He was surrounded by the lives of billions and yet could not touch or talk to them.

Some were simply the trivial complaints of trivial minds: Marissa said to me that *those* people had moved in down the street! Well, let me tell you that I want none of them by my . . ."

Some were pleasant reminders of the potential of life: "And with these words, the poet Michael Hawthorne, in his love for his children, spoke of our own love . . ."

There were far too many of them that were cold or dark or lustful for power, no matter what the cost: "Would rather see a radioactive wasteland than let one of those bastards push me around while I'm in office . . ."

"We've taken the native situation well in hand. The colonial government is setting up work camps in the frontier, where a final solution will be determined. . . ."

The vast majority, however, were merely slices of existence, slices that he envied, for they had something he could never have again.

Language did not matter; he understood all of them equally. It was hard, however, to concentrate on just one, especially when he wanted to listen closely. It would have been easier to hold back the tide on some jagged, stormy seashore.

Philo spoke out, shattering the spell of the voices. "Storm approaching, captain! Dead ahead!"

Dutchman's gaze snapped forward and his eyes fixed on a monstrosity that had not been there before, a monstrosity that filled him with fear each time it burst into existence.

"*The Maelstrom . . .*" he whispered. Each time he prayed never to see it again, always knowing that his prayers would be for naught.

It was little more than a speck in the distance at first, but it grew rapidly, becoming as large as a fist before another breath could escape Dutchman's chest. He did not need to see it clearly to know exactly what it looked like; it was impossible to forget such infernal majesty. The Maelstrom was Order and Chaos incarnate, a swirling mass in which the *Despair* could be engulfed as easily as the captain himself might swallow a single drop of water. The endless sailing was nothing compared to the agony of falling into the Maelstrom. He would survive, as he had each time before, but the cost was great. Worse, each time it happened, Dutchman found himself thrust into a place that was and was not his home.

Each time, he landed in a new version of his world, a world in a universe about to die.

As the panic and denial swelled within him, the *Despair* steered slowly toward the center of the widening maw, giving no doubt as to *her* intentions. Although it would tear her up as harshly as it did him, the ship would sail into and through the Maelstrom. She would sail Dutchman, Philo, and herself into the realms of madness and pain, places where the voices would seem a respite.

Now a true wind blew, a wind seeking to thrust them even sooner into the gaping crimson and black chasm fast approaching. Pushed forward, Dutchman, clad in hip-high, heavy boots, stumbled to the rail. The deck beneath creaked almost painfully. The wind had a cold, bitter sting to it. He drew his cloak higher, nearly to the brim of his hat, leaving only a narrow slit to see through.

The sails whipped back and forth. Dutchman wondered if he should give some order, for form's sake, but the sailing skills he had once commanded, and they had been great, were long forgotten, faded from lack of use and need. He was a captain in name only.

The Maelstrom moved closer yet, filling almost the entire horizon. Matter within it spun around and around, churning in a sea of fire that fell ever toward the eye of the monstrosity. A few loose fragments flew past the ship, pulled toward the Maelstrom. For the first time, the *Despair* slowed, as if more reluctant now that the vast fury was so close. Yet the ship did not deviate from its set course.

Dutchman could only stand helpless. Behind him, he heard Philo's mechanical curse. More to escape looking at the horrific wonder than because he was actually curious, Dutchman turned.

The ship shuddered, as if striking a reef. Philo stared to the side with one eye, but remained at the wheel. Dutchman struggled across the deck to the starboard side and leaned over, fully aware of what he would see yet compelled to look nonetheless. It was as he had expected. A good portion of the hull had been crushed inward. Leaning farther over the rail and glancing forward, he saw the huge rock that had caused the damage already continuing on toward the Maelstrom, undeterred by the collision.

A groan from below made him look at the damaged section again. Boards slowly straightened, the splintered sections beginning to seal. He could almost feel the vessel's pain as it sought to mend itself. Dutchman never saw sense in the futile task. If the ship did not want to be damaged, it merely had to turn them away from the Maelstrom before the latter's pull became inescapable. Yet, it never did.

Another rock flew past, striking a glancing blow to the opposite rail. Bits of wood joined the missile on the journey into the storm. The *Despair* began to work on that damage in addition to the hole below. As it did, the vessel shuddered and picked up speed. The acceleration, though, was not the work of the ship itself. The Maelstrom had them now. Once that happened, there was never any hope of escape. Now it was simply a matter of waiting.

A red, stifling darkness abruptly enveloped the *Despair*. The red was the color of blood, something with which Dutchman was all too familiar. Over the span of his exile, he had committed the unpardonable act of cutting his throat and wrists hundreds of times, but each time he had looked on in defeat and horror as only a trickle of blood emerged from the deep cuts. His wounds had always sealed within the space of a few breaths, although the pain remained with him for some time.

He was not permitted to die. That would have been too kind.

Dutchman glared at the horror swallowing his ship, and despite everything, found the anger and bitterness to cry, *"I only wanted to give us a second Eden! I did not know!"*

The wind howled, growing so fierce that he was forced to find more secure footing. Dutchman thought of lashing himself to the main mast even though he knew that it would mean nothing. Once or twice, he had even thought of standing defiantly at the bow, facing down his vast, roaring nemesis, but he was no such hero. A fool, murderer, and madman, perhaps, but no hero. As another rock struck, this one crashing into the deck near Philo, who simply glanced at it and then returned to his task, Dutchman struggled back to the door leading to the cabins below. Within the belly of the ship, he would buy himself a little time and comfort . . . before the destruction.

He did not see the rock storm until the first two crashed into the ship, one falling through the deck just before him and the other shattering the rail and deck above, where Philo still stood. These were not bits of earthly refuse that had been floating in the emptiness; these were huge masses of primal matter that had been tossed about within the Maelstrom like leaves in a wind. Compared to the Maelstrom, they seemed no bigger than pebbles, but some of these pebbles were larger than the ship itself. The rock that had earlier struck the *Despair* paled in comparison to the monsters now assailing the vessel.

Dutchman swore. He knew from tragic experience what would happen if one of these larger rocks struck the *Despair*. The vessel would shatter like a child's toy made of twigs. The memories of past disasters were still clear, the agony still real. The ship would rebuild herself, true, but—

Another rock crashed into one of the masts, tearing away the top section. Two of the remaining sails were in tatters. The roar of the ever-hungry chasm filled his ears. The wind threatened to suck him off the deck and into the maw. Each step became more of a struggle to complete. Another missile tore past him.

Something caught his attention. Philo was shouting, but the pandemonium made it impossible to hear. The animatron pointed behind him.

Dutchman started to turn.

A tremendous weight crashed down on him, flinging him into unconsciousness.

When he woke not more than a few breaths later, it was to find himself trapped beneath a section of one of the masts. Dutchman tried to breathe, but each movement made his chest hurt. His right leg was twisted at an awkward angle and his left he could not even feel. One arm was definitely broken and the other was pinned underneath him.

Heavy boots trod hard on the rocking, unstable deck. A shadow tinged in crimson covered him. "Captain?"

Philo's beak pressed lightly against Dutchman's cheek as the first mate checked his condition. With one hand, he touched his captain's shoulder, then the broken mast. Dutchman tried to speak, but his jaw would not work properly. He wished that the main mast itself had fallen on him. Then, at least, he would have entered the center of the Maelstrom in blissful darkness.

"Captain, I—"

Philo was *torn* from the deck. He disappeared from his captain's limited view almost instantly.

Dutchman shifted his head as best he could. They were entering the heart of the Maelstrom, the very gullet of the beast. The *Despair* trembled as if in anticipation and fear. Planks from the deck were ripped away and sent hurtling into the maw. With great force, the Maelstrom rent the ship piece by mangled piece.

The mast on top of him shifted slowly, reluctant, it seemed, to add itself to the flying debris just yet. The shifting allowed him to turn a little bit more. The Maelstrom was everywhere. It was even more terrible . . . and yet beautiful . . . this close up. The *Despair* was but a mote in its eye.

The sails were gone now and the deck was clear of all but the heaviest and most secure pieces. Even that would not last. The ship never journeyed through intact. The storm continued to tug at the mast that pinned him down. It was only a matter of time before that went, and when it did, Dutchman would follow.

The *Despair* shrieked as more planks were torn from her. The shrieking brought back fully the reason for his being here. He could see the people and the places, all gone long ago. The people surrounded him, watching his suffering. It was what he deserved, for it was because of his dreams that they existed no more.

Another shifting of the mast dispersed the ghosts, if not his guilt. Then the heavy mast lifted. Dutchman felt the weight lessen . . . and then vanish as the debris that had pinned him down flew off.

In desperation, he tried to seize hold of the cracked and battered deck below him with his one good hand. The wood gave way, though, and Dutchman was plucked off the ship. He watched helplessly as the *Despair* dwindled in size. The forces surrounding him pummeled and pulled at his already battered body, quickly pushing him beyond his limits of pain.

The Maelstrom swallowed him and, moments later, what was left of the ship. Then the gigantic maw also vanished, leaving behind no trace of its passage . . . or the existence of its victim.

2. THE ROAD TO NOWHERE

This was the high school. This was where the one he sought should be.

Gilbrin pulled the beat-up, dark blue Dodge into one of the parking places reserved for visitors, although who besides an irate parent would actually want to visit a high school was beyond him. Still, *he* was here, so the spaces were, for once, serving their intended purpose. Gilbrin considered himself lucky that any of them was empty, considering how often he, as a high school student himself only a few years ago, had parked in similar spaces whenever necessary. Anything to get a close spot.

He stepped out of the car, a short, wiry man with an old-young face, perhaps in his early twenties, perhaps not. Gilbrin's features were pretty enough to draw the attentions of many a female: a strong chin, a nose short but carved well, brilliant green eyes, and sandy hair parted on the side. In front, a few locks hung over his forehead at an angle while in the back the hair flowed loosely for several inches below the collar of his gold and orange windbreaker. He was clean-shaven, although now and then he liked to sport a mustache.

To complete his appearance, Gilbrin wore a blinding purple T-shirt and blue jeans. The sneakers he wore were bright orange. Save when circumstances demanded it, Gilbrin did not like to go unnoticed by those around him.

Bartlett. Aurora. Dundee. Schaumburg. Just four of a multitude of suburban kingdoms that he had scoured in the last month. When he rushed off from the familiar climes of Champaign, Illinois, leaving behind at the university a nearly perfect grade-point average and three girlfriends, Gilbrin had taken with him a misguided faith in his own reputation . . . or rather, the one he had had back home. In the Beginning.

The Scatterings had been teaching him otherwise ever since then, but Gilbrin was ever a slow learner when it came to himself.

North and near Chicago, that was all he had known when first starting out. Only when he had reached the southern kingdoms, the southern suburbs, had he realized the magnitude of his search. This was the largest population center that he had seen in several dozen Scatterings. The suburban areas were hard enough to search, but there had also been the added problem that she might work in the city, unaware of the dangers in the shadows and beneath the streets.

His hands in the pockets of his windbreaker, Gilbrin followed some of the school's returning inmates. Lunchtime made for the best chance to mingle in and avoid at least a few questions. Giggles and glances surrounded him. He smiled at one pretty young thing, wondering how she would react if she knew how old he truly was. A moment later, Gilbrin frowned, wondering whether age really had any meaning where he was concerned.

The head of a great cat, the totem of this school, snarled at him from a wall near the admissions office. Breaking away from the gaggle of bodies flowing toward the lockers, he stumbled into the office with somewhat less dignity than even he, often the clown, cared to reveal.

Gilbrin dismissed from his attention the pimply male student assistant and concentrated on the two elder, female employees. They stared back, reminding him suddenly of his own dark days of incarceration at a similar establishment.

Perhaps finally recognizing that the somewhat outrageous figure was not a student, the one seated nearest to the counter took charge.

"Can I help you with something?"

Gilbrin, also known as the Shifter to some, smiled innocently at them. "I'm looking for Maia. Maia de Fortunato. She's a student here."

With a long look of suffering on her face, the woman slowly rose. Gilbrin marveled at her slothlike speed and dexterity, awed that anything other than governments could move with such a sense of inertia.

"She's probably in a class if she's not in her lunch hour. Are you a relative?" There was a hint of suspicion in her voice. These days, one could not be too careful.

"Cousin. I'm visiting the family." He stared at both women intently. "Something's come up with her father and I can't reach her mother."

Whether it was his words or his eyes that did it, his inquisitor accepted the response. She walked over to a huge filing cabinet and reached for a drawer. "Fortunato?"

"De Fortunato."

She had him spell it out just to make certain, then pulled open the drawer. Gilbrin watched her fingers scurry through the files, his pulse rate rapidly rising. Why could she not have used the computer terminal on her desk? Surely all such records were contained within. He needed to find Maia.

After so long, only to find that they had been so near to each other all the time . . .

"We have no one by that name."

"Hmm?" He blinked in genuine confusion.

"We have no de Fortunato. Nothing close."

His mind raced. The names they received at rebirth were more often than not the same or at least in some way similar to their own. There was no explanation why; it just was that way. "Could you try under *F*? Fortunato?"

Both employees looked at him. Gilbrin had vague thoughts

of putting an end to the charade, but knew the danger of abusing his power. The Darkling might be near.

With the visage of a martyr, the woman pushed the drawer closed, then opened another. She thumbed through several files. After a short search, she shook her head. "There's nothing under Fortunato."

Nothing? Gilbrin belatedly realized that his mouth was wide open. He shut it quickly. "Are you certain? Wouldn't be the first time she'd been misfiled."

He could see that they no longer believed him a relative. In another minute, they would call security or the police. Despite the ever-present danger of the Darkling, Gilbrin had to take direct control. The student aide was gone, a fortunate thing, which left only the two women.

The Shifter quickly made eye contact with both, catching them off-guard with his sudden stare. Both women twitched, but did not otherwise appear different.

Taking a deep breath, Gilbrin asked, "Any names close to the one I gave you? Look around. It might have been filed out of order."

Under his control, she moved with much greater speed. Her fingers paused on a file. "I have a Maria Fortune. A junior. Her file was in the wrong place."

Success! He breathed a sigh of relief. His contact with Maia had so far been a fragmentary thing, which meant that she had not yet reverted to herself. Her rebirth identity still held. It was fortunate that he had been able to track her down so well; she could be just down the hall even now, but only when a brief involuntary summons, the first sign of awakening, touched his mind had he ever sensed her. The last time that had happened was more than a week ago.

Thank the stars that she's not reincarnated in this counterpart's thirteenth-century Asia! He had not enjoyed his time in that period. Living on the steppes and picking fleas off his body was not his idea of a life . . . but then neither was fleeing one variant Earth for another with no end in sight.

"Where is she at this time?"

"Her lunch period just started."

The Shifter swore under his breath. That could put her in a number of places. He himself had rarely eaten in the school cafeteria. If she or one of the many male friends she no doubt had owned a car, she could be anywhere within twenty miles of here. "Do you have her locker number?"

A minute later, Gilbrin was wandering the halls of the high school again, marveling at the changes since his own four years of hell. Things could have been worse, though, even worse than Asia had been. Even high school was not *that* bad.

The two women would not alert anyone to his presence. They barely recalled him now. He felt only slight remorse. Gilbrin was on what he considered a life-and-death mission and anyone who made him risk discovery of his presence deserved a little pushing. Besides, nothing he had done would permanently affect them.

Using his power had eased some of the tension within him. He very much doubted that even the Darkling could sense such use. The Prince of Shadows usually caught those more extravagant in their utilization of what this variant Earth termed "sorcery." Most of those fools had been taken long ago. The Scattered Ones still remaining tended to be more cautious or cunning . . . or, it was true, simply lucky.

More confident, Gilbrin again drew upon his talents, laying about him a sense of belonging that would make the instructors, monitors, and students see him as just one more young learner.

His eyes shifted back and forth as he read off the locker numbers. The ones he sought, Gilbrin soon realized, would have to be down the hall to his left. He turned there, counted twelve lockers, and located the one with the number the woman in the office had given him. Maia's locker.

One long, tapering finger stroked the combination lock. Gilbrin opened the door. Compared to what power he had already used, this act was negligible. Besides, the Shifter wanted to see what was inside. It could be that this was not

Maia's locker. It could be that Maria Fortune was simply Maria Fortune.

The locker was nauseatingly normal for a high school girl of this decade . . . not to mention the past few, he supposed. Besides the books and papers crammed into the top, there were various sundries important to her day. Magazines, makeup, brushes, a mirror, food, bits of attractive but hardly proper functional clothing, and cigarettes. The last made him smirk. The Maia he knew had always avoided such minuscule vices with a passion.

The inside of the locker door was covered with cut-out pictures of the latest heartthrobs. Gilbrin chuckled, then grimaced when he saw that one of the pictures in the upper corner was a photograph. A leather-jacketed stud. Likely he had about half the normal brain capacity for a human, but his face was the sort that high school girls dreamed about. The Shifter recalled the type well; they tended to treat women like garbage behind their backs and made men like him the butt of their foul sense of humor. When Gilbrin had awakened to his true identity and the powers inherent, he had paid back each and every one of his persecutors.

He rubbed his hands together, anticipating with some amusement the incident to come. That this Maria Fortune might not be his Maia was no longer a consideration; he sensed her through her belongings. Now he only had to wait. Gilbrin closed the locker and positioned himself against a blank wall a little farther down the hallway. He had come this far; a little more waiting would not kill him.

An aeon had passed. Gilbrin the Shifter was certain it was so, despite the school clock visible down the hall saying that only fifteen minutes had come and gone. Where was she?

Then he sensed her draw near. A moment later, he heard a deep yet melodious female voice laughing at something. Even though it was somewhat different, the lilt and tone were hers. Some things were consistent.

Two teenagers, both taller and more physically mature than

the norm, made their way around the corner. Their upper torsos were tangled together in the throes of young love. Somehow they succeeded in passionately kissing each other while walking. The male was the young stallion in the photograph; Gilbrin acknowledged that much about him and nothing more. What was important was that the female half-buried in his chest could only be Maia.

As the twosome slowly made their way to her locker, the Shifter had time to observe her. Maria Fortune was Maia de Fortunato; it was impossible to deny that. Even as a teenager in this variant Earth, she was larger than life, a goddess among mortals. Almost eight inches taller than Gilbrin's pitiful five-foot-four-inch frame. For some reason, he had always been shortchanged in terms of height. Only once had he grown past five-foot-six and that by only an inch.

Her hair was raven black, full and long. Her eyes were still the same silvery blue, the only worthwhile gift she had received from her father. Her lips . . . wasted on her nameless paramour . . . were red and full and her skin was dark, the latter giving her a Spanish cast. As for her proportions . . . Gilbrin grinned, being only human, after all.

When it became clear that the two would be clenched together for some time to come, the shorter man sighed and decided that he could wait no longer. Gilbrin suspected that Maia would even thank him for interrupting this scene once her true self had completely emerged. He hoped so, anyway. As for her paramour, what he thought or did was of no interest to the Shifter. The lad was, after all, only a transient life, not one of the Scattered Ones.

He started to speak, then thought better of it. A trickster at heart, Gilbrin the Shifter could not pass up an opportunity so rich in entertainment.

Unseen, he waited until they were locked together once more. When their passion was at its peak, he reached out and gently touched her shoulder, whispering only, "Maia, sweet, time to come out."

Power coursed through his fingers and into her body.

Although her face was only a tangle of hair from his perspective, he knew that he had succeeded when every glorious muscle in her body tensed. The moment stood frozen in time. . . . Then, with tremendous strength, she pushed the unsuspecting boy against the lockers, cursing him in more than a dozen languages picked up over centuries. Understandably confused, the boy started babbling incomprehensibly.

His sense of humor satiated, the Shifter quickly seized control of the lad's mind and froze him where he stood, the pitiful look still plastered on his face. Of course, no one had come to see what was happening. Gilbrin had prepared for that situation in advance.

"Carim and Disis! This is the worst yet!" Maia's epithets continued. She noticed neither the odd condition of her youthful lover nor the indifference of the few students wandering the halls.

Gilbrin stepped over to her. "The worst you say, sweet? I thought you were really enjoying him. Thought perhaps you might regret me waking you during such a romantic moment."

"Gilbrin!" she cried in surprise and anger as she spun around to face him. "You damned prankster—"

"I take no blame for *this* jest. The cosmos deemed that you would grow up so. As for your choice of lovers, animal drives will tell, sweet."

Gazing down at her body and the garish clothing she wore, Maia muttered another curse. "We just—" Her eyes smoldered as her gaze turned on her former love, but there was no longer any fondness in them. "We just . . . during lunch . . . in that vehicle of his! That . . . *van!*"

"Yes, I understand girls go for that sort of thing. I had a van my last year of high school and for the first two years of college." He winked at her.

"I'll burn him!" She raised her hand, but the Shifter caught her wrist before she could do anything foolish.

"Where is the levelheaded Maia who has always sought to keep me from allowing my own passions to rule? You'll do no such thing! I have attracted my share of attention in seeking you out and we really should be going now."

"He . . ." She lowered her hand, but the anger was still there. "Filth!"

"Your drives are still your drives, Maia, sweet. Never forget that. If you'd truly been seventeen . . . your original self, that is . . . you'd probably have been satisfied with him . . . for a time," he finished quickly, seeing her anger turning back to him.

"I want to leave!"

Gilbrin nodded. "By all means. As soon as we make a few adjustments. Is there anything you wanted to keep from your locker? The magazine cut-outs or something?"

She ignored his jibe, again staring resentfully at the mortal boy. Resentfully . . . but perhaps just a little wistfully, too. Gilbrin pretended not to notice. Maia could not help reliving her memories of this most recent birth . . . the good memories as well as the bad. He recalled a few himself, like the parents and sister he dared never see again. It should have been easy after so many times, but it never was. How many loved ones and friends had each of the Scattered Ones left behind? How many had he personally abandoned? More than he wanted to count.

"It's done," he whispered with some regret a moment later. Wiping away the past was never easy even when it belonged to someone else.

Maia finally met his eyes, silently thanking him for doing it for her. "The locker?"

"Empty. Broken lock that will take some time fixing. No clues left behind. Your records have been eliminated already and no one will recall my coming here. We need to stop by your home, though, and remove any clues from your room."

"It seems useless. We can't make everybody forget we exist."

He put a hand to her cheek, seeking to comfort her. "It buys us some time, Maia. That's all we can ever hope for, especially if the Darkling's dogs come a-hunting. Before long, maybe two or three days at most, you'll look like your true self . . . and no one will ever find Maria Fortune." His hand shifted to her arm. "Time to go, sweet. If I stay in one place too long, I get the itchy feeling that the Prince of Shadows is staring at my backside."

Mention of the Darkling set her into motion. Although she obviously had questions, Maia evidently knew that it would be better to wait until her companion said they were safe. The two started down the hall, the Shifter leading. Maia, however, glanced back at the locker that was no longer hers. The boy was gone. "What about Derek?"

"Derek?"

"My . . . *him.*"

"I've steered his thoughts toward another girl I found floating in the back of his mind," he responded with a grin. "Cherie something. If not for you, they'd be the item, as these mortals say."

"Good." However, her tone hinted at some resentment.

The duo made their way through the school, students and teachers ignoring them completely. Within minutes, they were in the parking lot, heading for Gilbrin's Dodge.

"Gods above and below, Gil! What's this?"

"A '73 Dodge. Get in! It won't bite and I had it fumigated just for you."

She obeyed without another word, which disappointed the Shifter, who always enjoyed making her react. "Where are we going?"

The smile returned to his youthful face. "After your parents' house? I've already dealt with my familial situation, so we don't have to go there."

"So where are we going . . . afterward?"

"I've no idea." Getting inside, he started up his beloved old horse. Oddly, whenever he was of the proper age and in this century, he always seemed to pick up an old Dodge from around the same year as this one. Tastes remained consistent.

"Then what . . . ?"

"We drive. Far away. Hope that the Darkling's got his eye

on someone else." Gilbrin took a deep breath and added, "He found MacPhee last time, by the way."

"MacPhee." Her beautiful face paled. MacPhee was one of *their* group, one of the ones hoping to make some sense of the Scatterings and find a way to take care of the dangerous leech in their midst . . . the Darkling. MacPhee had been close, or so he claimed, to finding a way to end their flight. That had been two literal lifetimes ago. "He never made it to this variant, then."

"The Prince of Shadows must've caught him just before that Earth perished. I've tried to sense him since I grew back into myself nearly two years ago. When I couldn't find him either here or in the past, I decided to wait until you made yourself visible, sweet."

MacPhee was dead. Of all of them, he had understood the most. He had discovered some of the reasons for their ability to leap from one Earth to the next, ever keeping just ahead of the destruction close behind them. Something within, some inner clock, sent their . . . souls, for lack of a better word . . . fleeing on to the successor world. However, the Scattered Ones, as they had begun calling themselves after the first few times, were spread not only across distances, but time as well. It was never the same era twice. Yet, many of them still maintained a strange sort of contact with one another regardless of the centuries separating them. If she concentrated on one of the others, Maia knew that she would locate that one even if he or she had been reborn a thousand years before. Contact between two refugees centuries apart was not very constant, however. The strain was too great for most of the Scattered Ones.

MacPhee had learned so much and now he was dead.

While Maia dwelled on the death of MacPhee, Gilbrin quickly pulled out. He wanted to finish with her present family and be far away from this area by nightfall.

The itchy feeling had already returned. If the Darkling or his dogs were not near already, they soon would be.

*   *   *

"Southwest would probably be best," Gilbrin commented, smiling at his rhyme. It was the little things in life that gave him pleasure . . . and the big things in life, like the Darkling, for instance, that kept trying to kill him.

They had been driving for more than two hours, moving generally west along one of the lesser highways. More and more the landscape consisted of trees and farmland. To Maia, born this time to a crowded suburban area, these lands seemed uncivilized. An odd notion, considering that at different times she had been reborn into medieval squalor, primitive bush, and expansive oriental splendor.

No one she had met in this variant would have recognized her now save the other Scattered Ones. Gilbrin had suggested that she choose to be ten years older than her seventeen years. Under his guidance, Maia had relearned her powers enough to age herself. Now she was even more striking, her features enhanced by a decade of maturity. She had also come to grips with her conflicting memories, although there would always be those that could not be erased. Her latest family would remain with her forever, at least in her thoughts.

They, in turn, would think of her only as someone who went away a year or so ago and never contacted them again. Maia had made certain that they knew she cared for them, but that was the extent of it. She had refused the Shifter's suggestion that a complete wipe of their memories was called for. The ebony-tressed woman knew that Gilbrin preferred a clean wipe mostly because he hated leaving anyone to grieve for him. That was not Maia's way, however. She wanted them to recall her, if only vaguely. That way, she would still be with them until either they passed away or the End came for this variant.

They had not spoken much since leaving her parents' home. Maia stared at the traffic, most of her thoughts turned inward. A red sports car being towed to a service station caught her eye; she belatedly realized it was the same model she had only recently begged her present parents to help her buy. A few more months and they would probably have given in. She had been lucky this time, having been born into a well-to-do household.

She had been especially lucky to have had a different father. That was one of the few benefits of her existence, in her opinion. *And where are you, August de Fortunato? Why couldn't the Darkling take you?*

Maia's mother had never jumped with the rest, but her father had. Each time she prayed that her father would not make it to the next variant Earth, but each time the bastard did. She cursed under her breath.

Hearing her, Gilbrin glanced at Maia, then smiled ruefully. Too soon to expect much from her. She was still adjusting.

The highway would eventually take them to one leading south. Gilbrin had chosen the route in the hope that the Darkling, if he was near, would concentrate on the major roadways such as 94 west, leading to Milwaukee, or 57 south, which would lead back to the University of Illinois. The going was a little slower on their present road, but not enough to matter.

He did not know if the Prince of Shadows was even aware of them, but it was better to assume that he was at least nearby. The Darkling was an unpredictable soul, if *soul* could be used in reference to him. It might be that he would even ignore their presence; not always did the Prince take those he discovered. Some he hunted down, others he merely acknowledged. It was almost as if he made the decision based on the flip of a coin.

The Shifter had no intention of being nearby if the wrong side of the coin came up for him.

The sun was shining. Spring was the Shifter's favorite time of year, a time when things grew and romance was in the air. He took his eyes from the highway just long enough to admire his companion. In the Beginning, before the first of the Scatterings, he and she had been lovers. Both of them had had many lovers since then, although there remained a special bond of friendship between them. However, permanent relationships between their kind were as dead as the Earth from which they had come. How could one have a permanent relationship when any moment might see them thrown centuries apart on yet another version of their world?

With endless road before them, Gilbrin allowed his thoughts to wander further . . . to the time when he and a few thousand others had found themselves ripped from the paradise they had created with their powers and suddenly reborn on an Earth that was similar but not quite their home. A duplicate world, a younger Earth. Slowly, they had managed to garner their resources even though they were spread across time as well as space. The new universe into which they had been literally reborn forced them to relive childhood; they did not even remember who they were until they were nearly two decades old. Only then did they become themselves, sloughing off the false identities.

Not all had made that crossing-over and a few were lost each time they had to do it again. None of them knew why they had survived, much less what had caused the catastrophe in the first place. They knew only that something had caused their world to die, but had spared some of them, at the same time giving those survivors an ability that they would only later come to appreciate. After the first leap, the refugees had assumed that they would live their lives out in their new world and that would be that.

They could not have been more wrong.

The force that had destroyed their home had followed them into their new world. What it was, they did not know. They knew only that suddenly they were painfully flung once more through time and existence into yet a second new universe. The second Scattering had pared their numbers down a fraction, possibly leaving some of them to share the fate of the last variant's inhabitants, but that terrible discovery paled with the coming of a new horror.

The Darkling Prince.

Gilbrin blinked, his attention suddenly returning to his driving. Best not to think of the Darkling any more than necessary, he belatedly realized. No one could say for certain whether thinking of him would attract his attention. The full abilities of the Prince of Shadows were a mystery that none of the Scattered Ones was eager to learn firsthand.

They passed another service station where some unfortunate's red sports car waited to be detached from a tow truck. The Shifter patted the door of his old Dodge, recalling simpler times. It had served him faithfully since he had bought it and he had come to think of it as a favored steed, not an overexpensive pile of junk like the sports car. *Some people must have their toys,* he thought wryly, *even if it means paying and paying.* Granted, his car had been enhanced by his powers—

"Gil?"

Suddenly, the Shifter's world seemed to brighten. "Yes, sweet?"

Maia had been half-asleep, but now she stirred. "Why southwest?"

"Why not?"

She gave him a foul look. "Despite your jests, despite your garish clothing, little man, I know you plan things better than you let on. Why southwest?"

He hesitated, not because he did not trust her, but because he was still uncertain of the validity of his reasoning. Still, if he could not tell Maia, whom could he tell?

"A thought occurred to me prior to our last exile, a thought about our friend and those he did not touch."

She leaned toward him. "What about those he didn't touch?"

"Most of the lucky ones seem to have lived in areas far from any major population center."

"Like Chicago?"

"Most definitely like Chicago. Rome, Beijing, that damned unpronounceable city of the Mayas, Jericho, Delhi . . . all major population centers of their times. I'm not completely certain, but he does seem to like the city life, sweet." He smiled knowingly at her. "I guess he's just a people sort of person!"

She pushed loose hair from her eyes, clearly unamused by

his attempt at levity. "So we have to find someplace fairly empty."

"But not too empty. Otherwise, we won't be able to search for the others. The desert areas of the west and southwest should be reclusive enough while still giving us some of the benefits of civilization . . . such as they are. MacPhee discussed something similar with me three or four Scatterings ago, but he never got a chance to pursue it, I guess."

"When did he—when did he get taken, do you think?"

"The last I knew, MacPhee was somewhere a few years after the last variant's American Civil War, the one that the English jumped into. I'd assume it was shortly after that."

"I was too many centuries back. It was hard to keep contact with anyone beyond the Crusades," she commented, her expression tightening. "I lived thirty-two awful years before I ceased."

Spread across the centuries, the Scattered Ones could physically die, but that did not necessarily mean that they would not jump when that Earth perished sometime later. The question of what happened to those who died and later were reborn was a thorny one that no one liked to delve into much.

Gilbrin nodded, then changed the topic. "I found that sniveling fool Orvan six months ago; he's a backwater priest, an evangelist, I guess they call them now, in the southern part of this nation. Also located Tres. She's a dancer back in Paris in the twenties."

His companion shrugged, caring for neither of the pair mentioned. They might all be suffering the same, but that did not mean that the various refugees cared for one another. "And my father?"

"I've not felt him. He's either not reached the waking stage or he's shielding himself. You know his skill."

Maia nodded, leaned back, and retreated into her thoughts again. Gilbrin watched the highway and began humming a little tune. It was a Phoenician sailor's ditty about an endless voyage. One of the Shifter's more pleasant incarnations. The third Scattering, he recalled. Aboard one vessel or another much of that life, he easily avoided the Darkling . . . though, he recalled, neither Boray or Hsi, both contemporaries at that time, had been quite so lucky.

How long must we run from you, oh Prince of Shadows? Through all eternity, all the while watching as billions of people, whole universes, perish?

Gilbrin glanced down at the gas gauge. Little more than a quarter of a tank left. It was always tempting to run the car on power alone, but for some reason he could never explain, it would have been like turning the Dodge into something other than what he desired. The Shifter knew that if he ever toyed with the old automobile's workings, he would soon after trade it in for something else. Something . . . still innocent.

A great desire to pull off overwhelmed him. The tall, gaudy sign of a fuel station beckoned from ahead, offering food and gas. He waited for the exit, then slowly turned off the highway.

"What are we doing?"

" 'We,' my lovely, have got to stretch our short, cramped legs and get some food for this blue monster and ourselves. You're welcome to join us."

The station was less than he had hoped for and Gilbrin began to have doubts about what sort of food they would find. The restaurant, a small thing, was barely visible behind the auto bay. Gilbrin slowed as a tow truck pulled out on another call. Business was good on the highway despite the lack of traffic. The mechanics were at work on two cars and two more were awaiting service, including—

Gilbrin wrenched the wheel around, sending gravel and dust flying, and immediately followed the tow truck back out onto the highway. He passed it quickly, not even looking at it. The Shifter's knuckles were white as he clenched the wheel.

Maia, who had been tossed about by the abrupt turn, righted herself. "Gil! Gods above and below, what are you doing?"

He did not answer at first, his eyes flickering back and forth between the road ahead and the service station gradually shrinking in the rearview mirror. At last, the station vanished over the horizon. The Shifter allowed himself to breathe again.

Maia leaned close. At any other time, the nearness would have stirred up some passion on his part, but not now. Not when their lives might very well be snuffed out at any moment like one of the splattered insects on the Dodge's windshield.

"Answer me, Gilbrin! What's wrong?"

Given full freedom, the blue Dodge voraciously devoured the miles. A tiny dot materialized in the distance. Gilbrin looked at Maia and then at the dot, which was just beginning to resemble a specific structure. What looked like a tall sign stood near it.

"Maia, sweet, that service station we left a few miles back. Did it look at all familiar to you?"

"This was the age of prefabrication, trickster. All of these places look more or less the same."

He glanced at her out of the corner of his eye. "Down to and including a red sports car just towed in?"

Her only reply was a puzzled look. Gilbrin nodded, his eyes always returning to the structure far ahead and to their right.

She still did not understand, but she was trying. "We passed the one with the sports car several miles back. I remember because I wanted my . . . I once wanted a car like that."

"You weren't paying attention, then, sweet. I just saw that same car in the station we were pulling into not more than a few moments ago."

"There are a lot of them. It's the hot car this year," Maia added, reverting momentarily to her seventeen-year-old incarnation.

"Between the station we just pulled away from and the one you remember seeing your car in, I recall another station with that same vehicle just being unhooked."

Her fingers dug into his arm. "Are you saying that we passed the same station three times?"

He nodded wearily. "And we're about to pass it again."

Maia followed his gaze . . . and saw the same buildings, the same sign, and the same red sports car, now parked, coming up on their right. Even then, even with the evidence before her eyes, she was unwilling to accept the truth. "We would've noticed something like that long ago! It can't be true!"

"It can be!" The Shifter bitterly spat out the words. "This smells like one of the Darkling's spell snares!"

As they passed the station, they studied it in silent horror. The red sports car glittered in the late afternoon sun. The tiny restaurant still peeked out from behind the other building. The tall sign continued to watch over everything, including, it seemed, two very trapped souls.

"Our minds are still our own," he commented. "This must be a self-activating spell. He might not be anywhere or any-time near here. One of his hunters must have set this up. I've got to try something now. Hold on, sweet."

There were few other cars on the highway at the moment. Smiling at his recklessness, Gilbrin twisted the wheel completely to the left, causing the tires to squeal and spinning the Dodge 180 degrees. Without hesitation, he planted his foot on the gas pedal and crushed it into the floor. Maia muttered a prayer of thanks to the inventor of seatbelts.

Gilbrin watched the road ahead, waiting for the service station they had just passed. This time it was on their left, of course, but otherwise everything was as it should have been. So far so good.

Both he and Maia remained silent for the next several miles. Each moment they waited for the same station to reappear over the horizon. It would have made perfect sense considering the Darkling's manner. Leave them trapped in a loop over and over. Gilbrin wondered whether the people at the gas station had noticed anything peculiar. Probably not. The Prince of Shadows was fairly thorough.

How much time passed, neither could say. A few minutes only, no doubt, but it seemed years. Maia was the first to spot the sign, but this time it was only one of the green ones announcing which destinations lay ahead. Topmost on the list was Chicago.

"We're out of it!" Maia whispered. "We've escaped!"

Gilbrin shook his head, wishing she were correct. Life, he decided, was becoming too serious for one of his nature. Once, all this would have seemed a game to him, despite the potential destruction waiting ever around the corner. Now, he was growing tired, weary.

"We've escaped from nothing, sweet. I'll wager the only open roads lead *into* Chicago. I'll wager we can't get more than three hours away from the city in any direction, Lake Michigan included. As far as we two are concerned, I'd say that all the other roads lead nowhere."

Her dark skin paled. "Population center . . ."

"Yes, Maia."

"Then . . . he's in there somewhere."

"Maybe. He might simply have set the snare and will come by later to pick us off at his leisure. This is too much just to catch the pair of us. The Darkling is probably using it to collect as many of us as possible. A new tactic for him. He's getting lazy in his old age; the hunt's beginning to bore him."

Maia stared into space. "If he's trying to gather more of us together so quickly, it could be that he fears something."

For once it was Gilbrin who did not quite understand. "What are you saying, sweet?"

"You know what time period this is, Gil. Maybe . . ." She hesitated, not at all eager to go on. "Maybe he's gathering us together like so much sheep because he thinks that another Scattering is about to take place . . . very soon."

He wanted to say *Not again*, not so soon after the pair of them had come to remember themselves, but could not. The End of the world was never dictated by their desires. It came when it came. It was just the luck of the draw.

"We wouldn't be the first to be woken just in time to have our souls ripped from our new home, sweet. You could be right. The world's never gone long past this century." Gilbrin scratched his chin. "Well, we won't know for certain until after we reach the city." He smiled. "I know a wonderful place for pizza that we should try when we get the chance!"

"How can you think of pizza at a time like this?"

His expression remained constant . . . almost too constant even for a trickster such as him. "How could I not?"

Maia blinked. They might have been lovers once, but that did not mean that she had ever completely understood the Shifter.

Entangled in their situation, the pair did not notice the lone figure wandering along the side of the highway, his destination also the city. Gilbrin in particular, had he studied the man with the aid of his powers, might have noticed something out of the ordinary. The man walked stiffly, almost mechanically, and his features, especially his nose, were very pronounced. In fact, to most mortal folk, he would have resembled a bird.

Gilbrin and Maia, had *they* taken a much closer look, would have seen more. They would have seen that the face of the wanderer did not just resemble a bird, but actually, under the glamour, *was* the face of a bird.

A parrot, to be exact.

3. SHADOWS OF CITIES PAST

The Maelstrom was gone.

How long? Dutchman asked himself first. Then: *Where am I?*

Questions. Always questions. Rarely answers.

The passage through the Maelstrom was a torn, confused memory. Again he saw the faces of the lost, crying out for peace they could never have. He could see the shadow cities, the cities of the past, present, and future of each of the now-dead worlds. He could see the death throes of each Earth.

His present world was one of darkness. Dutchman wondered what had happened to the light . . . then realized that the darkness came from within. His eyes were still shut tight. With both reluctance and anticipation, he slowly forced them open. There was no telling what he would see, but anything was better than—

There were people *everywhere*.

The world burst into sight and sound. He stood at the side of a busy street. People walked in every direction, heedless of where the sidewalk ended and the street began. The street was no less filled with people than the sidewalk was even though vehicles of all sorts, including animal-drawn wagons, moved blithefully along, ignoring everything and everybody in their paths. The people wore all manner of clothing, some of it so different in style that it was striking to see all of them in the same place.

Dutchman looked down at himself. He flexed a leg and found it in perfect condition. As ever, his injuries no longer existed once he landed. How and why they were healed, Dutchman never knew. He was only grateful that the pain had been stopped and that he could move again.

The people continued to walk by, paying no attention to his outlandish presence. Most of them could not see him, of course, lacking true Sight. If he called attention to himself, they might see him for a time, then forget him. One or two in the crowd glanced his way, humans with a touch of Sight, but even they did not see enough to interest them. Dutchman sensed no one around him with more than a fraction of ability. That meant that he could take a relaxing breath and observe.

There were so *many* colors. Reds, blues, greens, golds . . . so many colors and so many more shades. The clothing bothered him. It varied from pieces of material that barely covered to voluminous garments that threatened to envelop their wearers. Some of the males wore hats; others sported odd hair styles. Something was amiss, but he was at a loss as to what.

Then he saw an elegant coach run *through* a man and a woman, each of whom was as oblivious to it as they were to each other. Dutchman looked around and noticed that many of the vehicles and pedestrians moved through one another.

Shadows. Most of the people and vehicles around him were shadows of the past, although there were probably more than a few from the future as well. The cloaked wanderer looked up, noticing the contrasting structures that indicated at least a century of architectural change mixed madly together.

With some effort, he forced the shadows into the background, allowing himself to see the street as it was at this time. Hundreds, perhaps thousands of figures and vehicles ceased to be, but there were still crowds on the sidewalks and several lines of traffic moving slowly along the street. Automobiles, he recalled. An affectation of the late twentieth century, the last *whole* century, based on his prior landings.

That meant that there was no doubt that the End was near.

He sensed no instability in the world, no reason that it should suddenly tear itself asunder and take with it everything. Yet, it had happened so often before and each time with very little warning. Each time it had happened not long after his coming.

Dutchman pressed himself against the wall of a building, his thoughts unsettled. His drifting gaze fixed on a passing vehicle whose side advertised a newspaper called the *Chicago Tribune.* So Chicago it was that had been chosen to be his port of call. He knew the city from other variants, although never before had he been thrown into its midst. Chicago it was where the first signs of stress, the first signs of destruction, would appear.

Had Dutchman landed in a city in any other part of the world, it would have been just as simple for him to read the signs around him. All languages were one to him. It was a gift, so to speak, of his captivity. In his own Earth, the original version, he had only known one tongue, for that was all that had existed. Not until he had drifted to his third or fourth variant had Dutchman known that there could be another language. Why he had been granted such universal understanding, the exile could not say. Dutchman found no true worth in the gift, but then that might have been simply because he found little use in speaking to people who would soon be dead because of him.

He put a hand to his face as he wondered what to do now that he was here and the inevitable cycle of destruction had begun again. In landings past, Dutchman had tried to change the course of events, but each attempt had resulted in utter failure.

A shadow passed over the street.

Dutchman flattened himself further against the wall, his heart beating wildly. He peered up at the heavens, his eyes seeking a ghostly craft come to take him back to his empty prison, a ghostly craft whose coming would herald the beginning of the End for this Earth.

There was no sign of the *Despair*. What floated above was nothing more than a cloud. He knew that it was too soon. The *Despair* was still healing itself, seeking out its component pieces that had been tossed through time itself. It would sail back and forth through the centuries, gathering every original fragment of itself and invading the minds and souls of those individuals blessed, or perhaps cursed, with Sight. Legends of the spirit ship would abound throughout this variant's history just as it had in previous incarnations. He would gain for himself new names, new tales that were only shades of the fantastic truth. Along with the new would come the old names and stories that had been repeated over a hundred or more worlds.

The name he had chosen for himself, his own too cursed a thing even for him to bear, came from the most common legend that seemed to tie itself to him. His world was one where the ocean had once been paramount; the people had lived in harmony with it, knowing its value. It was not surprising, then, that maritime images meant much to his kind. Yet, there was one tale, spread over and over throughout hundreds of variant Earths, that stuck out, the tale of the mariner damned to sail until the coming of Judgment Day. Perhaps there truly was such an unfortunate captain, but Dutchman, cursed as he was by his own doing, had come to identify himself so much with that poor fool that it had seemed quite natural to take on the role. He had first called himself by the name as a sort of jest, but, after so long without reprieve, he had seen that he and the captain of legend were one. He was the Flying Dutchman, whatever his own origins.

Besides, playing the role meant thinking less about his own, long, lost life.

He began to wander aimlessly, caught up in the sudden change from eternal emptiness to constantly shifting sights and sounds. There were other things that Dutchman knew he should be doing, other matters made more important because of his limited time here, but the city was hypnotic.

Voices buzzed around him, but they were the voices of living folk, whom he could touch if he so desired. The voices of the damned had been, for a while, silenced. That was one benefit of his landing. Better yet, there were not just voices around him but the sounds of machinery, the calls of birds, and other noises that he could not identify.

Not all the smells and sounds were delightful, but Dutchman gladly embraced them. Even the scent of the sewage that lingered when he stepped near the curb was a gift.

"Life . . ." Dutchman whispered, inhaling the good and the bad together. "Life . . ."

He continued to stride along, drinking in all, as any man with so great a thirst would have done. The wind increased, but compared to the Maelstrom, it was a wonderful, delightfully light kiss. While others bowed their heads to avoid the full effect of it, he faced the wind gratefully.

His trek led him to a plaza where a monster of red metal bent over as if to seize a half-grown boy staring at it. Avians with mottled plumage ran amok in the nearly empty plaza, going hither and yonder depending on whether the wind blew or one of the few people there threw a piece of food or refuse to the ground.

The contrast between the statue and the glass and steel edifices flanking it was so striking that Dutchman turned toward the scarlet construct wondering what the artist had intended it to be. He was reminded of a bird, but not something as round as the scurrying forms at his feet.

The birds, of course, could sense him. With effort, Dutchman could have made them blind to his presence, but there was no need. He reached down, his interest in the construct momentarily abated. The avians were pigeons, creatures that thrived on every variant on which he had landed. Dutchman spread his hand palm up and positioned it before a pigeon with gray wings and a spotted body.

The bird strolled onto his palm and nestled. Dutchman

straightened, careful to keep his hand level. Most humans looked at such avians with either indifference or disdain, but he found that he admired them. They were survivors, living alongside humanity just as the less savory rat did. As lowly as both creatures were to humans, they were in some ways so superior. Simple but adaptable.

"I envy you, you know," he told the trusting pigeon. "But then, I envy everyone."

Dutchman stroked the back of the pigeon twice, then lowered it to the ground again. The bird rose and returned to the flock.

Straightening again, he glanced once more at the construct. A bird definitely. The artist had obviously been a fanciful sort of person, though, to have created such a thing.

As he walked toward it, the half-grown boy turned his way. Dutchman thought nothing about it until he realized that the boy was focusing on him. A glimmer of Sight touched him.

The youth, a swarthy child perhaps eleven years of age, blinked . . . and was gone. He had not run; he had simply vanished.

Ignoring the pigeons swarming around him, Dutchman made his way to the statue, his curiosity over the unusual encounter urging him on. He paused not more than an arm's length from where the boy had stood and scanned his surroundings. There remained no trace, not even a lingering tingle that sometimes marked where someone with Sight had stood. The youth had quite literally disappeared.

It was possible that he had come across a leaper, one of the refugees who journeyed from Earth to Earth in a desperate attempt to flee the destruction Dutchman always brought with him. He came across them now and then, although like the boy they tended to flee when he was near. Some of them knew by now that he marked the beginning of the End and they treated him for the most part like the pariah he was. Those who did not realize who he was simply knew that he was not one of *them,* and if Dutchman was not one of them, then to the leapers he was something that might be hunting.

There were things that hunted the refugees, things without conscience. Dutchman had come across them, too, and while he did resent being placed in the same category as the hunters, he understood the leapers' fear.

He had never come across a leaper so young. They were always adult or nearly so. They also left more of a trace, although it did vary.

Perhaps he had imagined the boy. He was not immune to delusions. He glanced around again, but saw nothing.

The plaza no longer attracted him. Dutchman retreated from the construct, choosing the nearest street and walking swiftly away from the plaza. He did not look back.

Once he was far enough away, Dutchman began to slow, his attention once more diverted by his surroundings. Again he grew fascinated by the sights and sounds of the city called Chicago. So *many* people. They were tall, short, fat, thin, old, young, black, white, and more . . . the variations astonished him even though Dutchman knew them all from each landing. Humanity always varied; it was one of its strengths, that diversity, although not all humans would have agreed with him.

None of that strength would matter at all when this world perished.

Again the wonder of his surroundings faded before the knowledge of the coming catastrophe. Dutchman froze in the middle of the crowd, the other pedestrians moving around him without realizing what they were doing.

What should I do?

Should he simply enjoy what little of this world he would be able to see before the End or try, once more, to find a way of escaping both his personal hell and the hell awaiting this unsuspecting world? Would it matter?

Why do I even try? What do I hope to accomplish?

It was tempting to just forgo the futile hunt, to pretend to ignore what was to come, in order to taste—

A mind that was not human brushed his own before quickly shielding itself.

Dutchman blinked, then turned his gaze to the crowds

around him. His first thought was that it might be the boy he had seen, but the boy, whether he was a leaper or not, had definitely felt human. No, the more he thought about it, the more the cloaked wanderer was certain that he recognized the mind from other variants. What had briefly caught Dutchman's attention just now had no right to be on this world, much less any of the other Earths where he had come across its like. The *Roschach* was what they called themselves . . . at least the one that had deigned to answer his question before it died.

It was out there among the humans, masquerading as one. It was hunting for someone, but not him. Dutchman had a suspicion as to who its prey was and that was enough to make him in turn seek out the hunter. As he began his search, his heart beat faster, but this time it was a good feeling. He was doing something even if in the long run his actions probably would not matter.

He again merged with the crowd. Any who noticed him at all would still see him as simply another suited man on his way to some occupation. The only ones who might see him otherwise were the Roschach and those on whom the inhuman creature preyed.

The leapers. This was indeed one of the creatures that stalked them.

Interesting that they should both be so close. Not a coincidence, perhaps.

Dutchman sensed it moving in the same direction as he walked. It was keeping pace with him, although not intentionally. He walked faster, cutting the distance between them until his prey, too, abruptly picked up the pace.

He had been noticed. Dutchman did not care. Let the Roschach feel what it was like to be hunted. He knew what sort of creature it was that pretended humanity, and to place it in the unfamiliar position of flight pleased him. It was not strictly out of altruism that he hunted it, either. Here was a creature on which he could vent his frustrations. Hunters like these moved from Earth to Earth without care for the life there, while he, the cause of so much death, wept for each person who died in the inevitable destruction.

One by one Dutchman eliminated the figures in front of him, seeing in them the humanity his quarry could not completely imitate. Sniffs, twitches, walks . . . it was the little actions that marked the differences.

His gaze at last focused on a swift but short figure clad in an oversized gray coat. By human standards, he was halfway through life and so very nondescript. Of course. How best to keep the prey unaware until it was too late.

Dutchman's stride increased . . . and so did that of the man in the gray coat.

At one corner, the Roschach hesitated. He glanced to his left, staring at another street corner. One foot twisted in that direction, but then the Roschach glanced over his shoulder. For the first time, a hint of his true self showed through, for to Dutchman, who had full sight, the man's eyes were striped black and white. Like himself, his quarry lacked pupils.

The man in the gray coat whirled to the right and vanished around the corner of a building.

Somewhere far to the left, Dutchman sensed the Roschach's intended quarry, another of the leapers. Again he wondered at the chances of so many outsiders like himself being nearby. Dutchman was tempted to investigate that one, but the leapers were, for the most part, victims and not threats, while the black-hearted hunters lived only to serve their function.

There was no sign of the Roschach when Dutchman finally turned the corner, but he still sensed the creature. The hunters did not have the degree of Sight that he did. It likely thought that it was now hidden from him, but its shields were insufficient at this distance. He knew exactly where it waited. He knew exactly how the hunters worked from when he had faced such on previous Earths. It was, in fact, only yards from him.

To all appearances, the store front it had chosen looked normal. Customers entered and exited through the doorway even as he approached. It was a clothing store, something that only vaguely interested him. He was not surprised by the choice; the Roschach often set their lairs over entrances through which many people passed. Dutchman had learned that in previous encounters. What he had never learned was why they wanted the leapers and who had sent them. The Roschach were astonishingly closemouthed, no matter what the secrecy cost them.

Pretending to be just one more human seeking to purchase garments, Dutchman opened the door and walked inside.

"A fool. A fool," croaked a deep voice.

For him, the door opened into a nightmarish yet peculiarly compact domain. Everything was blue, silver, or gray, or some combination of the three. The landscape was rocky and twisted. A ruined version of the store front loomed before the tall figure of Dutchman, but through the cracked windows he could make out the actual store, where humans continued to look at garments and make transactions. An elegant woman with dark hair, hair that reminded him too much of another woman still the mistress of his heart even worlds after her death, walked directly toward him. She reached the battered doorway of the nightmare version . . . and vanished the moment her foot stepped through.

Dutchman glanced over his shoulder. The woman was behind him, the door he had walked through already closing behind her.

He was in a world literally between the doorway and the interior of the building.

"Too late to go back. Too late to go back."

For the first time, he looked up at the wall near the ceiling. The small man in the gray coat clung to it like a spider, but now his limbs were long and thin and his hands and shoeless feet ended in tapering digits each with nails nearly a foot long. The grin on the Roschach's not-so-human face stretched so wide that it was a wonder the top of his head did not fall off.

His skin was as black as shadow.

" 'Welcome to my parlor . . . ' " Dutchman said, quoting

text from a hundred and more worlds, but the phrase was evidently lost on his audience, who leaped from the wall, all four sets of talons stretched out to seize the cloaked figure.

He could not say why, but the Dutchman thought that the Roschach evidently expected him to stand still for the attack. Perhaps there was a subtle magic that worked on the leapers and not on him, who was both more and less than they were. Perhaps they walked into the horror's snare unaware of their fate, then remained frozen in place, there to be hauled away to the hunter's mysterious master.

Ever so helpless during most of his cursed existence, Dutchman did not care even to pretend helplessness now. He reached out with his left hand and, as the Roschach fell on him, caught the monstrosity by the throat.

The talons scraped at him but did not find purchase. Both Dutchman and his cloak seemed too slippery for the Roschach to seize.

Dutchman squeezed just enough to gain the creature's full attention. It ceased its efforts to take him and just stared.

"We can simply talk if you are willing."

The monstrosity tried to spit in his face, but Dutchman squeezed tighter. His captive choked. Dutchman counted to ten, then eased his grip just enough to allow the hunter to speak.

"Why do you want the leapers?" It was the same question that he had asked other hunters before. He hoped for a different response this time.

"Because I do. Because I do." It was the same answer, more or less, that the creatures always gave.

"Who is your master?" He doubted that he would receive the answer he wanted, but it never hurt to ask.

The Roschach laughed, a painful, crackling sound.

"This accomplishes nothing. You serve no purpose by withholding the answers. Who is your master?"

The striped eyes glittered. "No prey are you. No prey are you. Other are you. Other are you."

"No," Dutchman agreed. "I am not one of your prey. I prey

on hunters with no regard for life. You do not belong here. You therefore have little choice; answer my questions or—"

Without warning, the Roschach fell apart in his hands.

The limbs broke into segments. The body, now so distended that it could never have been mistaken for something human, dropped afterward, turning to liquid as it touched the ground. Laughing again, the head fell backward, out of Dutchman's grip.

Intense pressure built up on all sides of him. It was as if a pair of giant hands was trying to squeeze Dutchman between them. The pocket world of the Roschach was collapsing. Dutchman did not fear death because he knew he could not die, but he was not immune to pain and to remain here was to invite much pain. He did not want to spend the rest of this Earth's existence trapped here.

He turned about and headed toward the doorway. He had almost reached the door when something caught first one foot and then the other. Dutchman glanced down and again was not too surprised to see the talons of the hunter clutching his boots at the ankle. Behind him, he still heard the head laughing.

"No one leaves. No one leaves."

The monstrosity was a more versatile model than the ones Dutchman had faced previously, but the creature still did not realize that it was facing something far different from the leapers. It had no idea what Dutchman could do.

"You are shadow, not substance," he remarked to the laughing head. Slowly, Dutchman raised one foot, which pulled through the talons as if they were molasses. Even as the Roschach's laughter turned into a hiss of dismay, he pulled the second boot free.

Without another word, Dutchman walked through the doorway. Just before he sealed the entrance behind him, he heard the hunter give one last cry of anger. Something struck the sealed entrance, but Dutchman did not turn to see what it was.

A breath later, he sensed the pocket world completing its collapse. With it perished its creator. Perhaps it had thought it would depart once the pressure overwhelmed its would-be victim, or perhaps it had intended both of them to die together. Dutchman did not know and did not truly care. When he had sealed the entrance through which he had passed, he had also sealed the other side in order to assure that the thing did not escape. The hunters disgusted him. They came from somewhere between or beyond the variant Earths. They were not so much alive as devourers of life.

He stood outside the store, no one having noticed his sudden appearance. A singularly disappointing confrontation. Again, the constant futility of his actions nearly overwhelmed him. He had disposed of one of the inhuman hunters, but as ever he had failed to discover where they came from or who sent them. More important, Dutchman knew that he had wasted time on something that brought no further answers to his ultimate challenge. So far, the world was still on schedule to be destroyed.

He shivered at the thought and could not help glancing back at where the Roschach had lurked. There would be more of them in this world and they would increase in numbers as the End neared. Dutchman did not fear them, but like the *Despair,* they were portents of the coming Apocalypse. That, along with his general disgust of the creatures, was the reason why he always sought to question them first, find out who or what was their master. He knew that they had one; they were not intelligent enough to cross worlds by themselves, and if they had come through some tear in the fabric of reality, then he certainly would have sensed that.

And why do I bother worrying about them? They are nothing. Parasites. Worth crushing, but, in the end, a waste of time . . . and there is so little time remaining. The words finally escaped him: "So little time . . ."

Soon would come the first ghostly passing of the *Despair.* He could not simply stand here and wait for that to happen. The Roschach had been a brief diversion, but even brief diversions cost him valuable time. If he was to act again, to pretend to save the world again, he had to start now.

Where was Philo? They were never cast too far apart, something for which he was always grateful. It was one of the few privileges evidently granted to him. He still marveled that he had ever been able to drag the animatron aboard. He still marveled that he had been able to keep the mechanical creature so long.

I should find him first. I should find him. I'll need his guidance. Perhaps *guidance* was the wrong word, but there was something about the animatron that calmed Dutchman, made him think more clearly. He needed to think more clearly if he had any hope of breaking the chain.

There was one problem, however. Dutchman could not sense his first mate in the same way as he had sensed the Roschach. Perhaps it was because Philo was a machine and not living, at least not in the most common sense of the word. More often than not it was the animatron who located his captain first.

So, searching for Philo was not the way to begin things. His first mate would find him. He had faith in the bird. Over the years, he had changed Philo into more than a simple mechanism. There was almost more of himself in the animatron than there was in the shell that was the bird's captain, so he sometimes believed. In many ways, Philo was more real than Dutchman.

Where to begin, then? How to commence with his quixotic quest *this* time?

The sky rumbled. Dutchman glanced heavenward again, troubled. There had been some cloud cover, true, but not enough that he would have expected any sort of storm. A storm generally preceded the coming of the *Despair,* but he neither saw nor sensed the ship. There was no reason to think that the rumble was anything other than an example of the changeable weather common in some regions.

No reason at all.

The clouds that had begun to gather floated low. Dutchman eyed them for a time, then stared at a building that stood tall among the rest. The uppermost portion of the grand edifice was obscured by the clouds.

He frowned, then reached out and took hold of the shoulder of one of the suited figures passing by. The man was startled and began to open his mouth, but a look from Dutchman quieted him.

"What structure is that? The tallest building."

"That? That's the Sears Tower," responded the other with the tone of one who recognizes someone not familiar with Chicago. Of course, Dutchman's informant saw him clad in a suit not unlike his own. Had he been aware of the tall figure's true appearance, the man would not have been so condescending.

Letting the other's tone pass, Dutchman released him. The man walked three steps, then settled into his previous stride. He had already forgotten his inquisitor . . . because Dutchman desired it that way.

The sky rumbled again. He studied the clouds a moment more, then started in the direction of the tower. The tower would give him a better view of the city and the clouds. He wanted to get a better look at those clouds in particular, not just with his eyes but with his Sight.

It was a beginning, at least, a beginning for his quest. He only hoped it was not already an ending as well.

From a distance that he knew was safe, the short, dark-haired youth watched Dutchman depart. He grinned. Like Dutchman, he was interested in the clouds. Unlike the other, the youth knew what the clouds, the sudden shift in weather, meant.

"He comes," the boy whispered in a voice that seemed too old for him, a voice tinged not with the accent his Hispanic features indicated but one that would have been difficult even for experts to identify. "He comes and the pariah is already here. Swifter than I thought, but that shouldn't matter. No, the Darkling might even be more rewarding for that knowledge."

He hurried off. There was so much to do and so little time

in which to do it. Not only did he have to prepare for his encounter with the Darkling, but he had to prepare for his daughter, who was drawing nearer to the city. He sensed her even though she could not sense him. He had made certain of that. Few of the Scattered Ones could match his skills.

August de Fortunato enjoyed surprising his dear, sweet Maia.

4. BIRDS OF A FEATHER

"Where are we going?" Maia asked as they entered the city. The traffic was slow, but not nearly as slow as it would have been had they been departing Chicago. The workers had finished their day and now headed home to their families. Tomorrow, they would return and begin the cycle again.

The two occupants of the Dodge simply wanted the chance to see tomorrow . . . and the next day, too.

"There are already a few of us in Chicago, sweet. I've never seen them and we've maintained minimal contact in terms of the link or telephone, but one of them MacPhee knew. We're going to see him."

"What's his name?"

"Tarriqa. Hamman Tarriqa. Never talked to him before. Have you?"

The name was not one that Maia recognized, but then, she could hardly know all of her fellow refugees. "Do you know anything about him?"

"Only that he might be the best chance we have of extricating ourselves from this situation. He knows some of MacPhee's work."

"Wouldn't he be trying to escape himself, then?"

Gilbrin shook his head. "He might not know what is happening, sweet. After all, we only found out when we tried to leave Chicagoland." He grimaced. "Of course, he might not even have any worthwhile knowledge to share. I'm hoping that he can at least provide us with temporary refuge."

Eventually, they escaped the expressway. Maia marveled at the way in which Gilbrin maneuvered the wide Dodge between the other vehicles, avoiding buses and trucks with as much ease as he did the smaller cars. What was more impressive was that he did it without the aid of his powers.

There was still light, but with the sun descending the interior of the vast city was a shadowed thing. Knowing that the hand of the Darkling had already touched Chicago, Maia eyed each of those shadows with trepidation. She knew that she was being foolish, the Prince of Shadows never struck so openly, but tales of other refugees being caught ran constantly through her mind. Some of them she had known well, others she had not. That hardly mattered; Maia had sympathy for them all. There was only one that she wished the Darkling would take and that was her own cursed father.

"Lake Shore Drive," the Shifter pointed out as they turned onto a much larger street. "We're close now, sweet."

"Good. I'm beginning to go stir-crazy, Gil. I keep thinking I'm seeing his dogs everywhere."

"Courage, Maia."

It was easy to say, but not so easy a command to follow. At least here on Lake Shore Drive, there was more sunlight.

She had only just calmed when Gilbrin abruptly slowed before a building. "This is it."

Even this near, Maia could only barely sense the presence of another of the Scattered Ones. Hamman Tarriqa was skilled at masking himself, even more than she or Gil. Once that might have encouraged her, but she recalled that while MacPhee had been skilled enough to completely shield his presence from others, he too had fallen victim to the Darkling's agents.

Still, she could not help becoming a little hopeful.

The structure had a garage built into it. The building was probably about fifteen or sixteen stories tall, the upper floors serving as dwellings for the affluent. It had been renovated at some time, but was probably at least seventy years old. Almost an infant compared to her.

She had no opportunity to study it further, for at that moment Gilbrin turned the massive Dodge into the entrance of the garage. A gate blocked their entry, but the Shifter touched the box where one either inserted a pass or took a ticket and the gate lifted.

"You are going to have to be more careful, Gil," she scolded. "Someone's going to notice you doing things like that."

His only reply to that was a mischievous smile. One of his most endearing qualities . . . not to mention also his most *annoying* quality . . . was the almost childlike attitude he frequently affected. It had drawn her to him after her first clash with her father, but had eventually proven to be too much. She cared about him, but could never, ever, bring herself to see him as a lover again. Maia regretted that in some ways, because the pattern of her existence was such that the only ones who would ever understand her were the other refugees, and so far she had found none who could fill the void within her soul. It was hard for any of the Scattered Ones to maintain relationships with one another, their predicament creating within each of them a sense of futility in such emotional ties.

Gilbrin drove up the curving ramp of the garage. Higher and higher they drove until Maia finally had to ask him, "Are we parking on the roof? We can't have much farther to go."

In answer, her companion suddenly turned the wheel, parked the Dodge in a random space, and turned to her. "We're here, sweet."

"Thank you for telling me. Isn't this someone's personal space, though?" She had noticed that all the spaces were marked with names.

"I'm sure they won't mind."

Knowing better than to argue, Maia climbed out of Gilbrin's car. The normalcy of their activities so far was deceiving even to her; they might have been a couple going to visit a friend rather than two worried and cautious wanderers seeking one of their own. The threat of the Darkling, not to mention the End of this world, seemed a bit more distant at the moment, although neither danger could be completely forgotten.

"Don't dawdle, dear," her companion called, already far ahead.

Shaking her head at Gilbrin's flippancy, Maia followed him through a door.

The dwellings might be lavish, Maia thought, but the hallways were, at the most, ordinary. There were not many doors on this floor, which said something about the immense size of the suites, and so it did not take long for Gilbrin to find the one he sought. This close, Maia now felt the definite presence of one of their fellows.

Before they could knock, the door swung open. A black, balding man, about twice the age that Maia appeared, looked the pair over well before saying, "Come in."

Hamman Tarriqa was, in this world, a man who had obviously done well for himself. The furnishings of his suite, which was even larger than Maia had imagined, were extravagant by the standards of the present time. A sense of natural beauty vied with high value for supremacy. Tarriqa certainly enjoyed showing off his wealth. The paintings, originals probably, and all the rest of the artwork portrayed wildlife or landscapes. The room was well lit, as if to best display his prizes. A huge window allowed a wide view of the city. Recalling some of her past incarnations, Maia felt a twinge of jealousy. Not for many Scatterings had she lived like this. Her most recent rebirth had been one of her best. This time, she could say that she had lived at least in comfort.

Gilbrin too showed some evidence of jealousy, but he quickly covered it. "Be it ever so humble, there's no place like home, is there, Master Tarriqa?"

"I was reborn a slave in the last world and the two prior to that I lived in such poverty that I killed myself both times, little man," the elder refugee snapped. "We take the bad and we take the good. I've made the good even better this time."

"I was just complimenting you on your lovely abode," the Shifter said, his face the image of innocence.

Tarriqa was not fooled, but he did relax some. "MacPhee warned me about you, jester. I suspect he was kinder than he should have been." He indicated that they should be seated. "I sensed you nearby several minutes ago, but I didn't know you were coming here until you entered the building." The tall figure eyed both of them, but especially Gilbrin. Tarriqa was not a small man physically and looming over them he was a bit overwhelming. "Polite guests call ahead in this variant."

"Polite hosts offer a guest a drink," returned the sandy-haired trickster with a twinkle in his eye.

"If it will get things moving . . ." Hamman Tarriqa glanced at a cabinet. The doors opened, revealing an array of liquor. He turned back to his visitors. "What would you like?"

"That looks good." Gilbrin pointed at a bottle of whiskey on the right side.

"I'll take water, if you please," added Maia, with a look of irritation directed at her companion. It was not advisable, she thought, to aggravate someone who might be important to them.

"A good choice, young woman. That's what I generally drink myself, but I keep stocked up for less health-inclined visitors like your friend."

"A little whiskey is good for the soul of the poet, my Philistine friend."

"As long as the poet's sole pursuit isn't that whiskey, clown." Tarriqa put both hands behind his back for a moment, then pulled them forward again. In each hand he now held a drink. "I believe this is yours, my lady."

"Maia, Master Tarriqa. I am Maia de Fortunato." As she took the water, she watched his reaction. Most of the Scattered Ones knew who her father was.

"My sympathy," was all the black man said in regard to her identity. "Please, call me Hamman." He handed Gilbrin the whiskey without any comment, then straightened. Reaching behind himself, Hamman Tarriqa brought forth another glass of water.

"And some call me a clown and showman." Gilbrin took a sip and smiled. "My compliments on the whiskey."

The wealthy refugee seated himself. "Now that you have your drink, perhaps you'll tell me just what you're doing here. I've not invited you and we've had no true contact. If you need some money to start yourself out, I can help you to a point, but I'm not a philanthropist. I intend to enjoy what's left of this world before it goes away."

"You know that it's soon, don't you?" asked Gilbrin, lowering his whiskey.

"How could I not? We're near the end of this century. The next one has never completed in the past worlds so why should we assume it will in this one? My estimates are another ten to fifteen years, with twenty-five the outside hope."

The Shifter leaned back and crossed his legs. Maia could not help but notice what a contrast his clothing was to their surroundings. She knew that Gilbrin enjoyed distracting from his surroundings. He had already shifted enough so that his right foot, which hung in the air, was directly in his host's line of sight. Hamman Tarriqa could not avoid noticing the bright shoe, although he gave no sign.

"You might wish to recalculate, Hamman." Gilbrin took another drink. His tone darkened. "I'd say we might have six months at the outside. More likely, we've only got weeks."

The glass nearly slipped from the black man's hand. "What do you mean?"

"Made any business trips lately?"

"My work at present requires my remaining in the city. I've got one trip planned next week, though. A flight to New York."

Gilbrin looked at Maia. "It might be interesting to see how far he gets and how he is turned back. An airplane is a lot more to deal with."

"Do you think he might be able to leave that way?"

"Possible, but not likely. Too obvious a means of escape. It wouldn't be allowed."

"What by Carim's lantern are the two of you babbling about?"

The Shifter was all too willing to relay the information to their host. Maia was glad about that; she did not care to be the one to tell such terrible news.

As he listened to the Shifter's tale of their own adventures, Hamman Tarriqa's face twisted from annoyance to disbelief and finally to resignation. His drink remained untouched, a direct contrast to Gilbrin's whiskey, which had to be refilled twice. For once, both men were in accordance. Even Gilbrin was shaking by the time he had finished.

"The Darkling . . ." whispered Tarriqa after a long silence. "I don't doubt what you're saying, jester, not if Maia here verifies it, too. I'd hoped for longer . . . but maybe I was just being wishful. You were right not to announce yourselves when you came here. His hunters could be out there even now and they can certainly sense us if we reveal ourselves too much."

"Hamman," interjected Maia, trying to keep the three of them from sinking into a quagmire of despair. "You knew MacPhee better than either of us. He was working on trying to understand the Scatterings and why we keep going from variant Earth to variant Earth with no end in sight. Did he tell you anything?"

"He told me many things, although how much was simply fantasy I can't say. You might not have realized it, but friend MacPhee did not always share his knowledge. There were things he knew about the Scatterings that I can only guess based on what he would *not* tell me. I think he knew far more than he indicated. I think MacPhee either discovered or already knew how it all started."

"And he said nothing?" The Shifter clearly had trouble believing that. "All of our lives in the balance and he said nothing?"

Tarriqa shook his head. "You didn't know MacPhee at all,

I can see. He was always willing to hold back things until he had everything in place as he saw it. Oh, he let out a few bits now and then to let the rest of us know he was making progress, but never anything substantial enough for us to use." He shook his head. "And I was supposed to be one of his closest associates."

"So we've come here for nothing." Maia slumped. "Nothing at all."

"Maybe, maybe not." Rising, the large man walked slowly to the window. Gilbrin started to follow, but Maia put a warning hand on his wrist.

"I can see the lake from here," Tarriqa continued, staring out. "It cost me over half a million dollars to live here, but I find it worth the money. It makes up for the past few lives." He shivered. "But I deserve to have it last longer. We all deserve it to last longer."

"If the Darkling's here, we don't really have any choice," commented Gilbrin, ignoring Maia's scowl. "And even if he's not, his Roschach must be for such a snare to be laid."

"Not everything points to the End just yet." The black man turned around. "No one's sighted the angel of death yet."

They both knew that he was not referring to the Prince of Shadows, although such a title could have easily been added to those the Darkling had already garnered. There was another harbinger, one many considered the cause of their endless fate.

On many of the Earths, he was called the Flying Dutchman. The Scattered Ones did not generally call him by that name, knowing that he was much more than a single legend. They called him mostly by the title that Tarriqa had used, but one other common one, favored especially by Maia, was simply the Boatman. It always reminded her of the dark character from many variants' Greek lands. To Maia, the Boatman was like Charon, who brought the souls of the dead to the underworld.

If that was the case, this Charon was busy indeed. He had worlds of souls to transport . . . and in the eyes of most of the refugees, was always eager to add another world to his list. Most believed that he was responsible for the Apocalypse, but Maia was not so certain.

"The fact that the Darkling himself has not yet been sighted means we may have more time than you think, jester. MacPhee made that clear and I think I agree with him." Hamman Tarriqa's hands vanished behind him and when they reappeared the glass was gone. In his left hand he held a business card. "I've some things to think over. When I have a better notion as to what to do, we'll meet again. In the meantime, you'll need a place to stay, I suspect. I've written an address on the back."

Gilbrin opened his palm. A moment later, he and Maia were reading over the address.

"We could just stay here, Master Tarriqa. You have so much room and so little to do with it." The sandy-haired figure studied the business side of the card. "Quite an entrepreneur, aren't we? Exports, imports, and more . . ."

Ignoring yet again his so-called guest's attempts at levity, the black man quietly responded, "I need solitude for my thoughts . . . besides, I have an appointment tonight."

The Shifter grinned. "You have a date, do you?"

"Gil." Her voice was quiet, but Maia made certain that her companion noted the annoyance in her eyes. To Tarriqa, she said, "We thank you, Hamman, but are you certain that we can't do more now?"

He remained by the window, resolute in his decision. "I wish MacPhee had told me more. For now, I can only say to watch for signs. Look for the ship that flies in the night sky. Keep an eye out for its unholy captain or anything that might be a sign of his arrival." Hamman Tarriqa smiled, but it was a smile that mocked both his grand lifestyle and the lifestyles of every other member of their refugee group. "And do keep an eye out for hunters and shadow princes."

Although he had not said as much, Maia knew that they had been invited to leave. She rose, pulling a reluctant Gilbrin from his seat. Tarriqa escorted them to the door.

"Listen to me, both of you," Tarriqa said. "I take everything we spoke of here very seriously, as should you." The last was said with a definite look at Gilbrin in particular. "Be wary, both of you. I've not noticed any hunters, but they could be anywhere. The address I gave you is a hotel nearby. They have a permanent suite set aside for whenever I need it. Simply give my name."

"Fascinating that they should do that for you," the Shifter commented, uncowed by Tarriqa's earlier glare.

"Business often requires such things . . . and a little influence helps," the man replied. The influence he spoke of was obviously related to his powers.

The door behind Maia and Gilbrin opened. The Shifter stepped through immediately, but Hamman Tarriqa put a hand on Maia's shoulder.

"Be especially wary. I almost forgot to tell you that one of the others thought he sensed your father in this region. I haven't felt his presence, but August de Fortunato could very well be quite near without my knowing it. He has the skill."

"Thank you for telling me."

"I'll be in contact with both of you in a day or two. I have a few associates I want to reach and not all of them are of this time period. This will probably take most of tomorrow."

Communication through time was taxing. Although the Scattered Ones lived what could have been called concurrent lives despite whatever century they had been born, their links with one another waxed and waned depending on many factors. Maia seldom tried to strengthen any such links, the strain often telling on her after the attempt.

"Thank you, Hamman . . . and good luck."

He closed the door the moment she was in the hallway. A few feet down the corridor, Gilbrin leaned against the wall, hands in his pockets and a typical mischievous smile playing across his features.

"Shall we be off?"

"You generally are."

He slapped a hand against his chest as if struck there by her verbal barb. "Faith! That must be the first time I've heard that . . . today."

Maia stalked past him. Gilbrin chuckled and followed closely behind her.

They made their way back to the Dodge and swiftly departed the building. Neither of them spoke until they were back on the street. By this time, only a sliver of light remained.

"Well, that was an exceptional waste of time," the Shifter remarked.

"What do you mean?" The visit had been short, but Maia thought that they had at least begun to plan. She had confidence in Hamman Tarriqa.

"He's as closemouthed as he says MacPhee was, sweet. I don't say that he won't try to do something, but don't be surprised if he feeds us bits and pieces." Gilbrin gave her a smile. "I guess what I'm saying is that I think we should continue our own efforts."

"And what efforts are those?"

"Well, first I think that we should take Master Tarriqa up on his offer of a place to stay. I've been driving a lot today, Maia. I'm about all done in . . . and I need some food to wash down this whiskey with."

In the growing darkness, she could not see his face well, but Maia knew that if Gilbrin was willing to admit to her that he was tired, he was *very* tired. The short, sandy-haired figure beside her was generally willing to extend himself beyond what most would do. His comical appearance hid a determined and dutiful man willing to aid his friends in any way he could.

Perhaps that's the part of him I once loved.

Maia leaned back in her seat and stared out the window. Whether or not her faith in Tarriqa was naive, she agreed with Gilbrin about taking up the other refugee's offer of sanctuary. She too had extended herself today, not only awakening to her true identity but also altering her form to one most like her original self. It was a wearying thing—

She blinked. For a moment she thought she had noticed a

bizarre figure turn around a street corner. Maia twisted around to try to get one last glimpse, but either the growing darkness had swallowed him up or he had not been there in the first place.

"What is it, sweet? What do you see?"

"I thought I saw . . . never mind. I'm tired, too. It couldn't have been anything."

Gilbrin frowned briefly, then returned his attention to his driving. Maia watched him for a while, but her eyes eventually drifted back to the window. She hoped that the hotel was not much farther; it was clear to her now that the day had ravaged her more than she had first assumed.

She thought that she had seen a man with the head of a bird. . . .

It began as an almost unnoticeably black light shining in an empty office in a building not more than two blocks from the tower toward which Dutchman had earlier journeyed. Only the Roschach knew of its existence and only they knew the reason for its coming.

The master was entering the world.

In the empty office, more than a dozen hunters of varying forms and sizes perched, hung, squatted, or knelt in obeisance. They were all equally dark and all had striped eyes without pupils. While they looked vaguely human at times, they were not even remotely related to their prey, much less any other living creature.

More than one hissed, anticipation running rampant. The hunters lived to serve the master. They knew no other purpose. Hunt the ones the master wanted and bring them to him. What he did with them afterward, they neither knew nor cared. They knew only that if they brought back a prize, they were rewarded well.

"Darkling . . ." hissed one.

"Darkling . . ." repeated several others.

"Prince of Shadows . . ."

"Prince of Shadows . . ."

"Shadow Prince . . ."

"Shadow—"

A gust of wind with no point of origin blew through the office, silencing the inhuman audience.

In the center of the largest open area of the office, an ebony sphere formed, a sphere that spun faster and faster, growing with each passing second. The creatures were still now, their alien eyes fixated on the expanding ball. Not a sound, not a movement disturbed the moment. The Roschach not only respected their lord, but feared him greatly.

Faster and faster the sphere spun and the faster it spun the more it expanded. From a tiny ball it grew swiftly to something larger than the largest of the dark creatures. It swelled, filling more and more of the office and forcing the nearest of the hunters to retreat lest they be caught by it.

Then, when it could expand no further, the sphere shattered, crumbling into dustlike fragments that spread across the room. Wherever they moved, the shifting fragments left a trail of pure white. The trails widened, covering even the most remote corner. The Roschach cringed but did not flee when the whiteness flowed past them.

In the center of what had been the sphere stood the Darkling Prince. Tall and completely shadowed despite the expanding whiteness, he slowly gazed around at his surroundings and his subjects. From head to toe, the Darkling resembled most a photographic negative of a man. His entire form was wrapped in what seemed a shroud of black mist that constantly swirled about him, ever obscuring some portion of his form. Even to the Roschach, who knew him best, it was impossible to say what exactly the Darkling wore or even if he wore clothing at all.

Of his face, there was only one visible feature, a most striking feature compared to the rest of his ebony form. One eye, the Darkling's right, stared at the cowering hunters. In contrast to the darkness, the eye was more pale than the room had become. It was a human eye, true, but so colorless that any other than his servants would have wondered whether the Darkling was a living creature.

"I am arrived in the world," he announced in a voice that did not come from exactly where he stood. His words echoed. "Let it rejoice."

His subjects emitted a variety of sounds in response, trying to show the Darkling their pleasure at this fact.

He graciously nodded his approval, then said to the gathering, "I will be seated."

One of the squat hunters scurried on all fours to a position just behind his lord. The creature shifted form, its torso flattening out and widening. The Darkling did not even look as he sat, trusting to his servant because the creature knew what would befall it if there was any error.

Shadows dancing around him, the hunters' lord held court. "Show me this Earth."

A tall, narrow Roschach shaped vaguely like a praying mantis came forward. The pale eye stared into the striped ones. The Roschach went rigid.

"Paris, Beijing, Cairo, Delhi, St. Petersburg, Manchester, Mexico City . . ." the Prince of Shadows muttered to himself. City after city joined the list until he had mentioned population centers in every corner of this variant world. They were all places where hunters existed and, therefore, all places where the Darkling had eyes. In mere minutes, he knew the planet better than most of its inhabitants.

He also knew which of his snares looked most promising.

The Roschach scuttled away the moment his lord broke eye contact. The Darkling looked around at the ebony forms, so out of place in the utterly white surroundings he had created. He pointed at a shorter, rounder Roschach, who immediately moved forward.

Time meant little to the Darkling in terms of this world's history, but it would have been inaccurate to say that time was not a precious commodity to him. Unlike the ones who jumped, he had no sure method by which he could determine how and when the variant would be destroyed. He entered each Earth in some specific century and worked from there, unable to reach back through time like the prey he sought. That was why he needed them. Although they themselves did not know when the collapse would occur, there was something inside them that prepared each for the leap to the next variant. By making use of their involuntary ability, which he had always suspected was no natural skill but one implanted, he could ready his own path. The jump always had to be timed precisely. His earliest escapes had been due more to luck than to knowledge. It was not until he had first encountered the refugees that he had found a way to avoid disaster.

Of course, the refugees, who called themselves the Scattered Ones, could hardly have been pleased with his discovery. Through them, through their ability to leap from world to world, he could time his own escapes. This meant sacrificing the life of the Scattered One he was using in the process. The sacrifice was a small one, however, for it allowed the Darkling to flee to safety before it was too late.

But someday I will be able to stop fleeing, he thought, not for the first time. *Someday, I will again claim a kingdom!*

"What success?" he whispered to the hunter.

Through the creature's eyes, the Darkling observed. The hunters he sent just before his own leap into each new variant were extensions of himself, a legacy of the wonders he had created before his own world had been torn apart and he had first begun his perpetual flight. He always sent them in packs. Just before he had fled the last dying world, he had risked twelve such packs, hoping that they would spread far.

Two of the packs had never reached the new Earth. The Darkling was not overly saddened; with each leap he expected some attrition. The Roschach were easily replaceable. However, there was only one of him. He made certain that his subjects remembered that at all times.

Of the remaining packs, all but one thrived. What had happened to them was unknown.

"Reveal to me."

The hunters had not been very successful so far. The Scattered Ones were even more scattered than usual and many of them had been cast into centuries he could not touch. They had prospects, though, and more than a few. Chicago seemed especially promising, although Beijing had points in its favor.

Chicago, though, seemed to call to him as no city ever had in the past. He had hardly needed his Roschach to guide him to this place; it had practically screamed for him to honor it with his presence.

Why was that? The Darkling dismissed the hunter, having learned nothing of great import from the creature. Everything was as it should have been; everything was *always* as it should have been. Why did he think that it might be otherwise this time?

Then, with much hesitation, a Roschach he had not summoned crept slowly forward. There was fear in the monstrosity's eyes; they all knew what it meant to anger their lord.

Nodding his head slightly, the Prince of Shadows permitted the scuttling thing to approach. It moved along until it stood before him, then stretched its head forward so that the Darkling could see as it did.

It was only a flicker of an image, but what it relayed spoke volumes to the Darkling.

One of his hunters had been eliminated, but the other did not know how. While now and then the refugees did kill his subjects, the Roschach who had reported sensing his death did not think it had been such a battle. This was the work of a different being, not one of the leapers. This same predator had eliminated other hunters in the past. The Roschach before him believed this to be the truth and after some consideration, the Darkling Prince agreed.

"Could it be . . . ? whispered the shadowed form, the Roschach before him already forgotten. It quickly moved away, grateful to have been spared.

His thoughts were disturbed by an intrusion into his chosen domain. At first he grew furious, wondering what fool would be brash enough to blunder into his sanctum, but then he realized that it could only be one fool in particular. The hunters knew better than to annoy him and no one of this particular Earth was yet aware of his glorious arrival.

"You may enter, August de Fortunato."

Into the whiteness came a short, wiry form, a form that coalesced into a boy perhaps eleven years old. The Darkling looked at his supplicant and chuckled. August glared but said nothing at first. He walked past the Roschach, patently disregarding their deadly presence. Despite his youthful appearance, de Fortunato moved as one long confident in himself, one who believed that when the battles were done, he would be one of those reaping the victories.

Standing at last before the Darkling, he gave a much too brief bow and said, "Hail to you, Prince of Shadows."

"You are looking very well, August de Fortunato. This place must agree with you, for you have a spring in your step and youth in your features."

De Fortunato scowled. "I woke to myself a little earlier than is normal, that's all. I chose to keep this form so far for a variety of reasons. Consider yourself fortunate that I did, too, otherwise you might've missed some opportunities, not to mention finding yourself in some possible straits."

"And what do you mean by that?" asked the Prince of Shadows, his humor fading.

"First, I need a chair."

The Darkling pointed a lazy finger at one of the hunters. The creature bent low and moved toward de Fortunato, but slowly. He waited until the Roschach had positioned itself, then sat down.

"Thank you. The second thing I need before I continue is one life spared by you."

"Other than your own at the moment?" The single pale eye of the Darkling Prince burned into August de Fortunato's soul.

"One other, yes," returned the dark-haired youth, refusing to be cowed. "I want the life of my daughter, Maia."

"Your daughter? Perhaps I have misjudged. Perhaps you are with heart after all."

"No." De Fortunato smiled. "I just want to deal with her myself. I've looked the city over. There'll be enough others for your machine. You won't need to dissect her."

Now the shadowed form chuckled again. "In that case, your plea is granted." Then, in a much darker tone, he added, "But that is the end of my goodwill. You will speak what you know now, August de Fortunato."

The boy steepled his fingers and leaned back. "Of course, Prince of Shadows. Of course . . . but first let me ask you one question. You are a fount of knowledge, but I wonder how knowledgeable you are about legends. . . ."

"Legends?"

"Legends . . . legends, say, like that of the so-called Flying Dutchman."

The Darkling Prince leaned forward, his shadows swirling about as if in sudden agitation. He said nothing, but his every movement demanded that de Fortunato get to the point or else.

At last slightly ruffled, de Fortunato blurted, "Yes, the one you really seek is finally here."

5. HUNTERS AND HUNTED

Whatever he had sensed near the tower had passed by the time he reached the top, but Dutchman remained there throughout the night, letting his thoughts drift as he stared down at the city. This was the closest he could come to sleeping and he savored the time.

It was not that he was idle during the night. Although Dutchman's thoughts drifted, they drifted with some purpose, seeking out any hints that the order of his present world was about to slip into chaos. More than once the cursed wanderer had sensed something, but whatever it was masked itself well.

As the first touch of light rose above the horizon, Dutchman's eyes opened. He had closed them but moments before and that only to assimilate what little data he had obtained. What he had learned put him no nearer to an answer to any of his queries, but at least it was now clear to him that there were others gathered in and around the city. A larger number than usual. Most of them were leapers. A few were unidentifiable. It was hard to tell where any of the latter were located; the most he could tell was that they were within the limits of the city proper.

There was still no sign of Philo, something a bit unusual, but Dutchman had faith that his first mate would find him soon. The parrot always did. Rather than wait for that to happen, however, he decided to descend to the ground and begin once more his trek around the city. In his bones he felt that something significant would reveal itself today and that it was more likely to do so if he made himself readily available.

"Maybe I just hope that. . . ." he muttered. Long ago Dutchman had given up trying not to talk to himself. Even surrounded by millions of living souls, his personal sense of loneliness was very strong. Each time he landed at a new port of call, his tendency to talk to himself increased. Not even Philo's company could put a stop to it.

His descent from the tower was swift, in great part because the elevator was under his direct control. The guard in the lobby did not note his passing nor did he see the door leading outside open for the cloaked figure.

As Dutchman stepped out, he caught wind of a wondrous scent. Food. Caught up as he had been in his arrival, he really had not yet thought of eating. While not a necessity to his body, it now became a demand of his mind and soul. The food represented a portion of life itself, a portion that Dutchman could actually partake in for a time. The city was only just awakening, so there was no crowd to slow him as he crossed the street in the direction of the enticing scent. The food establishments of this Earth were very unlike the ones that he had been familiar with when growing up, but after so many worlds, they were all more or less the same to his eyes. All Dutchman cared about was the fare they offered.

He walked into a small place that, besides tables, included several metal stools by the counter. A woman clad in a worn, white uniform poured water for one of a pair of men seated there. She glanced up when she heard the door, but looked down almost immediately after.

Walking up to the counter, Dutchman eyed the food on the plate of one of the other men. Simple fare, but a feast to him.

The server started to pass him. He lightly placed a gloved hand on her wrist.

She started. "I didn't see you! I'm sorry."

"I will have what he has," he told her, indicating the plate of his neighbor.

"Scrambed eggs and toast? You want orange juice or coffee?"

"Yes."

She looked at him for a moment as if seeing something other than another customer, than smiled and nodded. "Both. Okay. Just let me take care of something and I'll get your order right in to the cook."

Dutchman released her and seated himself two stools from the nearest other man. A few new people wandered in, but no one came within two seats of the cloaked figure.

Several minutes later, the server brought him his food. Dutchman inhaled, devouring the scents, then spent the next couple of minutes simply admiring the contents of the plate.

The server came over. "Is something wrong?"

Conversation still disturbed him. He was not used to speaking to anybody, save the animatron, for very long. "No. Not at all. It smells wonderful."

"I'll be sure to tell the cook. He doesn't hear that very often." With a quick smile at him, she turned to deal with a newcomer.

Her smile did as much as the food to lighten Dutchman's mood. He watched her walk away, not attracted to her but recalling his attraction to other women, especially one. A name he thought he had forgotten escaped his lips: "Mariya."

Tall, dark-haired, and the most beautiful thing to touch his life. Dead now long, long ago, he reminded himself. Her universe, *his* universe, did not exist anymore.

Rather than recall the painful memories any longer, Dutchman dug into his food. It was delicious. Anything was delicious after so long with nothing.

In what seemed far too short a time, he was eating the last of the toasted bread and sipping the remaining drops of the orange liquid the waitress had given him. By this time, the place was filled with patrons, many of them requesting orders to take away. Dutchman found their scurrying amusing. They acted as if the work they did every day had some lasting importance to the universe. Of course, they did not understand that their Earth had little time left and he saw no reason to inform them. They were happy in their ignorance.

One of the rushing figures looked directly at him. Dutchman ignored him for the most part, still caught up in the first true meal he had been allowed since the passing of the last Earth. The juice especially fascinated him, so different was it compared to the water he was used to drinking.

He realized a sip later that the other figure was still staring at him. Dutchman slowly turned his head in that direction, barely catching the other pair of eyes before the man looked away. It was too late, though. Dutchman had him identified just as the other man must have seen through the illusion cast around the ancient wanderer. The figure in the suit was well shielded, so much so that even now it was difficult to sense him for what he was, but there was no doubt that he was a leaper.

"Leaper . . ." He had not talked to any of the refugees in many landings and now faced by one so close, Dutchman's curiosity swelled. The cloaked figure rose, the remnants of his meal forgotten. The woman who had served him came by with a slip of paper, but Dutchman waved her away. She crumpled up the paper, removed the dishes, and went to deal with another patron. No memory of her tall, somber visitor remained.

Unlike the woman, though, the leaper had far from forgotten his presence. He was already at the door, his purchase left at the counter. Dutchman found himself mildly amused. He followed the other man outside, walking just fast enough to keep him in sight. Unlike the Roschach he had pursued the preceding day, Dutchman wanted neither to harm nor to cause harm to come to the figure. All he wanted was to ask him a few questions.

The leaper, a nondescript, brown-haired man who looked barely two decades old, picked up his pace. It was possible that he thought Dutchman one of the inhuman hunters, but there was no correcting that misconception just yet. Not until the chase was over.

Dutchman allowed the leaper to increase the gap between them to nearly a block, then stepped to the side.

A breath later, the leaper, still looking back, collided with the immovable form of his pursuer.

"There is no need for fear," Dutchman informed the panic-stricken man.

"Carim's blood! Damn you!" The leaper swung at him, more than simply physical power put into the blow. He radiated desperation.

Raising one hand, Dutchman caught the fist. Around them, people began to stare. Dutchman frowned. There had been enough excitement, he decided. Still holding the struggling leaper's fist, Dutchman looked around. As he did, interest in the encounter suddenly waned. Everyone had better things to do. They looked away and forgot that they had seen anything.

"There is no need for fear," he insisted again.

The leaper laughed, a laugh without hope. For some reason, he seemed not to take heart from the words. "I'm supposed to believe such a lie from the Prince of Shadows himself? You've got me; finish it!"

Prince of Shadows? He had heard the term before on other variants. Once before Dutchman had been mistaken for this titled figure although then he had not been able to ask why. "I am not this prince. I am another."

It was clear that his denial fell on deaf ears. The leaper stared at his trapped fist. A force tickled Dutchman's hand, but nothing significant enough to make him release his hold.

"I want only to ask a few questions." When his unwilling companion only stared at him, he decided to begin. "Have you sensed it? Is the End coming soon?"

"The End?" His quarry eyed him in outright hatred. "You would know better than I, wouldn't you? That's why you're here for me, isn't it?"

Dutchman cringed as if struck. It sounded as if the leaper knew that his captor was responsible for the cycle of destruction. The accusation was the deadliest barb that the other could have wielded. Dutchman almost released the fist, but recovered in time. From the look on the leaper's face, the man had realized that he had just missed an opportunity.

"I meant no *harm*," Dutchman told him, feeling the need to explain to someone who might understand. The questions he had wanted to ask had suddenly been expunged from his mind, but that did not matter at the moment. He felt a great need to explain somehow. He had to make one person see that he had not meant to destroy world upon world. Surely if anyone could understand, it would be one of the leapers. "It was supposed to open new vistas, new powers to us! I did not know it would open the floodgates! I did not know I would undermine the very fabric of existence! I thought I had planned for all contingencies! How could I have *known* that all this would happen?"

His captive backed away from him as far as he could. The outright fear in his eyes struck Dutchman. The memories of all those who had perished rose strong in his mind. Once more the voices, the condemning cries of the lost, whispered in his ears, growing louder with each beat of his heart. They had all died because of him . . . because of him . . . because of him. . . .

"I did not mean to do it!"

Overwhelmed by both the voices and his own sense of guilt, Dutchman bent over, trying somehow to hide from the condemnations. Without realizing it, he released the leaper's fist. All that mattered was fighting off the ghosts within his mind. The man could have struck him then and Dutchman would not have cared. It would have been light enough punishment for what he had done.

Instead of attacking, the leaper first watched wide-eyed as the cloaked, weathered figure fell against a glass window, all the while beseeching unseen souls to understand. Then, realizing that he was no longer under the stranger's control, the leaper regained his senses and ran away as fast as he could. Dutchman could do nothing to stop him; he did not even recall that someone had been with him. There were only the ghosts.

Only the ghosts . . .

"Hey, are you all right?" asked a voice that cut through those of the specters. "Mister?"

Other voices that might have been ghosts but sounded much too near, too solid, assailed Dutchman. Slowly his demons receded into the background. The struggling exile became aware of his surroundings again.

"What's he dressed like that for?"

"Someone call an ambulance or a cop! I think he's having a fit!"

"Don't touch him!"

"What's with the outfit?"

They can see me, Dutchman finally realized. *They can see me. . . .*

He had lost such control that he had come fully in tune with his surroundings. What must they think, the ephemeral souls around him? Did they suspect him of being insane? Surely that was the most likely notion under the circumstances. Even Dutchman was willing to concede the validity of such a suspicion.

"Mister, you need help?" The voice, Dutchman finally saw, belonged to an elderly, dark-skinned gentleman who was not quite tall enough to match the stricken wanderer's shoulder. "I think someone's called an ambulance."

Old . . . The very age of this would-be benefactor reminded Dutchman of what was going to happen here. Every one of the people surrounding him was going to die in a terrible catastrophe. Only he would go on, unless he pulled himself together and, for once, tried to do something concrete.

Taking hold of the elderly man, Dutchman whispered, "I'm sorry. I'll do what I can."

"What—?"

The cursed exile gently pushed aside the smaller man and stepped through the gathered crowd. They parted for him without thought, obeying his unspoken commands. Dutchman did not look back, but he knew that even as he reached the edge of the street, the folk who had tried to help him were beginning to go about their normal business. They would forget just as all the others he had confronted. He regretted that he could not turn back the aid they had summoned, but that situation would have to work itself out without his assistance.

Dutchman swore under his breath, berating himself for his handling of the situation. The leaper's words had stung because they echoed his own mind. It seemed that even the hapless refugees who preceded him to each world knew of his crimes and with each new catastrophe their hatred no doubt grew. Had Dutchman thought that they could have dealt proper justice to him, he would gladly have turned himself over for sentencing. Unfortunately, there was nothing they could do to him. His punishment was in the hands of others.

He had to find a solution, if only for everyone but himself.

There was no sign of the leaper, but Dutchman no longer cared. He had no desire to repeat the scene, no desire to relive the accusations.

Yet . . . one thing the man had said nagged at him a little. He recalled the title used by this leaper and by another on an older variant. That first time had been in the windswept regions of a place called Britannica. *Prince of Shadows.* He had also heard the name *Darkling* used with the same fearful tone. The leapers spoke the titles with conviction, as if they knew the bearer so well. How could that be when he barely ever contacted them?

For the first time, Dutchman wondered, *Is there another who truly bears the titles?* Out loud he added, "Is there really a Prince of Shadows?"

If there was, he seemed more than the leapers, almost someone who might have better knowledge of Dutchman's accursed actions and their terrible consequences. Perhaps this Prince of Shadows, if he existed, had answers of which Dutchman could make use.

They fear him, though. They fear him as much as I fear the voices. . . .

That made him think of the hunters. They preyed on the leapers and the leapers feared the Darkling. It made sense then that there might be a link between the inhuman creatures and this shadow man the refugees tried to shun.

So to find this Prince of Shadows, he might need only to find a Roschach. Not simple, but not impossible. Now more than ever he regretted his futile encounters with the creatures. *I will have to change my strategy should I encounter another of them. I shall have to avoid their destruction.* There had to be at least another in this city; Dutchman had never found only one. *The next hunter I will treat more gingerly.*

Glancing at the cloudy sky, the exile wondered again how long he had. This line of pursuit might turn out to be folly, a waste of precious time. The Darkling might be a bogeyman, a creation of the leapers' lack of understanding of the truth behind their eternal trek. It could be that he was nothing but a misrepresentation of Dutchman after all.

If so, then I will have failed. This world will follow the rest . . . and I will sail on until the next Earth prepares to die.

Hamman Tarriqa sat cross-legged in his living room, eyes closed and breath slowed.

Come on, Ursuline! Speak to me. Wake up, you old witch!

In his mind, Tarriqa no longer existed in twentieth-century Chicago. Now he floated unseen in a small room in a place he knew to be Paris in the midsixteenth century. While small, the room was elegant, even more so in some ways than the suite the black man owned.

Ursuline! Wake up!

Who's there? asked a sleepy voice.

Hamman. Why must you sleep at this time of day?

I prefer the night life, Hamman, you know that.

In his mind, Tarriqa watched a slim, attractive woman nearly as young-looking as Maia de Fortunato rise from a bed. She was not concerned that her ghostly visitor could see every detail of her body, but then, little concerned Ursuline in this life. She was the mistress of a very influential member of the court. It was a contrast to her last existence, when she had been reborn, much to her surprise and dismay, in the form of a man during the invasion of Europe by the Huns. Even the powers she wielded as a Scattered One had not helped her then. Now, in this version of Earth, she used those powers to aid her patron and, by doing so, herself. . . . In her present incarnation those same powers could have had her burned at the stake as a witch.

Secretly, Hamman Tarriqa feared for her. Ursuline was growing careless. Her attitude had become the type that attracted the attention of the Darkling.

There's news here. Let me tell you. He related to her what his recent visitors had told him, leaving out items he thought she need not know just yet. Tarriqa wanted Ursuline to contact a few of the others for him and filling her head with unessential information would only distract her. Maia and her buffoonish friend would have claimed he was withholding things, but like MacPhee, Tarriqa was certain that he knew better.

How disturbing for you, Ursuline replied when he was finished. She sounded only slightly put out. *I'm sorry for you, Hamman.*

Spare the pity and do me a favor. I need you to contact the others. He gave her the names just to make certain that she had not forgotten them.

I recall them all, she returned, her annoyance evident. *What should I tell them?*

Tell them to keep an eye out for the harbinger. Tell them I think that the ghost ship sails now. Tell them to watch out for the so-called Flying Dutchman.

That brought her completely around. There was even a hint of anxiety in her next question: *You've seen something?*

No, but I think he will make his appearance soon.

What do we do then? Ursuline was, Tarriqa was pleased to see, finally acting like her old self. He wished that she had been reborn in his time period, if only so that they could easier work together.

I've a notion, one that MacPhee was thinking of exploring. I want to speak to or, if necessary, capture the angel of death.

She knew that he did not mean the Darkling. *Are you serious? He is the signal of the—*

Their conversation was interrupted by a tremendous clanging noise. Tarriqa tried to maintain his concentration, but already Ursuline's room was fading. The last he saw of her was the woman, still naked, trying to block out the sound by covering her ears with her palms. Unfortunately, the sound was in her mind, for the source existed somewhere in the black man's suite.

Unable to maintain control any longer, Hamman Tarriqa broke contact. He opened his eyes and at last realized that the noise was the ringing of his telephone. With growing irritation, he reached over to the coffee table beside him and snatched the receiver off of its charger.

"Hammond Tarrez speaking." Only barely was Tarriqa able to recall his present name.

"Tarriqa! Carim's blood! What took you so long?"

"Rees?" The other's voice was unmistakable. Rees was one of those who believed his best hope of avoiding the Darkling's dogs was to keep his existence as separate from his counterparts as was possible. He called Tarriqa perhaps once a year.

"I saw him, Hamman! The Darkling nearly had me!"

Whatever anger remained after the interruption of his work drained away as Tarriqa absorbed what he had just been told. "You *saw* the Darkling?"

"Who else could it have been? He was in this restaurant I frequent before work, one of those—"

"Your insistence on living your way will be your end, Rees. I've warned you—"

"Spare me your sermons, Hamman! It's not very much different from your own ways!" The other refugee's voice had grown so shrill that Tarriqa had to hold the receiver away from his ear. "Do you want to hear this or not? There are others I could be contacting, you know."

"I do want to hear. I want to find out how you bested the Prince of Shadows so easily." Rees was far from the most competent of the Scattered Ones. In some ways his choice to live a mundane existence among the single-lifers might have been a wise one after all.

On the other end of the line, Rees calmed. "It was not as easy as all that, Hamman. He was sitting there . . . just *sitting* there and *eating,* for Carim's sake! No one else could see that he was different. Gods! He was the tallest person in the place, dressed in peculiar, old-fashioned garments, with a cloak that moved like it had a life of its own, and no one *noticed.* At the very least they should have seen his eyes!"

Tarriqa was mulling over the swift description of the supposed Darkling's clothing. "And what about the eyes?" he asked.

"Black as the shadows he comes from and no pupils whatsoever. I swear I felt I was about to be swallowed by them when our gazes met."

"In the restaurant?"

"In the restaurant." Rees swallowed. "Let me tell you everything that happened before it blurs."

Rees described his attempts to flee and the Darkling's toying with him. The Prince of Shadows had shrugged off his attack as easily as one might dust an insect from a coat sleeve. The tall figure had questioned him about the End. For a time, Rees had feared that his captor would tear his hand from his wrist, but then a startling thing had occurred.

"He did *what?*" Tarriqa interrupted, unwilling to believe what Rees told him next.

"Practically begged my forgiveness. Told me more or less that he hadn't meant for it to happen . . . then he doubled over as if someone was beating him! I swear he looked like that." Rees repeated his description of his last few moments with the cloaked figure. The Darkling had acted insane, moving about as if harried on all sides by unseen enemies. "I left before he could recover."

"Sensible, I suppose." Tarriqa would have made better use

of the time, perhaps finding a way to bind the other. There was something very odd about the encounter. This did not sound like the few descriptions MacPhee had gathered concerning the Darkling. He would have expected the Darkling to be more of a true shadow . . . as his other title indicated. From what he recalled of the fearful descriptions, the Prince of Shadows was murky, indistinct at times. With some exceptions, the Darkling that Rees had encountered could have passed for one of them.

If not the Darkling Prince, then who?

"Hamman? Are you still there?"

"Rees, where did this encounter take place?" As his counterpart described the location, he wrote down the address just in case. "I know it, I think. . . . Interesting."

"Interesting? That's all? *Interesting?* I nearly lost my life . . . permanently!"

"No, I don't think so."

"You were not there, Hamman."

He had a point, but Tarriqa was coming to believe that the only reason that Rees had been in any danger was due to his own attempt to lash out. "The reason I say that is because I don't think that the one who confronted you was the Darkling at all."

"Then who was it? None of us, I'm certain. A new sort of Roschach?"

That was a possibility. Maybe the Prince of Shadows now made use of more human-looking hounds. Still, the black man doubted that. "Could be, but I have another theory, Rees. I was just speaking to someone else about this when you called. I think . . . and it is only a guess at this point . . . that you have just reported to us the first sighting of the angel of death himself."

"The Boatman?"

"If you prefer that title, yes." He waited for reaction from Rees, but the man was silent. "I believe my theory makes more sense. The Darkling has never been known to be so . . . so regretful."

"It's the End, then."

Not until he had heard the other say the words did the realization truly strike Tarriqa. It echoed what that clown Gilbrin had said. For several seconds, neither man spoke, then Hamman Tarriqa very quietly said, "Soon, yes."

Rees grew upset again. "It's not fair! I've hardly had enough time with this life! I've only just established myself enough to enjoy it!"

Although he had lived longer on this variant Earth than had his counterpart and had accomplished much more, Tarriqa could only agree with Rees. It was *not* fair. They did not deserve to be uprooted so soon. That, however, was only a small point compared to the true dilemma: Once more they would all be cast out, their futures decided on the flip of the proverbial coin.

They would all feel the End, even those reborn centuries earlier. They would feel it through the link they shared with those present during the catastrophe. Communication might be difficult through linear times, but pure terror flowed along the links with ease. The leap would not take place until just before the final destruction, at which point he, Rees, Maia de Fortunato, the jester, and the others here would be at their wits' end, for it was never certain that they would all leap again. More important, there was always the fear that this was the *last* world, that beyond the destruction of this variant there would be . . . nothing.

Forever.

No one could explain how the process of leaping worked. Not even MacPhee had known everything. First an incredible swelling sensation in the chest, then a tremendous feeling of displacement, then . . . a blank time, when it seemed as if the leaper ceased to exist. If the leaper was fortunate, he would be reborn in a new world, eventually regaining his identity. If not, then he would never know.

Why some did not make it to the next variant was something else no one understood. They only prayed that they would do so.

"I want you to meet me at that restaurant in an hour," he commanded Rees. "Wait inside or stand outside, whichever you prefer."

To his surprise, Rees did not even argue. "I can be there in two. I . . . I need to get something."

"Fine. That will give me time to sort out some other details. I have something in mind, but it would be better if I had the chance to investigate the site of your encounter before I discussed it further. I would say it is safe to assume that your friend will no longer be nearby."

"Probably. I'll see you in two hours, Hamman." Rees hung up.

The black man eyed the receiver for a moment, then replaced it. Rees was understandably anxious, but hopefully not enough to make him useless to Tarriqa. He wondered what Rees would have said if he had known that Tarriqa was half-hoping to confront the cloaked figure there and then.

He considered contacting Maia and her companion but decided to wait until after his meeting with Rees. There was nothing the two newcomers could accomplish that he could not. Besides, they would keep asking questions and Tarriqa worked best when he had the time to think. Rees would be distraction enough.

Capturing the angel of death. You only thought about it, MacPhee, but I will do it . . . if necessary. The harbinger seems to want to talk this time. This could be what we've needed to do all this time instead of living in fear. This could be our way of changing our fates.

He rose suddenly, anxious to get on with things. Why wait for Rees? Why not go to the restaurant now and study the site in relative solitude, the other pedestrians notwithstanding? That way, by the time his companion arrived, Tarriqa might already have some information for him.

Perhaps by the time Rees arrived he might even have the Flying Dutchman in hand.

* * *

The restaurant was in a location that for some reason interested Tarriqa almost as much as the encounter that had taken place there. He looked up at the Sears Tower, impressive even to one who had leaped to hundreds of worlds, then to the northeast, where he knew the former monarch of the city, the John Hancock Building, loomed. The restaurant was in a perfect line of sight from one leviathan to another.

It was probably simply coincidence, but Tarriqa had not made his fortune entirely on the merits of what the inhabitants of this variant termed "sorcery." No, he had made his fortune in great part because he calculated things, looked for possible connections, and made hunches not entirely based on chance. In his own opinion, Hamman Tarriqa was MacPhee's superior. If the other had not been taken by the Darkling, the black man was certain that before long his work would have surpassed that of his associate.

There was no sense thinking ill of the dead, though, so Tarriqa decided to give MacPhee credit where credit was due and move on with his research. Rees had said that he and the stranger had first matched gazes inside near where businesspeople on the go ordered meals or snacks to be taken back to work. Therefore, the logical step was to go inside and try to sense anything out of the ordinary, such as energy residue. A being like the one that Rees had described would have had a unique energy signature.

The lunch crowds had not yet gathered, which made his task easier. Tarriqa quietly entered and walked over to where Rees most likely had stood. In fact, he could already sense his counterpart's recent location. If he was correct, then the one who might be the angel of death would have sat on one of three particular seats at the counter.

Making his way to the seats in question, Hamman Tarriqa sought in vain for some trace of the stranger. There was nothing. It was as if the seats had never been used. He could not sense even the normal traces that should have been left by the regular inhabitants. Even they, nearly devoid of the talent, generally left some minute evidence if only because so many sat there. Either the seats were new or something had absorbed the residue.

Absorbed the residue? The traces? Hamman Tarriqa found the notion both nonsensical and unnerving. He had never heard of something that absorbed such trace energy, but then no one really knew much about the Boatman. They assumed he was the cause because he always appeared shortly before the destruction. For the most part Tarriqa himself believed that.

"Can I help you?"

It was one of the waitresses. An idea formed in his head. He leaned forward. "Yes. A friend of mine thinks that he left something here. A tall, weathered-looking fellow with . . . with dark eyes."

She shook her head. "I've taken care of the counter since first thing this morning and I don't remember anyone like that. What's he lost?"

He stared into her eyes. "Let me describe him again. You should remember someone like him."

As Tarriqa repeated the brief description that Rees had supplied him with, the woman's eyes lowered and her breathing slowed. To all appearances she looked awake, just a little tired.

"Well? Do you remember him?"

"I . . . there might have been someone like him. I . . . let me think."

She should have been completely open to him. Her hesitation, her uncertainty, was completely without precedent to Tarriqa. The waitress should either have remembered the stranger or have said that she had never seen him. The hesitation alone was enough to verify that there had been someone unusual here, someone whose abilities were quite impressive.

He could hardly keep her under much longer, with so many others around. Once more Hamman Tarriqa repeated what little he knew of the Boatman.

At last her eyes widened a little. "Yeah . . . I think there was someone here like that. Yeah. Not bad-looking. Kind of weather-worn. Looked like my brother does. A sailor, my brother."

"What did he do while he was here?"

The Boatman's visit to this restaurant, it turned out, had been extraordinarily ordinary until the encounter with Rees. He had actually been eating . . . and enjoying the fare, according to the waitress. It was not until he noticed someone nearby that he had begun to act very strange, suddenly rising and leaving without a word.

"This was his seat." Her finger indicated the one just before the black man. "I don't think he paid . . ." she added.

"Don't worry about it." Tarriqa waved a hand before her. The waitress blinked and started to say something, but another waitress chose that moment to call to her.

As she departed, Tarriqa touched the seat. The absolute absence of any trace, he realized, was almost as good as a trace. Now that he knew what to look for, Hamman Tarriqa was slowly able to follow the trail back to the door. He opened it and stepped outside.

"You're here already."

He looked up into the anxious features of Rees "I thought I'd do a little preliminary study of the area. You're early, too, friend."

"Didn't take me as long as I thought to take care of things." Rees glanced around.

"I do not think he is here."

"Can you be certain?"

In truth, Tarriqa could not. Finally he just shrugged. "Show me the path you took when you ran from here."

"You would've run, too, Hamman, if you'd faced what I had," the other retorted. Nonetheless, he started along the sidewalk, trying to follow his earlier route. Hamman Tarriqa walked close behind, seeking out the same absence of trace energy. He was soon pleased to discover that his theory held water. Only one point made him curious and that was when the trail suddenly ceased.

Rees, intent on retracing his steps, did not at first realize that he had left his companion behind. When he did, he returned to Tarriqa. "What is it?"

"You saw him here, didn't you?"

"Yes."

"Where did he go from this point?"

Rees looked down. After a moment, he turned and pointed ahead. "Up around there. You can't quite see it in this crowd."

Lunchtime had begun for some and the sidewalks were crowded. Both Scattered Ones had been using their power to keep anyone from growing curious, so no one looked at them even now. Unfortunately for Tarriqa's purposes, he did not dare disperse even a part of the crowd.

He finally decided simply to accept Rees's word as to where he had next seen the tall figure. "So one moment he was here and the next he was there." He concluded, "So he can shift himself to another location." With great effort, some of the Scattered Ones could do that, but only over short distances. "Show me the area of the struggle."

It took only another minute or two to reach the spot. For the first time, Tarriqa was nearly overwhelmed by the strange sense of absence the Boatman left wherever he had been. Much had happened here.

"What's wrong, Hamman?"

Rees was not as skilled as his companion was, which was probably fortunate for him. He could not sense what Tarriqa could. "Nothing that I can't deal with. What happened after?"

"I ran off in that direction."

"Did you? His trail goes this direction." He pointed in a direction nearly opposite the one to which Rees had fled.

"I wouldn't know, Hamman. I went the other way before he recovered."

"Well, I think we should follow this trail while it is still fresh."

His companion shivered. "I was afraid you'd say that."

"You don't have to come, Rees."

"And I'm not. I'm no fool, Hamman. I don't walk into the spider's web. It was hard enough to come back here so soon."

He reached into his suit coat, revealing just enough of what he had hidden within it. "I guess I shouldn't have bothered coming back. I didn't want to. I even brought this, just in case of trouble here. It's not registered, if it matters to you."

"A projectile weapon? A revolver? Rees, are you insane? What did you hope to do with that?" Tarriqa pictured what would have happened had Rees come with him on the next leg of their search and they had actually run into the Boatman. *The fool would have shot first, that's what would have happened!* Likely the bullets would have had no effect, but the sheer recklessness of the man was a danger to them all. Tarriqa wanted a peaceful encounter. "You're absolutely correct, friend. You're not coming with me. I intend to confront the Boatman . . . or whoever this stranger is . . . and talk to him. He may provide valuable clues and information, not only concerning our existences, but perhaps even about the Darkling."

"He probably *is* the Darkling, Hamman!"

"I doubt that." He came to a decision. "You can return to your life for the time being, Rees, but I'd like you to do me a favor first, if you don't mind."

"What is it?" the other asked with some caution.

"Here." From his empty palm, Hamman Tarriqa produced a business card with an address scribbled on the back. "Go to a telephone . . . and I mean a telephone . . . and call this number. I have a couple of guests there. Let them know what happened and that I will contact them this evening, if possible."

"I can do that." Rees looked down at the address. "Nice hotel, but, Hamman, you shouldn't go alone—"

"I think it best that I do." In a gesture of faith, he put a hand on the other's shoulder. "Trust in me, Rees. Will you call them?"

"I said I would."

"Good. Then the only other thing I want you to do is put that gun away somewhere and practice patience. This entire situation requires care and forethought."

Rees put the card in a coat pocket. "I'll give them a call,

Hamman. I'll also keep the gun. It can be handier than you think."

It was futile to argue. The best thing that Tarriqa could do was hope that his younger-looking counterpart would stay out of the way until *he* had the situation in hand. "As you wish."

"Carim watch over you, Hamman."

The black man nodded. He watched as Rees turned and walked off, his suit coat drawn close. *Amazing that the fool has lasted so long.*

He dropped all thought of Rees, then, and instead concentrated on the trail the Boatman had left. It was strong, still fresh. The cloaked stranger could not be far.

As Tarriqa followed the scent, two dark-haired men in almost identical suits split from the crowd of lunchtime pedestrians. The first of them turned so that his path would bring him along the same direction as the black man.

The second continued on . . . his route identical to that which Rees had taken but a minute before.

6. ROOM SERVICE

At Maia's insistence, they waited most of the day for word from Hamman Tarriqa. It was not too hard to persuade Gilbrin; the suite came with its own bar and the room service was very courteous and prompt. The furnishings were plush and there was even a gas fireplace on one wall. More important to Gilbrin, there was also a Cubs game on in the early afternoon. Once seated before the television, the Shifter, who had become an avid fan of the team since watching the games on cable in central Illinois, might as well have been asleep for all he listened to his anxious companion.

At three in the afternoon, Maia, clad in black jeans and a stylish black T-shirt, began to pace. Gilbrin, cheering on his team, which was behind at the moment, glanced her way, then immediately returned his attention to the screen. She continued to pace for the next hour and it was only after the Cubs had come from behind to win by one run that the sandy-haired figure asked her what was wrong.

"What's wrong? We've been in this room all day, Gil! Hamman hasn't tried to contact us once by any method. It has me worried, that's what."

Gilbrin, dressed in battered blue jeans topped by a shocking pink Hole concert T-shirt, gave her only part of his attention. The news was another passion of his and he had already switched to one of the other local stations just in time to hear the headlines. "Now you should think about that, sweet. Master Tarriqa didn't necessarily say that he was going to contact us so soon. He might've had to recuperate, you know. Or maybe he didn't find out anything."

The television blared in the background: "A citizen's group lobbied today to keep the electric company from trying to raise its rates. . . ."

She looked at him, somewhat perplexed by his defense of their counterpart. "I thought you didn't trust him."

"Alderman Robert Sawyer denounced the State's Attorney's Office for what he called a 'witch's hunt' concerning questionable donations to his last campaign . . ."

Gilbrin twisted around, the better to face the pacing woman. "I don't. I'm just giving you some reasons to stop wearing a hole through the carpet with those attractive but rather pointy-heeled boots of yours. As far as I'm concerned, the only use Master Tarriqa will ever be is as the provider of this wonderful abode. I trust your bedroom was as opulent as mine was?"

"And police are looking into a series of shots fired near the vicinity of the Sears Tower. A gun has been recovered and although police have not released a statement yet, the suspicion is that it might be gang-related. . . ."

"Don't detour me with frivolous questions, Gil—and can you please turn that awful thing off? I've endured your fondness for sports, but I really have no desire to try to outshout the news."

With a snap of the Shifter's fingers, the television blackened. He smiled. "It's always worthwhile to remain informed, sweet. You never know what you might hear."

"Can we get back to the subject at hand?"

"Was it to do with our associate? We might as well be dealing with MacPhee. We'll get as far as we did with him."

Maia walked to the window and stared down at the busy streets. "You were the one who brought us to Hamman, Gil. You were also the one who first introduced me to MacPhee. Now you act as if dealing with either of them was a waste of time. I know you like to be contrary, but I wish you'd stop it. After our conversation with Hamman, you talked about doing something on our own, yet all I've seen you do is eat, sleep, and watch that accursed invention. I thank the gods that we never had such a devious device on our Earth."

"Frankly, I don't know what I did without television," the sandy-haired figure replied, his smile a deceptively lazy one. "I miss it each time we leap to an Earth where they forgot to invent it. I even tried to get some men interested in the concept on one variant, but they lacked the proper appreciation."

Maia, no longer paying attention to his comments, suddenly came to a decision. "I'm going to call him. By telephone."

"You might want this." The Shifter rattled off Tarriqa's telephone number from the card he had kept.

She purposely did not thank him. Maia pressed the buttons and waited for the telephone to start ringing. When it did, she glanced at her companion. Gilbrin's expression was unreadable, but the levity had vanished from it.

The telephone continued to ring. Just as Maia was about to put down the receiver, though, Hamman Tarriqa's voice came on. She almost spoke, then realized that it was only an answering machine message. Frustrated, she hung up.

"Not there?"

"Obviously not." She paused. "I'm going to try to link to him. It shouldn't be too hard this near."

"No." Gilbrin was on his feet now, his face awash with concern. "No," he repeated. "Don't try to link. If you want, we can go drive over to his place and see if he's come back, but I heartily recommend that you hold off establishing a mental bond."

"Why?"

"Because . . ." He rubbed his fingertips across his lips, as if looking for just the right words. "Because with the Darkling's soldiers possibly in the city, you never know what might intercept you . . . or him."

Now Maia understood what Gilbrin meant. "You're not

saying that you think that the Prince of Shadows might be the reason that Hamman's not contacted us yet? We saw him only yesterday! He's probably just out."

"He may very well be and I'm inclined to believe that over the other possibility . . . for now; but what I'm trying to point out, sweet, is that the link is probably the most obvious way we make ourselves known to the Darkling. Even a dozen minor spells do not shout out our existence the way one attempt to link does. That much I've learned without MacPhee and without Hamman Tarriqa. We can go to his abode and wait there if you like, but I would forgo linking."

What he said made some sense. Maia was tempted to accept his offer. "What about your own pursuits? You keep hinting about a different course of action."

He looked a little sheepish. "It's not quite jelled yet, I regret to say. I feel like something is not in place . . . that I'm waiting for someone or some incident. I have one idea, but so far it's too far-fetched for me even to offer out loud. That's why I'm still willing to see if I was correct in choosing to contact Master Tarriqa first. Believe me, sweet, I'd rather he had the answer, not me. I'm much too unstable a soul."

"So should we go to Hamman's?"

"Food might be suggested first since our associate's not yet at home."

She wanted to drive straight over there, but at last she nodded. Unlike Gilbrin, who could eat and eat and then eat again, Maia was honestly hungry, having had only some fruit early that morning. Until this moment, she had been too keyed up even to think of eating again.

At his further suggestion, Maia returned to her own room to rinse off her face and try to relax for a few minutes until room service brought up the meal Gilbrin was ordering. She had just finished drying off her face when she heard the television. The Shifter was watching the news again. Not at all desiring to spend her time listening to the ramblings of the announcers, the weary refugee fell back on her still-unmade bed and stared up at the ceiling.

She was on a sailing ship like none that had ever journeyed the seas of her Earth. A storm brewed around her and she grew afraid. There was no one else on board that she could see. Maia was not a fearful woman, but she knew nothing about sailing and the storm looked to be a fierce one.

Then, to her shock, a hand came to rest on her shoulder. A voice, as weathered in its own way as the ship on which she stood, asked, "Are you afraid? There is no—"

"Maia?"

Opening her eyes, Maia de Fortunato realized that she had fallen asleep and dreamed of a ship and someone on board. *But it felt so real. I smelled the odors and tasted the sea. . . .*

"Maia?" There was a knock. "Our meal has arrived, sweet."

Slowly she rose from her bed. "I'll be there in a moment, Gil. Go ahead and start without me."

"I'll try to leave you a few crumbs, but don't dawdle too long, love, or I can't promise anything!"

She ignored his jest, still trying to recall more details of her dream as she stretched. The only connection she could make between the ship and anything else was the brief mention of the legend of the Boatman toward the tail end of their conversation with Hamman. Why she should dream of him was beyond her. Too much anxiety, she supposed. Although the Boatman . . . or Flying Dutchman . . . did supposedly exist, Maia had neither met him nor ever seen the ghostly vessel that supposedly haunted the skies after his coming.

I'd better eat something. It was lack of food that made her dream such peculiar scenes.

Maia smoothed her clothing and departed her room. Knowing Gilbrin as she did, he would be fast at work on the meal. While he was not likely to eat her food, she did not want him sitting around staring at her as she chewed. It made it hard not to rush, which Maia did not like to do.

"I hope you haven't touched—" was as far as the dark-haired woman got as she entered the living room of the suite.

Gilbrin was seated with his back to the covered cart on

which the trays of food had been brought, his attention on the news. In his lap was a plate. The Shifter, caught up in the day's topics, barely paid attention to the meal he was stuffing into his mouth.

It was not the sight of her companion eating that had stilled Maia. Rather, it was the covered cart. The trays still atop it, the cart was *growing,* rising higher and higher. When she had entered, it had already reached a height nearly equal to her own.

Worse, it was moving slowly and silently toward Gilbrin's back.

"Gil! Look out!"

The cart hissed and a black appendage ending in long, needlelike talons burst from beneath the covering. It shot through the back of the chair, reaching for the short figure seated there.

Its prey was no longer there, however, having rolled off the chair before Maia could finish her warning. In an instant, Gilbrin the Shifter was on his feet, facing his attacker.

Maia was already reacting. She focused her attention on the cloth that covered the thing and used her power to cause it to burst into flames. A second black appendage reached from the back of the cart and pulled at the burning cover, tossing it at the woman. Maia dodged the flaming missile, then worked quickly to smother it before the fire could spread.

Revealed at last, the thing beneath the cover was shaped to conform to the cart under which it had hidden. It was black with a long, flat head and four incredibly lengthy limbs. The monster had a mouth full of teeth and striped eyes with no pupils.

"Roschach!" snarled Gilbrin. "Darkling's dog!"

"Come unharmed, come harmed. Choose . . ." mocked the hunter, still growing. Its limbs were at least six feet long and as supple as those of an octopus. How all of it had fit so cunningly under the cover was a mystery, but not one especially important to either of its intended prey. What was important was that the deadly monstrosity seemed capable of dealing with both of them with virtually no effort.

"Go willingly to your prince, my would-be cephalopod?" The Shifter shook his head. "And people think that *I'm* daft! We're not yours for the taking, no indeed."

In response, the Roschach opened wide its flat mouth. A thick, ebony tongue as wide and round as Maia's arm shot out at Gilbrin. He raised his arms to deflect it, but as he did, one of the other limbs snaked over to his leg, winding around it with astonishing speed.

Maia saw what was happening, but another limb was already racing toward her. She leaped just barely in time to avoid being coiled and as she landed, the heels of her boots jammed into the Roschach's appendage.

It shivered in pain, the bizarre tongue momentarily flailing wildly before Gilbrin's face. Maia's companion ignored the lessened threat of the tongue, concentrating on the limb wrapped around his leg. His hand fairly glowed, but the hunter's limb was unaffected.

The hunter had retracted its injured limb, nearly sending Maia falling backward. Unwilling to let her triumph simply fade, she tried to stomp on the retreating appendage, but the monster's tongue suddenly altered course and darted for her chest. She ducked the grotesque, saliva-covered tongue and tried to blind the Roschach with a spell, but the stripes shifted as light burst before the creature. For a moment, the thing's eyes were red and black, but they returned to their former coloring once the illumination had dwindled.

From above her, the tongue struck, the Roschach trying to knock her senseless. Maia twisted to the side, but was not completely successful. She was batted over, practically falling on top of the now scattered plates and dinnerware that had rested atop the Darkling's soldier.

The tongue wrapped around her waist.

Maia tried to clear her head, but now she could not breathe well. To her side, unseen, she heard Gilbrin shout, "I *said* let go of me!"

The tongue quivered as if shocked, then loosened its hold on her somewhat. It was enough for Maia to recover her breath. Able to think at last, she looked around desperately for some weapon. Her power was failing her. However, the only weapon in sight . . . and in reach . . . was one of the forks that had come with the food. Unable to kick at the appendage holding her, Maia decided to seize the fork. Only the fact that the metal tips of her bootheels had injured the hunter's limb gave her hope.

Another limb snaked toward her. In the back of her mind, Maia found herself wondering just how the Prince of Shadow's creature could maintain its balance. Then her curiosity faded as she realized that if the new limb caught her arm, her makeshift weapon would be of no use to her.

Driving her hand down with as much force as she could muster, the desperate refugee buried the prongs of the fork into the limb. To her surprise, the prongs sank in with ease, going as far as the full length.

Hissing, the hunter again retracted. Maia, urged on by her success, attacked the tongue. She jabbed again and again with the fork, caring only that each strike garnered some damage.

Uncoiling, the dripping appendage retreated all the way into the maw of the Roschach. The monstrosity's eyes flared.

Something moved just at the edge of her field of vision. It was Gilbrin, heading toward the fireplace. Maia had no time to wonder what he planned, for once again she was attacked. This time the Roschach seized her arm before she could prevent it and shook loose the fork. The makeshift weapon fell out of her reach.

"Blasted doors!" the Shifter growled.

"Gil!" He did not hear her. Maia kicked at the hunter, but could not connect with any of its appendages.

The Roschach's macabre form filled her view. Even though it looked her way only part of the time, it was able to concentrate enough attention on her to keep her from either freeing herself or creating some viable counterattack. Maia knew that with each passing second she was losing precious ground.

"Ha! Got it!"

A blazing brilliance filled the room. Maia smelled smoke and gas. The hunter opened its mouth and unleashed a shrill squeal of anguish. One of the limbs uncoiled, giving Maia some freedom of movement. She pulled at the other appendage, which did not resist as much as she had expected. The Roschach was still squealing, an ear-piercing noise that made her wonder why every soul in the hotel had not come to see what was going on.

"I don't like my meals being interrupted, my cuddlesome friend! It rather burns me up . . . and I see the same can be said for you!"

A second burst of brilliance illuminated the room. The Roschach curled back. For the first time, Maia saw the flames racing over its black body with incredible speed and thoroughness. The hunter tried to douse the flames, but they spread too rapidly for it to have any chance of success.

Gilbrin stood by the fireplace. The decorative doors were wide open and from within shot a steady stream of blue-tinted fire directed at the cringing, burning monster. Maia's companion stared without blinking at the flame, guiding it along, but otherwise not affecting it.

Once more the bizarre creature squealed . . . then it began to shrivel and crackle, drawing into itself like a dying insect. It grew smaller and smaller until it was no larger than the cart. Even then it continued to shrink, the rubbery appendages curling up.

Maia scrambled over to Gilbrin, but did not disturb him. The intense expression on his face bothered her almost as much as the presence of the Roschach. Gone was all hint of merriment. Gilbrin did not move, did not relax until nothing remained of the shadowy creature.

"Ashes to ashes, dust to dust," he finally murmured. The exhausted refugee peered down at the spot where the hunter had been. There was no residue, no trace of it. "Although in our friend's case, that evidently doesn't apply."

Nothing else in the room had been affected by the flames.

The only signs of the hunter's presence were the toppled cart and the scattered dishes.

Maia put a hand on his arm. "Gil! Are you all right?"

He gave her a tired but typical smile. "Oh, fine! The Cubs won today; what could possibly bring me down from that?"

"Talk sense, Gil. I worried about you."

To her surprise, the sandy-haired man gave her a gentle hug. "Maia, sweet, it should've been yourself that you worried about. By the way, I wouldn't have been able to do what I did if you hadn't injured this inkblot in the first place." He released her and peered again at the Roschach's last location. "Interesting. It was impervious to direct attacks with power, but metal and indirect attacks both affected it."

"What are you talking about?"

"You might not have noticed, sweet, but I tried four times to attack it with my power. Direct assaults. I know that you tried at least once. Those all failed, yet your metal-tipped boots, that fork, and my directing the gas flame from the fireplace all harmed it. Fortunately, I only directed the flames where to go and didn't try to enhance them in anyway. If I had, it probably would've failed."

Looking around at the mess, another thought struck Maia. "No one's come up to see what happened."

"Our friend's doing, no doubt. Some shield blocking sound, perhaps. Possibly that's the reason why no one ever noticed the disappearance of others of our group in the past." He grimaced. "Which leads me to ask the question on everybody's lips: How did the thing know we were here?"

Maia voiced what she knew Gilbrin was thinking: "Hamman! Something might have happened to him!"

"A very distinct possibility. I'm sorry if so, Maia; we might've annoyed each other, but I wouldn't want any of us to fall into the Darkling's clutches. Mind you, we don't know that's what happened."

"We have to go find out, Gil. We have to see if something happened."

He thought it over for a minute, then nodded. "I do believe

you're correct, sweet. Besides, I for one do not feel at all comfortable here anymore. Room service has gone to hell."

They departed almost immediately, taking only enough time with their power to put the living room into reasonable shape. All the way to the lobby, Maia looked around uncertainly, wondering if yet another hunter lurked in the vicinity. It was hard to believe that the person who had prepared the cart had not noticed the horrific thing lurking under the cloth. Of course, Gilbrin had not noticed it, either. She posed the possibility of a second Roschach to Gilbrin.

"We'll just have to keep our eyes open," was his not-so-satisfactory reply.

Traffic was steady, the rush hour advanced but by no means over, but Gilbrin always found a path . . . or influenced one when he could not. It was not that far to Tarriqa's home, but it still took a good deal of time before the Dodge pulled into the parking garage.

Hamman Tarriqa did not open the door when they arrived nor did he respond when Gilbrin dared to knock. The Shifter touched the doorknob, but nothing happened.

"He's sealed it. Doesn't mean anything, of course. Do you want me to break in?"

Maia thought that her companion sounded too eager to do so. "I don't sense him in there. Do you?"

"No, but that doesn't mean that there might not be a clue to his present whereabouts." He straightened. "Give me a moment."

She watched as he closed his eyes, concentrating. Not certain what Gilbrin planned and not at all certain that she would like it, Maia attempted the lock with her own power.

Something in the door clicked. Maia looked at Gilbrin, whose eyes had opened wide the moment of the click.

"What did you do?"

"I opened the door for us," she remarked, giving him one of his own smiles.

Without waiting for him, the tall woman gingerly pushed the door open and stepped into the suite.

Everything was as it should have been. There was no indication that the black man had been disturbed by an intruder. Everything pointed to Tarriqa's having departed in peace.

"No trace of any assault that I can sense, sweet. How about you? Anything out of place? Any peculiar sensations?"

"Nothing. It all seems as normal as it looks."

Gilbrin studied some of the artwork in the front room. "I don't know if I'd ever consider this a normal abode, but I agree." He wandered farther into the room. "Well, we could wait here if you like, but I don't know if I want to be at any address connected to the man who gave us the use of that hotel. If the dogs knew we were there, I suspect that they know about Master Tarriqa's home, too."

There was no arguing that, but still Maia found herself hesitating. She followed Gilbrin around the room, gazing at the furniture and the decorations as if they might tell her something. Her eyes drifted briefly to the telephone . . . and focused on something written on the notepad next to it. An address.

"Gil, do you think this is something?"

He came over to study it. "Good possibility, sweet. Why don't we go and see what this place looks like."

"You really think this might be where Hamman is right now?"

"As I just said, it's a good possibility. Quite frankly, I'd also like to be anywhere but here, Maia, love. I can't help feeling that we're treading on the edge of a spider's web and that if we don't leave soon, the spider will come along."

Maia understood exactly how he felt. She tore off the slip of paper with the address on it. "Then let's go."

Despite their fears, nothing slowed them as they left Tarriqa's building. The shadows had grown long by now, reminding her of yesterday, when they had just left the black man's company. Maia looked around, almost expecting to see the man with the bird's head. That was nonsense, though. She had been hungry and exhausted yesterday.

And I am hungry and exhausted today, too, she reminded

herself. The hunter's attack had prevented her from eating her meal.

"If Tarriqa is not at this address," Gilbrin began, as if reading her thoughts, "then our next stop is somewhere to sup. I'm so famished I can barely hear the engine over my growling stomach." That he had eaten just prior to the attack seemed not to occur to him.

Traffic was not nearly so terrible by the time they reached the address, which proved to be a restaurant very near the Sears Tower. While Gilbrin located a place to park, Maia looked up at the metal and glass leviathan, marveling at its size. Although variations on it had existed on some of the other Earths, she had never been able to visit it. *Like standing next to a man-made mountain.*

As she thought that, a peculiar sensation passed through her. It felt as if she had crossed an area of utter absence. Maia abruptly began to cry. She felt her mood darken. To be alone for so long . . .

"A pity. Looks as if the restaurant is closing."

Gilbrin's comment stirred Maia from her depression. It vanished so abruptly that she could not be sure that she had even suffered it. Why such a feeling of loneliness?

"Maia, sweet? Are you still here?"

"Let's hurry with this," she snapped, climbing out of the old blue Dodge so quickly that she left her companion gaping after her.

It appeared that Hamman Tarriqa was not nearby, but Maia tried to see if she could sense his past presence. After several attempts, she thought she noted something, but whether it was a trace left by Tarriqa's passing she could not say.

While she studied the area outside, Gilbrin had gone inside. The restaurant might have been closing, but the Shifter was very persuasive, power or not. Maia glanced inside and saw him speaking to a waitress who was all smiles. Shaking her head, Maia de Fortunato forgot her companion and decided to walk a short distance from the restaurant. Perhaps she would have better luck from another location. Hamman might not have actually entered the place, but rather observed it from, say, across the street.

Crossing put her next to the tower itself. Maia glanced at the restaurant, then at the surrounding storefronts. Nothing unusual caught her eye, but then much of what she sought was not visible. Once more she concentrated on trying to sense some trace of the black man; for one of the Scattered Ones, Tarriqa was gifted. If he had shielded himself well, her efforts might be worthless. Maia had to try, though.

Again she was struck by a sudden sense of absence. It made her think of her dream, for some reason. The image of the ship drifted through her mind.

That will not help Hamman, the black-tressed woman scolded herself. As if some subconscious part of her took the scolding to heart, Maia suddenly sensed what she was looking for. Hamman *had* stood here at some point.

Better, there appeared to be a trail. Whether she was backtracking him she could not say, but the trail was definitely stronger when she looked to the west.

I should wait for Gil. However, now that she had discovered the trail, she was afraid that if she abandoned it for even a few minutes, she would lose it. She also feared that she would lose the trace if she turned her power to linking with Gil. *I'll only follow it for a block. If it is still strong, I can summon him then.*

Convinced that she had chosen the correct course of action, Maia de Fortunato started down the street in the direction the trace indicated. Her connection to the trail grew stronger as she headed farther west, so strong, in fact, that she continued past the tower and all the way to one of a series of bridges that crossed the murky green waters of the Chicago River.

Maia hesitated before the bridge, knowing that she should contact Gilbrin before proceeding . . . and yet, she felt compelled to go on. Inhaling deeply, she swore that once she was over the bridge she would turn back and inform her companion. All she had to do was cross the bridge.

The few other pedestrians paid her no mind as she started

over. As far as Maia was concerned, no one else existed. More and more she felt certain that she was about to discover a valuable clue.

Midway across, a new sensation of emptiness washed over her like a wave.

She stumbled against the sturdy side of the bridge, unable to control her emotions. There were people walking nearby, but Maia felt as if she were the only being left in the world. Her heart pounded and her breath came in small gasps.

Gods! What's become of me?

Staring skyward proved too disorienting. With as much force as she could muster, the stricken woman turned around, her view shifting madly until at last it settled on the river below.

At first she looked at the shifting water without seeing. Then, as her senses returned, Maia saw reflected in the water a thing that should not have been possible. She stared, unable to fathom its reason for being there and yet frightened that she knew why.

In the dull reflection there sailed a vast ship . . . a ship floating among the tops of the nearby buildings.

Maia looked up again, searching the sky for the ghostly craft.

There was nothing. Other than a few clouds, the darkening sky was clear.

She turned and once more stared at the river. To her horror, the ship was still there, part of it obscured by a passing cloud.

Maia looked up yet again, but the ship was not visible. She kept her eyes on the heavens for a longer period, yet was not successful in catching sight of the ominous vision.

When she dared look down at the river again, the ghost craft was no longer there.

The Boatman! she thought. *The Boatman! I saw the ship—*

Had she? Had she truly seen the ghost ship? She knew its vague description from the tales of others of her group, but not all the sightings could be claimed to be legitimate. Considering the attack she had just been through, Maia thought that perhaps she was imagining things. Hamman was missing, they had been attacked by a Roschach, and they were trapped in the Chicagoland vicinity. Small wonder that she might have imagined something as dire as the legendary mariner. Had not Hamman mentioned him only yesterday?

The sensation of absence was fading. Breathing easier, Maia peered into the river again. There was no sign of the ship, but even if it had been there, it would have been harder to see by now. The light had dimmed enough that only with effort could she even make out her own reflection.

Nothing at all. I must have imagined it. It couldn't be true. I don't even believe in the Boatman, the angel of death, the Flying Dutchman, or whatever legend he is supposed to be. There is no creature. He's as imaginary as the man with the bird's head who I thought I saw yesterday. Thinking of it in these terms allowed her to relax further. *As imaginary as the bird man.*

"Pardon, lass," interrupted a gravelly voice from behind her, "but I think you might be a help in finding my captain."

Maia did not want to turn, but her body had a will of its own, forcing her gaze from the river. She wanted to close her eyes rather than look at the speaker, but even that was forbidden her.

He was taller than her. He was clad in simple garments that spoke of a hundred old sea films that Gilbrin had no doubt watched over and over on his beloved television. One that Maia recalled from her most recent life, a movie with Errol Flynn, seemed most appropriate. That movie had been called, if she remembered correctly, *The Sea Hawk.*

Of course, to be accurate, the figure before her had the head of a parrot.

7. SPIDERS

He recalled firing the gun over and over. There had been some effect, but not enough. Even wounded, the horrific black thing had still been able to take him, the pedestrians around them unaware of the frantic battle taking place.

What had first alerted him to its presence, Rees could not have said. Perhaps it was a paranoia that had developed from his encounter with the cloaked character, or perhaps simple luck.

Rees had tried his power first, but the creature had shrugged that off. In desperation, he had pulled out the weapon that Tarriqa had so condemned him for and fired at his attacker. The first shots had gone wild, but four had hit. The monstrosity had bled, if black ooze could be considered blood, but the shots had only stalled the inevitable. Even as Rees had tried to reload, the Roschach, for that was what it was, had completely enveloped him.

That was all he recalled. He did not remember it carrying him away or when they had come to this place of whiteness. Rees did not even remember being hung on what seemed an invisible, vertical rack, his arms and legs pulled tight. His coat had been taken from him and his pockets emptied, but otherwise he was still clothed. That knowledge did nothing to ease his tensions.

His limbs ached. He sweated even though his surroundings were not warm.

Rees knew that he was a prisoner of the Darkling and was scared. Very scared.

Out of the white a small figure appeared. It seemed to grow from a tiny dot of darkness. By the time the figure reached Rees, it had coalesced into a young Hispanic lad. However, the expression on the youth's face was anything but innocent. Rees stared at his visitor and knew him even though the two had never met.

"De Fortunato . . ."

The boy smiled. A chill ran through Rees. Most of the Scattered Ones knew of the evil among them. August de Fortunato had done the unthinkable: He had purposely slain other members of the refugee group. Worse, it was known that he had dealt with the Darkling himself.

"I don't think I know you, but that doesn't matter. I just wanted to ask you if you knew my daughter."

Rees shook his head.

"You had a business card in your pocket, with an address on the back as well as the front. Do you know who those people are?"

"Just . . . some business associates," the prisoner ventured weakly.

"I doubt that someone you and Hamman Tarriqa deal with would simply be a business associate." De Fortunato shrugged. "The Roschach has already been dispatched there. It should return soon with an answer . . . and more guests."

"For Carim's sake, de Fortunato! Why the Darkling?"

The boyish face grew grim. "He has a hold over me. I can no more disobey than you can escape." The face suddenly became jovial again. "Well, the last part is true anyway . . . your hopes of escape, I mean."

With that said, August de Fortunato walked away, vanishing into the whiteness.

Rees barely had time to recover before another form materialized. This one began as a swirl of mist that danced before his eyes, ever increasing in size. As it swelled, from within there seemed to grow a human figure . . . or at least the form was similar. Larger and larger it became, until what stood before Rees, half obscured by the lively shadows that seemed a part of the immense figure, was the Darkling Prince.

Rees could not move, not because of any spell on him, but because of the incredible fear that had seized hold.

"You are in my august presence," announced the Prince of Shadows, floating closer. Rees found his voice disconcerting; it came from a different direction. "However, you are granted the option of not kneeling."

"I've got nothing to tell you!" responded Rees. "I don't know anything!"

"I am aware of that deficiency." Now the voice seemed to come from a new location. "I regret it; you must understand. It ever leaves me no other choice. The answer lies . . . or may lie . . . inside."

"What are you talking about?"

"About the End of this world and all those worlds that preceded it." The Prince of Shadows floated closer. The one pale eye looked the captive over. "And your part in aiding myself to know when to bid this most recent Earth farewell." He stared at Rees's chest. "Do you feel any urge to leap to the next variant? Is there yet a tremor within your heart?"

That was, in fact, one of the signs. Rees did not want to know how his captor had come to know that. "I don't know when I leap. It just happens."

"You feel as if you die, do you not?"

He did. They all did. Although the leap saved their existences, it was a terrible experience. Rees kept silence.

"I must know if I have time still. I realize the inconvenience it will cause you; but know that I will cherish the memory of your sacrifice when I next cross into the new frontier, the new variant to follow this one."

Behind the Darkling, a black light flared, disrupting the whiteness. The word *sacrifice* blared loud in the mind of the imprisoned refugee.

"I swear I don't know anything! Ask the damned Boatman if you need an answer! Ask him!"

The light, which had almost come to focus on his chest, suddenly ceased. His shadowy captor floated so near that Rees could not help but stare into the single, unsettling orb. "And have you seen this Boatman?"

Hope sprang to life. Rees quickly nodded. "I did. In the city . . . not far from where . . ."

"You have served me well by telling me this." The Darkling backed away to roughly arm's length. "This encounter I must know about."

"Please . . . just let me go and I'll tell you everything."

His captor blinked. Then, in a tone that almost hinted of amusement, the Prince of Shadows replied, "But there is no need of that. Now that I know to look for it, it will be a simple task to have the machine draw that knowledge from you as I draw out the other answers I seek. I shall see to it that your honesty was not in vain, believe me. It may be that this encounter with the one you term the Boatman will provide me with the ultimate solution to my quest. For that, you may go knowing you have my *undying* gratitude."

The black light flickered back to life and without hesitation focused on Rees.

Gilbrin the Shifter had exited the restaurant with more than the few clues he had expected to find. Careful questioning and a quiet study of his surroundings had helped him piece together an interesting yet puzzling tale.

Master Tarriqa had evidently been investigating certain events at this inn, another of the Scattered Ones with him. Who the second one had been, the jester could not say. He recognized neither the vague description he had culled from the servers nor the power traces left behind. Gilbrin doubted that the identity of the other refugee was as important as the reason for the pair coming here. Unfortunately, there the tale grew most hazy.

He sensed the directions in which both men had departed.

For Gilbrin, the trails were not difficult to follow, as it had not been long since the pair had split up.

He looked around for Maia. She was nowhere in sight, but Gilbrin was not unduly worried. It was quite likely that she had simply gone around the corner in search of some clue. Maia was more levelheaded than he was, the Shifter was willing to admit; she was not the type to go charging off on her own.

Desiring not to waste any more time, Gilbrin concentrated on her. The Roschach already knew that they were in Chicago; there was no sense in hiding from them. Better that the two of them keep moving.

Maia, sweet! Come back to the restaurant. I've found something.

He could not sense her. That was impossible. Of all the other Scattered Ones, she was the most familiar to him, the most intimate . . . the only one who would really put up with his mischievous nature.

Gilbrin hurried to the corner and peered around. No Maia. He hurried to the opposite corner and studied both streets there. Still no sign.

You are a fool, Shifter! he suddenly scolded himself. Here he was running around searching like one of the ephemerals of this world. Most of them lacked the power he had to search with his mind, not simply his eyes.

Her trace was childishly simple to locate now that he was sensible enough to look for it. Still chiding himself, Gilbrin fairly leaped across the street. Because of the Roschach, Maia was no doubt shielding herself from their detection. She *was* more sensible than him.

Her trail continued past the tower and all the way to the river. *How far afield have you flown, sweet? Even I wouldn't have gone this far away!*

He could not see her on the other side of the bridge, but her trace indicated that she had gone there. Gilbrin steeled himself and started across. She was on the other side; she had to be.

Midway across, her trail simply ceased.

Nothing. It just ended.

Gilbrin walked past the final location, relocated the trail, and tried again. It ended in the same place. He could sense only that she had paused here.

"Gods, Maia!" he whispered. "Not you!"

Racing across the rest of the bridge, he paused at the end and quickly scanned the area. No sign. Gilbrin could not detect her trace. There was something, almost a sense of emptiness, but it was so faint that he found it unimportant. It might have nothing to do with her.

The Roschach took her! The Darkling has her! The brightly clad figure shivered. The Darkling had Maia. . . .

"No. I don't know that for certain." Panic would avail him nothing. Maia was talented enough to cover her trace completely; after all, as much as she hated to admit it, she was the daughter of August de Fortunato. Traitor he might be to his fellow refugees, but his skills could not be denied. The reason he still existed was that he could conceal himself so well.

Could her sire have her? Another unnerving thought, but one that Gilbrin believed in even less, although he could not say why. Perhaps it was because he would have expected August to take his daughter in a much more spectacular fashion. Gilbrin also believed that August would not have passed up the opportunity to capture him as well. He had never forgiven the trickster for helping Maia escape him back in their original world, when the evil of the man had already been apparent. The first leap had actually saved the life of the elder de Fortunato, for he had been involved in activities that had condemned him in the hearts of many.

Thinking about August de Fortunato's past crimes was not going to help Gilbrin find Maia, though. The Shifter thought matters over carefully and finally glanced back at the other side of the bridge. There was no trace of his companion, but perhaps there was still hope of locating Tarriqa. The other Scattered One was unimportant unless it proved impossible to find the black man. Then and only then would Gilbrin try to track that other one down.

Urged on by growing anxiety, Gil hastened back to the restaurant. Hamman Tarriqa's trace was still clearly evident and only seconds later Gilbrin was well on the black man's trail. In his opinion, Tarriqa had not made sufficient effort to shield himself, an action that the jester thought verged on cockiness. Tarriqa might be highly skilled, but it was never wise to underestimate the Roschach or their master.

One by one he passed streets. LaSalle, Clark . . . Gilbrin briefly wondered if he would ever see another Cubs baseball game. . . . Dearborn . . .

A straight line so far, but unless you took a dip in Lake Michigan you've got to turn somewhere, Master Tarriqa.

It was getting very dark now, but Gilbrin believed that he had no choice but to continue. He almost felt sympathy for any Roschach who might try to take him. They would find the Shifter more than willing to strike back.

At Michigan Avenue, the trail suddenly turned north. Only when he paused there did he realize just how far he had walked. He was still far enough south, but Gilbrin calculated that if he continued in a northerly direction, then headed east to Lake Shore Drive, he would not be far from Tarriqa's home.

No, that had to be nonsense. Hamman Tarriqa would not have come all this way and then simply walked the long distance back to his suite. Something else must have happened.

Gilbrin was about to make the turn when a wave of dizziness swept over him. He recognized what it was almost immediately and braced himself against the side of the building.

Another scene overlapped the image of the dark streets. He was in a chamber in a house at least two centuries old. It was, if Gilbrin recalled correctly, Russian. A row of intricately painted eggs lined the top shelf of a hand-carved wooden case. In his present century, their value would have allowed Gilbrin several years of extravagant living. A wolf skin served as floor decoration. Several animals' heads dotted the walls, seeming to stare mournfully at all onlookers. Two long, fairly gaunt hounds rested near a fireplace. In contrast to the general look of the room, there were art pieces and weaponry displayed that spoke of another distinctive culture, one that was generally anathema to all who called themselves Russian.

A burly male figure clad in what looked like fur-trimmed hunting clothes sat before the Shifter, an amused smile peeking out from under a thick black mustache. *"Guten Tag,* Gilbrin."

"I think you're confused, Mendessonn. You look Russian. I know the variant well enough. It never seems to change much."

"Yes, but my heart will always belong to my more Germanic incarnations." Mendessonn had a scar on one cheek. He seemed to invite duels no matter what time and place he was reborn. Perhaps it was because he knew that nothing human could permanently kill him. Like the other refugees, he would be reborn in the next variant Earth . . . unless he was one of the few who failed to make the crossing, or unless the Darkling took him.

Gilbrin saw no reason to take further chances with his own existence, but Mendessonn had always been one to seek challenges, to play with his life because he believed himself invincible. Of course, he kept his activities to the mundane level, rarely utilizing his abilities. Mendessonn was a risk taker, but he was no fool. His skill with weapons would not save him if the Darkling ever crossed his path.

Unfortunately, it was Gilbrin who had to deal with the Darkling in this incarnation.

"What do you want, Mendessonn?"

The smile vanished immediately. "Ursuline has been trying to reach someone I believe you know, a Hamman Tarriqa."

"I know him." The Shifter saw no reason yet to mention that he was presently searching for the same person. He wanted to know exactly what Ursuline, who he recalled had also been intimate with MacPhee, wanted to relay to the black man.

"She could not find him, little man. Hamman Tarriqa contacted her only a short time earlier, but was interrupted. Ursuline tried to contact him as soon as she could gather the strength, but nothing happened. She turned to me for assistance."

Now Gilbrin recalled that Ursuline and Mendessonn had had their fair share of liaisons, more so than most Scattered Ones could manage considering incarnations. Mendessonn was also one of the more skilled of the refugees, even if he tended to keep to himself more than most. "And what does that have to do with me?"

Mendessonn sniffed. "It should have nothing to do with you, Herr Eulenspiegel. I was seeking Tarriqa and thought I had discovered him. When I concentrated harder, though, I reached you instead. I trust this is no trick on your part. It is him I seek, not you. I only decided to link with you because I thought it too coincidental that you would be so nearby."

"While I graciously accept your compliment," Gilbrin replied, referring to Mendessonn's naming him after Till Eulenspiegel, the Germanic trickster of legend, "I've played no prank. If you can't find Master Tarriqa it's because he's not to be found. I've been looking for him myself. Is there anything more? I don't know about you, but I don't like long, useless conversations, especially with the ever-present possibility of the Darkling sensing us."

"The Darkling?" For the first time, Mendessonn's expression turned nervous. "You know something! Has Tarriqa been taken?"

"I don't know, friend Mendessonn. I follow his trail even as we speak . . . and the sooner I can return to the hunt the better. What did Ursuline want? I'll pass it on to Master Tarriqa when I find him."

"She insisted on dealing with him alone. I don't know if I should tell you—"

A car drove through the background, seeming to run over both the dogs and the fireplace. As they had spoken with each other, Gilbrin had kept a constant eye on the real world. It was ever a disconcerting process, but he dared not lose sight of the danger of a Roschach suddenly striking. It was better to end this conversation as swiftly as possible. "And if Tarriqa *has* been taken, what then? Best to tell someone, Mendessonn, even if it's me."

He knew that the other man could not argue, however much he might dislike Gil's playfulness at times. "All right. Ursuline told me that if I contacted Tarriqa I should tell him that no one has seen the ship."

Gilbrin knew exactly which ship was meant. Master Tarriqa had obviously been telling the others to watch for the signs presaging the End of this variant. It made sense. "And is that all?"

"One more thing, prankster. It's about August de Fortunato. Hwong, who's a member of the Khan's court in China this time, said that—"

The grand room, its trappings, and its occupant vanished, leaving Gilbrin back in the streets of Chicago. The abrupt shift left his head throbbing and his vision blurry.

What in the name of—? was as far as his thoughts progressed before he felt the new mind touch his.

No, not one new mind, but *two.* A second, more intense set of thoughts touched him, obscuring all evidence of the first contact. In contrast to the first, the second mind was not human.

Roschach.

The inhuman thoughts were dwindling away, as if the Roschach was fading. Gilbrin could not detect another trace of the first mind, but he thought it might have been Tarriqa's. There was only one way to find out.

Gilbrin continued his pursuit, but at an even faster pace. The trace left by Tarriqa was again his only clue to the black man's whereabouts. The Shifter grew more nervous the longer he failed to reach the end of the trail. Block after block he passed and still the trace urged further searching. Worse, there was no replay of the momentary mind link. The Roschach might already be well on his way back to his master, Hamman Tarriqa soon to be the Darkling's latest victim. For all his differences with the black man, Gilbrin hated the thought.

He turned another corner . . . and paused. The trail went a little farther, then diffused, disappearing before a series of office building entrances.

Suspicious, he studied the doors. The buildings should have been locked tight by now. They should have been locked tight when Tarriqa had passed this way. The Shifter grimaced. He knew a bit more about Roschach than did many of his brethren.

"Into the shadow of the valley of death . . ." Daring what very likely was a trap, Gilbrin took a few tentative steps toward the first true doorway. To all appearances it was perfectly normal, but the Shifter detected inhuman thoughts coming from within. He paused a foot from the door before daring to plunge forward. A hint of something inhuman lingered around the doorway. The Roschach seemed to be inside. . . .

As he touched the door handle, Gilbrin's world changed.

A twisted version of the building stood before him. The walls jutted at impossible angles and the doorway was bent toward him. The office building now stood some distance away and the landscape between Gilbrin and the structure was a rocky, pale parody of the sidewalk. The Shifter looked left and right and saw that only the building in front of him existed. The sidewalk ended in silvery haze a few yards on each side.

What is this place? What've I stepped into? His reserve slipping, Gilbrin the Shifter looked wildly around, half-expecting a legion of the black hunters to come charging from the mist.

He had sensed a Roschach here and somehow this looked just like the sort of place one would find the abominable creatures. This had to be one of their lairs. He *had* to have stepped into a trap . . . yet where was the spinner of the web?

It took him a few seconds to discover the horrific form of the Roschach.

The fiendish creature was dying. What could have killed it in the place where it supposedly would be most powerful? The monster lay in a pool of black ink . . . no, it *was* the black ink. Gilbrin, only a few feet from the macabre figure, backed away in disgust. The Roschach was melting slowly into a puddle of ooze.

The striped eyes flared to life and the one appendage not yet turned to ink tried to reach for him.

Gilbrin had no difficulty eluding its grasp. The Roschach hissed, then collapsed again. The eyes dimmed. It was still not dead, but the end was not far off.

What's going on here? The Shifter gave the Roschach one more glance, but it was clear that he had nothing more to fear from the Darkling's dog. Whoever or whatever it had battled had been very thorough, very powerful. Gilbrin suddenly had a great desire to be anywhere but in the dying Roschach's lair.

He whirled about and started for the entrance through which he had come. It was not far away. Only a few steps and he would be safe. The Roschach was no danger now, but something about the pocket world still worried him. He felt a pressure on his back and chest, a pressure slowly increasing with each passing moment.

Something caught his attention. It was at the very edge of the haze to his left. Gilbrin paused, not eager to stay any longer than he had to, then finally stepped toward the mist.

A moment later, he was rushing over the unstable surface. What he had barely noticed was a body. A human body.

The Shifter knew it was Tarriqa even before he reached the man. Tarriqa lay still, his left hand just disappearing into the haze. Gilbrin put a hand on the other's chest, but he already knew that his counterpart was alive. Hamman Tarriqa appeared to be in some sort of coma. A quick check revealed that there was only one apparent injury, an ominous mark on the neck that resembled a puncture wound.

The pressure on Gilbrin's chest grew more insistent and he

found that he was having trouble breathing. The entire pocket world looked smaller, more compact. He had a terrible suspicion that it would look much smaller very, very soon.

"Time we were off, Master Tarriqa." Gilbrin hefted his unconscious companion over his shoulder. Despite his size, he was stronger than many of the other Scattered Ones. Still, the black man's weight was a strain on him. Tarriqa was a large, muscular figure. Gilbrin thought about utilizing his power to hasten their escape, but was afraid what effect it might have on the obviously unstable lair.

He glanced back. The Roschach was still alive, but barely. It did not even notice him anymore. More than two-thirds of its body had dissolved into thick, black ooze. Gilbrin realized that the lair's stability was tied to the hunter's life force, which was rapidly fading.

Steadying his load, the small man trudged toward the doorway. Despite the shrinking of the pocket world, it seemed farther away than ever. He knew that was not so, that it was only the weight of his burden that made him think the distance was more, but Gilbrin could not help thinking that the pair would not make it to the doorway before the Roschach's last bit of life melted away.

As if to confirm that fear, the pressure again increased. Gilbrin gasped and nearly lost his hold on Tarriqa.

This is not how I want to go! I am not a grape to be squeezed into wine!

He stumbled again. The lair was definitely much smaller. The doorway still beckoned, but Gilbrin doubted he would make it unless he used his power after all. Things were already too unstable; surely the use of power could not hurt matters further.

Concentrating, Gilbrin the Shifter focused on the doorway. If he could hold it open long enough for Tarriqa and him to reach it . . .

The entire area shook. Bits of the landscape rose and fell as if an earthquake had begun. Gilbrin managed three more steps before collapsing, Hamman Tarriqa's inert body half-pinning him to the ground.

"Damn!" was all he could think to say as he watched the doorway start to shrink. It was nearly impossible to breathe, so heavy was the pressure squeezing him from all sides. His head throbbed and his breath came in gasps.

He was going to die.

A hand . . . at least Gilbrin *thought* it was a hand . . . pulled the black man up, then did the same for him. Weakened, Gilbrin could not have protested even had he wanted to. He caught glimpses of a pair of high boots and a long, flowing cloak, but then the pressure became so overwhelming that it was all he could do simply to look down at the shifting ground.

They reached the doorway. Gilbrin was certain that it could not possibly be large enough for the three of them to pass through, but as he lifted his head to look, he saw that unlike the rest of the pocket land, their escape route was now expanding. It was his rescuer's doing; he could tell that even though he did not sense any use of power.

The doorway ceased expanding when it was about half of its original dimensions. Gilbrin sensed his rescuer hesitate. The collapsing world was defying even this miraculous visitor's efforts. They still might die.

Then the mysterious stranger lifted both refugees high and without pause threw them bodily through the small opening.

A brief sense of emptiness coursed through Gilbrin as he flew beyond the Roschach's lair. The pressure vanished from his chest and back. He was only barely able to rejoice, for the next moment it occurred to him that he was flying without any knowledge of where he would land. Gilbrin's mind raced frantically, trying to forge a concentration strong enough to allow him to soften his landing.

A second later he struck a hard, but fortunately carpeted, floor.

"Carim's blood!" He rubbed the shoulder that had made first contact with the floor. Gilbrin knew that he should be grateful to be alive, but he decided that he could save his gratitude for a time when every bone in his body did not feel as if it had been rattled loose.

It took another moment before the battered refugee could identify his surroundings. When he was able to, Gilbrin the Shifter blinked in surprise. He was in the front room of Hamman Tarriqa's suite.

Thinking of the other, Gilbrin shifted onto his back and propped himself on his elbows. He had a good view of the room now, a view that included, much to his relief, the still form of the black man reclining on a luxurious couch. Tarriqa looked as if he had been gently dropped onto the couch, which made the Shifter even more annoyed regarding his own landing.

His annoyance ceased as a hole opened up in the middle of the room, a hole floating about four feet in the air. The opening was as large as one of the reclining chairs on the other side of the living room and its edges shone like the sun.

A cloaked figure lowered a leg through the hole, then stepped completely into Hamman Tarriqa's suite. The opening shrank to nothing the moment the newcomer was through.

Gilbrin looked up into black orbs with no pupils and for a minute he thought that what towered over him was some new form of Roschach or some other sort of hunter employed by the Darkling. He even wondered if it was the Darkling Prince himself, but the vague descriptions he recalled seemed to contradict that notion.

The clothes were archaic, even for one who had been reborn in multiple centuries. They were not exactly like anything Gil had come across in his own lifetimes. In fact, the figure before him reminded him more of home . . . that is, his *original* home.

The weathered face at which he stared remained unreadable. Gilbrin was reminded of a corpse that had forgotten to die. The broad rim of the hat often shadowed the upper half of the face, further increasing the sense of unliving.

For some reason, despite his fear of the figure, Gilbrin the

Shifter also felt a trace of pity. There was something about his rescuer that spoke of a soul lost forever.

Then it came to him who it was who had rescued him and Tarriqa from the collapsing lair of the Roschach.

The Boatman. The angel of death. The Flying Dutchman.

The End of the world was at hand . . . again.

8. COLLECT CALL

"The ship will be passing near again."

The comment was made in so matter-of-fact a manner that Maia de Fortunato could scarcely believe that her companion had said the dread words. Of course, to the bizarre creature she traveled with, the event likely meant little. It probably simply waited to board the ghostly vessel and proceed to the next port . . . or, in this case, Earth.

They stood atop the roof of a strange structure that was part of the University of Illinois. What he . . . it was hard not to think of the creature as a *he* instead of an *it* even though a close look clearly revealed that her captor was mechanical, not living . . . expected to see in the dark night, Maia did not know. She knew only that she was tired and more than a little anxious. Never in her existence had she come across the creature's like, but then, never in her existence had she come across anything associated with the Boatman. The dark-haired woman wanted to flee. At the same time, she felt compelled to discover more.

Of course, since the thing that called itself Philo had a literal grip of steel on her wrist, her choices were moot. He did not seem intent on hurting her, only keeping her nearby. For some reason, Philo could not find his master. This disturbed him . . . yes, Maia was certain of the truth of the emotion . . . very much. She gathered that the mechanical creature was very much used to knowing where his master was at all times. This time was different, though. This time, Philo imagined that Maia alone possessed the key to locating the "captain."

"A full moon this night," announced Philo, peering heavenward with one great, round orb. He reminded her of the amazing robots, the animatrons, she had seen during the Fortune family's visit to Disneyland four years prior. "The moon of madness."

"*That's* an understatement," she returned.

"An ill wind blows, lass."

The shivering woman tried to duck low. "Every wind blowing up here is ill. Is there a need to be here?"

His gaze shifted to her. She could almost have sworn that there was exhaustion and defeat in the eye that met her stare. "No, lass. We can be moving along to the next port of call."

Without warning, Philo seized her with his other arm. Then, before she could even begin to struggle, the animatron stepped forward and *off* the top of the building.

They landed gently on the sidewalk, the parrot-headed golem barely missing a step. The sidewalk was not even cracked. Philo proceeded to drag his stunned companion along.

"Hold on!" she called. When Philo continued to ignore her pleas, she added, "You'll hold on or I'll make enough of a fuss to break through the shield you set up around us!"

The threat caused the animatron to stop and cock his head to stare at her. "You are not cooperating, lass. Things would be smooth sailing if you would just try."

"I do not even know *how* to try! I have been trying to tell you that, but you never listen!"

Despite her loud words, no one came to see what was happening. It might have been city apathy, but more likely it was because Philo had surrounded them with an incredibly strong shield that made them nonexistent to others. Any of the Scattered Ones could create a shield, but not one as durable or widespread as this. Maia doubted that she could have followed through on her threat, but she was not about to reveal that to the one who technically was still her captor.

"You know. You feel the wake of his passing, lass. The emptiness of a thousand dead lifetimes. We have to find him before the ship comes to retrieve him. He's my captain. I owe him everything."

Again she was struck by the fact that Philo seemed more flesh than machine. He acted as if he were alive. Possibly that was true in some sense she could not explain; possibly it had to do with being a thing of the Boatman's, a thing imbued with his power. Maia sensed the same emptiness that had allowed her to trace the legendary harbinger, who apparently preferred to be called Dutchman.

The trace . . . A ploy to free herself of her erstwhile companion's grasp, a ploy that had the ring of truth about it, blossomed to life in Maia's thoughts. "You just reminded me of something, my avian friend. A reason why I cannot find the captain."

"What is it?" The eye stared at her intently. Maia had constantly to remind herself that Philo was technically nothing more than a complex puppet.

"You're the problem. You are a part of him. The reason I cannot find him is because you keep fouling up the trail. I sense you instead of him."

"I cannot release you, lass. You would, I daresay, run away. Now that would be the truth of it, wouldn't it?"

Damn! Maia shrugged. "You think it over. You'll see I'm telling the truth. For some reason, you cannot sense him. I could, although I don't know why. I suppose I've always been a little more sensitive than most of my kind." She dared to plant her index finger in the tall figure's chest and discovered that if Philo was not made of metal, then he wore a very thick breastplate beneath his pirate's clothing. "But as long as I remain in contact with you, I'll keep sensing you instead."

"You would run."

"I want to find your captain, too, but it has to be my way." She gave him what to any normal male would have been an enticing smile but to the animatron was nothing. "My way or none at all."

Philo raised her imprisoned arm and for a moment Maia wondered whether she had pushed him too far. Perhaps he had decided that she was not worth the time and trouble anymore. Perhaps he intended now to dispense with her and search for another Scattered One who might be more amenable to his needs.

The animatron released his grip. Maia was so relieved that she simply allowed her arm to fall. Philo, his eye still set on her, took three lengthy steps back.

"Begin . . . but know that I'll be watching you like a hawk, lass."

Humor? Does he know what he just said? In the short time that she had traveled with him, Maia de Fortunato had heard the parrot spout more than one possibly humorous statement. *How real are you, First Mate Philo?*

Maia turned from him, then hesitated. Everything she had told her companion was true. She *did* want to find his captain. Here was the potential to discover not only some of the truth behind the legends, but also the hope of finding some release from the endless leaps. If Dutchman was more than a harbinger of disaster, if he was the cause of their eternal flight, perhaps he also held the key to ending it all.

And if I have to kill him to find a way to free all of us, I will. It was a thought that had slowly been rising in her mind. Any creature responsible for the deaths of countless worlds, countless universes, was worthy of death, especially if it put an end to his reign of destruction. *I could save us all. . . . The Darkling would even stop hunting us since he wouldn't have a need to flee.*

Maia did not pause to consider what the Prince of Shadows would do if he no longer had to flee. Her thoughts centered on how to deal with the angel of death once she located him . . . which she was certain that she could do now. Even this close to the animatron, she could now sense Dutchman's trail. Maia took two carefully planned steps farther from her companion. The feeling of emptiness grew, causing her nearly to gasp.

It's . . . distinctive. Not the same as what I feel near Philo . . . not quite.

Distinctive? How could emptiness, absence, be distinctive? It made no sense and yet it was true. Maia sensed what she knew to be Dutchman somewhere farther to the east, back in the core of the city. She was fairly certain that if she concentrated, both to focus and to keep the emptiness from overwhelming her again, she could locate him before the night was over.

"Ready to set sail? Is the course set?"

Maia nodded. "I think so. I do."

The parrot said nothing more. He simply stood there, staring, until Maia felt compelled to go. She took one step, then another. The farther east she journeyed, the stronger the trail. Maia heard Philo following, his steps even and unhesitant. His pace matched hers. Maia knew that he would keep the distance between them constant.

It was odd, but the more she focused, the easier it became. Maia's pace quickened; it was almost a compulsion. The nighttime city faded around her; only the trail held true meaning to her. Philo was merely a following shadow.

Before Maia realized it, they had reached the Chicago River again. On the bridge she faltered. Remembered images of the ghostly ship forced her to peer down once more at the murky water. Fortunately, even in the reflection of the moon she could see nothing.

"It's not yet time, lass. Soon, though. She'll be making a sweep by."

Maia looked up at Philo, who still maintained a distance of several paces. "But I already saw the ship once."

The parrot head swiveled left, then right. "It's not yet time."

She wanted to argue or at least ask him to clarify what he meant, for if anyone would know the truth it had to be the mechanical figure, but it appeared futile. *It must have been my imagination. It must have been because I was sensing the Boatman himself.*

Yet, Maia remained unconvinced.

There was still activity in the city, of course. Chicago was like New York, Paris, Tokyo, or any other large population center. There was always something going on. However, while vehicles continued to cross their paths, Maia and Philo passed fewer and fewer pedestrians. Most Chicagoans now journeyed elsewhere for entertainment. In this part of the city, much of the area closed down after business hours.

What must Gilbrin be thinking? Maia had not contacted him since first encountering the animatron. It was doubtful that she could have done so in any case, for Philo's shield apparently could nullify nearly anything the parrot desired it to. Gil was probably scouring the city for her.

Guilt made her come to a halt. Philo dutifully paused.

"I'm sorry, but I have to contact someone."

"I must find my captain."

"And we will. In fact, the person I want to contact could aid us in many ways." In truth, Gil likely had a better notion of how to deal with the Boatman than she did. She needed him if she hoped to take on both the angel of death and his companion.

Philo stood motionless for so long that Maia nearly screamed from impatience. At last, the animatron's head swiveled from side to side. "I cannot. There are pirates and knaves in the city and your call will be a siren song to them."

She was not certain that she understood what he meant, but his denial of her request was obvious enough. Maia desperately thought of a compromise.

"There's a telephone, a communication device, over there." She pointed across the street.

The parrot's head turned nearly halfway around so that he could briefly view the object. Maia wondered if he had ever seen a telephone before or understood how it worked.

"How far away is this person located?"

"I don't know. He can't be far."

The parrot blinked at her. "You don't know where he is, lass. What makes you think you can reach him?"

"There are two possibilities." The hotel room and Tarriqa's suite were the only places that she could imagine Gil being if he had given up searching for her. It was unlikely that he was at either location, but she had to try. Besides, she hoped to test the limits of Philo's shield.

There was only one way to find out, provided that he allowed her to use the telephone. Maia had discovered that Philo was far swifter than she. She could not outrace him. Trickery, which was more Gil's method, was her best hope.

"Very well. We will cross together."

It was not what Maia had hoped for, but she noted that at least Philo maintained the same distance between them. At least she had that much distance with which to begin.

When she reached the telephone, she discovered that it was broken. Vandals. The receiver was still attached, though, and the basic mechanism appeared intact. Another notion occurred to her.

"I need to use my power. Just a little. Enough to make this telephone function."

"Very well."

"You'll have to step farther back. I can't do anything while you're this near." This was not true, but she hoped that Philo would not realize it.

To her silent joy, the animatron slowly backed up three more paces. It was possible that he was at the limits of his shield, or perhaps he feared that if she ran he might not be able to catch her now. Whatever the case, Maia felt some sense of triumph.

She touched the receiver. Numbers beeped. A breath later, a voice answered. It was the operator at the hotel where she and Gilbrin had stayed. Maia quickly gave their room number, her gaze drifting to the waiting Philo.

The telephone rang once, twice, ten times. There was a momentary click, then the ringing continued.

Maia cut the connection. She pointed again. Once more a telephone began to ring.

After four rings, a voice came on. Hamman Tarriqa's. Maia started to speak, then realized it was only the black man's voice on his answering machine.

The message was followed by a beeping noise. Maia hesitated, then: "Gilbrin. If you get this, I'm all right. I—"

Philo seized the telephone receiver. The very human-looking hand crushed the device without the slightest effort.

"What—?"

"We are in deadly waters," Philo said. He dropped the broken receiver and seized her wrist again.

The telephone began to ring.

"This way." Philo said pulling her back across the street. Behind them, the telephone continued to ring. Even across the street and a block farther east, the ringing could still be heard.

"What is it?" Maia finally managed. "Why did you do that?"

If the parrot had planned to answer her, his response was cut off by the sudden silence of the telephone. Philo glanced behind him as if the silence was a sign of impending doom.

"Maybe someone just picked it up," she offered.

What exactly Philo feared she did not know, but only one thing came to mind: The Darkling . . . But why would the telephone call put them in such danger?

Another telephone rang. Maia fairly leaped and even the unliving creature beside her seemed to take the sound as a terrible danger. The new telephone was some distance ahead of them, one of a set of three near a street corner along their intended path. *Sheer coincidence, she thought. Telephones ring all the time.*

The two other telephones began to ring. Then, from around another corner, Maia heard another set begin wailing.

A lone pedestrian, a young, leather-jacketed man whose hair had been shaved off on both sides of his head, paused before the trio of crying telephones. He eyed all three, then reached for the center one.

The lives of the ephemerals should not have meant much to her, but Maia found herself crying out a warning: "Leave it! Don't pick it up!"

At first she thought he was ignoring her, but then Maia recalled the animatron's shield. She whirled on him. "You have to let him hear me! You cannot—"

"I think it's too late, lass."

Maia turned back to where the young man had been standing.

The receiver he had been reaching for hung loose at the bottom. The two other telephones continued to ring, but she thought that the one in the middle might be silent now. Of the man who had answered, there was no trace.

The telephones abruptly ceased ringing.

"Is it over?" She did not want to think about what might have happened to the hapless mortal, but in truth his disappearance mattered less to her than did the fate that might await her.

"The calm before the storm." Philo's voice sounded detached. If he seemed unconcerned, Maia reminded herself, it was only because he was not capable of the fear that she felt creeping through her.

Amid the stillness, she heard footfalls. Maia peered into the dark streets and saw nothing. Then she noticed a young figure, hands in pants pockets, walking nonchalantly toward them from far down the street. At first Maia paid him no mind, assuming that the boy was simply walking in their direction. Then she realized that the youth was staring at them.

He paused well out of reach, raising his chin so that Maia especially could see him. There was a glint in his eyes that belied his young form.

"You're looking well, my dear, but I cannot say much about the company you keep these days. "

It was only Philo's grip that kept Maia from trying to seize her father by the throat. It mattered not what her father looked like; there was no innocence left in the young shell. Even if he had been brought to her as a newborn, she would have willingly throttled him because of the past horrors he had committed. There was no redemption for August de Fortunato.

Of course, it was more likely that he would have killed her instead . . . after a time.

"I am looking for my captain," Philo announced.

"And I can help you find him," August de Fortunato returned. "Simply put yourself in my hands. I will take you to your final destination, where your answers await."

"Don't listen to him," Maia warned. "He's the Serpent of Edos himself."

Philo fixed one eye on the short figure of August de Fortunato. "I must find my captain. Please step aside."

"I see you're determined in your effort." De Fortunato took three steps back. "Well, let us find your captain together, shall we?" The youth reached out an inviting hand. "Come with me willingly . . . or come with me as I choose to take you. You won't like the latter, my avian friend. Just ask my darling daughter what I'm like when I'm not obeyed."

"You're filth, August!"

"*Tsk.* Shouldn't talk to your daddy like that, my darling. Your mother talked to me like that and you know what happened."

Again Maia tried to attack her father and again Philo held her back. She glared at the animatron, but he simply cocked his head and said, "Time to set sail, lass."

De Fortunato's eyes narrowed and his sinister grin widened. He lowered his head and stared at the pair from under his brow. "Oh, you think you're leaving me?"

The telephones rang again. Maia glanced at the nearest. Sparks burst from first one receiver and then the next. The ringing died away, but as it did, something dark and fluid oozed from the receivers. It gathered in pools, more than half a dozen, with yet more of the liquid still pouring from the telephones.

In mere seconds, the first of the Roschach took shape, the

striped eyes opening and peering at the two beings before August de Fortunato.

"How can you do it?" the dark-haired woman demanded, her gaze trying to burn its way into the evil mind of her father. "How can you deal with the Darkling, father? Even you should be unwilling to trust the word of the Prince of Shadows!"

"Did I say I trusted him?" De Fortunato raised his right hand, then pointed at Maia and her companion.

The Roschach moved closer. Maia counted six, seven, then two more. She looked at Philo, but he gave no sign of his thoughts. Even if the Roschach destroyed him, his avian visage would remain expressionless.

He is only a machine. Worry less about him and more about yourself!

Her sire would turn the animatron over to the Darkling, but would keep *her* for his own amusement. August had no insidious attraction to her . . . there was at least that to be thankful for . . . but his adamant belief that she had somehow betrayed him by not remaining his obedient daughter was enough to have long ago sentenced Maia to a lingering fate. August de Fortunato was the great betrayer of the Scattered Ones, but heaven forbid if anyone dared to betray him. The double standard by which her father lived was simply one more factor that she felt revealed the extent of his madness.

Philo released her and reached for something at his side. "I *must* find my captain, scurvy knave."

The dark-skinned youth laughed. "You are amusing."

The animatron pulled a sword—a cutlass, of course—from nowhere. The tip glowed blue.

De Fortunato frowned. The Roschach paused; then, under the boy's savage gaze, they reluctantly started forward again. The creatures came in all shapes and sizes, some of them boxy, some tall and much like insects in form, others constantly shifting. There had to be more than a dozen now. Maia prayed that no more would join the ranks . . . as if that mattered. She was not capable of taking on more than two and even that would require as much luck as skill.

One of the more daring Roschach scrambled nearer and opened its mouth. A needle-thin tongue darted swiftly toward Maia. Philo reached past her, moving swifter than a human, and sliced into the sinister tongue. The sheared portion dropped to the street, where it dissolved. Its owner quickly retracted the remaining portion, hissing in pain. All the Roschach backed up a pace.

"Simple-minded buffoons!" snarled de Fortunato. He raised his right hand again and made a cutting action with it.

Philo nearly toppled over as both his sword arm and the cutlass seemed suddenly drawn to the ground. The animatron pulled, but could barely keep the hilt of the weapon off the street.

"Now take him . . . if you fools can."

More confident again, the Roschach advanced.

"No!" Maia clenched her fists, her mind building to a frenzy. Her only hope to compete with her father was to use her rage, her hatred of him in a focused, careful way. Maia hated to do it, but August and the Roschach were too powerful otherwise.

Her power extended to the foremost of the Roschach. The monster's striped eyes widened and it hissed. Nothing else happened save that it no longer moved forward. Maia concentrated harder, recalling what it had been like to be the daughter of an ambitious dictator and murderer, a brutal man.

A gleaming white light burst from the Roschach's center. Its kindred halted again, turning as one to stare. The affected creature hissed louder, but the hiss was drowned out by a searing noise as the white light spread quickly across its victim, a miniature sun burning away the foul night. A breath later, nothing remained of the creature save a wisp of smoke that drifted off.

"There are moments when I am very proud of your skills," her father interrupted, drawing her attention and breaking some of her concentration. "There are times when I see the worthiness of my daughter."

"I never *wanted* to be your daughter!"

"You have no choice."

A horrible, gut-wrenching force shook Maia, disrupting her remaining will. August de Fortunato walked slowly, almost casually toward her, the Roschach moving with him. Through tear-racked eyes she looked to Philo for aid, but the animatron was still struggling with the sword. Her father was that powerful.

Then, just before he could reach out and seize her, a fierce, howling wind ripped down the street. The Roschach found it impossible to advance further and even August de Fortunato could not continue far enough to take his daughter. However, the wind also threatened to throw Maia toward him, forcing her to grab hold of Philo, who seemed the only one able to stand in place.

The animatron paid her no mind. He had abandoned the sword, his attention now on the dark sky. "This is her doing. She's come early for some reason."

Maia followed his gaze.

A half-ruined sailing vessel floated among the clouds, the bow haloed by the moon. Great portions of the ship were missing. The hull had gaps large enough for a car to drive through and most of one mast was gone. Oddly, the tattered but serviceable sails of that mast were in place, as if some invisible twin held them there until the true one could be found. There were gaps in the rail, too. What else might be missing was impossible to say; Maia was amazed that she could see as much as she did.

An anchor lowered, unattached to any chain. The ship began to descend.

"Run unless you want to be shanghaied, lass," Philo declared, his voice as calm as ever. However, his actions were anything but that. He pulled Maia away, breaking the spell of terrified fascination the ship's coming had caused, and ran with her down the nearest side street.

"Stop them!" roared her father. The Roschach, however, were being pushed farther and farther back, and some of them now began to retreat. They had no idea what this ghostly vessel was and what its coming meant. Their master had said only to obey the short human; nothing had been mentioned concerning this.

"What's happening?" Maia glanced over her shoulder. The ship continued to descend. To her surprise, although the vessel looked solid, she saw that it passed *through* the nearby buildings. There was also a new sight: Four rope ladders, two on each side, hung down. Already the ends nearly dragged on the ground.

She saw one other thing: the small but fleet figure of her father racing away from them and into the shadows. Maia doubted that he had abandoned the hunt.

The ravaging wind followed them, tossing trash and dust around. The few pedestrians on the street paid no attention to them and none of them even raised an eyebrow at the coming of the spectral craft. To them, the wind had simply picked up.

"The *Despair* is collecting its own," Philo uttered, finally answering her question. "And sometimes what it considers its own is a matter of whim."

"But why are you running from it? It's your ship!"

One eye fixed on her as the animatron increased their pace. "The *Despair* carries us, but it is its own creature. So my captain says and so I agree, lass."

"I don't understand!"

The parrot turned his gaze from her. "No one does."

A long, green vehicle turned the corner, heading in the direction of the ship. Maia watched as she ran, trusting Philo to guide her. Not at all to her surprise she saw the car, unimpeded, drive through the anchor and the rope ladders. The *Despair* was intangible to everything, it seemed.

She did not want to test that theory in regard to herself. Maia knew that for her, the ghost ship would be very, very real.

The wall ahead of them burst, tendrils composed of solid

brick and metal reaching out to seize the pair. Philo was thrown against a lightpost. Maia was lifted into the air and held there.

"You shouldn't go running off without asking your father for permission, Maia!" From a shadow created by the streetlight emerged August de Fortunato. He rose from the shadow in much the same way as the Roschach had come out of the telephones, but in some ways his coming was even more terrible. She had never heard of such an ability. With effort, some Scattered Ones could transfer themselves from one point to another, but moving from shadow to shadow . . . that had to be yet another gift of the Darkling.

Is nothing beyond him? With such power why does he even need the Darkling . . . or is it that his power's been made greater by the Prince of Shadows? Certainly she had never known one of the Scattered Ones to travel through shadows cast by streetlights.

"I told his royal darkness that I didn't need his pathetic ink stains for this, but he wouldn't believe me."

"August, you are a fool! Didn't you see the ship? It might take all of us!"

"Then we shall have to be gone soon, won't we?"

"I must find my captain," Philo insisted despite his predicament. "I must find him."

De Fortunato smirked, ignoring the wind that buffeted them. "You are growing tedious, my toy soldier." He peered behind them and suddenly scowled. "Looks like your ship has finally come in. I think that means that it's time for us to fly from here."

Maia knew that the ghost ship had to be directly behind them. She struggled to be free, wondering which fate would be worse, her father or the spectral vessel. Out of the two, she decided that the *Despair* was probably the lesser evil. Better to sail forever than suffer her father's tender mercies for even a time.

Maia fixed her mind on the tentacle that held her. All she

had to do was weaken one area, but her father's stony creation made it hard for her to breathe, much less think.

The appendages drew her nearer to her father. August de Fortunato reached out a hand to her. Philo was still held by the brick tentacles. A pair of Roschach that seemed to have materialized out of nowhere came up behind their master's ally. De Fortunato noticed them and pointed at the animatron.

"Quickly now!" he shouted over the terrible wind. "Your master will not like it if you lose that one! We must be away now, do you hear me?"

The Roschach seized the struggling Philo. August de Fortunato prepared to take hold of his daughter.

Maia glared at the tentacle holding her, forcing her will on it. It suddenly began to quiver.

It cracked in two just before he could grab her wrist. Her father shouted something. One of the Roschach holding Philo abandoned its grip and reached for her. The foul monster missed, but Maia's good luck was short-lived, for the remaining brick that bound her did not crumble as she had hoped. The imprisoned woman tumbled over and started to roll. De Fortunato lunged after her. In desperation, she pushed herself along with her feet, rolling away from the grasping fingers and not caring at all what happened to her save that she avoid her father's touch.

Despite the herculean wind pushing against her, Maia rolled faster and faster. The world spun around, repeating images of the street, the night sky, Philo in battle with the Roschach, and, most terrible, her furious father in pursuit.

Then something tall and solid cut short her almost absurd flight to freedom. At first Maia thought it was another lamp post, but by twisting she was able to see that it was a man, a tall, weathered man clad in a long cloak, who looked down at her with eyes blacker than the night.

Before she could speak, he reached down and picked her up, bonds and all. The brick tentacle shattered as he raised her, the fragments blowing away in the wind. Although suddenly free, Maia was too stunned by the appearance of her rescuer to do anything. She knew that he could only be one person.

He whispered something that sounded like her name, but the wind carried it away. Behind the black eyes, which Maia saw had no pupils, she sensed something akin to surprise and possibly sorrow.

A sinewy shape fluttered behind him. Maia's eyes widened. It was one of the rope ladders. She quickly looked up at the ghost ship, which now loomed almost directly above them. The ladders snaked down from it, but they were not tossed by the wind. Instead, each moved toward her rescuer and her as if alive or, at the very least, appendages of the *Despair*.

Maia tried to call out a warning, but the tall figure who held her was already turning. It was too late, though. Her rescuer, who must be the Flying Dutchman, turned just in time to see one outstretched ladder only inches from him.

The tip of the ladder touched his cloak even as he tried to twist away.

The world vanished. Maia found herself still in the tall figure's arms, but now he stood on the half-ruined deck of a partially transparent sailing ship.

Around them there was nothing but black space.

9. FIRST TREMOR

Dutchman had found it more difficult to locate another of the hunters than he had expected. He had searched but found only traces of their passing. His trek had taken him all over the core of the city. It was as if all of the Roschach had heard he was near and had gone into hiding. How was he supposed to find this Darkling if he could not find the creature's servants?

Then he had come across the black man. Even from a distance Dutchman had recognized him as one of the leapers. The man was powerful, but too caught up in his present concerns to realize that to someone like the mariner, he radiated power. To his own kind this newcomer was likely as invisible as Dutchman was now to him. Oddly, the black man had also appeared to be hunting and after a few moments of observation, it had occurred to Dutchman that the leaper very possibly was searching for *him*. The irony was enough to make him smile, briefly.

Caught up in his observation of the other, Dutchman himself had had a momentary lapse. He had failed to notice the Roschach that suddenly crept around a corner, coming up directly behind the leaper. Dutchman had nearly called out, but it was too late to prevent the Roschach from seizing its prey.

The black man had turned at the last moment, but the action had only made his capture easier. A clawed appendage had clamped around his throat. The monster had opened its mouth and a needlelike tongue had shot out and pricked the captive in the neck.

The man had collapsed immediately.

Disgust had caused Dutchman to pursue the beast without care. It had fled perhaps a block with its captive, then, predictably, had created a pocket lair in which it hoped to hide itself and its prey until its pursuer gave up. It had not counted on Dutchman knowing its kind. He had not even paused, charging through the facade it had built and entering the world secreted between the edges of the true doorway.

The lair had been just like that of the first. The Roschach stood in its center, the black man's inert form still in its clawed arms, the humanoid form of the monster now having given way to a crablike shape with four legs. It had scuttled toward the haze and deposited the refugee's form there, then stalked toward Dutchman, claws clacking.

"I only want some questions answered," he had told the Roschach in an attempt to prevent battle. "And I must take him, too."

This Roschach had said nothing, attacking but a moment later. It had been a more versatile creature than its predecessors, shifting shape at least half a dozen times in the first few breaths. Dutchman's greatest difficulty had been trying to keep hold of it, for the Roschach had melted each time he seized a limb or even the torso.

"This is not necessary," he had insisted. "We do not need to fight."

It had not listened to him. The needle tongue darted out again and again, barely missing him until Dutchman, finally annoyed beyond his limits, had seized it and, before the Roschach could change again, tore the tongue from the monster's maw.

At that point it had howled and, reshaping, had tried to escape.

"I want your master, creature. Tell me where I can find him and we can end this without further harm."

The Roschach had stilled then, staring at Dutchman with such intent that for a moment he had believed it would agree.

A moment later, it had re-created the pincers . . . and driven them into itself. There had been a flash of energy, enough so that Dutchman had thrown the beast away out of sheer surprise. It would not betray its master even at the cost of its life. He had not expected it to act so.

The Roschach had still been alive even after its very effective suicide attempt, but when he walked over to it, he saw that it was melting . . . this time, forever. Disappointed, Dutchman had turned to the unconscious figure.

The dark-skinned refugee had reminded him of someone he had known long ago when he had been a human being like everyone else. In every world he saw those who reminded him of faces from his past. Sometimes he wondered whether the confrontations were the work of the ship or even possibly of those who had cast him aboard the living prison. Were the encounters designed to remind him again and again that his overconfidence had caused him to attempt to master forces that, when he had finally lost control of them, had begun this horrible, endless sequence of destruction? If so, he needed no such reminders. The memories of his folly were ever with him.

Despite his efforts, the black man had not awakened. Dutchman had touched the other's forehead and found his thoughts. There had been visions of a luxurious abode and half-formed images of more than one person. The unconscious figure had stirred slightly as Dutchman read through the vision, which meant that his mind had still been clear and healthy. He had not appeared to be injured; whatever the Roschach had injected him with simply kept him in a coma-like state. It would pass, of that Dutchman had been certain, but what to do with him in the meantime . . .

His solution had come in the form of another of the leapers, an amusing and energetic little man who had walked right by him, studied the dying monster, and then tried to rescue the black man on his own. At first Dutchman had been willing to let him do so, but then he had realized that the small man would not be able to drag his companion out in time. In fact, the lair had been shrinking so fast that he had suddenly wondered about his own escape. He still did not desire to know what would happen to him if he failed to escape. Not death, but pain, definitely. Or perhaps he would never be able to escape, even after the coming cataclysm had destroyed this Earth, including his makeshift prison. The *Despair* would simply retrieve him as she had so many times in the past. The *Despair* always found him.

Seizing hold, he had dragged both to the collapsing opening. The streets he did not trust . . . not with other Roschach about . . . so Dutchman had chosen an image from the black man's subconscious, the obscenely plush living quarters of the refugee, and twisted the entrance a little. It was a process that had strained him hard, but he had succeeded. First one and then the other had gone through. Then, after a struggle to keep the doorway open, he had followed after them.

"Who are you?" was the wiry little man's question when he first looked up at the cloaked figure. Dutchman had told him. He had not been at all shocked when the colorful character had blanched.

His fear aside, however, the one who called himself Gilbrin the Shifter had been more concerned with what had happened to the black man. He barely listened as Dutchman related the Roschach's attack and the confrontation in the lair. It was clear that Gilbrin did not care much for his rescuer. Small wonder, since he evidently knew that the cursed mariner was the cause of all of their troubles.

"Why did you bother?" Gilbrin had asked as he looked over his friend. "We'll all just begin over, anyway, now that the End is near. Might as well have left us to die there. That's what you want, isn't it? For everything to die?"

Dutchman doubted that the man would believe his tale, that in that other life he had worked for the good of his world, and so he had simply turned away from the pair and replied, "No."

A few tense minutes later, the black man had opened his eyes. He had been unable to say a word, but his steady stare at Dutchman had spoken volumes.

The room had abruptly resounded with a piercing noise, one that made Dutchman want to cover his ears. The black man wanted to rise, but Gilbrin had not allowed him to do so. The wiry little figure had simply stared at a device on one of the tables.

"We don't know who might be on the telephone, Master Tarriqa. Trust me on this."

The telephone had ceased its racket shortly after, but another machine had come into play. Dutchman heard a voice that announced itself as belonging to Hamman Tarriqa. Then a second voice had snared his attention.

"Gilbrin, if you get this, I'm all right. I—"

Dutchman had known that voice. It was a part of him that he could never have forgotten . . . but the voice was that of someone long dead. It could not possibly have been her.

The wiry Gilbrin had leaped at the telephone, but all of them heard the crackle just before he touched the machine. Something had destroyed the link from the other end.

"Maia!" the clownish young man had uttered.

"Mariya . . ." Dutchman had corrected without realizing.

"Something's happened! We have to get to her!" Gilbrin had turned back to Tarriqa, who had managed to sit up. The black man had waved to him, indicating, as far as Dutchman could tell, that he would be safe without them.

Dutchman had put a hand on Gilbrin's shoulder and when the other had looked into his timelost face, the cloaked figure had told him, "You will take me to her."

"I don't know how! I can't sense her! She's either shielded or . . ."

Dutchman had refused to hear of it. "You will take her to—"

A chill wind had coursed through the room . . . no, not through the room, but within him. Dutchman had known what it meant and the coincidence had been too much for him. The call and the coming of the *Despair* were tied together.

He knew where the damnable vessel was and that *she* must be there.

"Come with me," he had commanded Gilbrin, tightening his grasp as he quickly took his reluctant companion from the room.

It had been an effort and at first glance he had almost regretted the action because of the chaos before him. The *Despair* was hunting, which made no sense, and it was clear that what it was hunting was Philo and a dark-haired woman whose features he could not make out in the dim light of the street lamps. A short, insidious-looking youth faced them, the same one he recalled having seen near the massive sculpture.

The following moments had been a blur. Before his eyes, she had freed herself, but not the way in which she had intended. He had tried to save her, but his actions had been marred by emotions he had thought long buried. Dutchman had saved her, but at the cost of forgetting the more imminent danger to both of them.

He had forgotten about the *Despair*. One glance at the face of the woman he had picked up from the ground and even the dread vessel, his eternal prison, had faded from his thoughts. Only one thing came to mind.

Mariya. His long-lost love.

He could have stood where he was until the End of that world, staring at her beauty returned to him. It was not simply a resemblance; it was she.

He had said her name, expecting her to respond, but instead she had looked beyond him. For a brief moment, Dutchman had wondered why . . . and then he had turned to see the *Despair* reach out toward both of them. A rope ladder it might be to the eyes, but Dutchman knew that it was not the wind that blew it toward them.

But by then it was too late. Instead of the city street, they abruptly stood on the deck of the damnable ghost ship.

He had failed more miserably than on any world past.

Worse, he had now condemned her to his miserable fate . . . and another world to its death.

Hamman Tarriqa sat up on the couch, still groggy but gradually recovering. He recalled nothing of his time as a prize of the Roschach. If not for the presence of the infamous angel of death, the Boatman, he would have thought that Gilbrin had been telling a tall tale.

Tarriqa!

He groaned as he struggled to come to grips with the mental call. The link was not complete, for he sensed only thoughts, not images, but Tarriqa knew who it was who tried to contact him. Steeling himself, he acknowledged his caller. *What is it, Gilbrin?*

The jester's tone was frantic, something not surprising considering the circumstances. *Tarriqa, how good are you at transference?*

Transference? He had seen the Boatman . . . no, Dutchman . . . make use of the ability as if it were very simple. For the Scattered Ones, however, the skill was rare, the gift of only the most powerful or foolhardy. Tarriqa had used transference, teleportation, or whatever one wanted to term it only once and that had left him ill for a day. He could certainly not do it now, not on his own.

Not on his own?

Give me a moment, Gilbrin.

I can spare a moment, Master Tarriqa, but not much more! I think August de Fortunato is growing tired of my whimsical nature!

August de Fortunato? All traces of lethargy burned away as the black man straightened. *Gilbrin! Give me your mind! Link with me fully! Let your strength be mine to use!*

Anything else you'd like while you're at it? My virginity's long gone, I have to tell you! the other refugee quipped with obvious anxiety. *He's getting nearer. . . .*

Do it!

Suddenly the full thoughts of Gilbrin the Shifter filled Tarriqa's mind. Never had he felt such a childish jumble of patterns. It was a wonder that the buffoon could function at all . . . and yet, thoroughly embroidered into the jumble was a cunning, devious mind that used the childlike attitude and thoughts to excellent effect. At another time, he would have dearly loved to explore the full thought processes of the wiry little man, but first he would have to rescue Gilbrin.

Follow my lead! Hamman Tarriqa commanded. What he intended should be possible. The Shifter was also powerful, much more so than he had expected. It was possible that in his own way Gilbrin was as powerful as Tarriqa himself.

Gilbrin understood what he planned, but suddenly added, *I'm not alone, Tarriqa! I'm holding on to—*

All right! Don't worry! The black man needed no further explanation. Gilbrin must have had Maia with him. Who else might need help? Certainly not Dutchman. He knew where Tarriqa lived and could get there easier than any of them. It had to be Maia, but since Tarriqa could not sense her mind, she had to be unconscious or worse.

He closed his eyes. A brief wave of dizziness struck him, but he fought it down. His anger at having been so easily snared by the Roschach gave him the strength. *Come to me, Gilbrin. This is the way.*

At first there was resistance, but then suddenly he felt the oncoming presence of the sandy-haired trickster. There was also a second presence, but it was indistinct, which bolstered his notion that Maia was unconscious, perhaps gravely injured. The presence of Gilbrin seemed to rush toward him, growing bigger by the moment.

Energy crackled throughout the suite. Tarriqa felt every hair on his body stiffen.

"Carim's children! What a ridiculous way to get around!" bellowed the familiar voice of the Shifter. There was a loud thumping sound, then the black man felt the field of energy fade.

Hamman Tarriqa dared to open his eyes. He felt as if a train had parked on top of him.

Gilbrin the Shifter stood by the telephone, in almost the same location from which Dutchman had taken him. He looked much worse for the wear, his brightly-colored clothing torn in some places and covered with dirt and dust in others. An inky substance dripped from one sleeve and there were two long but shallow cuts on his right cheek.

The figure standing next to him was not Maia. It was not even living, as far as he could tell, although it certainly pretended well.

"You couldn't have been a little faster, could you?" Gilbrin asked with a tired smile. He reached out with one hand, catching a bottle of whiskey that suddenly flew toward him. With much gusto, the weary refugee sipped directly from the bottle.

"What the devil is that beside you, prankster? What's happened to Maia and the Boatman?"

"The *Despair*," remarked the tall figure, as if that answered everything.

It was human in shape, but with the stylized head of a parrot. To Tarriqa, it was as if one of the characters from Disneyland had escaped. Then he took a closer look at the creature and saw that while one might first take the mechanical mariner as simply a humorous oddity, there was a sense of being, of some sort of existence within, that marked the animatron as possibly more than either he or Gilbrin could imagine.

"I've never seen anything like it," Gilbrin the Shifter began, ignoring his bizarre companion's remark. That anyone could be termed "bizarre" next to the color-clashing refugee was itself amazing. "It was a ship . . . the ghost ship. It didn't even touch them."

"The rope ladders." The parrot eyed Tarriqa.

"The ship and . . . and both of them just disappeared."

"Shanghaied, lad, although I can't say why."

"Shanghaied?" the black man said. The mechanical man looked ready to explain, but Tarriqa waved him silent. He had so many questions to ask about Dutchman, the ship, and the parrot's role, but there were other questions he needed to have answered first. "Just tell me: Is the woman unharmed?"

"Aye."

"That will do for now, then."

"That will *do*?" Gilbrin looked at him as if he had gone mad. "How can you say that?"

Tarriqa stood. It was an effort, but he wanted to face the Shifter with some semblance of strength. "I can say that because they are both apparently alive and well, if . . . elsewhere." He did not want to consider where *elsewhere* actually was. It might be that Maia de Fortunato was forever gone, cursed to sail through time alongside the man who had possibly caused the death of countless Earths. He could not think about that . . . just as he had tried since waking not to wonder where Rees might be. If a Roschach had been following Tarriqa, then it stood to reason that one might have also been following—No, no thinking about that. Not now. "You said that you barely escaped from August de Fortunato, Gilbrin. I gather he was working directly with the Roschach."

"He was commanding the blotty things!"

"Things are certainly different this variant. So all pretense is off. De Fortunato has chosen to be direct with us. I wonder why, after so many lives of subterfuge and hiding in the shadows. They knew that you were at the hotel, didn't they?"

A hint of Gilbrin's old self returned. "I will never order room service again. I prefer eating my meals, not my meals eating me."

They must have Rees, Tarriqa could not help thinking. He shook off the fate of the other man just as he had in the past been forced to shake off any emotions concerning friends and associates snared by the Darkling. Rees was dead; that was the way to look at it. "I suspect that we are not safe here." From what he could see, Gilbrin had had the same thought. What the animatron thought was anyone's guess. "We have to go elsewhere."

"Probably so," Gilbrin agreed, obviously still deep in thought concerning Maia. "He . . . the Boatman . . . he in-

sisted on rescuing her. While old August was distracted by
them, I pulled this one out. That little bastard didn't know
which way to turn, he wanted everyone so badly. You should
see him, Tarriqa; de Fortunato's just a nasty-looking kid, but
he's as deadly as ever." He indicated their new companion. "I
contacted you just before August was about to make both of
us into truly scattered ones and I'll tell you that I'm very, very
grateful you did what you did."

"You were probably in less danger of destruction than you
think, jester. I don't believe that August de Fortunato would
have damaged our friend here, although you, on the other
hand, I can't say for certain."

"You have no idea how much you've relieved me on this
matter," chided the Shifter.

Tarriqa tested his limbs. He still ached, but he was confident that he would be able to keep up with the others. "We
need to discuss this further, but it's time to go. I have a place
in mind that I think should be safe. There we can plan."

"I must find my captain."

The two Scattered Ones looked at the animatron, who
cocked his head and studied them in turn.

"As you indicated, they are lost to us," Tarriqa countered.
"We need to be concerned about our own welfare. At the very
least, we have to stay out of the Darkling's clutches until the
next Scattering." It sounded cowardly, but it *was* something
they had to consider.

"Not yet," the parrot insisted in his calm voice. The grating,
almost movie-pirate tone with which the mechanical creature
spoke was all that gave his voice any emotional tinge, but Tarriqa still found the calmness a bit much to take at this time.
"The *Despair*, the cursed lady, she'll be still coming in to hunt
for the rest of herself. The Maelstrom's a rough lover; he scat-
ters her over all of history each time they meet."

It was the longest, most elaborate response either of them
had heard from the animatron. Gilbrin, however, was only
momentarily impressed. "Now what does that mean, my fine
birdbrain?"

The wide, unblinking eye stared at the Shifter until he was forced to look down. "My captain named me Philo. It was the name of a man, a friend, he once knew, although he has probably now forgotten that." Philo turned his attention to Hamman Tarriqa. "The ship will materialize again. More than once. The End of your world is not yet here. Soon, but not yet."

"How . . . No, never mind. I don't want to know how long we have left just yet." Tarriqa nodded. "So they may be able to escape."

"May." Philo shrugged. "There is a first for everything, sir."

Tarriqa looked at his watch. "How long until it returns?"

"A day . . . possibly two. It has an entire history through which to hunt."

"An entire—" Gilbrin shook his head. "It's going to go back in time? Just like that?"

"She was designed to sail every sea, lad, including that of time itself." The animatron suddenly clamped shut his beak, as if he had said something he was not supposed to reveal.

Tarriqa was not concerned with possible secrets. He was busy making calculations. "This will bear thought later. Now it is time to adjourn to the safe place I mentioned." He paused. "Will you come with us?"

Philo seemed to consider the question . . . at least he was silent for several seconds. "Aye, sir. With pirates haunting the waters, it behooves us all to sail close together."

"Have you ever watched Errol Flynn?" Gilbrin asked with a tired but still mischievous expression.

The animatron only looked at him.

Concentrating, Hamman Tarriqa searched the nearby vicinity for any sign of the Darkling, August de Fortunato, or the Roschach. He found none. Unfortunately, it was all too possible that the ones he sought were shielded.

"The sea's calm right now," Philo announced just as Tarriqa opened his eyes.

"You're sure?" he asked.

The animatron shrugged and said nothing more.

Both men were without their vehicles, the cars having been left in the vicinity of the Sears Tower. Gilbrin expressed some interest in salvaging his beloved Dodge, but the other would not hear of it. Neither vehicle could be trusted now that de Fortunato was known to be nearby.

Much as Tarriqa hated to admit it, the easiest thing for them to do was to borrow . . . *steal* being such a distasteful word . . . one of his neighbor's cars. Transference took too much out of him to do it again even with Gilbrin's aid and the animatron, unlike his captain, seemed bereft of the ability. At least, Philo had not given any indication of possessing the skill.

The vehicle they chose, which belonged to a neighbor two floors down, was large and roomy, the latter a necessity when traveling with a creature as tall as Philo. The hour was late, so no one noticed them take it. As they departed the building, Tarriqa again made as thorough a scan as he could for any sign of Roschach, de Fortunato, the Darkling, or anything else unusual. Nothing. Despite that, he drove along the empty avenues with a feeling of uneasiness.

"Do you sense anything?" he asked Gilbrin and Philo.

"No," replied the shorter man, who had appeared to be half-asleep. "I've been searching since we left your place. I haven't noticed slime nor hair of dear August and his inky pets."

Philo simply shook his head.

"Now can I ask where we're going?"

"A place I keep on the South Side. I don't go there much."

"I wonder why. Why don't you just drop me off at Cabrini Green? I'm likely to get just as lovely a reception there as where you're going."

"What's that supposed to mean?" The black man glanced at the jester, sudden anger threatening to bubble to the surface.

Gilbrin scratched his pale face. "My tan's just not what it used to be."

"I could drop you off right here, you cursed little joker. I don't abide such comments, no matter what my lifestyle might otherwise indicate. If you have trouble with skin color—"

"Not *me*," Gilbrin protested, holding both hands up before him. "I'm afraid someone there will take offense of me, that's all."

"Only of your personality and dress sense, Shifter. Not your pasty skin."

"At ease, lads," came a voice from behind them. "Let's not be turning our guns on each other."

"A good point," Tarriqa responded. "We're all nervous. We've nothing to worry about down on the South Side, Gilbrin. No one will even know that we're there."

The sandy-haired figure slumped back down in his seat. "I hope so." His eyelids drooped. "Sorry."

The mumbled apology made Tarriqa smile. "We're in this together. We just have to keep remembering that for all our sakes."

"I'm worried about Maia."

"I know. I—"

The car shimmered . . . and stretched wide.

Tarriqa suddenly found himself sitting next to himself, who, in turn, sat next to himself and so on to infinity. Somehow, interspliced in the infinity of Hammans was an infinity of Gilbrins. The look spreading across the features of each of the legion of jesters was of shock, expressions that no doubt mirrored the faces of each Hamman.

In the backseat, an entire aviary of parrot-headed animatrons stared blankly.

The condition was not restricted to the vehicle and its occupants. The street, the lights, the city, Chicago itself was now an infinite string of metropolises.

Hamman Tarriqa, brain afire and eyes strained beyond their limits, fought to maintain control of the car, but everywhere there was a street there was also a sidewalk or curb.

"Tarriqa! Watch out for that lamp post!" roared the army of Gilbrins.

He saw the posts, but how to avoid them when they were

everywhere was a question he could not answer. Worse, the buildings seemed to be closing in on all sides, squeezing the widened vehicle between them.

"Away from there, man. This storm's too much for any but an old sea dog like me to be at the wheel."

A long arm stretched past Tarriqa from the backseat. Philo seized the steering wheel. The black man leaned against the door in order to allow the animatron . . . or animatrons . . . better mobility.

"Put the brake on!" the Gilbrins cried.

"No," returned the Philos. "Do not drop anchor under any circumstance. Ride out the storm or we're all for it." He steered past one light, then another.

Then, as suddenly as it had happened, the madness vanished. The street was back to normal. There was only one vehicle and only one of each of them inside. Ahead of them lay only empty streets. The buildings had all reduced to their original size.

"Is it over?" Gilbrin's voice was muffled. He was wrapped in a ball as if trying to hide from what had happened.

"Storm's blown over, lad." The animatron released the wheel.

Tarriqa quickly seized it, then maneuvered the car to the side of the street, parking there. He was amazed that his sandy-haired companion could even speak. His own breath came in hurried gasps and it was more than three minutes before he could speak.

"Is . . . is everyone all right?"

"Define 'all right.' My insides feel like scrambled eggs, Master Tarriqa."

"I would rather you did not mention food at the moment." The simple thought of it was enough to turn the black man's stomach. He stared out at the darkened city, so quiet and seemingly unaware of what had just happened.

Tarriqa knew. He had no doubt that Gilbrin and the animatron knew as well.

"It's begun," announced Philo in his typical flat tone. "A bit early," continued the parrot, "but it's definitely begun. The world's going to crumble sooner than I thought. The ship, she'll stay around a few days after she returns. She always does, just so the captain knows she's watching him watch the End. That doesn't give us long. I'd say maybe a week, lads, and then again maybe not even that."

The two Scattered Ones glanced at each other. *It's begun.* A simple sentence to describe so terrible an event. This would not be the last such disturbance. In fact, this was likely to be the least of the disturbances. As time went on, each shock would grow in intensity, causing worse and worse damage to the structure of reality until things finally snapped.

The animatron leaned back in the car seat. "I must reach my captain. It is your only hope."

10. PARADISES LOST

"Where are we?" asked the woman who looked like his Mariya. "Where are we?"

They were surrounded by night sky, not the emptiness through which he and the *Despair* normally sailed. These were unusual but not entirely unfamiliar waters the damned ship now plied. Sometimes the *Despair* seized him before his time, stole him away before the devastation occurred. Not often, no, but enough so that at least he had some notion as to what was happening.

She repeated her question. To her credit, she was more confused and angry than frightened. Just like his Mariya. Had he not relived her death over and over in his mind, Dutchman would have been willing to swear that his love now stood on the deck of the spectral ship, fists on her hips and growing annoyance in her expression.

"The seas of time," he finally told her.

"And what are the seas of time?"

Dutchman shrugged, not having a good enough definition. He knew what happened during these periods but not *how* it happened. That was a secret of the *Despair*. "The ship . . . she will sail against and with the current of time, piecing herself together and drawing strength. When she is done, when the world is nearly done, she will take me back into her cursed bosom and sail on into limbo again."

She obviously understood only a little of what he said. Turning away, Mariya . . . no, her name was Maia . . . stalked to the still broken rail and peered over. "There is nothing down there but more stars. Are we in space?"

"No."

When he did not elaborate, the dark-haired refugee looked back at him. Perhaps there was something in his expression, but the anger in her seemed to melt away then, to be replaced with something more akin to sympathy.

It was Dutchman's turn to look away. He did not want sympathy from her, for she so reminded him of the woman who had died because of his folly.

"Thank you for rescuing me."

It was not what he had expected. No one ever thanked him for anything. "You've no reason to thank me. I've cursed you to a worse fate than any that originally awaited you."

"I doubt that. You obviously never met my dear, deadly father. That was him you saved me from. The boy."

He remembered the boy. The boy unnerved him. The boy was evil. Her *father?* "Is he the one called the Darkling?"

"The Darkling? Hardly, but he's as good as the Prince of Shadow's lapdog. Those were the Darkling's creatures with him. Dear daddy made a deal, I guess; he got me and the Darkling got your . . . your first mate." Her brow furrowed. "So that they could find you, from what I understood."

"This Darkling wanted to find me?" The irony of the situation fit so well within the usual pattern of his existence. The one Dutchman had sought had also sought him . . . and now both were as far apart as any two creatures could ever be. Once again, his chosen path had become a dead end and his failure had condemned another Earth.

"Be thankful that he did not. It is death to fall into his hands. He hunts us because we . . . or maybe our souls . . . seem to know when the world will end. We leap and are reborn into each new variant Earth . . . but you knew that, didn't you?"

"I knew that."

He said no more, hoping that she would not ask him just how much he knew.

For a time, neither spoke. Dutchman was afraid to do so and Maia appeared to have satiated her curiosity for the moment. She moved from the rail, studying what she could of the *Despair.* Dutchman watched her, wanting at least to walk along with her, but a fear of her had risen within him. She was not his Mariya, but she seemed a variation of her. That was enough for him. Her anger, her condemnations when she learned that she was forever trapped aboard this vessel, would pain him as if they came from the very lips of his beloved.

"It looks so very old." Arms folded tight against her chest, she walked the entire deck, pausing only when she reached the steps leading up to the wheel. Maia put one foot on the first step, then turned and asked, "Are you really the Boatman?"

It was another of the titles he had accumulated, but not one of his favorites. "I am sometimes called that. I am sometimes called Charon, the Eternal Mariner, Landlost, and the Flying Dutchman. My names are nearly infinite."

"What do you call yourself?"

"I prefer Dutchman."

"Dutchman . . ." She returned to him, not stopping until they were only a step apart. Maia was as tall as Mariya had been, but she still had to look up to match his gaze. Her eyes were as vivid and as beautiful as Mariya's. "So you're a Dutch sea captain who swore to sail around the cape or something?"

It was too close a proximity for him. He finally stepped back, ashamed but untrusting of what effect her closeness would have on him. "No. I simply prefer that name over others."

"I see." Maia took another step forward, defying his obvious unease. "If you won't talk, then can you take me to my friends? I'm afraid that they might be in danger."

The question he had tried to avoid. *Can you take me to my friends? No, I cannot take you to your friends; we are here forever.* Dutchman took a deep breath. "No, I cannot."

"Cannot or won't?" The anger was back. When he did not answer her, she asked again.

Unable to face her with such dire news, the cloaked outcast turned from Maia and walked toward the bow of the ship. There were stars all around the *Despair*, a much more pleasant sight than the nothingness. At first he wished that his prison looked like this, but then he realized that after a time he would yearn for the blank surroundings. Novelty wore off quickly when one was condemned for all eternity.

A feminine but quite strong hand took hold of his arm. Behind him, Maia insisted, "I asked you a question."

"Cannot."

Her hand slipped from his arm. It returned, accompanied by the other. Maia attempted to turn him to face her and this time Dutchman yielded. "Say that again."

"I cannot, Maia de Fortunato. You are here forever, just as I am, a prisoner of the *Despair* and her makers."

The confidence that she had exhibited thus far faded, revealing it to be nothing more than a mask, a veneer hiding the woman's strong fears. "I don't believe you."

"I am sorry."

"This is your ship!"

"I am captain in name only. I no more sail her than you do."

"I don't believe you!" Maia looked up at the wheel, then suddenly ran toward it.

Dutchman made no move to stop her. She would learn the truth of his words soon enough.

Reaching the wheel, the determined woman turned it with all her might. The wheel groaned and gave way. Maia was momentarily triumphant, but her pleasure quickly dwindled as she noticed the lack of effect. The *Despair* did not alter course, no matter which way or how much she spun the wheel.

"My first mate has turned that wheel to no better success, Maia de Fortunato. Before that, I, too, failed to persuade my infernal lady to accede to my desires even once. We are trapped here and I can only say that I would never have allowed this to happen to you if I had only had a choice. I sought to rescue you, not condemn you to my cursed fate."

By the end of his speech he had reached the top of the steps, but there Dutchman paused. Maia eyed him with complete distrust. She edged away from the wheel and him, not pausing until the rail prevented her from going any farther.

"This is all insane! I want to go back! I cannot leave Gil and the others!"

"There is nothing I can do."

Her hand stroked the rail. She looked over the side, clearly contemplating leaping over. Dutchman knew what would happen to him if he did as she dreamed, but as to her fate, he could only guess. It might be that by leaping Maia would commit herself to an eternity of floating helplessly in this starlit limbo.

To his relief, she finally stepped away. Once more Maia smothered the fear, even going so far as to return to him. Dutchman reached out a hand in order to escort her down to the deck, but she folded her arms and made her way down alone. Dutchman followed her at a respectful distance, understanding some of what she must be suffering.

His new companion muttered to herself as she came to grips with the certainty of her situation. Names . . . Gil, Hamman Tarriqa, August, and others. Dutchman wanted greatly to comfort her, but doubted that Maia would accept his touch just yet. It hurt him more than ever to watch her, for she was still every inch his Mariya in form and attitude. There was no doubt in his mind that eventually she would overcome her fears. What she would do then, however, was a mystery. Shun him, perhaps.

"You are certain that there is no way back?"

"I have witnessed the deaths of more worlds than I can count. Do you think that I would have let myself suffer so if there was a chance of escape?"

A dark look crossed her features. "I don't know. If you are the angel of death, the Flying Dutchman, then aren't you the one responsible for their destruction? Don't you *want* to watch worlds die? Don't you look forward to the devastation?"

Her words were as sword thrusts, each of them through a vital organ. Coming from her, this Mariya who was not his Mariya, it was more painful in some ways than the journey through the Maelstrom. At least the Maelstrom was an unthinking, uncaring monster. It tore him apart without regard of who he was or what he had done.

Despite the pain of her hatred, Dutchman rebelled. Whatever he had caused, however many deaths could be laid at his door, he did *not* enjoy them. He had never taken satisfaction in the murder of a single human being. Each death was torture to him. "Yes, I am the instrument of their destruction," he snapped. "Yes, I am the angel of death! I played with the fabric of reality and opened up such instability that the chain reaction has coursed ahead, tearing apart variant after variant of my world! Yours was only one; as many as you have lived upon, I have walked a hundredfold more, all *dead* now, too!"

Fear returned to the expression of the beautiful woman, but Dutchman was so caught up in his protest that he cared not how much worse she might think of him. He was a monster, yes, but he was not the Maelstrom.

"My world was the wondrous, the most perfect of the Earths I have trod. There was only one major land, Gondwanaland, and she was jeweled with exquisite lakes and rivers and surrounded by an ocean of glittering blue!" He looked past her, seeing instead the high, majestic mountains, the green fields, and, most important, the ocean, the waters, so important to the civilizations of his Earth. "We harvested from the seas and, knowing the importance, cared for it as we would a loved one. It supplied us with so much. Our lands were not always rich in food and fuel, but what we lacked from the land was made up for by the water. Power from the rivers . . . and the golden sun . . . food, as I said, pleasure and sport. There was knowledge, too, to be gleaned from a life so associated with the water. In time, we had built ourselves *paradise*."

In those days he had worn another name, one that had already become known for great achievement. Dutchman had excelled in everything he had attempted, his only failure being his impatience to reach those goals at the rate he desired. He had garnered for himself more than anyone could have asked. Yet he had not been satisfied with paradise, no, not *him*. He had to investigate things that others saw no sane reason to pursue. Life had come into perfect balance; why toy with perfection?

It had started with a peculiar energy trace that he had come across purely by accident, a form of energy that had the potential to allow him—called "scholar" on his Earth and "sorcerer" on other variants—to manipulate the elements. Each day he pushed a little more and learned a little more and that continuing bounty of knowledge encouraged him to ignore safeguards others would have put into place at the very beginning.

Maia no longer stared at him in fear. Fascination—morbid fascination—Dutchman believed, had replaced the fear. He was grateful for the change in emotion even if he believed the reprieve only temporary. When she learned fully what he had set into play, her fascination would turn to hatred again. Regardless of his regrets, he *was* the angel of death, the harbinger of the Apocalypse.

The Four Horsemen in one cursed form.

The *Despair* sailed on as Dutchman related the tale of his arrogance to his unwilling companion. Once the floodgates had been opened, it was impossible to keep the words in check. He had to tell the story that he had spent so many eternities trying to forget and if there was anyone Dutchman had to tell, it was this female who could have been his loved one.

"There was a woman . . . much like you, Maia de Fortunato. Her name was Mariya. She was my morning, noon, and night. I would have done anything for her . . . except surrender my interest in the power I had discovered." Dutchman walked past Maia and leaned on the rail.

Mariya would have warned him about his folly . . . if she had known about his work. She was everything to him and yet he had not told her what he was doing, for fear that she would tell him to abandon what he had discovered. Early on, to stop had become unthinkable.

"I saw myself as the one who would make fact of what we still dreamed of accomplishing. I saw myself as the explorer who would pave the way for miracles such as none could ever believe possible. My name, my glory, would shine forever. Mariya would look on me with greater love, greater pride."

A voice whispered in his ear. At first he imagined that it was Mariya's, then he thought that it was the voice of his present companion. Only after it was joined by another did he know that yet another part of his curse had come again into play. Why not? The view might be different, but this place was otherwise much the same as the emptiness with which he was more familiar.

He would not be distracted, though. He wanted to tell her everything, regardless of her reaction. She deserved to know.

With effort that surprised him, Dutchman pushed the voices back. They were still there, but now only as the buzzing of gnats.

Maia evidently saw his silence as hesitation, for she finally asked, "So what happened? What did you do wrong?"

What did I do wrong? "Everything. From the lies to the presumptions. I knew what I was doing. Oh yes, I did. I knew that I had the right of it."

The voices grew stronger, but he had their measure this time. Dutchman buried them deeper within his soul, then proceeded with his confession. This was the moment when the woman beside him would hear of his greatest folly, the beginning of the End for worlds to come.

It had started with a calculation that he had made based on his progress. So many doors had been opened; so many miracles had been his not only to behold, but to create.

To better focus his work, Dutchman had moved to a secluded islet a day's journey from the city that he had called home. It was far away enough that he was not bothered by others and yet near enough that he could maintain contact with those few he cared most for, especially Mariya. Once a week he returned to his home both to clear his mind and to live something of a normal existence. To him, this proved that he was aware of all that he did and that his work was therefore safe from error on his part.

He could not have been more wrong. Soon Dutchman grew dissatisfied with his progress. The miracles, vast miracles by the measure of others, began to pale. It was clear that with more access to the forces he had discovered he could perform even greater feats. There had always been interest in harnessing more power for the betterment of civilization. Unfortunately, the energy that he had been able to draw upon so far, while almost sufficient for his desires, could not possibly aid his people.

"And so," Dutchman related to Maia, forcing himself to look at her, "I determined that to achieve everyone's dream, or at least what *I* believed to be everyone's dream, I had to enable a greater stream of power to come through into our world." He clenched his fists, still unable to believe, even after so long, how arrogant and self-important he had been. That was one more reason why he had abandoned his name; the man who had worn it was unworthy of memory, only condemnation. "It was not so difficult a thing, I discovered. The energy itself provided the starting point. It came from elsewhere and so the hole, the rip in the fabric of reality, already existed. I simply had to enlarge it. An easy thing for someone of my skill to accomplish. It only took a matter of time, you see."

Still the raven-tressed woman said nothing. He both appreciated and feared that. Although she was willing to listen . . . in fact, had little choice but to listen . . . likely her silence also covered growing dismay and disgust. When Dutchman briefly tried to meet her gaze, Maia's eyes shifted to the partially reconstructed sails of the ghost ship. However, she was still listening. That he sensed from her posture. Maia de Fortunato just could not look at him . . . for which he could not blame her.

There was nothing more to do but go on to the bitter end. After all, they had all the time in the world.

"It took only four days to seal the fate of that first world, my world. How did I do it? I had the finest devices and the power itself to work with. I divined the point where the energy emerged and focused the stream back upon itself. I used its own force to further weaken the boundary between my land and, for lack of a better word, *there*. I did not care where *there* was, only that it had gifted me with so much and would gift me with more.

"Near the end of the fourth day I succeeded in widening the breach. Now more than double in size, it allowed a veritable flood of energy to escape. For two days I did nothing but play with it, test it out in various ways. After that, I honestly believed that I understood and, in fact controlled the forces I had admitted. With the utmost confidence in my ability to keep everything under control, I worked out a method to funnel the energy into more mundane uses. Power to move vehicles . . . to illuminate cities . . . to aid in cultivating the land and water without ruining either.

"I could not have been more satisfied with my results. I would revolutionize the world, give it everything, and, of course, reap some recognition and reward for my accomplishments. Mariya, who had lately begun to question what she termed my 'overzealous dedication,' would see that my work was so vital that it *demanded* my full devotion."

"Everything you've told me so far sounds wonderful," Maia interrupted, momentarily returning her gaze to him. "What went wrong?"

"I was overconfident, the bane of every scholar everywhere. I thought that once I had opened the floodgates, it would be an easy thing to shut them again." Black eyes blinked. In the background, Dutchman still heard the voices, more of them now, but they meant nothing so long as he had the story to tell. "I was a fool."

It seemed so simple a task to seal up what he had torn asunder. The energy flow returned to its previous level with no evident difficulties. Yet, although the triumphant scholar had apparently conquered this new source of power, he knew little about its origin. Desiring to be thorough before announcing his discovery to the world, Dutchman deemed it necessary to return to the university where he had been taught. If there was anywhere in the world where he might find the theories or information he sought, it was there. The journey would take days, but that was of no great concern at the time. Everything was under control.

"I went there without even talking to her, you know. I thought it more important to rush to the university than to stop and see the woman I loved for even one day. My plan, you see, was to prepare everything for the grand announcement, then return to her and allow her to be the first to know." A shiver ran through the cloaked wanderer. His legs felt unsteady, but he did not move. There was only the story.

"I buried myself in research the moment that I arrived. I cheerfully lost track of life outside the university. There was so much to read, so many theories to study, then categorize as either of interest or not. I had always loved research. In fact, I loved it so much that it was not until two days after it began that I heard the news." He looked at Maia, but her eyes had again drifted to the sails. However, when she realized that Dutchman had stopped talking, she looked at him. Although there was no hatred in her expression, she did not permit him to stare long at her, turning back to her study of the sails. Dutchman could not see what fascinated her so much, then lost interest as he continued.

There had been a disaster. An earthquake ripped apart the islet where he had worked. There had been damage to some of the surrounding region but nothing much else.

To most, the news was interesting but not worrisome. To him, however, it was enough to banish all thought of triumph. It was too coincidental, too convenient. He made arrangements to depart for the coastland nearest to his former abode, determined to see the devastation.

The next day, it was announced that a terrible hurricane had struck that very region, destroying everything. More than four thousand people were believed dead. The hurricane had risen without warning, crushed the coastline, and vanished without a trace.

Before the day was over, three more disasters of increasing magnitude struck the continent, each one farther from the devastated islet than the previous. A volcano rose and erupted in the fertile plains where much of the land's foodstuffs were grown. A major river flooded and drowned several communities even though the water level had been normal only two days earlier.

A tornado in the middle of his people's largest city . . . the city where Mariya lived.

"I no longer even thought about the damnation that I had unleashed." Dutchman closed his eyes, recalling the events. *Why can I not forget them? It was so long ago and yet still it replays with the same cursed vividness!* There was no forgetting, however, and, in truth, he knew that it was his own doing, not that of any invisible jailer. He alone was responsible for keeping the memories so sharp. "I only cared about what had happened to her, to my Mariya. She *had* to live. She had to."

More and more, everything that his people had come to accept as normal turned upside down. Storms rose and struck, only to fade away just as quickly. Quakes shook even the most stable regions. The water, which had always been so cherished and treated so reverently by all, now turned ungrateful, tearing coastlines apart and wrecking ships.

Mariya was alive; that was the one bit of good news amid the many catastrophes. He did not find her, but discovered word that she had gone to relatives in the northland, where things were most stable. Dutchman gave thanks, assuming her safe for the time being. Once more his mind returned to what he had unleashed. There was no doubt that the disasters were caused by the very forces that he had played with earlier. Dutchman could sense those forces with very little effort. More important, so could others. Unfortunately, none of them had anything to offer. He heard speculation after speculation, but no concrete advice as to how to combat the situation. For a short time, he hoped that he would not have to reveal his link to the disasters, but when it became obvious that no one else knew as much as he did, he stepped forward.

They did not believe him at first. Then, when they finally decided that he was telling the truth, the condemnations started. Rather than listen to his findings and utilize them somehow in an effort to reverse things, his counterparts chose to turn him away. He decided that he had to resolve matters himself.

"It had to take place at the point where I had first opened wide the breach. Under another name, since mine was already becoming anathema, I hired a vessel, very expensively since the owner doubted I would return, and set sail for the remnants of my islet."

"What about Mariya?" Maia stood very close to him. It was funny; he could not recall her coming so near.

"Once again, I did not have time for her, only time for a scribbled note." What would have happened if he had gone to her instead? Probably nothing save that perhaps he, too, would have perished. Dutchman shook his head. "There was a storm, of course. I had to sail the vessel by myself; not even a madman would take my coin. Despite the tempest, I made it to the rocks that were all that were left of the islet. I could not only sense the forces bursting through, I could see them. Brilliant crimson and black waves pouring out of nothing and spreading in every direction. The only reason I was not caught up at that moment and destroyed was that I knew how regular the pattern of the energy was. In a sense, I rode that pattern, enabling myself to garner both the time and the strength I needed. I was still confident. I knew my earlier mistake, when I had believed the tear all but sealed. This time, I would multiply my efforts and strike when the pattern was at its weakest."

Instead of the voices, Dutchman heard again the tempest that had rocked his craft and threatened to dash it against the

rocks of his former sanctum. He sensed again the foul forces
that he had allowed greater access into the world; once more
recalled counting the pulses, measuring each in order to know
when the flow was at its weakest. The intensity with which
the alien force flowed into his world verified something that
he had up until that point only suspected: Unless it was turned
back soon, the resulting instability would permanently deteri-
orate the fabric of reality. His world . . . and perhaps more . . .
would collapse.

"Each world talks of Apocalypse in some form or another,"
Dutchman whispered, no longer noticing if the woman was
listening. "But I was witnessing the potential of it there and
then. I knew that I could wait no longer. It was still possible
to seal the gap completely. I could rectify some small part of
what I had caused . . . and so I steadied myself and reached
out, striking when I knew it would be best. The effort was terrible. More than once I believed my heart would truly burst.
Yet, slowly but steadily the tear shrank. The danger lessened.
My efforts still strained me, but I saw success imminent. I
only needed one last effort. I gathered my will and pushed."

The *Despair* creaked. It was possible that she turned, but,
if so, the shift in course was so slight as to be unnoticeable.
Dutchman looked out at the starlit heavens, lost in the dread
moment from his past. Only belatedly did he feel the moisture
coursing down his weathered face. It could not be tears. He
was lifetimes past tears.

"I gathered my will, pushed . . . and was pushed back.
Pushed. My own power used against me. I could not believe
it. I would not be denied this. I pushed again, harder than before." The storm again battled him. He stood on the deck of
his ship, the rocks ever closer, railing against the forces that
he had once so easily manipulated.

This time, however, the determined scholar was not simply
pushed back. This time, in answer to his assault, the heavens
blazed with a sudden outburst of such energy that his tiny ship
was thrown over the remains of the islet, Dutchman a helpless
missile tossed from its deck.

He landed in the water, barely maintaining consciousness. Wild waves attempted to ram him against the rocks, but Dutchman seized hold of one and, with effort, pulled himself up top. His vantage point was precarious, but it allowed him to see what had happened.

Instead of sealing the hole, he had made things worse. The fabric had torn more; energy poured through into his world, disrupting everything nearby and spreading farther and farther in all directions. Dutchman screamed, but there was no sound. All sense of reality, all matters of established physics, altered. The water rose up and flew. Rocks melted. There were a thousand of him, each attempting to maintain hold of a thousand identical outcroppings.

Through the rupture burst a vast white comet, so blinding that even with his eyelids closed the light pained the helpless castaway. It soared on, leaving in its wake boiling sea and strewn matter. He felt the ground beneath him quake and parts of his own little domain begin to crumble into the churning water. His foothold slipped. The sea reclaimed him.

"My last thought as the water closed around me was that Mariya would die knowing only that I had created the means of our destruction. She would never know how I had tried to make amends."

The *Despair* creaked again. This time Dutchman sensed the cursed ship alter course ever so slightly.

But if we have changed course, she will be heading back to the latest variant. She is still gathering herself together. We will return to the Earth.

He could not leave the ship, but was his companion trapped? Perhaps, just perhaps, she might be able to disembark. The Scattered Ones had abilities of their own. If they could near the time period from which she had been snatched . . .

"There is hope."

At first she did not comprehend what he was saying, her expectations no doubt having been to hear the rest of his tale. Dutchman had no more time for tales, though, not even his own. Not if there was a way to free the woman. In some sense, he felt as if he had a second chance to save his Mariya, if only for a time. Better the life this Maia de Fortunato and her companions lived than the nonlife he suffered.

"What do you mean by that?" she finally asked.

Turning to face her, Dutchman tried not to look too hopeful. Much of what he contemplated was theory and from his own past crimes he knew how well his theories and suppositions held up. He pointed at the sails. "The ship is turning."

"I know. I . . . I noticed that it follows the voices."

Now it was his turn to look confused.

"The sails, the lines, the whole ship seems to follow them. Not all of them, though. I noticed it while . . . while you were telling me about . . ." she trailed off, apparently not wanting to talk about it.

The ship follows the voices? Dutchman stared at the sails as if they had somehow betrayed him. *How could I not notice that after so many worlds? How could I miss something so obvious that she saw it almost immediately?*

That did not matter. What mattered was that he might be able to save her from his fate. "Listen to me, Maia de—"

"Maia. Simply Maia. Don't call me by that last name. When you say it you sound too much like my sire introducing himself. . . . I cannot stand to hear it."

"I am sorry." He shifted uneasily, beginning to understand a little how she had come to adjust so quickly to her adverse situation. Her father, who wore the form of the dark youth, was an object of terror to her. She had suffered at his hand. Suffered, but also been tempered by it. Instead of breaking her, he must have made her stronger. That had to explain how she had so swiftly overcome her fear of him, who was rightly damned by those of her kind.

He tried again: "Maia . . . Maia, there is hope of escape for you. I had . . . forgotten . . . that the *Despair* must return again to this variant. She is not yet whole and until she is she cannot leave. She will come in contact with time and reality again and when she does, you, with the aid of those you know, might be able to abandon ship."

"Are you jesting?" Sudden hope shone in her dark eyes.

She could not wait to be free of him. Dutchman fought back the unexpected wave of disappointment. He could no more expect her to stay with him than he would have expected the woman she resembled to have done. Maia was not Mariya and neither of them deserved to suffer alongside him. Maia had suffered enough, cursed as her kind was to forever flee his apocalyptic curse.

"I am not jesting. There is hope, but I cannot promise if you will be able to return to the time from which you were taken. It could be any century—"

"But I *must* go there! Gil and Hamman are in danger! I cannot abandon them!"

It was possible. Certainly the *Despair* would sail close. She might be able to come within range of the same decade, possibly even the same year. Still, it was too much to hope that Maia might be able to reunite herself with her friends.

"Waiting until the period from which you were taken is risky. If we pass it by before you can extricate yourself from my lady *Despair*, then you may truly be trapped on board here forever."

For the first time, true sympathy for him spread across her majestic features. "Is it really that terrible?"

"It is nothing more than I deserve." He spoke with what he hoped was enough vehemence to make her think twice about asking again. He did not want her to concern herself with him.

The voices were growing louder. Around the *Despair*, the peculiar, starlit universe began to ripple. The effect was disorienting even to Dutchman. Maia was even more affected; she lost her equilibrium and toppled into the cloaked figure. Dutchman barely caught her, his own equilibrium a precarious thing.

"We are beginning planetfall," he announced.

"Where?" his dazed companion blurted. "Where?"

"The *where* is not so important as the *when*. Sometime after the discovery of fire and before the firing of Rome. Hardly ever later." He knew variant Earths where humanity had never risen past the building of the pyramids. They could find themselves in a hundred different lands in any of countless periods of time.

The *Despair* shook, rattling as if a giant child had taken it in hand. Maia held on to him tightly. Dutchman did not dissuade her, both for her own comfort and the rare feeling of human warmth against his body.

The stars faded. The Earth slowly formed, a rippling ghost that simultaneously solidified and grew. By the time it had completely formed, it overwhelmed their view of all else.

Undaunted, the *Despair* sailed directly toward the leviathan. Dutchman knew that unlike her descent into the Maelstrom, the ship did not now sail toward destruction. This did not make it any easier to watch.

The wind picked up, tousling her hair and causing his cloak to flap like a mad magpie. The *Despair* rode upon waves of radiant energy, her descent ever swifter. Gravity guided her along, inviting her to even greater speed. It was both thrilling and frightening.

"Your tale!" Maia shouted. She had to shout; even next to each other it was now impossible to hear over both the wind and the cursed voices. "You never told me what happened after you were swept into the water."

"It can wait."

"No! Tell me!"

Now was certainly not the time to tell her what had happened after he had been washed back into the sea. The Earth loomed ever more vast. Dutchman tore his gaze from the swelling sphere and looked down at the night-tressed woman whose arms were wrapped tightly around him. There was fear in her expression, but, as his Mariya would have done, Maia was trying to find some way to loosen fear's grip. By having him continue his tale even in the face of such a spectacle, she no doubt hoped to turn some of her attention away from their fall.

She could not have chosen a worse direction in which to divert her attention. Dutchman quickly returned his gaze to the variant Earth. It would be soon. . . .

"Tell me!" Maia repeated, this time even louder. A mismanaged chorus of voices nearly shouted her down, but to emphasize her interest, she reached up with one hand and forced the taller figure to look her in the eye once more. "Tell me what happened. *Please!*"

Dutchman tried to renew his study of the wondrous and terrible sight ahead, but Maia would not be denied. Even the fearsome grandeur of the blue planet could not compete with her demanding stare. He faced her again, black, starlit eyes filled with loss.

His voice was barely more than a whisper, but somehow it managed to carry to her. "I died."

11. LINKS

In the Australian bush when men in the western half of Europe were slaughtering one another in the name of Caesar, an aborigine slaughtering his kill suddenly had a vision. He looked up to the heavens and, ignoring the curious stares of his fellow hunters, cursed his present existence in a language that some born centuries later might have identified as similar to Portuguese.

In Egypt, as Ramses II sanctioned yet the greatest statue of his illustrious self, one of his advisers suddenly took ill. Apologizing profusely to his august majesty, the adviser, a bald, wizened man, rushed from the chamber. He did not pause until he was well away from watching eyes.

When he was certain that no one could hear or see him he muttered to himself, "What the devil was that? What did it mean?"

The language he spoke could nearly have passed for English in many variant worlds

As one, whether awake or asleep, the Scattered Ones, no matter in what century, suffered the vision. Some recognized parts of it, others began to cry out to their brethren for explanation. No member of the refugee group escaped experiencing it. Those who had some understanding did not always give council to those seeking to understand. However, only a handful had an inkling as to the true origin of the startling vision.

It was a ship, a sailing ship, dropping from the heavens onto their present refuge, the latest of the variant Earths.

No member of the refugee group escaped experiencing the vision.

August de Fortunato had recoiled from the sight, inwardly fearing that the ship had now come for him the way it had taken his daughter. The way it had seemed almost to stalk the stupid girl reminded him too much of a predator. August de Fortunato preferred to be the hunter, not the prey.

"Something ails you, August?"

He cursed his weakness. Naturally, the damned shadow master would notice him even when he had his *back* to his short ally. De Fortunato wondered whether the swirl of shadows that surrounded the Darkling served as more than appendages. Perhaps they served also as eyes. The Prince of Shadows was still too great an enigma, which was why Maia's father made no attempt to betray him just yet. Once he understood enough about the Darkling's power, though, that would change. The Darkling had the method by which August de Fortunato could finally put an end to his damned cycle of rebirth after rebirth. If he could travel as the Prince of Shadows did, then he could at last do more than simply survive world after world.

It was a prize the Darkling held high out of his reach, the price for his aid in solving the shadow man's own problem. Until the Scattered Ones, the Prince of Shadows had been forced to rely on calculations that were not entirely accurate. More than once he had escaped the destruction of a variant by the barest of miracles. The Scattered Ones provided a method of better knowing when that precise jump moment occurred, but that meant that they continually had to be hunted down on each Earth. That, in turn, meant relying on the Roschach and in de Fortunato's opinion, the inkblots were more bite than brain. Under the renegade refugee's guidance, however, they were generally much more efficient.

Did that earn him his desire, though? Of course not. The Darkling knew that he could trust de Fortunato only as long as he withheld something of value from him.

"I am waiting, August de Fortunato."

The youthful renegade gathered his wits. If his ally thought that he was losing control, the same Roschach that he commanded for the Darkling would be turned on him. De Fortunato was powerful, especially with the increased abilities with which the Prince of Shadows *had* rewarded him, but he was not ready to confront the beasts and their master. "Something's just happened. Something concerning the harbinger."

The shadows shifted. The Darkling was suddenly staring at him with that one dead-white eye. "You are commanded to speak."

Each time the dark figure "commanded" him, de Fortunato found himself wondering what kingdom it was that his ally had ever ruled. If not for the Roschach, the Darkling would be a prince without subjects to command. "I had a vision. The ship falling to this Earth."

"And are you often subject to such visions?"

"I am *not*." The response came out somewhat sharper than he had intended and despite the fact that the two of them were alone in the white brilliance of the Darkling's domain... well, there was also the one called Rees, but he was mostly here in just the flesh, not the spirit... de Fortunato thought he sensed the Roschach tensing. He knew that they could materialize at a moment's notice. "This was... I felt my daughter's presence involved in the vision, somehow."

"Your link," the shadow man interjected, floating nearer but slightly above his ally. He looked down at de Fortunato. "Your so interesting link between each other. The same link that has been so great an aid in the pursuit of my needs."

With one of the Darkling's devices, they had been able to turn the natural mind link between various of the Scattered Ones into a method by which the refugees could better be tracked. It was a system devised in great part by de Fortunato, the first offering he had made after having sought out the Darkling. He had felt no remorse about betraying the others; his reputation from the days when his Earth had been the true one had condemned him in their eyes. Thus he saw their deaths as a necessity. Had any of them captured him, he had always known that he could expect no mercy. They might not be able to kill him, but there were worse things than death.

"She must've reached out without thinking, possibly without even realizing what she'd done."

"To her dear progenitor?"

"To no one in particular, your majesty. My darling, sweet Maia wouldn't think of disturbing her father if she could avoid it." He rubbed his head, which still throbbed a bit. "On the ghost ship . . . sailing to Earth . . ."

The Prince of Shadows turned from him, floating to a point some distance to de Fortunato's right.

The Scattered One called Rees formed in the brilliance. There was not much left of him. The Darkling's prisoner looked as if some great spider had sucked the fluids from his resisting form. His clothing hung loose, especially where the shadow man's device had eventually burned through the material and branded the captive's chest.

Carried higher by his shadows, the Darkling positioned himself so that Rees's head was even with the shadow man's chest. The Darkling seized hold of the unfortunate's hair and tilted the head back so that Rees could look at him . . . if the man still had the strength to open his eyes, that is.

"Awaken."

Somewhat to August de Fortunato's surprise, Rees obeyed. However, the eyes did not quite focus and very little was left of the mind.

"You have served me well. I shall always remember your commitment to me. Now there is one last service that I require of you. Tell me if you have just dreamed."

Rees continued to stare.

"Maybe he doesn't hear you."

"He does. I will not permit it to be otherwise. If he has seen the ship falling to this world, he will tell me."

"Sh . . . ship." The words were so soft-spoken that the youthful traitor could barely hear them.

"You see? Yes, the ship. Did you dream of it?"

"Ship . . . falling . . . the girl . . . the . . . the angel of death with her." Not once did Rees look at his captor. It was possible that he could no longer see.

This was more than de Fortunato had experienced. Perhaps the prisoner's present condition had somehow opened him up further to the force of the vision.

"Very good. You shall be rewarded for everything now."

The Darkling planted his hand on the prisoner's head, clutched it tight, then gave a sudden twist.

The snap was very audible.

De Fortunato remained very still as the Darkling turned back to him. "You see, my dear August, I am compassionate to the weaker. His suffering is at an end."

"You also already had everything you could have gotten from him."

"A minor quibble. The matter is of no more import." The shadows that flittered about the lower half of the Darkling suddenly extended toward the body, catching hold of Rees's legs. The bonds that had held the captive vanished.

De Fortunato watched in silent fascination as the corpse was quickly drawn into the mass of shadows. There should not have been enough depth to the darkness to envelop the entire body, but in only a few seconds the late Rees was merely a memory.

"A notion of great import to my search has occurred to me, August. A notion which involved the harbinger, your daughter, and the three who escaped you."

"They did not escape me so much as they did your simple-minded oil smears. How you managed to cope with them before I came along I don't know." He would *not* take the blame for the escapes. The black man should have been captured not long after the other Roschach had taken Rees. Maia and her juvenile ex-lover should have fallen to the creature stalking them at the hotel. More important, if the inkblots had obeyed him to the letter, he and the Darkling would now have the harbinger, the Flying Dutchman, in their hands.

"My Roschach are loyal followers, friend August." As the Prince of Shadows spoke, one of the murky creatures formed. It crept toward its master, its head bowed. The Darkling put a hand on its head, then nodded.

A second Roschach formed. Before that one was even complete, a third joined it, then a fourth. They gathered about their master like hounds. "My Roschach are loyal followers, friend August," the Darkling repeated. "Never do I have to question *them* in that regard."

Roschach continued to gather. De Fortunato did not recall ever having seen so many of them and he suspected that there were even more elsewhere. Despite his best efforts, he grew uneasy. It seemed that each pair of striped eyes was studying him. Given one simple command, the Roschach would have gladly torn him apart.

"I've no trouble with their loyalty; I question their ability at times. If not for me, they'd have lost more of their prey. If they'd listen better, we'd have the one you really want."

No more of the dark creatures had formed, but what had gathered was already a small army. Their shadowy master did not respond to de Fortunato, instead spreading his arms wide and looking down at his so-called subjects. The Roschach responded instantly, moving toward the swirling tendrils that had just a moment earlier claimed a full-grown man.

The foremost of the creatures touched the tendrils . . . and was absorbed into the darkness in the same way that a sponge might absorb a small spill. A second Roschach vanished in the same manner, to be followed in swift succession until not one glimpse remained of the inhuman legion. There was only the Darkling Prince.

"We are ready to depart."

"Depart? Where?"

"A few moments ago, one of my oh so clumsy and inefficient host located two of the Scattered Ones in question and, most important of all, the clockwork bird man. They have moved to the southern part of this metropolis to a rather squalid residence."

De Fortunato had sensed nothing of the missing trio in the city. This Hamman Tarriqa was strong, although it was possible that one or both of the others were aiding him in shielding all of them from Maia's father. He had known of Tarriqa through MacPhee, but had never been certain just how powerful the black man was. "You are just going to go in and take all three of them? That could be messy. You could lose the parrot; he won't go willingly and he's got some sort of power of his own."

"Your gracious request to volunteer your services in the capture is noted and accepted, my loyal friend. It saves me from having to otherwise command you."

"Wha—?" What had he just talked himself into? He had just been through one debacle; let the Darkling see what it was like to command these stupid dogs.

Before he could protest, smoky tentacles stretched forth, seizing him by the limbs. They kept his arms and legs stretched apart, the better to immobilize him.

"You are correct, of course, in some of what you said, and it would also be a shame to risk damaging the mechanical creature. Therefore, I think they need to be drawn out and possibly tricked into separating. You, who would *also* never be disloyal to my desires, will surely be able to devise an appropriate plan."

"Now see here!" roared the traitorous refugee. He was strong, but the shadows had him in too tight a grip. They quickly dragged him to their master. "I want to know—"

That was as far as August de Fortunato got before the tendrils pulled him within the swirling mass. The Darkling Prince chuckled throatily, always enjoying such discomfort in others. Then, he folded his arms and allowed his shadows to overwhelm him. The tendrils rose until he could no longer be seen, then they quickly faded away.

Along with them faded away their master.

* * *

No member of the refugee group escaped the vision.

It struck Gilbrin as he sat before an old television . . . one that was not even connected to cable, much to his dismay . . . watching the local news for any hint that someone had noticed what had gone on during the previous night. Suddenly a headache that he was certain presaged his brain exploding sent him reeling. He clutched his head and slumped on the worn but serviceable couch he had earlier chosen as his seat.

The pain suddenly vanished, to be replaced by the image of the sailing vessel that already haunted his dreams. It was falling quickly toward the planet. At the same time, he sensed the presence of Maia. She seemed frightened, but otherwise unharmed. Nearby he also sensed what he believed was Dutchman.

It ended just as he began to understand.

"Carim's sake!" The world swam, but Gilbrin knew that what he felt now was simply an aftereffect. He remained still until the vertigo passed, then carefully shifted back to a sitting position.

"Gilbrin!"

Eyes still a little blurry, the sandy-haired Shifter looked up at a somewhat disheveled Tarriqa. The black man had been resting in one of the two bedrooms, still recuperating from the bite of the Roschach. Now he stood in the narrow, dusty hallway looking much the way the slighter refugee felt.

"I apologize if I cried out and woke you, Master Tarriqa, but I—"

The other cut him off. "Gilbrin, did you just see the image of the Boatman's ship?"

"Saw it and felt it."

"Was it a message from Maia, do you think? You know her much better."

Gilbrin pondered that. While he assumed that Maia would contact him if she could, he doubted that the abrupt vision had been some message. Oh, it had come from her, but probably not with the express intention of alerting either him or Tarriqa. He said as much to his companion.

"Then what does it mean? Why did both of us experience it?"

"The she-devil is coming into port."

Both men turned to look at Philo, who had spent their entire time in the old house Tarriqa owned staring at the wall. The mechanical man fixed one avian eye first on Gilbrin, then on Hamman Tarriqa.

The Shifter half-rose from the couch. "You mean that she's back? Maia's back again?"

Philo's head shifted back and forth. "No. Not here. The *Despair* docks for a short time in another time, another place. Far, far in the past, lad."

Gilbrin sat down again. Maia was back, but in another century. "Can we contact her?"

"I would not try that just yet," Tarriqa interjected. "If she's very far back, then we would have to try to link with others. I cannot see August de Fortunato or his dread companion missing such activity."

The point was a valid one, but Gilbrin did not like surrendering so easily. Maia was back on Earth . . . or at least back in reality. "There must be something we can do."

Philo started to answer, but then both men were struck by a sea of demanding voices. Scattered Ones from every century and land were demanding explanations concerning the vision. They were not trying to contact either man specifically; most were simply asking *anyone* to explain what had happened.

Shutting the voices out of his head, Gilbrin started to speak to his host. However, Tarriqa was looking elsewhere.

"Hold on." Tarriqa's face smoothed. The Shifter knew the look; his companion was in contact with someone. The black man nodded, then briefly focused on Gilbrin. "I need to go back to the bedroom for a few minutes. I must speak with someone."

Gilbrin needed no further explanation. To facilitate his link with the other, Tarriqa needed privacy. Better concentration aided the conversation, especially with so many other voices now intruding. *Has to be someone he trusts if he's willing to risk catching old August's attention.* That probably meant the woman Ursuline or gruff Mendessonn.

With effort, Gilbrin blocked the last, most demanding voices from his thoughts. Let someone else deal with them. He wanted to concentrate only on Maia and Dutchman. It was strange, but he felt almost as sorry for the dread mariner as he did for his old love. When the weathered figure had been with him that had not been the case, but now that the Shifter had had time to think about the stranger, he realized that Dutchman was as much a victim in his own way as the Scattered Ones were.

This is the man who has set the deaths of worlds into motion? Perhaps he has changed since then. Certainly it has been long enough! Still, Gilbrin could not believe that Dutchman had so changed. Rather, he was willing to believe that there was some other cause and that the cloaked figure was simply a scapegoat. *But he does appear just before the end of each variant, so maybe it is his doing. . . .*

"Night's fallen."

"Hmmm?" The gaily clad Shifter twisted around on the couch. Philo was no longer staring at the wall, having without a sound moved to one of the windows. Gilbrin did not worry about anyone seeing the animatron. To the eyes of those living in the neighborhood, Philo would appear perfectly human.

"Night's fallen."

"You said that. I appreciate the announcement, but I noticed that about an hour ago. You would've, too, my fine feathered friend, if you'd not been admiring the wallpaper all afternoon."

"The moon is shrouded, the stars are hidden. It's a night for black deeds and pirates sailing quietly into unsuspecting ports."

That just about summed up the plot of the old pirate movie one of the smaller local stations had been showing before the news. It had not been an Errol Flynn flick, but it had been

passable. Apparently the animatron had been paying attention
to it even while he had been staring elsewhere. "And Black-
beard is outside our door with his beard on fire and his cutlass
raised high to slice off our heads?"

"No, but there is a dark-skinned youth watching the house
from across the street."

"Oh, one of the neighborhood punks. Maybe I should give
him a little discouragement." Gilbrin had been itching to do
something; since Maia's abduction and their escape, he had
felt useless. A failure. There was something different about
this conflict with the Darkling and dear old August. It was not
simply that this time he and his friends stood a good chance
of dying permanently. Something bigger was happening,
something that none of them understood. He hated feeling so
ignorant.

Then the parrot's words struck home. *A dark-skinned
youth?*

Bolting from the couch, Gilbrin joined Philo by the window. He squinted, trying to make out detail in the darkness
outside. "Where is he?"

"Gone. He was there." Philo indicated a post across the
street.

Gilbrin sensed nothing, but if it *had* been de Fortunato,
then the trio was in terrible trouble. He continued to scan. The
homes here were crammed together and in various stages of
deterioration. The streets were full of trash. Fences were
mangled and more than one house looked abandoned. It was
not so much the fault of the residents. Many of them made
barely enough money to support their families. These were
the only houses that they could afford, but that meant living
with the constant threats of sickness, drugs, and crime, the last
most apparent in the form of gangs. The vast majority of the
people were good, decent folk, Gilbrin suspected, but they
were cautious and often distrustful of strangers.

And there's few stranger than us, he managed to quip
silently. His humor had faded, though, despite the fact that the
streets seemed perfectly normal. There were even some folk

sitting on a doorstep a few houses down the street. They were obviously enjoying their conversation. Gilbrin envied them.

He sighed, then stepped back from the window. "What did he look like?"

"Young, black, shaved head. He wore a bright jacket, the lad did. Definite pirate."

Street gang. Not de Fortunato, then. "You remember the one who nearly captured you? The one your captain had to rescue Maia from?"

"Aye."

"Did you see him at all?"

"No. If I had . . ." As Philo trailed off, he raised his hand.

The Shifter found himself staring closely at the edge of a glimmering cutlass. He wanted to touch it to see if it was real, but knew better. Nodding, he backed away a step or two from the animatron. "Very nice. Now put it away please."

His mechanical companion complied. The blade vanished into some hole in reality. Gilbrin was impressed. More and more he was convinced that Dutchman's first mate was more than a simple mechanism animated by the wanderer's power. Philo thought and acted too much like a living creature.

That's absurd, though . . . isn't it? It had to be his overenthusiastic imagination at work.

Philo suddenly leaned toward the window again. "The boy has returned with two of his mates."

Peering through a window that from the boys' point of view would appear dark and unoccupied, Gilbrin saw three youths, perhaps fourteen years old, sneaking their way toward Tarriqa's house. Their intention immediately became clear; the car parked in the narrow drive by the house was a much more expensive type than those generally found in this neighborhood. Tarriqa had added a fence that closed off both yard and driveway from the street, but the obstacle would seem minor to the trio. They intended either to steal the car or to strip it.

"Oh, this will be good." He rubbed his hands. It was not as satisfying as rescuing Maia or throttling August would have been, but at least it would enable him to burn off a little nervous energy. Besides, this trio deserved whatever he gave them.

Two of the youths were dark, the other a pale contrast. It was a bit ironic to think that the gangs had brought together two different colors, but that was sometimes the case. Still, racial harmony did not require condoning theft. Gilbrin felt no guilt concerning what he planned.

One of the darker gang members stood a little back, acting as lookout. The other two neared the enticing vehicle. The Shifter had no doubt that his host had already put some contingencies of his own in place, but that would have taken all the fun out of Gilbrin's ready hands. He would save Hamman Tarriqa's efforts for any later hoodlums. These were his.

Tarriqa had securely bolted the gate, so the pair had to climb over the low, rather rusted chain fence. No trouble normally, but Gilbrin had other notions. The first boy got a toehold on the fence, but as he pushed down, the metal gave. It did not break, but rather stretched earthward, as if made of soft taffy or rubber. Because he had expected to leap over, the juvenile slipped down unprepared, slamming his elbow on the hard metal rail of the fence.

His partners looked aghast and the closest of them whispered something that almost began an argument. The argument died, however, as the victim of Gilbrin's prank pointed at the car again. The pair renewed their efforts, this time testing the wire before beginning to climb.

Not wanting to repeat his first trick, Gilbrin waited until they had reached the top of the fence, then focused.

Both youths found their hands and feet stuck to the metal. They pulled as hard as they could and for a moment he was tempted to let them pull themselves free so that they would fall backward, but then the third boy joined his companions. When everyone was where he desired them to be, Gilbrin finally released one of the trapped pair.

The hoodlum fell on top of his would-be rescuer, the two

toppling to the ground. Gilbrin released the remaining one. That one slipped and fell back, crushing his partners.

The Shifter chuckled as the threesome extricated themselves, glanced back at the fence, then turned and ran. They had abandoned their efforts much too soon, but at least they had been entertaining. He moved away from the window and looked at Philo. "That was much too quick. I was barely warmed up. Still, not bad for a little light amusement."

Turning his head, the animatron resumed his one-eyed gaze out the window.

Rather annoyed at Philo's lack of appreciation for the little pleasures in life, Gilbrin opened his mouth to push his point, but Hamman chose that moment to return.

"What have you been up to, Gilbrin?"

"Just protecting the fort."

Tarriqa shook his head, then slumped into a chair. "I've just been talking to Ursuline."

"And how is our delectable little minx?"

The black man ignored the question. "Ursuline tells me that everyone seems to have suffered the same vision. *Everyone.*"

It took a moment for Gilbrin to digest. "When you say 'everyone,' do you mean *everyone?*"

"Each and every Scattered One throughout history. You should not find that too hard to believe, jester. You heard the voices just as I did."

"Everyone." It was impossible . . . or should have been. "But how can that be . . . and why?"

Tarriqa rubbed his chin. "You know Maia better than I do, Gilbrin. Is she so very powerful? She seems the only source for such a vision."

"She's got the potential, but she's held it back." He thought about their years together and the lifetimes since then. Despite their breaking apart, they had always remained close. He had watched over her during good times and bad, including a few drastic encounters with her dear sire, August. "I think she felt that it made her too much like her father. He was . . . is . . .

very strong. She might be even stronger, since her mother also had great ability."

"August de Fortunato murdered her, did he not?"

"Only because she heinously betrayed him by trying to take his daughter away from his vile influence." A grim smile played across Gilbrin's features. "By killing her he guaranteed that Maia would never obey him again . . . so in the end Natalia did triumph."

"Small victory."

"No, my dear Tarriqa, it was a great victory." The Shifter did not want to think what Maia might have been like had she remained under her father's tutelage.

"Be that as it may, it seems that Maia is in fact one of the most powerful of us, if this is any indication. She must be the only reason for this vision. The angel of death has journeyed to many, many variants, but this is the first time we've experienced something like this." The black man paused. "At least we know she's in fair shape."

Gilbrin had not thought of it, but he had to agree. "I felt fear, but no pain. If Maia had been injured, I, at least, would've felt something, I think."

"She's making her first port of call," Philo interjected. He had moved just enough from the window to be a part of their conversation, but his attention clearly remained on the street outside. "The lady *Despair* has come back to this world."

"Yes," Tarriqa added. "Ursuline also reported one firsthand observation of what might have been the ghost ship . . . though it was difficult to verify, for with the panic brought on by the vision, the observer might simply have confused reality with impression."

Gilbrin was on the edge of his seat. "Was there any message? Any sign? Did anyone escape the ship?"

"The report mentions only a sighting, Gilbrin. The ship materialized, then faded away a moment later. The time was quite far back. The peak of the kingdom of Ur, which is approximately around the —"

"Spare me the historical timeline, Master Tarriqa."

The black man nodded.

Maia was alive and likely well, but she had not taken the first opportunity to leap off. Why? *Because she's trying to come here, you fool!* Gilbrin told himself. *That's just like her, isn't it?*

It was possible that Dutchman held her prisoner or . . . or the ship itself did. Maybe Maia *couldn't* escape. Maybe she would reach this century and watch helplessly as the ship floated on, this time probably toward the next variation of their world. Soon after that, of course, the final ruptures would begin literally to tear apart this unsuspecting copy.

"All right, bird." The Shifter turned to Philo. "You gave us some hope before, but is there really a chance that Maia can escape? Is there?"

It took some time before the animatron answered. "It might be smooth sailing, but the risk of storms is greater. Aye, she has the chance, but she'll have to risk all for it."

"What about your captain?"

"He will do what he does."

"And that explains so much." Gilbrin was again getting annoyed with Philo. *And people complain about the way I answer questions.*

"There is one other thing to consider, lad."

"And what is that?"

"Our visitors outside."

The sandy-haired jester's spirits rose. He needed something to keep him from worrying too much about Maia. Until the ship returned to this time period, he could do nothing. "Are they back again?"

"What's that? Who?" asked Tarriqa, obviously not caring for the expression that had crossed Gilbrin's face.

"Some would-be car thieves, my dear host. Some brave and foolhardy ones. Just something to take my mind off the situation for a time." Gilbrin rose with a flourish, his mind already full of methods by which he could further harass the young gang members. *With any luck, perhaps they've brought some friends along! The more the merrier!*

"Leave them alone, Gilbrin. I have wards on my vehicle and this house. No punk will even get fingerprints on the door handles."

"I'll just soften them up a little, then, all right?" He really needed to do something and the return of the car thieves was a blessing.

"Gilbrin—"

"It is not—" the parrot began.

The Shifter paid them no mind. He had to take his attention off Maia's predicament. Toying with the gang members would better allow him to think. Moving back to the window, he peered out into the darkness, his mischievous grin back in place.

The grin vanished. "Carim's blood!"

"What?" Tarriqa rose.

"Your safe house isn't so safe, Master Tarriqa," Gilbrin muttered, eyes shifting to Philo. "I wish you'd learn to be a little more specific, my feathered friend. 'Visitors,' indeed. Those sophomoric hoods were visitors! These are . . ." He trailed off, frustrated, and returned his gaze to the window. "Come see this, Tarriqa."

The black man had already moved to the window and was leaning down to get a better view.

Gilbrin stepped away. He was shaking. "What do you see?"

"I see a young boy sitting on the steps of one of the houses. I see the streetlight and the shadows formed under it by—"

"Can you see what's forming the shadows?"

"No." Hamman Tarriqa nearly had to choke the word out. "No, there's nothing creating the shadows . . . and they are moving slowly toward the house."

Something caused the roof to creak. The two men and the animatron looked up.

"On the roof, too." The sandy-haired refugee grimaced. "I would venture to say that we're surrounded."

A powerful mind suddenly attempted to thrust its way into Gilbrin's. He gritted his teeth and fought against it as best he could. Through slitted eyes he saw that Tarriqa was doing the same. Philo watched both humans with . . . with no visible emotion.

It was Tarriqa who managed to spit out the cursed name: "de Fortunato!"

De Fortunato, yes, but Gilbrin recognized another power behind the renegade, a power that could be only one creature.

The Darkling.

12. THE BELLY OF THE BEAST

For a time, Maia could not even think about Dutchman's cryptic and, admittedly, unsettling response. The fall of the ship demanded precedence. How could it not? With each blink of the eye, the Earth appeared to swell to greater proportions. The gravity pull became more intense. *Surely we'll break up before we strike the planet!*

They did not. Suddenly the *Despair* shimmered. The sphere below shifted. To her amazement, they were no longer falling, but rather floating in the sky among the clouds. Somehow the ghost ship had leaped down into the atmosphere and found calm waters.

Calm waters? I almost sound like I belong here.

The *Despair* sailed through the clouds, moving along almost serenely. Slowly it became evident to her that the vessel was still descending, but at a rate that was hardly worrying.

Probably won't go low enough to let me jump, though. The hunt in Chicago had been an exception, of that she was certain. She had hoped it might be otherwise. Perhaps there would be another. The actions of the *Despair* could not so easily be predicted.

Maia realized that she was still clutching the tall, weathered figure and immediately let go, backing away from him until she was out of arm's reach. Now that the terror of their fall had greatly lessened, his words echoed in her mind.

I died.

What made things even more horrible was that she believed him. Maia could not look at him without seeing the truth of his words.

I died.

Still, she had to ask. "What did you mean when you said that?"

He did not ask her to clarify. That alone was enough to indicate to her what his answer would be. "Exactly what I said, Maia de Fortunato. Exactly what I said."

Dutchman did not attempt to close the gap between them. Rather, he turned from her and started back to a door leading down below. He did not invite her to follow.

Whatever truth in his macabre statement, Maia did not want to be left alone on deck, even with things momentarily calm. Nor did she really want to go below, which seemed like walking into the belly of a beast. "Wait!" she called out as she started after Dutchman, wanting to catch him before he reached the door.

He continued on.

Anger mixed with fear. "Dammit, don't you run from me!"

Now at last he turned. His face was still expressionless, but Maia, watching the unsettling eyes, thought she saw much more: Dutchman was afraid of her. That made her slow down.

"I want to know what you meant. I want you to tell me now."

"There are far more immediate matters to deal with, Maia de Fortunato. There is the slightest chance that you can abandon this ship in this or one of the other landings. You should stand ready, in case she draws low enough for you to act. You—"

"We are at least a thousand feet up. I do not dare try anything for now and so the only thing I have to pass the time is your explanation." She took a deep breath. "Tell . . . tell me about your death." Saying the last made her shiver, but she remained resolute. Dutchman was not some monster, whatever his past. She just had to keep telling herself that. In some ways, the cloaked wanderer was a sad figure, more adrift than the Scattered Ones. What he had done was terrible, but he did not revel in it. Not like the Darkling Prince probably did. Dutchman's remorse was very deep.

A crackle of energy interrupted them. Maia turned around to the source of the noise. A portion of the deck that had been missing was ablaze with light and in that light several planks suddenly burst into being, perfectly filling some of the gaps.

Another crackle from above made her look up. The mast that had been missing was now there . . . at least part of it was. The upper portion now existed, but much of the lower two-thirds was still absent.

"She gathers herself bit by bit."

"What do you mean?" Maia was beginning to feel like the parrot that Philo so resembled. She was tired of asking questions; she wanted answers.

"Each time, the lady *Despair* is shattered by her lover, the Maelstrom. I have never understood why she would suffer her own destruction simply to make me watch yet more worlds die because of me, but she does. Her damage is never permanent, though. The *Despair* always rebuilds herself. She will leave this time soon and fly on to another, where she will gather more of her pieces. By the time she reaches the period from which you were taken, I judge that she will be nearly complete." He frowned at his own words. "The rate at which she pieces herself together this time likely means that she will not need to complete a third journey after she reaches your period. If so, then this variant has less time than I imagined."

More good news. Maia clenched her fists and, not certain why she did so, hurried to the rail. Her eyes widened. They had fallen lower than she had thought. A city was visible below. It reminded her of one she had lived in during an incarnation in ancient Persia. They seemed to be in the Middle East, but exactly where and when she could not say.

Even as she watched, the sight began to fade. The weary

captive blinked, but the view did not sharpen. If anything, it grew even less distinct.

"We are moving on to her next port of call."

She nearly fell over the rail, so startling was it to hear Dutchman's voice next to her. Sometimes he moved so silently. Maia whirled on the wanderer. "Where will that be . . . and when?" she demanded.

Dutchman shrugged. "I only ride as a passenger, Maia de Fortunato."

"I asked you to call me Maia. Nothing more."

He nodded.

"How long until the next port?"

"Time is rather confusing where the *Despair* is concerned, but I do not think it will be . . . long."

Already the ground had vanished, to be replaced by a peculiar gray fog. Maia expected the starlit emptiness to reform, but instead the clouds thickened. Nothing could be seen above, below, or around the ship. Maia counted to two hundred, but the scenery did not alter.

Dutchman waited while she adjusted to this most recent change.

He was not horrible to look at, she suddenly noted, once one got past his incredible age and the ravages caused by his eternal trek. He was not reborn as the Scattered Ones were; he had simply continued to exist, universe after universe.

Then Maia recalled again that he *had* died. Again the need to know conquered all else. She steadied herself. "Tell me."

His expression hinted at resignation. His tone left no doubt. "I died. It was impossible not to recognize that. I felt torn away from myself, soul without body, body without soul. There was nothing left of the world . . . nothing. I vaguely recall the water overwhelming me and the inability to breathe. My heart burst and my lungs filled with the entire ocean. For me, that is proof of my death."

"There has to be more to it than that. What happened *after*?"

Even now, it obviously distressed him to remember. "I

knew such pain as I feel no one has ever experienced before
or since. I may have screamed; I have never been able to recall with certainty, but it surely must have been so. I floated
for an eternity . . . maybe longer." He blinked, his ebony
eyes growing more human as he related the pain and terror.
"Eternity does not seem so long anymore. I've lived so
many eternities."

The ship creaked, but when Maia glanced about, she saw
no change. It was evidently not yet time for the next "port."

Dutchman began anew the moment her attention returned
to him. He stretched forth an arm to indicate the mysterious
vessel. "I was suddenly not alone anymore. *She* came, a
silent, determined shadow that I could not escape. I could
only watch as she swelled, growing larger as the distance between us shrank. My first thought was of some hungry
leviathan come to take me. I did not understand what she
could possibly be, only assumed that this was my punishment
for causing the End of a world. What else could there be for
me in the afterlife? It was what I deserved." Dutchman
smiled, but there was no pleasure in it, just memory. "When
she was near enough, my eternal lady swallowed me whole."

"Swallowed?" Suddenly Maia had a great desire to pull her
feet free of the deck. She felt as if at any second a hole would
open up beneath her and she would vanish forever into the
bowels of the *Despair*.

He must have noticed her dismay. Dutchman shook his
head, then reached up and removed his wide-rimmed hat. The
graying hair fluttered in an alien breeze. Without the hat, his
appearance became yet more human and much less imposing.
"You have nothing to fear about that now, Maia. The *Despair*,
so I personally named her after my grief, is not like she was
then. This ship, this sailing vessel, is the creation of my own
damnation. It was drawn, I realized eventually, from different
images from my background."

A creation of his own? Maia studied the ship, seeing the
vines, the age, the care with which the *Despair* seemed to
have been crafted. Everything about her said that she had al-

ways been a sailing ship, yet Dutchman had just said . . . in an almost matter-of-fact tone . . . that when he had first confronted her she had worn another shape. Maia wanted to believe that she had been mistaken, that he had said something else, but she knew better. "What did the ship look like when you first saw it?"

Dutchman closed his eyes. His concentration was visibly intense. Maia began to fear for him. Perhaps pushing for so much information about his past had put too great a strain on the mariner and former scholar.

At last, he opened his eyes again. "It's strange, but I don't recall with certainty. It was white, very bright . . . like a sun." An expression of honest perplexity spread across his visage. "I can recall every cursed moment before that damnable encounter, but I cannot recall the specifics of my deathly lady before she became this fine, unyielding vessel. But then, I tried very hard to forget so very much."

Knowing that the *Despair* had once been something other than a sailing ship intrigued her. Knowing that the ship had taken him aboard intrigued her more. Why had it done so? Was it, as he had said, a part of his punishment? *I cannot believe that.*

As if hearing the silent question, Dutchman added, "I did not know why I was swallowed. I did not understand why I lived when I knew that I had died. I especially did not know how it was that when I woke, it was to find that I now slept in the cabin of a fine sailing ship, one like those I had dreamed about as a boy."

He had wandered the length and depths of the ship for what seemed years, trying to learn about it. The first thing he discovered was that he no longer needed either sleep or food. There was water, but Dutchman needed it only on rare occasions. His time on board went from surprise and fear to tedium to the realization that he was trapped aboard her with no end in sight to his trek.

"I lie when I say I did not sleep after that first time. There was one other time, very early on, when I slept long and deeply. I do not know why. I only know that one moment I stood upon the deck, still trying to adjust to my fate, and the next I suddenly woke up in the cabin that had apparently made itself my own. I awoke recalling a dream, one in which I lay in darkness while something spoke to me. I could not understand the words, but there were images and I recognized the condemnation in the tone of the voice. Somehow I knew that a world had collapsed into itself, all things dying with it, but it was not my world . . . and yet it was." Dutchman held high the wide-brimmed hat. Then, before Maia realized what he was doing, the tall figure tossed it over the rail. He did not even watch it fall from sight. His voice grew more pained, guilt-ridden. "It took much consideration, but at last I pieced together what the voice was trying to convey. The discovery was monstrous. I had succeeded not only in destroying my world, but also after that *another*."

A gust blew up so suddenly that Maia clutched her head and ducked a little to avoid its force.

Something dark and winged fluttered onto the deck from the opposite side of the ship. Maia at first believed it a creature, but when it remained still, she saw that what had landed was a *hat*. Dutchman's hat.

"The first time, almost immediately after my discovery, I threw *myself* over that very rail, Maia. The first time, the second, the third, the twelfth . . . and after each attempt I was returned to the ship in just such a manner. There *was* no escape. This was to be my prison, my punishment for my past crimes and my crimes to come. Not for a period, however long. Rather, forever."

The clouds around them had begun to thin as he finished. Dutchman turned to retrieve his hat. Maia chose to return to the rail. In part she wanted to see what lay below now that the clouds were clearing, but she also needed time to think over Dutchman's latest revelation to her. She only hoped that she would not suddenly be overcome by a desire to throw *herself* over the rail.

Mountains. High mountains. They reminded her of the

ones that, in various incarnations, she had known as the Alvis, the Grossen, and, on the present variant, the Alps. Judging by the sun, the *Despair* was heading south. There were villages here and there, but what period they belonged to, she could not yet say.

Dutchman stepped to her side again. More and more he seemed one of her own group, one of the Scattered Ones. Had she met him without knowing who he really was, he would have struck her as little different, sometimes even more normal than, say . . . well, to be blunt, *Gil*.

"That first time the ship brought me to a new world, I did not know what to think." He looked out at the clouds. "I will not speak of my first journey through the Maelstrom. Suffice to say that it is a terror, a monster, that I pray you will be able to avoid, Maia. It came when I had given up hope of any change at all in my existence, tore the ship and myself asunder, and cast me out. When I recovered, I found myself on *land*. My first thought was that I had been freed. I had been forgiven by my unknown jailers. I was overjoyed. I wandered this new variant, marveling in the differences and the similarities between it and my Earth." He swallowed. "Never had I felt so alive."

The landscape below was nearer. What made the *Despair* choose the level at which she sailed was a puzzle to Maia, as was the fact that since she had been aboard, Maia herself, like Dutchman, had come to call the vessel a *she*. It was true, though. Maia sensed that somehow the *Despair* was very much alive. Not alive in the same way as her two reluctant passengers, but definitely alive.

She realized that Dutchman had fallen silent. Maia considered his most recent words. She could guess what came next in his story. Not knowing exactly why she did so, the tall woman reached out and took his hand in hers. He looked startled, but did not protest.

"How long before your new world began to collapse?" she asked.

Dutchman was clearly reliving the second Apocalypse. He

almost withdrew the hand, but Maia tightened her grip. "Thirteen days. The signs were subtle at first, noticeable only to me. I wondered, but did not understand until the first rupture." He bent down so that their eyes almost met. Each word he spoke pleaded for some small measure of forgiveness for his crimes. "I only then recognized the source of the freak disasters that had occurred one after another since I had arrived. It was the same disruption in the fabric of reality, the same intrusion of alien force that I had allowed into my *own* variant. It was happening again. *Again.*"

The crackling sound began anew. Maia watched a portion of the rail repair itself, then another section of the nearly completed deck appeared.

Once more, the clouds gathered.

"So short again," Dutchman muttered, his breakdown momentarily forgotten. "She usually stays longer. I wonder what her hurry is?"

His nature is very mercurial, Maia noted, *shifting from calm to anxiety to calm in only a breath or two.* It was a wonder he was sane at all . . . or perhaps he had gone insane long ago and had gradually returned to sanity when his madness ran out of strength. *Of course, I am not much different, am I? Maybe he's still insane and I'm too insane now to notice the difference. Certainly I've come to accept all of this much easier than I should have.*

She did not ask him to relate the rest. She and the other refugees knew all too well what happened when the worlds collapsed. Each time the sequence of events varied, but the overall effect was the same. The quakes, the storms, the shifting of all laws of physics as everything that had been accepted now ceased to function . . . the Scattered Ones had suffered them over and over.

There was, however, one thing she did want to ask. "Where did you find Philo?"

"Him?" The question actually startled him, as if he could not believe that she would find the subject so interesting. "I found Philo on a variant that had all but killed itself without my aid. He was an amusement left partially running. I salvaged him and, to my surprise, was able to bring him aboard. Rebuilt him using what power and knowledge I had. He is not real, but I have worked on him for so long I sometimes think he has come to life. Not possible, of course, but he has saved or possibly rescued my sanity many times."

His words and tone indicated a fondness for the animatron, but also, to her surprise, an honest belief that Philo was little more than he appeared. In the short time that Maia had known the mechanical creature, she had come to think of him as much more. Had she been imagining something, or had Dutchman simply failed to believe that his first mate could become more than a mechanism?

Philo sounds like the only thing that he's brought aboard, the only thing of substance besides myself. Her mind racing, Maia de Fortunato glanced at the wheel of the ship. An unsettling notion blossomed. For some reason, she was fairly certain that the only reason he had been able to bring Philo aboard was because the *Despair* had allowed him to do so. *Now why would she do that, I wonder?*

As the clouds surrounded them and the land below faded away, Maia asked, "How often does she usually stop?"

"At least half a dozen times. Possibly more, although I cannot promise that. It varies."

"Will she get any lower, do you think?"

"That depends on her whim."

On her whim. He was not jesting. Their chance for success lay in the whims of the *Despair,* a ship that Maia suspected was far more aware of what was happening than should have been possible. Dutchman was not a stupid man, but she wondered if he had become too used to his helplessness, too used to suffering the whims of his living prison. The *Despair* had no doubt done her best to break him.

Maia was not yet so complacent. "We have to be ready, anyway."

" 'We'?"

"If we get as low as we did this time, could you transport

us both to the ground without killing us? You can transport from one spot to another, can't you? That's how you appeared so suddenly during the fight, isn't it?"

"I can with some difficulty, but, Maia—"

Dutchman was the taller, broader, and no doubt stronger of the two, yet she pushed him back and forced him to listen. "I know that you've probably tried something similar in the past, but perhaps if you link with me as we Scattered Ones do, then we can work together to increase our chances of success. We have to try, don't you agree?"

He stared. "You are . . . much like her."

She felt herself redden, but forced her mind back to the matter at hand. "Is it worth—"

Maia?

She had come to ignore the voices as much as was possible, but this one was different, touching her in her mind.

Maia?

"Who is it?" she called, not realizing that she spoke aloud.

"Who—?" Dutchman began, but she signaled him to be still.

Maia . . . it's Temin . . . soldier . . . Greek . . . listen . . .

Temin. Maia knew him fairly well. Short, dark, and stocky in his original life. An artist, then, but if she understood correctly, a soldier now. The Fates loved games. "Temin! Where are you? You sound . . . not right."

Below . . . I think! Been trying to . . . hours! Sensed . . . above, but no . . . Listen . . . I was told that if you . . . should tell you that . . . Tarriqa and the Shif . . . your . . .

That was all. The link snapped, leaving her with a mild headache. Maia realized that the *Despair* had abandoned the time period to which Temin belonged. He had made contact with her too late.

Beside her, Dutchman wore a look of mild puzzlement. As she explained what had happened, he listened with growing interest.

"It may be that your hope of escape is not so much a dream, then. If you and your kind can contact one another even at such a point, it may be that, with their aid, we may yet abandon the *Despair*. I cannot promise, though, that we will be able to return to the same time from which we left."

Heartened by his newfound hope, Maia scanned the ship, studying each incomplete section. The *Despair* had repaired much of herself, but many pieces were still missing. According to her companion, the ship would completely recover her missing parts and fix herself before abandoning this variant. In Maia's opinion, that meant that she had only to wait. The ship would return to the same place and time as she had been taken from. She was certain of that even if Dutchman was not. Even if the *Despair* recovered every piece of herself before Maia's time period, there remained one component that she felt the ship must collect before departing this variant.

Philo.

She closed her eyes and tried once more to focus on the mechanical first mate. *Found on a dying world.* What were the odds that Dutchman would have discovered him? How had he managed to salvage him and why had he chosen to do so?

Trying to make order out of so much confusion only added to the pounding in Maia's head. *I need to rest. I cannot concentrate anymore.* There was nowhere to rest, though, was there? She could hardly relax on the deck.

What about below? The ship had shown no signs of desiring to harm her; it had virtually ignored her once she had been taken aboard. Why should it harm her if she went below?

There are cabins down there. There must be a bed on which I could rest for a short time. She could not stay down there for very long. Soon they would return to the twentieth century and she had to be ready.

Just a little rest. It sounded more and more inviting with each passing moment.

As ever, the tall figure beside her waited in silent patience. She looked up at him, which still surprised her, for Maia rarely needed to look up at men. "You said that there were cabins below?"

"Yes."

"Is there one that I could use? I need a brief rest."

His eyes widened a little, but he responded without hesitation. "The first cabin on the right is the one I use. You may choose that one or do as you will." He studied the enshrouding clouds. "I will make certain that you are here when you need to be, Maia. Rest assured of that. I will not see you forever condemned to this vessel. I could never forgive myself."

The last was said with such determination that Maia could not respond in words. She touched his arm, then, on impulse, leaned up and kissed him on the cheek.

To her amazement, his face reddened. Maia felt flushed. She quickly turned and headed for the door. She was in such an anxious state that she did not even think about her earlier fear of the areas below deck. Swinging open the door, she descended in a rush. She did not even notice the sound of the door closing behind her.

Only when she had reached the foot of the stairs did it occur to Maia to look around. With the unnerving exception of the gaps in the walls and floor, the view was quite ordinary. The interior was as weathered and ancient-looking as the exterior. There were several doors, only two of which she could immediately identify as belonging to cabins, and another set of steps at the end of the short hall, these descending deeper into the ship. A strange design. Maia had no desire to go anywhere near them and so turned to her right and entered the nearest cabin.

Only after she had entered did she recall that this was where Dutchman rested. She began to retreat, but then something slowly drew her forward into the center. The cabin was so much larger than Maia had imagined that she almost thought it was some sort of trick of the eye. *But of course, this is no ordinary ship.*

There were shelves with a few books, something she had not expected. Maia decided to look them over after she was through investigating the rest of the cabin. She found the bed hard but serviceable. A small, round pillow and a heavy blanket lay atop it. Not the most luxurious of accommodations.

The bed was built into the wall and below it were several cabinet doors. She opened each, but found nothing. Still suspicious, Maia opened all of the other cabinets in the room.

All were empty but one, and in that she found only a lantern with a candle. That made her wonder about the light already illuminating the room. A quick glance around revealed two wall lamps burning near the door. The weary refugee frowned. Not only did the lamps have no discernible power source, but the cabin door was now closed. She knew that she had left it open.

When she tried it, the door opened for her. She quickly stepped out into the hall. Then, chiding herself for being so weak, she ducked back into Dutchman's quarters. She would not let the *Despair* affect her so.

There was no porthole, which did not bother Maia overmuch. The only thing left to investigate before she retired was the tall, narrow closet in the wall opposite the foot of the bed. Maia opened it carefully, curiosity shifting to disappointment when the contents proved to be nothing more than several cloaks and another blanket, folded and tucked into the bottom.

All in all, a very spartan existence. Even the wooden walls spoke of austere living. They were plain, with no decoration or paint. There was nothing terrible about the quarters and yet they managed to deepen her sadness for Dutchman. To live with only this for so very long . . .

Her head pounded again, a reminder of why she had dared come down here in the first place. Slightly dizzy, Maia had to put a hand against one of the walls for support.

The wall rippled beneath her hand, turning a brilliant white so blinding that she instinctively shut her eyes and pulled away.

When she dared look again, the wall was normal.

Did I dream that? There was only one way to find out.

This time she narrowed her eyes before reaching out. If she was wrong, nothing would happen, but if she was correct, then Maia did not want to take the chance of permanently blinding herself.

Her fingertips touched the wall.

Under each tip the wall shifted again, returning to the brilliant white illumination that she had seen the first time. Maia pressed harder. The results were staggering. She did not even have to plant her palm on the wall; the fingers alone were enough to begin a transformation that swept over the entire side of the cabin, altering everything in its path.

Fascinated, Maia could only watch. Now not only the wall but the ceiling and the floor were affected. What little decor there had been faded, including the bed. Only the door remained and as the whiteness crept toward it, the wary woman almost removed her fingers from the wall. If the door vanished, would she be trapped in this brilliance forever? With her eyes barely open, she could hardly see. Maia could not imagine being trapped in here even for a moment, but still she could not bring herself to pull free.

The whiteness swallowed the door. Maia tensed.

The illumination lessened, becoming more tolerable. Some sense of intuition finally made her pull herself free.

The whiteness remained . . . but Maia no longer felt frightened. To the contrary, she felt safer, more secure, than she had in some time. Here she need not fear anything. Not the Darkling, the Roschach, her father . . . even the End of yet another innocent world. None of that was worth worrying about.

"What am I thinking?" Maia suddenly realized that it was from the *room* that the sense of comfort radiated, not from herself. It was affecting her mind. Immediately all feelings of relief vanished. She started for where the door had been.

There was no trace of the entranceway. For that matter, there was no wall. Maia ran a distance far, far wider than the tiny cabin and yet she *still* could not find a barrier.

Once more, the sense of comfort sought to overwhelm her. She struggled, but it was a mighty battle. The power trying to overwhelm her was very strong.

A voice called to her. Maia focused on it. Although the language was not familiar, after a moment she began to understand something of what it was trying to relate.

A feeling of loss. A feeling of justice denied. A desire to hunt. Regret. Mistakes. Need. Desperation. Determination at all cost. Death.

Death. Shadows. Some of what Maia was experiencing slowly began to make sense. She needed only a little longer to understand.

A repeat of all the sensations, the feelings. It started to make sense. . . .

"Maia."

She blinked . . . and woke to find herself on the bed, her head on the pillow.

"Carim's blood . . ." Maia de Fortunato muttered to herself. Everything was as it had been before she had touched the wall. All that was different now was that she lay sprawled on the bed, as if she had slept for quite some time.

"Maia."

Dutchman. He stood on the other side of the door, evidently respecting her privacy.

The blinding illumination. The transformation. The voice. Had they all been part of a dream? Maia shook her head, trying to clear it. She had not been lying down. She had been standing by the wall and when she had put her hand against it for support; the entire cabin had blossomed into light.

Then how is it I woke just now? I must have gone to sleep. That has to be it.

She stared at her fingers, then slowly turned them toward the cabin wall. Holding her breath, Maia touched the wood.

The cabin did not transform. There was not even a flicker of change.

"Maia, are you well?"

Dutchman. In her confusion, she had left him standing outside. Maia rose from the bed and opened the door. The face before her was just shifting into the first stage of worry. However, now Dutchman broke into a surprisingly vivid expression of relief.

"I'm sorry," she began, uncertain as to whether she should make any reference to what had happened . . . or had *not* happened . . . in the cabin. Until she was certain that something *had*, she decided to keep the details to herself.

He peered around the room, almost as if he knew what had happened. Maia thought about his own experience with such a strange dream and wondered whether she had simply incorporated that into some product of her overtired imagination.

"You are all right?"

"Yes, but—" She still wanted to say something.

A gloved hand seized her wrist. "Then come with me. Quickly."

He spoke quietly, but his eyes hinted at urgency. Maia pushed aside her own worries and immediately followed him up the steps. However, as they neared the door to the deck, she heard a strong wind.

"Stand ready!" Dutchman shouted as he pushed open the door. He had to shout. The howling of the wind grew so great that it was nearly impossible to hear him otherwise.

"What is happening?"

"She's turned! She's changing course!" His hat flapped against his face as wind rushed into the stairwell. He finally removed it and threw it down the stairs. Starlit eyes met her own. "I hear the voices, but different this time! Not the voices of the lost! They are the voices of your time, your place! Your chance is coming!"

Maia could barely recall being down below; more time must have passed than she had imagined. "We've already stopped at the other time periods? I slept so long?"

"You have barely slept at all!" Dutchman led her toward the rail. The going was slow, the wind whirling like a tornado around the deck. From his expression, it was clear that he had not expected this. "I can't say why, but she's changed course! She *abandoned* the other ports, never stopped at them at all!"

Never stopped at them at all? Maia forced herself to not listen to the voices. She had to concentrate on what he was trying to say. "But why?"

He grabbed hold of the rail and brought her up next to him. Gesturing for her to seize hold herself, he called, "We may never know . . . and it truly does not matter now! All that we need to know now is that you must be ready! It may be already too late!"

"But surely this is a good sign?"

He shook his head. His voice was filled with such dread as she had never before heard. "An ill sign if any, Maia de Fortunato! If my lady is in such haste, I fear that the time is fast approaching! It may be already here!" Dutchman bowed his head in dismay. "Another world about to die!"

Something huge and dark suddenly jutted through the cloud cover just ahead of them. Not a mountain, but a building. Maia stared at it. A skyscraper. To be exact, the John Hancock Building. Even as the realization dawned on her, the clouds slowly began to part. It was night, but strangely enough she could see everything, almost as if the sun still shone. Below her lay the entire metropolitan area, even the lake.

They were back in twentieth-century Chicago, but were they too late?

13. HOME INVASION

A headache. August de Fortunato was trying to kill them by giving them the grandfather of all headaches.

Gilbrin the Shifter fell to one knee as a tremendous force sought to squeeze his brain. He thought that what de Fortunato sought to do was probably more complex and deadly than some grand headache, but that was all that he and Tarriqa had suffered so far. Of course, if the pressure became unbearable, then the headache was all that Maia's father would have to give them. Gilbrin was already almost willing to give in to the pain. How nice and inviting the floor looked. How nice and calm unconsciousness promised to be.

Maia.

The sandy-haired trickster saw her face in his mind. It was almost as if she were here now, so vivid an image it was. He could not surrender to the traitorous de Fortunato or to the power behind him, the Darkling. Not only would that mean Gilbrin's death, but then he could not help Maia.

"Steady, lad." Hands with a grip of iron . . . *of course!* the irreverent part of him still managed to jest . . . lifted Gilbrin from the floor.

Through his tears he could make out Philo's unchanging expression. The animatron had his head cocked to one side. Gilbrin tried to focus on the large, staring eye. It helped to do so.

He grabbed Philo's shoulder and gasped, "The Darkling! The Darkling's out there, too!"

The mechanical man said nothing, but even as confused as the Shifter was at the moment, he thought he felt Philo tense. That was impossible, of course, since such an action would have indicated human emotion in the creature . . . but then had Gilbrin not thought about Philo's humanity just a short time before?

Worry about that later! Worry about surviving now!

"Gil . . . brin!" Tarriqa's voice, sounding very far away. Miles and miles away. "They will be coming . . . from all sides!"

"What do you suggest, Hamman? We each take a side of the house? That'll still leave too much unprotected!" The more they talked, the more Gilbrin found himself able to concentrate. Unfortunately, he could still do little else. He hated to think how little he would be able to defend himself when the Roschach invaded the house . . . which they were sure to do very soon.

"No! If we separate . . . they'll take us! We should stay together!"

Gilbrin was about to argue that staying together meant that the Roschach would trap them in one room, but Philo chose that moment to throw him to the floor.

A black tentacle shot past them, striking the wall behind. Philo kept him pressed against the wood while he pulled the cutlass out of thin air and used it to slice cleanly through the menacing appendage. With a loud hiss, the owner of the tentacle quickly retreated with what was left. The remnants flopped about on the floor for a second or two, then dissolved, leaving no trace.

"Very predictable they are, eh, lad?"

"Oh, yes," muttered Gilbrin, trying to rise. He still had the taste of dust in his mouth. "They're ever so boring." It occurred to him that he had no trouble thinking now. The assault on his senses had passed. August was no longer trying to drive them mad. The Shifter doubted that the cessation of effort was a good sign. "Master Tarriqa! He's stopped."

The black man sat against one wall, still rubbing the back of his head. "We have to try to shift to another location. With your power and mine, we should be able to do it."

Gilbrin eyed the back hall. Was it darker back there, darker than it should have been? He could see the shattered doorway where the first Roschach had broken through, but nothing moved. *Which doesn't mean the beasties aren't there!* "Now why don't I think that our dear friend August will let us get away that easy? Not to mention the Darkling, of course."

"Can you think of anything else to try?"

"Prayer?" he joked weakly. Hamman Tarriqa was correct, of course, however slight their chances of success.

"The brigands are on the move again," Philo informed them.

Gilbrin had neither heard nor sensed anything and it was clear that Tarriqa was just as much at a loss. Still, if the animatron claimed that the Roschach were on the move, then . . .

A black, tarry substance oozed up through the floorboards, spreading quickly over much of the surface.

"Chair!" roared Gilbrin, pointing at one only a few feet from the other Scattered One. Tarriqa moved instantly, leaping from the floor onto the chair. The Shifter rolled toward the couch. Only the animatron stood his ground.

"Philo!"

The tar formed quickly into two massive heads with maws large enough to take Gilbrin's entire arm. Striped, inhuman eyes sprouted.

The parrot cut off the nearest head before that Roschach could even orient itself. The creature collapsed, its substance pouring back through the minute cracks.

However, the second Roschach had used the moment to form arms and legs, its final shape something like a thin crab trying to transform into a man. *A centaur, only with a crab's body instead of a horse's,* Gilbrin decided. It moved with caution toward Philo, the cramped room almost assuring that it would have to attack if it made more than two more steps.

"Gilbrin! The duct!"

The Shifter looked behind him. Out of the duct poured more liquefied Roschach, enough, he estimated, for at least two of the infernal monsters. Just how many did the Darkling have to throw at them? *More than he'll need, no doubt.*

Recalling the Roschach in the hotel room, Gilbrin wondered whether these, too, would be somewhat protected against his power. He had only one way to discover the answer to that. Sighing, the wiry figure crawled to the far end of the couch, the better to put at least a little safe distance between himself and the creatures, and concentrated.

"Time to turn on the air-conditioning," he muttered. His eyes fixed on the thermostat. *Thank Carim, Master Tarriqa had managed to buy a ramshackle house with central air!*

A strong gust of chill wind burst through the air duct. As it did, the Shifter reached for a book lying on a side table. The living puddles reacted instantly to the air, the first one streaming away before Gilbrin's ploy could touch it. The second one was slower than the first, however, and suffered the consequences. The cold air struck it as it tried to pull the last of itself free. Immediately the back end of the puddle froze. Part of a Roschach head formed, as did one handlike appendage. The Roschach tried to drag its frozen portion along with it, but it could not move swiftly enough. The cold quickly spread across its protean form.

When it had completely solidified, Gilbrin threw the book at it.

The Roschach shattered, showering both Gil and its companion. The other creature ducked low. It began to shape itself for an attack, several clawed appendages beginning to sprout at various points all over its body.

Out of the corner of his eye, the Shifter saw that his companions were equally at odds. Another Roschach had seeped through the floor, forcing Philo to confront one on each side of him. The animatron shifted his cutlass back and forth, momentarily causing a stalemate. Beyond him, Tarriqa was pinned in the hallway that led to the side door of the house. A Roschach resembling a serpentine arachnid hung from a crack in the ceiling. It was trying to snap at the black man's hand, but some invisible wall prevented it from doing so. However, each time it attacked, it got a little closer. Tarriqa, on the other hand, was obviously weakening.

Gilbrin had no more time to consider his companions' fates, for his own adversary was fast readying itself for an all-out assault. Only the death of its companion had caused it any hesitation.

Gilbrin had to do something about that . . . but what?

The monstrosity did not allow him time to answer that question. It leaped at him.

In desperation, the Shifter did the only thing he could think of. From within the couch he drew every spring and screw he could free and sent them flying toward the ceiling. Of course, between the ceiling and the couch was the Roschach, which received the bulk of the deadly missiles. The projectiles peppered its body as it flew over the couch. With a hiss of pain, the Roschach tried to turn itself out of the path, but by then it had suffered the bulk of the savage attack.

The monster tumbled to the floor just inches from where Gilbrin crouched on the sofa. It was not dead, but it was sorely wounded. It was also furious. Without even trying to rise, it snatched at the figure just above it.

Beware the Bandersnatch . . . It had been years and more than one variant since Gilbrin had read any version of Lewis Carroll, but if there had ever been any such creature, it must have looked much like the Roschach. *Maybe the multitudes of Mr. Carrolls who wrote about it dreamed of one of the Darkling's pups!*

The Roschach snatched again and this time came up with Gilbrin's ankle. For the first time, it spoke. "Little man, little man! Master wants you, master wants you . . . but he will take you just alive, he will take you *just* alive."

"Well, *that's* certainly a comfort!" Gilbrin used his free foot to kick his attacker in its flat, toothy face.

The Roschach hissed, more annoyed than hurt by the kick, and slowly rose, still holding Gilbrin's ankle. Black fluid dripped on the floor from more than a dozen holes. Gilbrin had never seen anything resembling internal organs in a Roschach. It was a wonder that the beasts could even be termed "living."

That term would not apply to him soon if he did not extricate himself from the creature's grip. Up until now, he had been working on indirect attacks, letting the air-conditioning and the metal workings of the tattered couch serve as weapons. Now it was time to see if direct force would do as well.

"You're making a mess on the floor," he chided the Roschach. "Master Tarriqa hates messes . . . which means he's going to be very annoyed at me for this."

Gilbrin seized the Roschach by the appendage that held his ankle just as it reached out with two more hands to grab him. Gritting his teeth, he put the full force of his inner power into the attack. There was terrible resistance at first, but then he felt it melt away . . . and with it the Roschach. Talons scrambled for his arms and legs, tearing his garments and leaving bloody scratches that threatened to shake his concentration, but the Shifter held on. He held on until the other claws pulled away and the one gripping his ankle grew soft and pliable. The Roschach melted back into a puddle, looking all the while like some parody of the Wicked Witch from *The Wizard of Oz*. It did not stir.

Gasping, Gilbrin the Shifter slumped back on the couch and, without meaning to, shut his eyes for a second. The effort against the Roschach had taken more out of him than he had expected. Given a moment, he would regain some of his strength, but—

"Well, well, if it isn't my daughter's clownish little former lover."

The weary refugee opened his eyes just enough to see the

short, deadly figure standing where the Roschach had only just melted. "August. You know, it's terrible I never was able to call you 'dad-in-law.'"

The boyish features of Maia's father twisted into an expression of disgust. "Tearing away from you was one of the few things my darling get did that made sense. You as *my* son-in-law? The disgrace would have been too much!"

"As opposed to murder, greed, and madness, I suppose." He had to keep August de Fortunato talking. From the sounds of things, Tarriqa and Philo were still doing battle. There was still a chance. All Gilbrin needed was a few more moments and he would be ready to assure that the overaged juvenile delinquent before him never got another chance to grow up into a monster. There were ways to permanently kill a fellow Scattered One and Gilbrin knew some of them. Of course, his adversary likely knew *all* of the methods.

De Fortunato glanced down at what little remained of the one Roschach. "Disgusting, incompetent creatures. Good for cannon fodder and not much else."

"Oh, I don't know. They might be good for greasing the axles on my Dodge." Gilbrin felt his strength returning.

"There is that," the youthful traitor agreed with a chuckle. "You can make the suggestion to the Darkling yourself. We'll see what he says." De Fortunato's eyes narrowed.

"I'll pass on that, thank you." The Shifter raised a hand.

August de Fortunato moved at the same time. His attack was not visible, but suddenly every bone in Gilbrin's body shook. He gasped, almost but not quite losing control of his own attack.

Compelled by Gilbrin's power, the oily remains of the Roschach rose up and washed over de Fortunato. The youthful villain choked back a cry of surprise and worked to repel the foul substance. His attack on Gilbrin faltered, but the jester could hardly move, so violently had he been shaken.

"If he didn't want you alive, joker . . ." August de Fortunato dispersed the tarry mess and glared at his foe. He took a step forward, his power already building.

Pulling himself up, Gilbrin prepared for what would probably be an insufficient defense. He was exhausted. Still, he would not go down without a struggle. Not to one such as Maia's father.

A burst of light shot past Gilbrin's couch and struck de Fortunato full in the chest. The renegade flew back against the wall, striking it with a loud crack as he broke through the drywall and even some of the wooden skeleton underneath. Gilbrin doubted that someone as well protected as de Fortunato could be more than stunned, but even that was a great reprieve.

He peered back over the couch at his rescuer. Hamman Tarriqa, still gasping, slumped against the hallway wall, the only sign of his Roschach adversary a small smoldering black pile several feet down the hall. His face had visibly paled, though, and the strain he had been through was clearly evident. He looked nearly as terrible as Gilbrin felt.

"Gilbrin! We have to . . . join hands! All of us!"

On another side of the room, Philo backed away from two more inky creatures that had somehow seeped through the cracks around the window. The animatron had a vast puddle at his feet, attesting to his ability with the astonishing cutlass. Perhaps he had heard the black man's words, for he was backing up in a direction that would put him exactly between the two humans.

Certain that every cell in his body ached, Gilbrin pulled himself over the back of the couch. August de Fortunato was still recovering and the Roschach were momentarily at bay, but they had yet to hear from the worst of all, the Darkling himself—

A brilliance so white it almost blinded even when their eyes were closed spread across the entire house. It was everywhere, filling even the places where there should have been shadows. Even Philo, who Gilbrin had not thought would be affected, cringed against the terrible illumination.

"Tarriqa!" Even through slitted eyes, it was so bright he could hardly see across the room.

"Here . . . Gilbrin!"

Vaguely, he saw the black man. It struck him as ludicrous that he would have such a difficult time locating a man as dark as Hamman Tarriqa in a room so extravagantly lit.

Then the illumination lessened slightly as a patch of darkness formed in the center of the brilliance. Gilbrin had a sinking feeling that he knew what this presaged. He doubled his efforts to reach his companions, but his body moved as if caught in molasses. *It's the light,* he realized. *The light is making it hard to move!*

"Give me your hand, lad." It was Philo, of course. The animatron moved through the light as though unaffected, although he had to shield the eye that faced the source.

He was only barely able to obey, so Philo pulled him forward . . . and not a moment too soon, for behind him the Shifter heard the sinister snarl that warned that August de Fortunato was up and functioning.

"No more . . ." hissed the renegade. "I don't care if his highness wants you all alive! He'll have to settle for the bird. You're both dead!"

"That is . . . very presumptuous of . . . you," Tarriqa called. He had ceased trying to reach Gilbrin and instead stared at their foe.

Grunting, de Fortunato went down on one knee. It took Gilbrin only a moment to realize that Tarriqa was giving the traitor a taste of his own medicine. Still, while the black man was strong, he was probably not strong enough to keep de Fortunato down long. *But the two of us might be able to make a quick end of this battle!*

They needed to finish it quickly. The darkness within the brilliant glow was swiftly shaping into something more human in form. It was only the defenses that Tarriqa had placed around the house that slowed the approaching apparition. They had to end this now.

Even as de Fortunato started to rise, pain replaced by anger, Gilbrin added his attack to Tarriqa's. August de Fortunato fell back to the floor, but, much to the Shifter's surprise, he did not collapse. Instead, with much more of a struggle, the renegade slowly began to rise again.

"It's no good, lad, it's—"

"Fool!" de Fortunato said, focusing his anger on what he evidently considered the greater threat, Hamman Tarriqa. "My power is superior!"

Tarriqa trembled. At first Gilbrin thought it was from effort, but then he saw that his companion could not control his trembling. Sweat dripped down the black man's face. The battle with Maia's father had become a personal duel between the pair and Tarriqa was now clearly the weaker.

Try as he might, Gilbrin's own attack slowed de Fortunato only a little. It was impossible. None of the Scattered Ones should have been capable of such ability . . . but then, none of them had the power of the Prince of Shadows behind them.

"Forget me!" the frantic trickster commanded Philo. "Help Tarriqa! Help him!"

The animatron visibly hesitated, then, with a nod, released Gilbrin. He took a step, not toward their comrade, but rather toward the attacking renegade. Once more, the cutlass materialized.

August de Fortunato broke off his assault on Tarriqa and turned his baleful gaze to the parrot. Gilbrin watched with horror as the black man slumped to the floor. Tarriqa might not be dead, but he had to be near it, if Gilbrin was any judge. With Philo snaring the youthful traitor's attention, the exhausted Shifter dragged himself toward the still figure.

"Preparing to repel boarders," the animatron remarked.

His offhand manner made de Fortunato take a step back, but the uncertainty did not last long. De Fortunato gestured for Philo to come closer. "Come to me, parrot! I'll pluck every painted feather off of your mechanical body, you overgrown clockwork toy! Then, I'll shake every gear loose until you're nothing but a pile of rusted, twisted metal!"

In response, Philo pointed the cutlass at his foe and increased his pace.

Gilbrin reached Tarriqa. The wounded refugee was still

alive, but barely. He was conscious, however, and when he felt the Shifter touch him, he managed to open his eyes and whisper, "Get . . . him out. They want . . . the . . . Philo . . . badly."

"Easy, Hamman. Can you grab hold of me at all?"

"Do not waste time . . . Gilbrin."

The Shifter tried to make light of matters. "Don't go dying on me, Master Tarriqa. I won't let you forget this when we get to the next variant. Besides, you might be poor again on that one. You wouldn't want that."

The eyes of the other Scattered One fixed on Gilbrin's. "Not going to be reborn . . . I think . . . feels different . . . he's turned something inside out."

"Listen to me, Ha—"

There was a flash of light even brighter than the first, near-blinding brilliance. It caused both their conversation and the battle between Philo and August de Fortunato to falter.

"I am not pleased," said a voice that echoed from everywhere. "I am not pleased with any of you."

The ebony figure floated a good three feet off the floor and should have been touching the ceiling . . . save that there was now a great gap in the ceiling. It was as if someone had taken a knife and cut into it the way one would cut into a cantaloupe. In fact, the very room also seemed wider. Gilbrin would have sworn that it was at least twice as large as it should have been.

Philo turned from de Fortunato and tried to slash at the newcomer. The black figure casually raised one hand to waist level. The animatron's hand twitched and the cutlass fell from his grasp. It faded the moment it touched the floor. At the same time, a gesture by the newcomer sent Gilbrin's mind reeling. It became difficult to understand his captor's words, much less to concentrate on escape.

"I am the Darkling. Bow to my will," the creature commanded. "I am your will, your desire. I control. It is your duty to obey."

It was impossible to make out much of the Darkling's

lower half. Moving shadows shrouded his legs and feet . . . assuming that he had feet.

"I told you that you couldn't trust those damn stains to do things right," de Fortunato interrupted. "If I hadn't gone in, these three would've escaped!"

"And instead," countered the Prince of Shadows, "you decided to eliminate all of them, counter to my command." The Darkling sank lower until he was only a few inches above the floor. For the first time, Gilbrin saw the dead-white eye. While Maia's father did not appear to notice the subtle mood shift, Gilbrin was certain that the Darkling was growing very, very tired of his erstwhile ally.

Keep it up, August. You may talk yourself right out of a life. If there was anything that would make being captured by the Darkling tolerable it would be to see Maia's mad sire finally, once and for all, pay for his many crimes. Death at the Darkling's hands was always permanent.

"There would've been enough left for your purposes."

To the Shifter's horror, the Darkling suddenly swerved his way. He tried to back up, but whatever hold the Prince of Shadows had on him was much too strong. Only at the last moment did he see that the ominous figure was interested not in him, but rather Hamman Tarriqa.

"Enough left?" The Darkling stretched forth a black hand. The shadows by his feet reached out, snared Tarriqa's limp form, and brought it to what was approximately shoulder level for the sinister figure. "This one looks a little overdone, friend August. I daresay he has nothing left worth saving." The eye shut briefly. When it opened, he concluded, "Sparks of life, but the core, that which knows when the time to leap comes, is blacker than a Roschach. You've broken him too much, friend August. He is of no need to me now."

The shadows released Tarriqa's body, which struck the floor with a heart-wrenching *thud.* Gilbrin stared at his companion. Had the black man's life force ebbed away or was Hamman so skilled an actor? Unfortunately, the answer was likely the former. *I am sorry, Master Tarriqa. I know that I got on your nerves, but I like to think we got along splendidly despite that.*

"This one, however, you have fortunately not damaged much." Suddenly, Gilbrin was airborne . . . no, the shadows had taken him just as they had Tarriqa, but the Shifter could feel nothing where they held him. As far as his sense of touch was concerned, he was floating. "Yes, he still has the potential to do me a great boon."

"That one isn't worth any damned trouble! You'd be better off snapping his neck now. You've got the parrot; what do you need this pathetic clown for?"

"Maybe he prefers my company over yours," Gilbrin managed to blurt. He was pleased to see a slight gleam of amusement in the Prince of Shadow's otherwise chilling eye. It was indeed only a matter of time before the Darkling and August de Fortunato turned on each other. Gilbrin hoped that it would be soon. Perhaps then there might be the opportunity to escape.

"The parrot is a means to the ultimate End, friend August, but I dare not assume that it shall be reached on this appointed variant. I may have to bring the clockwork man with me to the next, where I can make better use of his secrets and the link between himself and his master."

"I do not serve with pirates," Philo stated. "And I will not betray my captain. I will walk the plank and visit Davy Jones' Locker first."

"You have the soul of a poet, my feathered friend. I shall enjoy our discussions." The shadows of the Darkling reached for Philo. "Now come along."

Tendrils snared the animatron's arms and one of his legs. Gilbrin thought to act, but then he, too, was suddenly entangled in more of the murky appendages. Try as he might, he could not tear himself free. Slowly he and Philo were drawn toward the mass of writhing shadows.

Without warning, the entire room warped even more than it had with the arrival of the Darkling. Gilbrin realized instantly that it was another shock wave preceding the End of the world, a shock wave far stronger than either de Fortunato's attack on their minds or the earlier wave that had nearly caused Tarriqa to crash his car. The floor twisted and swelled, the ceiling curved and bowed. The walls rippled. The furniture stretched wide. Even those within were affected. Gilbrin looked at himself in horror as his arms grew long and spindly while his legs swelled to the size of ripe watermelons.

Even the Darkling suffered some distortion. His shadows grew thicker, seeming to be made more out of clay than darkness. The pale eye widened until it encompassed almost a third of what passed for the Prince of Shadow's visage.

Gilbrin tried to take advantage of the chaos, but the Darkling was not disoriented as he had hoped. Rather, the shadow master was the one most in control of himself save Philo. It was actually the animatron who did what the Shifter could not. The parrot looked much changed, but his reactions were no slower than before. He twisted out of the grip of the now nearly solid tentacles, then turned and seized the ones grasping Gilbrin.

"Look out!" de Fortunato called.

He need not have bothered, for the Darkling reacted only a blink after the animatron's actions. Gilbrin glanced over his rescuer's shoulder to see a new set of deadly appendages racing for them. He reacted as best he could, countering with whatever raw ability remained within him. To his relief, the shadows suddenly shot up into the ceiling. The reprieve would no doubt be only momentary, but Philo was already pulling him to his feet.

Gilbrin expected to run with the animatron, but Philo surprised him by lifting him over his shoulder and carrying him along. The Shifter could hardly argue, not only because of his injuries, but also because of the disorientation caused by the warping.

"Batten down the hatches, lad! We're going through the window!"

"But the window's too small—"

Philo leaped. Gilbrin waited for the inevitable collision.

The window was only wide enough for one body to pass through and even then the jumper had to crouch. What gave Philo the notion that he could get them both through?

Glass shattered. Gilbrin felt brief resistance from a thin, metal netting ... then somehow the pair was outside.

Even in the darkness, the Shifter could see the distortion caused by the warping and he now knew why the parrot had been confident. Hamman Tarriqa's sanctum looked like something from the works of Salvador Dali. The walls were swelling in and out, the roof was sinking, and the window ... what was left of it now ... was nearly ten times its original size. Small wonder that Philo had chosen to leap through it.

A black form jumped out at them as they landed, but Philo shifted and the Roschach went crashing into the fence.

From the front of the house burst the macabre form of the Darkling. The distortion had spread, making him longer, more spidery. His pale eye was so long that it reached down to his jaw. The entire scene might have come out of some terrible nightmare.

"Hold tight," Philo commanded.

Suddenly they were flying ... no, not flying, but rather leaping onto the roof of the car and from there jumping over the fence. A Roschach near the car tried to snare Philo by the legs, but it was too slow, too encumbered by the changes the warping had caused. Gilbrin breathed a sigh of relief even as he was jolted by yet another hard landing.

There were no people around. Whether they were hiding inside their homes out of fear or because the Darkling had shielded all activity from their minds, Gilbrin could not say. He knew only that he could not expect any aid or interference from the ephemerals, whom he wanted to stay away so that they would not be hurt. On other variants, at other times, many ephemerals had died because of the Prince of Shadow's whims. Probably a few had already died in this world.

Trailing close behind the Darkling was August de Fortunato. If his own circumstances had not been similar, Gilbrin would have laughed at the comic way in which the renegade was forced to move. He looked like an escaped cartoon character. Of course, Gilbrin did not look any better. He was grateful that the mechanical man was strong enough to carry him without losing stride. The Shifter doubted that he could have moved much faster than Maia's father was moving now.

Two confused Roschach sprang from the shadows. Both moved slowly, but one was near enough to snag the animatron's ankle despite its obvious disorientation. Philo lost his balance, Gilbrin falling backward as the parrot toppled to the pavement.

It was at that moment that the world abruptly stabilized.

"Carim!" gasped the Shifter.

It was a pleasure to be able to look at his body and see normal arms and legs, even if just beyond those legs lurked a suddenly rejuvenated Roschach. Gilbrin took advantage of his recovered reality to pay back the menacing inkblot by weakening the base of a street lamp. Still adjusting to the return to normalcy, the creature did not notice the street lamp until it had already started to tip over. Caught between its desire to flee and the commands its master had given it, the Roschach moved too slowly. It finally released its hold on Philo and started to shift backward, but by then it was too late.

The lamp caught it on one side. The glass casing shattered and the current still running through the light now coursed through the unfortunate attacker.

Well, I know one thing, Gilbrin thought, covering his nose from the stench. *Roschach smell much better if barbecued. Frying definitely brings out the fragrance in them.*

Beside him, Philo rose. Gilbrin gave him a hand, but that was as far as they managed to get before the Darkling appeared behind them.

"It is most unbecoming of a guest to simply run away, friends. I have not yet been able to present you with the hospitality that I am famed for. I would hate you to leave this world thinking that I was unable to afford you less than my most gracious." The shadowy tendrils reached out again. There were dozens and they spread out as they moved, ensuring that it would be next to impossible for either figure to dodge them for long.

Philo reached to his side, but his cutlass was gone. One avian orb fixed on Gilbrin. "We're done for, lad. Our only hope is for the captain to come through for us."

Gilbrin glanced up at the night sky, almost expecting the ghostly ship to suddenly materialize and Dutchman and Maia to come help turn the tide. There was no sign of the flying vessel nor did he sense Maia nearby. He should have known better than to hope. Maia and the wanderer were probably trapped forever elsewhere, regardless of what Philo had earlier hinted. *No John Wayne cavalry rescue for us. The Indians have us.*

That was unfair to the Indians. There was nothing as dark and deadly as the Darkling.

The shadows seized them. Both the Shifter and his companion struggled, but this time to no avail. The Prince of Shadows began to draw them toward him. Behind the fearsome figure, August de Fortunato chuckled at their misfortune. Gilbrin wished that he could have dealt at least with the renegade. His capture was bad enough, but to have to listen to dear August's mocking tone was too much.

"Laugh all you want, August," he called out. "Just remember, eventually you'll be joining us."

The darkness swallowed him after that, but he had the minor satisfaction of hearing de Fortunato's chuckle suddenly die.

14. DOWN TO EARTH

Dutchman watched Maia. He felt as if he could do nothing else. It was not simply because she reminded him of his lost Mariya. Although they were very similar, Maia revealed subtle and even not-so-subtle differences. The differences were intriguing and even admirable.

She kept him off-guard. He was not used to that. His world had been one of constant repetition, the same cycle of destruction running over and over again. Maia de Fortunato had shattered that cycle by her very presence. In some ways this disturbed him, but in others it made him feel alive, a true person and not simply a timelost ghost.

It would have been nice to know her longer, Dutchman decided. Perhaps they could have been friends . . . then more than friends.

You are still a dreamer, are you not? Even after so many eternities, you still dream of renewed life, love, and reprieve. You should know better.

He could see her planning, trying to calculate her best chance of success. The contact by one of the other Scattered Ones had given her reason for hope and him reason to marvel. Dutchman had not expected such an ability from the refugees. He wondered in what other ways they could surprise him.

Does it matter? Nothing should matter but helping her.

They sailed on, skirting the tallest buildings. Dutchman

was certain that his ship had returned to the twentieth century in order to watch *this* Earth die. That meant that they had only a short time before the true destruction began and the tide became irreversible. *The first shock waves should have begun by now. Only the most sensitive will experience them, though. The rest will not realize what is happening until the final day . . . when everything falls apart.*

"We're dropping."

He nodded, almost putting a comforting hand on her shoulder but recalling himself at the last moment. *You must not allow yourself to become too close!* "Are you prepared?"

"Yes."

"What will you do now?"

"Wait for her to go lower. In the meantime, I want to try to contact Gil and Hamman."

When she mentioned the name of the comical little man, Dutchman felt a twinge in his heart. She and Gilbrin had been very, very close at one time. They were still close; that much was evident. Not lovers, but good friends. So he hoped.

Again the forbidden thoughts. What kind of fool are you to dream what you dare not dream? Forget her. There is no escape from this ship. You are married now and forever to your lady Despair, *and she is not one to give up her mate willingly.*

They continued to descend. Maia took a deep breath. "That is odd. I do not sense them." She gave Dutchman a suddenly fearful look. "Do you think that the Darkling might have them?" Before he could respond, the worried woman moved on. "They could be shielding. That has to be it. I'll have to try harder. Maybe if I push to my limits one of them will notice."

She was very nervous, which was certainly understandable. Not only did they have to hope that the *Despair* would descend low enough, but neither knew for sure whether Maia would be allowed to escape. She did not need the added strain of worrying about her friends.

He watched as she concentrated on linking with her companions. At first, she seemed to have little success even though the *Despair* was sailing over the center of the massive metropolis. This close, it should have been a simple matter for her to contact one or more of her friends, yet precious time continued to evaporate without any sign of hope. Dutchman, unable to resist the urge any longer, gently put a comforting hand on hers.

A voice suddenly filled his head.

Who is that? it asked.

"Maia de Fortunato," his companion replied with a sudden rush of joy. Like the questioner's, her voice resounded in his head. In some ways the questioner, a male, sounded like one of the voices that haunted Dutchman, but in other ways it was as if he spoke from the far end of a long tunnel.

Maia de Fortunato? I am Mendessonn. It is good, fraulein, that you have found me.

"Mendessonn!" Maia grew excited and through his contact with her, Dutchman was immediately caught up in that excitement. "I need to send a message to—"

Quiet, please! Where are you! You seem so very . . . distant. You are not in my time and yet you are.

Dutchman resented his manner, then realized that he had also picked up on Maia's resentment. It was hard to tell who was feeling what, but he found that it did not matter much to him. Never had he felt so much a part of another, not even with—

Maia's response prevented him from having to complete what would have been a blasphemous thought. "Never mind where I am, Mendessonn. Listen to me. Do you know Hamman Tarriqa?"

Yes, I do. I have, in fact, talked to him not long ago, fraulein. About you, in part.

"You're part of his group, then." The dark-haired refugee sighed in relief. "I do not have much time. Can you contact him? I can find no trace."

But why not? You are supposed to be twentieth century, are you not? You sound . . . close yet not. What is happening—

Looking down at the oncoming landscape, Dutchman

frowned. "Maia, you must hurry. I do not know how much lower she will descend and for how long."

Who is that?

"Never mind!" Maia unconsciously seized Dutchman's hand tightly as she fought down the frustration of dealing with Mendessonn. "Listen! Find Hamman or Gilbrin the Shifter for me! Quickly now! Tell Hamman that the ship has returned! I think that I can abandon—"

Dutchman felt the link snap, a mental sensation so abrupt that he pulled away from Maia, snapping that link as well.

"Damn him! If he would have just stopped interrupting, I could have told him everything. I hope that he can at least pass along what I managed to tell him! At least Gil and he will know that I'm all right." She suddenly looked at her hand, then at Dutchman. "I felt a change when you touched me. You added to my strength."

"I did not expect to." He was afraid that his face was crimson. Ridiculous, he knew, but the fear would not go away as long as she looked at him like that.

"I know that our kind can do that, but only with great effort and only if both are strong enough. Still, our link was stronger than I would have expected." She mulled over the matter. "Mendessonn spoke to me from another time and place. Odd that I could reach him but not Gil or Hamman."

"As you indicated, they may be purposely hiding their presences."

"I would like to believe that." She looked at her hand again. "I also felt something else when we linked. I felt you. What you are. Something of what you think . . . but not all." When he did not respond, Maia quickly returned to the subject of their escape. She peered down. They had not descended much farther in the past few minutes, which to Dutchman meant that time was short. "She's slowing, isn't she?"

"Yes."

"We have to do it now, then." Maia pushed stray hairs from her face, then glanced around. "Do you think it matters where on the ship we begin?"

Just like that, she was ready to start. Once more he wondered how she could even pretend such confidence. Why should the lady *Despair* wish to rid herself of a passenger whom she had only just brought aboard? He should never have given Maia such hope. There was no chance of escape.

Still, in response to her question, he said, "No, it would not matter where."

Maia smiled at him, which made him feel all the more guilty. She reached out her hands. "We will probably have more chance of success if we hold hands."

Dutchman nodded, taking hers in his own. Maia closed her eyes, but he could not. He knew he should say something. He *had* to say something.

"Maia—"

The fierce wind that had assailed them earlier swept over the deck of the *Despair* again.

He quickly pulled her to him, fearing that she might be caught up by the gale, but the act was a futile one, for the wind was so great that it lifted *both* figures from the deck. Maia screamed in surprise and even Dutchman yelled, so unexpected was the terrible force.

It was only because they clutched each other tightly that he could hear her. *"What . . . is happening?"*

Dutchman had no answer. Even as the wind threw them farther and farther from the floating ship, threw them high over the streets of Chicago, he could think only that this madness was the lady *Despair*'s doing. Why she was behaving so, he could not understand. He knew, though, that whatever happened next, it would be because it was what the ghost ship desired. Their fate depended upon her mercurial nature.

The wind ceased.

They plummeted to the streets.

Maia woke with a jolt, then scrambled madly for a few moments, the awareness that she was about to strike the earth still with her. It was only when she felt the solid street beneath her and was able to focus on the tall, dark buildings around her that the woman realized that she was not only alive, but unharmed.

It cannot be possible! The thought raced through her mind again and again. Tossed madly into the air high above the streets, she had been unable to concentrate enough to save them and she doubted that Dutchman had been of much better mind.

Dutchman! Maia gasped and, rolling over, searched for him. She did not see him at first and began to panic, but then her gaze fixed on a large, cloth-covered mound several yards from her. In the dark it had looked like a tarp, but as Maia's eyes adjusted, she realized that it was indeed Dutchman. The long cloak had obscured most of his form.

More relieved than she could have imagined, Maia crawled to her feet and stumbled toward the motionless figure. Her relief shifted to anxiety as she noticed how still he was. Doubts rose. Had it actually been his doing that enabled her to survive the fall? If so, had it been at the cost of his own life?

But he cannot die . . . can he? Dutchman himself had indicated that many things were occurring that were not part of the normal cycle he suffered. The ship . . . that *horrid* ship! . . . was doing things she had never done before. Would that include his unexpected death?

She placed a tentative hand on his back and to her joy he stirred. He tried to rise, but would have failed without her aid. With Maia allowing him to lean on her, Dutchman slowly made it to his feet. His face was even more gaunt than before and his skin was nearly as pale as the whiteness Maia had encountered in the cabin.

"Can you stand?" she asked.

He tested himself. Maia saw pride in combat with weakness. Somehow, Dutchman did manage to stand on his own, although he was clearly more worn than she was. That further strengthened her belief that it was by his doing that she had suffered so little.

Dutchman looked her over. "Are you all right?"

"I am, thanks to you."

He shook his head. "I did nothing, Maia. I could do nothing even though I did try. You . . . we . . . are here, safe and more or less whole, because that is what she desires . . . although I can't say why she would behave this way."

That made no sense to Maia. "Why would she take us aboard, only to return us to the very same location? Is she mad?"

"My lady *Despair*? I sometimes call her mad, but I suspect that she is saner than anyone else. I do not speak whimsically, either. If she has released us, it is because there is some agenda, some very good reason, for allowing us to be here." Again he shook his head. "Although I cannot fathom what that reason could be."

"Well, *I* don't care what her reasons are." The spectral ship could do whatever it pleased as far as Maia was concerned, as long as it did not interfere with her. Unfortunately, she was fairly certain that her future and that of the vessel were now severely entangled. "Dutchman, can you locate Philo?"

"That ability is beyond me. It is generally he who seeks me out."

She found that more than a little intriguing. The animatron was truly a versatile creation, much more so than he should have been. "Perhaps I am wrong, but I think that your ship will not leave until both you and Philo are aboard. I think that she came back in part to find him." When the tall figure did nothing but stare at her, Maia's resolve began to slip. "Of course, it is only a notion. I'm probably wrong."

With what seemed some difficulty, Dutchman finally looked away. He sighed, rubbing his unsettling eyes. "No, Maia, I do not think you incorrect, but I think that there might be more to it than what you say. I have learned in the short time we have known each other to trust much of what you say. You have an agile mind, something which I too once claimed to have."

"I wish I could believe that." She looked up at the night sky. The *Despair* was nowhere in sight, but she was not the only thing Maia searched for. How many days had passed?

Had any days passed? Lowering her gaze, she spotted a pair of newspaper machines on the corner of the street.

The first she peered into was empty, but the second still held a few papers. The date, when she finally made it out, was the day after she had been carried off by the ship. Time obviously was a tricky thing aboard the *Despair*. There was still hope of dealing with matters.

"But how?" Maia murmured as she straightened. "What can I do?"

Dutchman came up and put a comforting arm around her, then suddenly stiffened and carefully removed it. A wave of disappointment coursed through Maia, but she forced it down, reminding herself that she still had to find either Gilbrin or Hamman. How, though? She had tried aboard the *Despair* and had actually reached one of the Scattered Ones in another century, but of her two friends she still sensed no trace.

Hamman Tarriqa's suite. It was the only place that she could think of to start searching. During their sojourn aboard the sinister ship, Dutchman had related to her how he had come to be there during the attack by August and the Roschach. He had been with Gil and Tarriqa when Maia had tried calling. Through that telephone call, Dutchman had transported Gil and the black man to the scene.

"How are you feeling?" she asked.

"I am better. What is it you desire?"

"The suite. Hamman Tarriqa's home. Do you recall it?"

"I do. You desire to go there now, don't you?"

Feeling guilty for pushing his strength so, Maia looked around. "It's late, but maybe we can still find a taxi. I think I still have some money with me—"

He caught her wrist and turned her to face him. "Maia, I will do this. Time means much right now not only to you but to me. This variant is in the first throes of death, but something is different. My lady *Despair*'s—"

"Please stop calling her that."

Dutchman blinked. "Calling her what?"

"Please stop calling that ship 'my lady *Despair*.'" She shivered. "You talk like you are forever married to her, like she dictates your life . . . like you are hers to do with however she pleases."

"And is that not true?"

Maia had no answer for that. What she wanted to say was that he deserved more than his fate. He deserved to walk among people, live a normal life, even die a normal death. In frustration, she returned to the prior subject. "All right. If you think that you can handle taking us both there, I would appreciate it. I have to find out what happened to them."

Dutchman straightened and as he did so, he seemed to grow both in size and in power. Suddenly, he was more the mysterious, mythical figure of so many legends. With one sweep of his arm, he enshrouded Maia in his cloak. "Have no fear, Maia. We will find all of our companions. We will find Gilbrin."

She wondered if there had been a catch in his voice when he had spoken Gil's name, but before the dark-haired woman could mull it over, Dutchman's gloved hand pulled her close to him. Maia felt his entire body tremble.

A hole opened up before them. She barely had time to register its existence before the man looming beside her led her into it. She felt every fiber of her being tingle as they touched it—

And then they were standing in the center of Hamman Tarriqa's plush suite.

Only the suite was not so plush anymore. Every item, every piece of furniture, had been torn asunder, as if by a pride of hungry, angry lions.

Of course, it was more likely that what had destroyed Tarriqa's abode had been a pack of Roschach.

Reflecting her thoughts, Dutchman muttered, "This place looks and smells of the black hunters."

"It was the Darkling's dogs that did this, all right." Maia wandered about the room, trying to sense what had happened. Had the Roschach surprised them here and taken all three away? That did not seem the answer. The destruction here did not strike her as having been caused by battle. It more resembled an act of frustration. The furniture and artwork . . . and what a waste the destruction of Hamman's treasures had been . . . had purposely been torn apart, not accidentally destroyed in combat.

"There is no blood." Dutchman touched the ruined couch, then paused a moment before a painting that had been scratched apart by very long, very sharp claws. "This was done more to be malicious. To make up for their own failure, I think."

"Meaning that, like me, you think that the Roschach didn't find anyone at home. That seems to be the case." She glanced at the door. "And I suppose none of the other residents heard or saw a thing, which is probably fortunate for them."

"What do you wish to do now?"

"I don't know." She put a hand on her forehead and tried to think. Standing still made her too nervous, so she began to pace. It elevated her pulse rate, if not her thinking. "They must have shielded themselves since I can't sense any trace. Hamman didn't mention any other homes, although I don't doubt that he has at least one other residence. They would not go back to the hotel that Gil and I stayed at or for that matter any other hotel, I guess." Again she looked over the devastation. "If there was any information here, I cannot imagine the Roschach or August missing it. They are very thorough."

Dutchman was not paying attention to her. He knelt low, touched a shattered statuette, then ran his fingers along the ripped backside of the couch. "The stench is very strong. Your friends shielded themselves well, but the hunters did not bother to hide their trail at all."

Maia stared at him. "Are you saying you can follow their traces?"

"Yes . . . perhaps."

"But that might just lead us to the Darkling and . . ." The notion of confronting August in the Darkling's own citadel was daunting to say the very least. She did not think that she was ready to face August there, not in a place where the advantage was certainly all his.

Dutchman rose and the expression on his face frightened her. "I would welcome a meeting with the Prince of Shadows, Maia." His expression softened then, as if he had just come to realize how he must look to her. "But I think that I can differentiate the traces. I can . . . sense, as you call it . . . minute traces of your companions' passing presences. It is difficult, but I think that between the two, I can trace the proper—"

The telephone rang.

In the midst of such desolation, the sound was startling. Dutchman froze. Maia, nearer to the telephone, leaped back, every fiber of her being screaming that they should flee the suite immediately. She fought down her panic as a second ring resounded through the room. It was one of the portable telephones, the type that could work for hours without being connected to a charger. For all she knew, it was simply one of Hamman's mortal business associates or even one of his friends. The best thing to do was to let it keep ringing. While the telephone still functioned, the answering machine was broken. Eventually the ringing would just stop.

It did not. It rang a third, a fifth, even an eighth time. When it rang for what Maia counted as the twelfth, she could no longer resist the temptation. She reached down and grabbed it, only at the last moment recalling that she had to press a button in order to speak to whoever was on the other end of the line.

"Hello?"

"Is this the residence of Hammond Tarrez?"

She recalled the name on Hamman's business card. "Yes, but he's not in."

"Ma'am, this is Detective Andrews of the Chicago Police Department. Are you Mr. Tarrez's wife?"

"No. No, I'm just a friend of his." Her mind raced. Why would the police be calling his suite? "Has something happened to him?"

"We're not quite sure. Does Mr. Tarrez have any relatives that we might be able to contact?"

Maia's concern grew. "I don't know his family, detective. I only know him. Tell me, please. What's happened?"

Andrews hesitated. "I should've waited until things were a little clearer, Ms.—"

"Mar . . . Maia de Fortunato." She cursed herself for nearly making the complete slip. Despite Gil's efforts, it was possible that enough memory of Maria Fortune had been left behind to cause someone to alert the police to her absence. The odds were slight that this detective would have recognized the name even had he heard it earlier, but Maia did not want to take a chance. Better her true name, which only another Scattered One would recognize. "I'm a friend. Hammond is letting me use his extra bedroom for a couple of nights while I look for a place of my own."

It was not the best story, but she wanted to give Detective Andrews a reason for her being in Tarriqa's suite before he became suspicious.

"How long have you known Mr. Tarrez?"

"Not too long. Detective, I'd really like to know what's going on. You are making me nervous. What has happened to Hammond?"

"I'm sorry I called this way, Ms. . . . uh . . . de Fortunato. I don't know what possessed me. This isn't quite procedure. Listen, if you will wait there, two—"

Maia had had just about enough. "I'm going to hang up if you do not tell me right now what is going on! Is Hammond all right? Where is he?"

Andrews exhaled. "All right, I'll tell you, but please sit down, ma'am. Is there anyone with you?"

"No." She glanced anxiously at Dutchman, who had so far remained silent. There was no need to include him in this. "I'm alone."

"Then please sit down."

Maia did no such thing, but responded, "All right, I'm sitting. Tell me, please."

"Ms. De Fortunato, I'm at a house on the South Side." He rattled off an address that Maia nearly forgot to memorize. She knew enough about the city to know that it was not one of the good areas. What were Gil and Hamman doing there? "We have a man here, badly injured, who may be Mr. Tarrez."

"How badly?"

"Very badly. He's been beaten something terrible, ma'am. To be honest, I'm surprised that he's still alive at all. Listen, this isn't the way you should be informed about this, but something made me call this number. I'm sorry."

"I appreciate that," Maia returned. "I'm glad you called, detective." Something had made him telephone Hamman's residence. She was fairly certain that the particular something had been the black man himself. "What do you think happened?"

"Looks like several persons broke in and trashed the place. Naturally, none of the neighbors heard very much." From his tone, the detective's opinion of such neighborhoods was clear. "Someone did finally claim to hear a window break and a couple of people running away, but that's all. They've had trouble with gangs there recently, ma'am."

But never gangs of Roschach. August must have used a very strong shield. "Where is Hammond now?"

"The paramedics are still working on him. . . ." Something in his tone indicated that the paramedics were not quite doing the job that they were supposed to do. "Listen, he'll be taken down—"

Any entanglement with the Chicago Police Department was minor in comparison to what the Darkling was doing. Maia had heard all she needed to know from the detective. Before he could finish his statement, she covered the mouthpiece and held the telephone toward Dutchman.

"You found me after my telephone call. Can you do the same with this one?"

He took the device from her and held it high. Maia could just hear Detective Andrews calling her name. She would worry about him later.

Later might not even come to this world.

Dutchman stretched out a hand to her. Maia seized it with all her strength. He held the telephone for a moment more, then put it on the couch.

A hole opened up before them. With Dutchman leading the way, they stepped through.

It was as simple as that. On the other side of the hole was a rundown neighborhood that, while normally dark this late at night, was presently the scene of much activity. Fire trucks, evidently unneeded, were now pulling away. However, there were two paramedic units along with at least five marked police cars and three unmarked, which probably belonged to detectives, including Detective Andrews.

Men were moving all about, trying to make sense of what they would never truly understand. A pair of officers took down words from some of the neighbors. Other officers were combing the front yard for clues. Next to one of the unmarked cars, an older, slightly stout man in an overcoat angrily tossed what looked like a cellular telephone into the front seat. *Detective Andrews,* Maia realized. "Can they see us?"

"No. I doubted that you would want it so."

"No, it would only make matters worse." To her surprise and pleasure, she suddenly sensed a familiar presence. Maia looked around, then fixed her gaze on one of the ambulances. "He's in there."

Her companion nodded. The pair of them wended their way through the police officers until they finally reached the ambulance. Nearby, two men were arguing.

"I didn't leave it back there, Joey! I brought it with me! You probably just can't see it in the dark!"

"It isn't here, buddy, and we can't hook him up without it. Cripes, this guy's got the worst luck! First the handles on the carrier snap off, then I trip on that damn loose step, and you can't get the monitoring equipment to work right."

Maia definitely sensed Hamman Tarriqa inside. However, he did not respond to her mental queries, which increased her fear for him. She hesitated. If Hamman was badly injured, he needed the paramedics' aid. Yet, the only way she could reach him was if she sent them away, which would endanger him further.

While she was debating the issue, Dutchman walked over to the paramedics. He stood behind the one called Joey and said, "You left the equipment in the house. Both of you had better go inside and look for it. Search thoroughly."

"We'd better get that equipment or we'll get hell from the hospital," Joey's partner said.

"Yeah, I don't want to have to go paying for that stuff."

Both men hurried off. Maia looked at Dutchman. He had rid them of the paramedics, but possibly at the cost of Hamman's life. *Was I wrong? Is he so inhuman after all?*

"He wants us here, Maia. Can you not feel it? The men spoke of mistake after mistake. Too many coincidences. He should have been attended to and taken away to a place of healing long ago. This pair has been having too many difficulties for it to be mere coincidence."

She had to agree with him, but it was difficult to think that they might cause the death of the other refugee. In the short time since she had met him, Maia had come both to like and to respect the black man.

I'm wasting time . . . not only Hamman's but everyone's. Steeling herself, she approached the ambulance door. It was open and an interior light illuminated the inside. The change in lighting forced Maia's vision to adjust and it was several seconds before she could focus on Hamman.

When she did, she gasped. She had suspected much from the brief description Andrews had given her, but Hamman Tarriqa looked both better and worse than she had imagined. He lay on his back, a tube in one wrist. He was beaten up, true, but she had expected every inch of him to be a bloody mess. Instead, while he was bruised all over, there were hardly any cuts or blood to be seen. He had required only a few bandages.

The true damage lay within. When Maia looked inside Hamman, it was to find an emptiness of such intensity as she

had not felt since being shanghaied onto the *Despair*. This
was a different sort of emptiness, though; this was the emptiness preceding death. Permanent death. There would be no rebirth for Hamman Tarriqa in the next variant. Someone had
torn out the very core of his being, the very thing that made
him one of the Scattered Ones.

"August . . ." she said quietly, "and the Darkling. *Damn
them!*"

Tarriqa's eyes fluttered open.

"Maia . . ." His voice was a light breeze. She knew that he
spoke her name only because of the way his lips moved. Maia
wondered why the paramedics had not put him on some sort
of respirator.

I would not let . . . them. This time, the voice came from inside her head. He clearly did not have the strength to communicate any way other than by thought.

"We have to get you help, Hamman," she insisted, moving
closer to him. His eyes widened as he looked past her and
Maia assumed that he had noticed Dutchman.

*Do not waste . . . time on . . . me. I have been ebbing . . .
away since they left. I was left for dead . . . or rather, dying.
Your father made certain . . . that I was no use for
the . . . Prince. Carim's blood, Maia! What a creature the
Darkling is . . . but not much worse than your sire. . . .*

"There must be something we can do for you, Hamman!"
She looked to Dutchman for aid, but one glance from him told
her that he could do nothing. Saving Tarriqa's life was beyond
his abilities.

The black man's eyelids fluttered again, then drooped so
low that it was barely possible to see that he was still looking
at them. The voice in her head grew fainter. *No . . . I cannot.
I wanted to reach you . . . Maia. I wanted to be certain . . .
that you knew everything I could tell . . . you. I thought I
sensed you . . . then I felt the . . . the call of old Mendessonn.
I knew that you . . . were coming back. I knew he . . . would
try to bring you . . . back.*

It was astonishing that Hamman's mind had managed to remain so intact, but then, his physical injuries were not as terrible as they could have been. It was what they had done to his inner being that was killing him. He was like a flashlight working off a fading battery. The light was still there, but it was flickering and soon, much too soon, it would simply stop. He had held on this long for her and her alone.

Hamman reached out, trying to grasp her hand in his. Maia seized it and squeezed.

Be interesting not to . . . come back. Maia . . . they have Gilbrin and . . . the parrot. They seemed especially interested in . . . Philo. I—" His mouth actually managed to form a brief smile. The effort cost him, though, and for a moment it seemed that Tarriqa had faded away. Then, he forced his eyes completely open. His mind voice grew stronger. *Two things, Maia. The Darkling left himself open . . . to me. He thought I was nothing. Nothing. I tried to look within, but his shields are incredible. I did . . . catch some stronger surface thoughts. A tall building . . . one of the tallest in Chi-Chicago. Gods, I think I'm drifting off. . . . Could be the Sears Tower, the Hancock, or the Prudential, but not many others . . . in city. Also . . . he had plans . . . for Gilbrin and . . . all of the—*

From within came the sound of at least two men arguing vehemently. Maia and Dutchman looked up. The paramedics were returning. She quickly turned back to the dying refugee. "Hamman, you have to—"

There was nothing. Tarriqa's eyes were still open and he breathed shallowly, but of the mind and essence, there was nothing of substance left. For all practical purposes, he was dead. Forever.

In some ways, you're probably the luckier one, Hamman. She would have liked to grieve, but there was no time for that. Gilbrin and Philo were in terrible danger. Their lives could still be saved, even if it meant the death of yet another variant. Maia did not want these people to perish any more than she had the people of her own Earth, but if their deaths were inevitable, those of her friends and even the animatron were not necessarily so. It was a terrible, personal choice to make and Maia felt great guilt, but she knew of no way to save the world. That left her only the rescue of her companions.

"We must leave the ambulance," Dutchman reminded her. "We can delay no longer." The paramedics were just outside, but were so intent on their argument that they had not checked on their patient.

Maia and Dutchman climbed out of the ambulance. The paramedics did not notice them, but as they stepped away from the vehicle, someone else did.

"You two! What the blazes were you doing in there?"

All four looked to the distant figure of the man Maia had taken for Detective Andrews. He was rushing toward them, a flashlight in one hand. The beam was aimed not at the paramedics, but at Maia and Dutchman.

"We're going! We're going!" snapped the one called Joey. "We've had some problems!"

"Not you! Those two!"

The men glanced in the direction the detective had indicated, but they did not see the pair. Joey's partner eyed the law officer as if he had lost his sanity. "*What* two?"

"Those two, the one dressed like Dracula and the—" Andrews looked around. "They were here a minute ago! They climbed out of the ambulance!"

"Jesus!" blurted Joey. "The beaten guy!"

Both paramedics hurried to the back of the ambulance. The detective took a hurried look around, then joined the pair.

Maia and Dutchman, standing nearby, watched for a moment. Andrews had a particularly strong mind. She hoped that whatever Dutchman had done would hold until they were far away. Fortunately, no one else had taken notice of them. Few ephemerals were sensitive enough to require much effort; it was surprising that it had taken a second attempt to deal with the detective.

Dutchman finally broke the silence. "He said a tall building and mentioned names. Do you know the names?"

"I do. We saw one of them from the ship. That was the Sears Tower."

"The ones we seek are there."

"Or at one of the other buildings, yes." Maia continued to watch the ambulance. Detective Andrews climbed out, shaking his head. A blink later, one of the paramedics closed the door from the inside and the ambulance pulled away.

Somewhere overlooking the city, the Darkling and August de Fortunato held Gilbrin and the animatron. Somewhere inside one of the tallest of the leviathans, they no doubt also waited for Maia and Dutchman to come searching. Even though August had witnessed her kidnapping by the ghost ship, Maia was certain that for some reason they would expect her to return.

But maybe I'm wrong. Maybe this is to our advantage. Maybe the Darkling and August will not be expecting us. Maybe we can catch them by surprise and rescue Gil and Philo.

So many *maybe*s. Maybe she was completely wrong. Maybe this was all an elaborate trap. Maybe all they would be doing was turning themselves over into the hands of their enemies.

Maia thought of Hamman Tarriqa's death. Maybe they would be envying the black man's fate before long.

15. NIGHTMARE IN BLACK AND WHITE

Gilbrin the Shifter awoke to a nightmare in black and white.

He squinted, but even that was insufficient. It was like staring into a sunlit snowbank. No matter what part of his prison Gilbrin turned his gaze to, the brilliance threatened to blind him.

That was the white.

The black was the Roschach.

There were more than a dozen, possibly as many as two dozen. They hung from invisible rafters, crouched on what passed for a floor, perched on stands that were not there. . . . Each one, whether it stood, hung, or floated, was different from the others. The only constant was the striped, animalistic eyes. Even their toothy maws varied, although the prisoner did not long dwell on that subject.

Gilbrin himself hung, but when he looked to see what held him, there was nothing. Essentially, he seemed to be floating. His arms and legs were stretched out in the shape of an X. His limbs were pulled tight, making even the act of turning his head uncomfortable. His clothing remained intact save where it had been torn or burned in the battle. All in all, he was in surprisingly good shape.

He just wished that the Roschach would quit looking at him as if he were a side of beef hung up to cure.

Of Philo, there was no sign. Gilbrin tried but failed to banish thoughts of the animatron slowly being dismantled. The only more dominant image was of *him* being slowly dismantled.

Both images were enough to make him try to pull free. He succeeded only in straining his already worn muscles and in earning looks of hungry interest from the Roschach. When he attempted to use his other abilities to free himself, he not only failed again, but this time several of the creatures stirred, one of them even moving closer to investigate.

"Down, doggy," he muttered.

The Roschach coming toward him moved on six antlike legs and its mouth was one of the toothiest he had seen. It hissed at his words, then in a buzz-saw voice said, "Bad man, bad man. Mustn't leave, mustn't leave, before master is through with you, before master is through with you."

"Would that be considered bad form, then?"

All around him, the Roschach began to hiss violently. It took Gilbrin some time before he realized that they were *laughing* at his response. Even the one nearest him seemed amused.

At least I'll go out making them laugh.

"Still flippant to the very end, jester?"

Out of the brilliance emerged August de Fortunato. The Roschach instantly quieted and Gilbrin thought he noted many looks of hatred among the monstrous creatures. *Guess they can't be all bad, then. At least they have some taste.*

"And a good morning to you, August. You're not looking very youthful today. Voice change yet?"

De Fortunato's lip curled, but otherwise he ignored the jibe. Even Gilbrin found it one of his weaker ones, but a few of the hunters gave some indication of renewed amusement. They definitely did not like Maia's sire. *And how can I make use of that, I wonder?*

"Out of the way!" the renegade commanded a pair of Roschach in his path. They moved aside, but with obvious reluctance. August walked past them, apparently oblivious to their hatred. He kept walking until he stood only a foot from the captive. "You look very uncomfortable up there. Good."

Gilbrin tensed, fully expecting Maia's father to strike him. To his surprise, though, August simply looked him over, as if checking to make certain that he was still secure. When he had satisfied himself, the youthful villain backed up a few feet.

"And to what do I owe this honor, dear August? Or have you just come to hang around with me?"

"Your quips are as pathetic as their originator, clown. Fortunately for all of us, we won't have to hear them for very much longer. One way or another, the Darkling will deal with you."

"Not you, August?" Gilbrin dared a look of comic realization. Had one of his hands been free, he would have even slapped himself on the forehead for extra effect. "Of course! Silly of me! Your master didn't give you permission to play and we certainly can't do *anything* without the master's permission."

"I don't need anyone's permission for anything, clown. I do what I decide." He stepped forward again, reaching out to touch Gilbrin's midsection. "I can cause you great pain and even kill you simply because I choose to do it."

His words did not settle well with the Roschach. They made no move toward him, but every inhuman visage hardened to the point where Gilbrin knew that only a few more careful words, accompanied by a few not so careful words from de Fortunato, would send the creatures into a frenzy the youthful traitor might regret.

"You'd better *not* disobey, August. The Darkling might still need me even if he gets what he wants from the animatron. He wouldn't sit well with you damaging any *more* precious commodities. You wasted Tarriqa already. He may not forgive you for that."

"I neither need nor desire his forgiveness. I don't need his permission in regard to you."

An electrical shock coursed through Gilbrin. He gritted his

teeth, forcing himself to remain silent. The shock continued for several seconds before August de Fortunato finally removed his hand.

Tears ran down Gilbrin's face, but he was proud of himself for not having so much as grunted. August looked annoyed. He reached toward his captive.

"Not to damage, not to damage," snarled the Roschach that had spoken to Gilbrin earlier. "The master will not forgive, the master will not forgive."

"Be quiet, you abysmal blot. Don't tell me what to do, do you understand?"

A second Roschach stirred. "Must not damage."

Forgetting Gilbrin, the traitor confronted the creatures. "I think you may have me mistaken for someone who cares what you say. Stand back and be silent! You fear your master, but you would be wise to remember to fear me as well."

The Shifter watched with growing interest, careful not to make the slightest sound or movement that might turn attention to him. Things were fast heading toward conflict. August de Fortunato's natural tendency to look down on all other creatures, especially those already considered servants, was about to get him into a hot situation. Gilbrin could only estimate the combined power of the Roschach host, but it had to be enough to cause de Fortunato trouble . . . maybe even kill him permanently. In the chaos, it might even be possible that Gilbrin could discover a way to freedom.

As one, the Roschach host tensed. De Fortunato clenched both hands into fists, a sure sign that he was summoning his strength for an attack. This was evidently not the first time he had come into near conflict with his erstwhile ally's minions.

Just a few moments more and they'll be at one another! Now if only—

A voice resounded from every direction. "All will cease their childish antagonism or suffer my most royal wrath."

—the Darkling doesn't show. Gilbrin's hopes plummeted.

He was there, in their very midst. He floated above all, even those Roschach hanging from invisible roosts. The shadows darted and danced toward both the Darkling's servants and the angry but suddenly silent August de Fortunato. The threat in each of those appendages was clear. It said something that Maia's father had immediately quieted. It said that the Prince of Shadows was an even more terrible figure than the renegade had ever been.

I am going to die. I am going to die forever to serve the black prince. His only relief so far was that Maia had escaped the clutches of this most dire pair. She was probably in the one place that even the Darkling could never reach.

"I will have this Dutchman and his vessel before very long, friend August."

His words caused the Shifter's eyes to widen and every muscle to tense.

"Then will you finally give me what I've been waiting for? We made a deal."

The pale eye focused not on the renegade but on Gilbrin. "I will reward all accordingly. Time is short, though. The window of opportunity will be slighter than I would have desired, which is why it is still essential that this one be kept whole, intact, friend August."

"Nothing I did would have had a lasting effect on this clown."

"I cannot permit the risk. Do you understand?"

De Fortunato was surprisingly contrite. "Of course. I'll be careful."

"Leave us now, friend August. I would communicate with this one who shall sacrifice so much for me so very soon." The Darkling drifted closer to Gilbrin.

Looking past the approaching shadow master, Gilbrin watched de Fortunato's expression go through a variety of changes. Maia's father so clearly wanted to teach the Darkling to respect his power, but it was just as clear that he had too much respect for the Prince of Shadow's own abilities. After a few moments of inner debate, the wiry little figure spun about and marched off into the brilliance.

"He is so given to emotional actions," the Darkling commented. The black figure's voice was still disconcerting. Sometimes it came from the side, sometimes from behind. On rare occasion it actually came from somewhere near its originator. "But I am certain that he means well most of the time."

Despite his predicament, Gilbrin's flippant side rose to the occasion. "He means as well as any serpent, I guess. You'll just have to forgive him if he accidentally bites on occasion."

"Friend August knows his place . . . and when he forgets, he will be reminded." The Darkling was near enough that he could have reached out and broken the Shifter's neck. The lively shadows stretched, twisted, and coursed around Gilbrin's body. The weary prisoner regretted his mention of serpents; he could not avoid seeing all those tendrils in that light.

To take his mind off the inquisitive shadows, Gilbrin forced himself to look up again. The choice was little better; he now had to make contact with the one pale eye of the Prince of Shadows. The Darkling looked as if he had died long ago. In truth, he seemed more what Gilbrin would have expected the captain of the ghost ship to resemble. Here was a most deadly phantom.

"Gilbrin is your name."

"Astonishing that you discovered that so swiftly."

The Darkling chuckled, a sound made all the more unnerving by the fact that it came from many directions at once. "You are a brave little man, harlequin, a brave, bright, little man. I am amused by you."

"I'm gratified."

"As you should be. My good grace is all that preserves you for the time. It may be that I will not need you as I did the others in the past. It may even be that if you cooperate, I will reward you for your services."

He could see why the Darkling had dismissed August de Fortunato. The Shifter could just imagine August's ire had he heard his shadowy ally offer freedom to Maia's former lover. It almost made the Darkling's offer something to consider. "And what service do you need from me, my lord?"

It was very possible that the Prince of Shadows missed his sarcastic tone, for the dark figure nodded his head once, as if pleased by his captive's cooperative attitude. "I have been speaking with the clockwork man. Philo, I believe you call him. A most fascinating creature. It will be tragic when he is dismantled, but it seems necessary in order to achieve my goals."

So Philo was still whole. That was good to know. "And does my cooperation in part have to do with speaking with him, drawing some truths from him?"

Shadows darted to caress Gilbrin's face. Their touch was light, but oh so cold. He shivered despite a strong effort to ignore them. "Very astute. I knew I chose correctly when I decided to offer you my goodwill in return for your efforts. The avian and I have already talked at length and while some of his secrets have been revealed, some others have been only hinted at. This captain, this quaintly titled *Dutchman*, I knew of only as legend, story, for my time has ever been much too short for each world. It was not until our friend August came to me with his offer that I learned there was more to the tales."

"You believed something August de Fortunato told you? That can be very foolish, my lord."

The Darkling cocked his head. "I have researched his tales, discovering the truths and the lies. There were mostly truths, I discovered. Friend August also offered other things, useful things, in exchange for not only his continued existence, but added power as well."

"You're playing with a scorpion, my lord," Gilbrin insisted. "August knows no loyalty but to himself. He left our world with a long, bloody trail behind him."

"Yes, there is that aspect of your group. I ask this of all of you, including even August. Do *you* know why your group was spared the death of your variant? Do you know why you are able to leap from world to world? I have only been able to isolate that which causes you to move on; I have not been able to discover either its source or, if necessary, how it could be adapted to myself."

"I wish I knew, believe me, I do." *But I still wouldn't tell you, you damned monster.* He could only imagine the threat the Darkling would pose if he no longer had to concentrate his efforts simply on surviving from one world to the next. "I don't even know why each world turns unstable after a time."

"You do not, do you?" The Prince of Shadows warmed to the topic. In fact, his tone grew almost desperate. "It is a question whose answer has eluded even my most strenuous efforts." He moved closer, as if speaking to a trusted confidant. "I have been forced to retreat from more worlds than I care to recall, friend Gilbrin. Far more worlds than even *you* have seen. My respites are not long, for soon the End draws near on each variant." The dead eye narrowed. "Earth after Earth. Universe after universe. From each I have been forced to flee like some insignificant insect. I! The Darkling! The Prince, who once commanded galaxies! The man who learned to harness the very essence of the universe! Despite all my vaunted power, despite all my skills, still I was forced to abandon my subjects, abandon my empire, when that very universe began to tear itself apart."

So the title is real, eh? Gilbrin probably now knew more about the Darkling Prince than any of the other Scattered Ones, not that it would do him any good if he did not survive the encounter. So much power under the guidance of one madman, unless *madman* was truly the key word and all the Darkling had just told him was the product of the shadow master's imagination. Yet, the Shifter felt certain that his captor was not lying when he said that he had once commanded such power.

The Darkling looked up, supposedly at the heavens, and intoned, "If I could only stop this world from perishing, I would create for it an empire such as it has never seen. All would gratefully kneel before myself, their savior and their master. I would make this world be as it could only be under my complete, just guidance." He looked back down at the imprisoned refugee. "It would be *glorious*."

Around them, the Roschach hissed their approval of their

master's dream. Any dream that included the hunters, though, had to be more of a nightmare, Gilbrin thought. The Prince of Shadows did not strike him as a benevolent dictator. Under the Darkling's rule, the Shifter imagined a world where everyone lived or died strictly for the sake of their master.

Some choice for this poor variant, then. Either the imminent destruction of all or a torturous existence serving the greatest of megalomaniacs. Imminent destruction sounds more and more enticing.

"I do not recall your world, friend Gilbrin. Was there something significant about it that I missed, despite my watchful eye? Was there an essence there that chose to allow some of you this intriguing existence?"

The Shifter tried to shrug, but could not. "As I more or less said before, I know as little as you, my lord."

With a slight wave of one hand, the Darkling dismissed the subject. "Then we should return to the glorious opportunity that I have offered you. Can you get for me that which the clockwork man refuses to divulge? I have offered, I have cajoled, I have even been forced to threaten, something I do *not* care for." The eye snared Gilbrin's gaze and would not release it. "I truly do not like to be forced to threats to achieve what I desire, friend Gilbrin, because then I fear that I must prove that such threats are not simply empty air. I must deal harshly and you must believe me when I say it rends my heart to have to be so cruel to others."

His voice was so sincere that the Shifter almost thought that the Darkling believed his own words. "I will do what I can, my lord, but if he will not tell you, then I cannot promise that he will tell me."

A black hand reached up and cupped Gilbrin's chin. The dead eye blinked once, the first time that it had done so to the prisoner's recollection. "But you will try, friend Gilbrin, and you will try hard, because if I cannot extract the answers from the avian, then I may have to make do with what I can extract from you."

"What . . . what exactly is it you want me to ask him?"

"Very good. Many things you must recall, friend Gilbrin, many things concerning this remarkable ship, its captain, and my suspicion that it will return before this variant perishes. In order of significance, the following specifics . . ."

Gilbrin could not say how long it was before Philo was brought to him. The overwhelming brilliance made it hard to keep track. For all he knew, time might not flow the same in the sanctum of the Prince of Shadows as it did outside in the real world. All Gilbrin knew was that by the time the animatron appeared, the Shifter was cold with sweat. He was, as hard as it was for him to admit even to himself, scared to death.

This did not mean that he had given up hope nor did it mean that he would not fight both the Darkling and August if given the chance. Gilbrin knew the difference between fright and cowardice. A frightened man could fight well. In fact, it was generally the very brave who died first, simply because they took foolish chances. By nature, the trickster was a fool, but he was not *that* type of fool. At least, so he hoped.

The Roschach had departed with their master, but now two of them brought forth the animatron. With his unchanging expression, Philo looked no worse for the wear. It was questionable whether the animatron even felt pain. Still, looking at him, the Shifter recognized signs of what seemed like fatigue, even distress.

Philo moved automatically, obeying each dictate of the inhuman guards. They made no attempt to bind him as had been done to the human. The pair of Roschach merely turned and moved off again, fading away into the light.

"Are you all right?" ventured the Scattered One.

"I function, lad." Philo turned in a complete circle, the huge eyes taking in every lack of feature of their prison. When he finished, the parrot focused on Gilbrin.

"I don't suppose you could get me down from whatever it is that's holding me?"

In response, the animatron reached out. Midway out, his

hands stopped as if presented with some obstruction. A barrier that Gilbrin could not see surrounded Philo.

The Shifter frowned. How did the Darkling expect him to accomplish anything from where he hung? More to the point, how could he hope to free both Philo and himself from the shadow master's grip if he could not even get down?

Philo spoke then. "Are you well, lad?"

"I've had better days."

"Keep your head. We're not sunk yet."

"Are you programmed to be so optimistic?" Gilbrin tugged his left arm. Whatever held it did not loosen in the least. "I'd say it looks very bleak."

"My captain will not leave me. My ship cannot leave me."

There was something in those two short statements that piqued Gilbrin's interest. He ceased his attempt to free himself long enough to ask, "Are you saying they'll return?"

The animatron's gaze shifted for the space of a breath before returning to Gilbrin. "Aye, they will return. They must. *She* must, lad."

"She will?" He grew confused. Was Philo referring to Maia? He doubted that. There was no other "she," though . . . or was there? Mariners often called their vessels "she." He could not recall whether Dutchman or Philo had earlier used the pronoun for their ship, but then, he could not recall much of anything at the moment. However, Gilbrin was now fairly certain that the "she" was the ghost ship.

Again there was the subtle glance around. "Aye, she will return and with her my captain. She must make him see the End of this world; she must make him live it."

Gilbrin automatically tugged his arm while he listened. For someone who had evidently given little information to their captor, Philo was being very forthcoming. He was making Gilbrin's supposed task much too easy. Did the animatron not realize that the Darkling might be listening? "The ship'll do that?"

"She'll do that and then she'll leave. The ship always knows when to leave; she's the safest way from one port to the next, lad." The parrot glanced, cocking his head; he did not peer long. "But she'll look for me first. She has to. I'm part of her, you know."

"No, I didn't." Gilbrin pursed his lips. He was learning some fascinating things, information he was not certain that he wanted the Darkling to know after all.

"I'm the only one that can steer her, you know. The captain, good man that he is, can only command. It's me who sails her for him, though."

"Sounds like a much more attractive way to go from variant to variant than what we have to use. Being reborn in a different time and place each world can get on one's nerves after a while."

"It was the best the captain could do, lad."

Gilbrin was not certain that he had heard correctly. "What did you say?"

Again Philo cocked his head. "The captain. It was his doing that got your lot moving. Wasn't supposed to turn out the way it did, which is why he doesn't realize he succeeded at all."

All thoughts of the Darkling's desires were briefly pushed aside. The animatron had just confessed to the fact that Dutchman, however unknowingly, had created the Scattered Ones. The cursed wanderer had given no sign that he even recognized the force that kept the refugees leaping from Earth to Earth and yet his first mate, a mechanical creation, spoke of it as if it was not even the least of secrets. "You're not serious."

"I am, lad. Now and then, he gets it into his head to try to save a world. He can't help those who've lost what some call the 'magic,' but there was one place, your place, that teemed with the force. I recall well. He was actually enthusiastic then. Thought he'd save a world at last, maybe free himself of the curse." Philo cocked his head to the other side, but his gaze never wavered. "What he tried to do was to use the natural power of its people to throw the devil force out of that world. You'd repel it, that's what he said. Your very selves would cause it to go . . . elsewhere. Only he had to hurry and the

plan, it got turned around. Wasn't the devil force that got repelled, it was a goodly number of you folks. Happens again
each time the foul stuff grows too strong in a variant. The
spell kicks in and you're shanghaied off to the next world.
The captain, he never made the connection, but I did, lad."

Gilbrin did not know whether to believe the fantastic explanation. It was very glib in some ways, but . . . why would
Philo make something like this up? "Why haven't you told
your captain, then? Seems to me you should have mentioned
it to him right away."

"And what good would that have done, lad? To know that
he'd cursed you to such an existence? He's best not knowing,
so's he doesn't repeat it again. Wouldn't have worked proper,
anyway. He'd just have made a bunch of new ones like you,
poor folks of this old Earth who're better off dead than that."

The animatron's words continued to startle him for many
reasons, but one was foremost. Gilbrin wanted to know why
Philo was telling him all of this so readily. If the Darkling was
listening . . . and it was almost a certainty that he was . . .
Philo was sealing his own fate. The Shifter tried to return to a
previous subject. "You think that the ship'll really come back
soon?"

"Oh, aye. I feel her already. It'll be soon and then I'll be on
my way again."

"You're forgetting our hosts. They'd really hate to see us
run off so soon." Gilbrin strained to free the one arm. For one
second, he thought he actually felt the invisible bond give, but
then it held. All he succeeded in doing was pulling a muscle.
Just one little aggravation to add to the big ones.

Philo watched him intently. When it was clear that Gilbrin
had failed, the parrot nodded solemnly. With his index finger,
he touched the invisible barrier around him. "Aye, there is
that, lad. True are your words, that our hosts would hate to see
us leave. I fear that I may have to miss my ship after all if
that's the case. You're drawn and ready for quartering, while
I'm helpless here in the brig."

Gilbrin would have replied, but at that moment Philo did

something that made the startled prisoner clamp his mouth shut for fear their captors would take note.

The animatron slowly and calmly pushed his hand forward, index finger first. As it touched the barrier, a bright, yellow halo formed around the digit. Philo pushed more. His finger moved on. In less than the blink of an eye, the animatron's entire hand was through the barrier. Only when the halo had reached his wrist did Philo cease his efforts and carefully withdraw his hand.

One eye remained fixed steadily on Gilbrin. Artificial the orb might be, but there was no mistaking the look of warning in it.

"Aye," the animatron concluded, his tone no different from when he had last spoken. "There's no way out for us. We're helpless."

Gilbrin could only stare. Whatever Philo was, the Shifter was now certain that he was *not* simply the mechanical man that any of them, especially the bird's captain, assumed he was.

The question was, *what* was he?

"It's a trick, I tell you, and if you continue to fall for it, I know something'll happen!"

The Darkling ignored him. August de Fortunato hated when the shadow master did that, for it was yet another reminder of who was truly in charge. That jackanapes Gilbrin had struck a tender chord, especially since he had spoken the truth and before the Roschach yet. It was bad enough for them to watch their master treat him like a lackey, but to hear such talk from so helpless a prisoner as Maia's former lover . . .

Still the Darkling did not respond to him. The Prince of Shadows was instead listening to a conversation that the renegade found suspiciously fortuitous. When the Darkling had informed him of what he had arranged, August de Fortunato had been tempted to ask him just big a fool he was. Did his supposed ally really believe that Gilbrin would willingly work to get the animatron to reveal the secrets that even the best coercion had failed to produce?

Yet here was the voice of the animatron now, speaking of the ship and his captain with little apparent concern about eavesdropping. The Darkling did not miss a word. Now and then he nodded. The shadows surrounding his lower half moved slowly, but always seemed drawn toward the voices of the captives.

"Do you seriously think that the bloody clockwork bird doesn't know that you're listening?"

Tentacles of smoke turned toward him. Slowly, the Prince of Shadows turned. The Darkling dropped to a level that almost enabled de Fortunato to unkink his neck. That was another thing that annoyed de Fortunato, the other's constant demand that the renegade always look up to see him. It would not have mattered had he boosted his present body to adulthood; the Darkling would simply have floated a little higher to make up for de Fortunato's increase in height.

"Save," the shadow master commanded to empty air. The prisoners' voices became muted. Some part of his sanctum would now record every word spoken between the two, however quietly whispered. August de Fortunato had never seen such a mechanism sort in the Darkling's domain, although he supposed it must exist. The entire thing could not be made of light . . . at least, he supposed it could not be.

"Your concern is noted and appreciated, friend August. Truly I must say that it is heartwarming to see you so concerned. Your concerns are for nought, however. Did you think that I would so naively expect the harlequin to obey my dictates even under duress? It is not his nature. He is one who follows an old, rather romantic tradition, despite his foolish look. He is one who considers himself a heroic rebel, no matter what cause it is he rebels against. Frightened he might be, but unfaithful to himself? Never."

"Then what's the point of this charade?"

The Darkling shook his head at de Fortunato's lack of comprehension, which made the renegade all the more bitter.

Some day very soon, he was going to teach the black prince proper humility.

"The point, friend August," said the Prince of Shadows, sounding far too much like an old school instructor, "is to listen to and study the speakers by what they do and do not say. I learn more by doing that."

"Why not do what you did to that other one? Rees. You got information out of him with that device."

"The device, while capable of many things, will not work effectively on this construct. I would be more likely to rattle him apart, thus ruining any value he might have once had." The dead-white eye narrowed. "The only things more valuable to me are his captain and his ship, and neither are so valuable at the moment as to make me consider the avian's destruction. Nothing must happen to friend Philo, not until I know all."

In August de Fortunato's eyes, the bird was bait and nothing more. On one thing they did agree: The bird gave every indication that the angel of death would return. It was the one bit of information the mechanical creature seemed more than willing to admit and the only bit that de Fortunato had any faith in. He only wanted to know why the damned bird was so anxious to betray his master. Logically, the first mate should have kept quiet, the better to allow his captain to attempt to catch his enemies unprepared.

"And what've you learned, if anything?" August asked.

"That this Dutchman does not fully comprehend what surrounds him. His ship, his first mate, they are part of something more. He is . . . a point of focus for them. Something that enables them to direct their energies toward some end. However, they act independent of him; we have seen that." The Darkling rubbed his chin. "What that end is, I almost feel I know. A little longer, perhaps. The bird is waiting for something to happen, something imminent."

"Something other than the End of the world?"

"Oh, yes, friend August." The Darkling began to float upward and as he did, the voices grew audible again. "Now please go somewhere and be alert, friend August. I suspect that things will not be boring for very long. In fact, it would not surprise me if everything fell into place before the sun rises over this city . . . and a good thing, too, for I suspect that there are few sunrises left in store for this world."

"You think the harbinger will come for his bird man."

"I think that many things will happen, but yes, that is one of them." The Darkling rubbed his chin again. "The avian is impervious to my techniques, but his master, however immortal, is still human. If necessary, I think through him I can reach the bird and through the bird, I will have the ship—" The Prince of Shadows broke off, eye widening momentarily. "The ship . . ."

"What is it?" August de Fortunato had never seen the Darkling behave so.

"Something . . ." The pale eye relaxed. "Nothing. Just a brief sensation. Anticipation, nothing more. Nothing."

De Fortunato waited, but the Darkling had become engrossed in what the renegade considered the worthless babblings of the two prisoners. Here time was running out and the shadow master was wasting precious moments on the pair. De Fortunato abandoned the Darkling, heading for where he knew the exit would be.

The black prince was waiting for the harbinger to return. So was the youthful traitor, but not because of the Darkling's needs. It had occurred to August de Fortunato that there was no reason why the ship and its secrets should not rightly belong to him, rather than to the homeless tyrant whose only subjects were a bunch of mindless ink stains. As for the rest of the Darkling's concerns, once de Fortunato had the ship, he would no longer have to worry about them. Let this world collapse, be consumed by flames, or whatever. Under *his* guidance, the ship would take him where *he* wanted to go.

The Darkling intended to use the animatron as bait, then as a hostage for the wanderer's cooperation. The thing was a machine, though, however well it could mimic a man. August de Fortunato had something better in mind to use. In the few moments during their confrontation, he had come to recognize a few traits in the legendary traveler. First and foremost . . . and what he counted on . . . was the so-called Dutchman's obvious care for others, especially, it seemed, de Fortunato's *daughter*.

He looked at her as if he had known her all his life. He was human at some point; it must've been some memory.

Memories could be played upon. He was skilled at that. Whatever the reason the wanderer cared for Maia or others, it would be his downfall. He would turn over the ship to de Fortunato, who would *not* be content simply to be a passenger. The ship *would* learn who its new master was.

As for the Darkling . . . the renegade smiled. *Your promises have been nothing but air lately, your highness. With the ship in hand, I can finally remind you to keep them.*

And then he would kill the Prince of Shadows . . . along with the rest of them.

16. THE TOWER OF FEAR

They had just reached the Sears Tower when Maia was struck by a pain in her chest so terrible that she thought she might explode from within.

Dutchman caught her just as she collapsed, but although his action saved her from striking her head on the concrete, there was nothing he could do to relieve her of the agony. It was as if her very core were on fire while at the same time someone tried to rip her open. It grew so great in intensity that Maia actually pleaded for it to finish her. She knew somehow that if it did, she would go on to another place where she could start anew. The pain would be gone. She would have a new life, be reborn.

The horrible sensations finally passed. Maia took a deep breath and looked up to see great concern etched into Dutchman's face.

"It's . . . it's over." The weary woman took another, deeper breath. She suffered from lingering effects. Her entire body tingled save for her right arm, which felt slightly numb. Raising her head caused some dizziness at first, but Maia fought against it.

However, when she tried to stand, her legs threatened to collapse. Dutchman immediately carried her to a place where she could sit. Maia tried to stand again, but he forced her to remain where she was for the time being.

"You are no good to yourself if you do not rest. You would be no good to your friend Gilbrin, either."

Maia had to admit that he was correct. In truth, she doubted that she could have taken more than two or three steps before the strain made her collapse again. It felt terrible to look so weak. She was embarrassed even though there was no reason to be.

What happened to me? She had never experienced anything like that before . . . and yet, it *had* reminded her of something. What? The sense of displacement, the feeling of leaving herself and moving on to another life, another—

"Another world," Maia whispered. "Being reborn again on another world." Night-tressed hair flying, she quickly turned to her companion. The action was enough to cause a brief return of the dizziness, but Maia refused to be overwhelmed again. It was too important that she tell Dutchman what had happened. "It almost *happened*. I almost did it!"

"Did what?" He carefully controlled his expression, but his concern continued to show through.

Maia seized part of his cloak. "I almost—" Even now she could scarcely believe it. "I almost *leaped*."

The starlit eyes studied her as if struggling to believe. Dutchman finally looked away, his gaze drifting up to the sky. Maia wondered whether he was searching for the *Despair*. At last, he responded, "But it is too soon."

There she agreed with him. "It still happened, though. It took me a little time to recognize the feelings, but they were the same. The only difference was that instead of taking only a few seconds, barely enough time to really feel them, they kept going on and on, as if slowed down. I thought I was going to go mad from pain."

He put his arm around her. "I understand what you must have gone through. The Maelstrom . . . it would be much like that, only the pain would continue even longer and instead of simply feeling like you were being torn apart . . . you truly *would* be."

Maia thought of what she had experienced and tried to multiply the effect in order to understand what he had suffered in the past. The very thought made her shiver. Dutchman held her closer.

"This world is different," he finally declared, again looking heavenward. "Something is terribly different."

"It must be the Darkling. It can only be the Darkling."

"Perhaps. But if it is this Darkling, then why? He has hunted your kind on other variants. What is different now?"

"He's got Gil and Philo." Maia straightened. She had nearly recovered, although the memory of her torture promised to remain with her for some time to come . . . provided that there *was* time to come.

"Philo . . ." Dutchman pondered the capture of his first mate, evidently having decided that Gilbrin could not be the reason for the changes. Maia had to agree; Gilbrin was a unique personality, but he was still only one of her kind. There was nothing special about him.

Philo, on the other hand . . .

Dutchman rose. "We must find this Darkling's sanctum." He turned to Maia. "Are you recovered enough yet?"

She read the urgency in his voice. He understood little more than she about the situation, but both knew that each passing moment brought them closer to chaos. The answer, so she hoped, lurked in the citadel of the Prince of Shadows. It was the only place to look. It was also the only thing to do if they hoped to save their companions, Philo especially. As much as Gilbrin meant to Maia, she was positive that freeing the animatron from the hospitality of the Darkling was of greater import. Never before had she felt such pain. Never did she want to feel it again.

"We should go to the top of this great tower," Dutchman suggested. "Even if his sanctum is not here, which I suspect is the case, we will be better able to locate it from above."

"I agree." She moved slowly, her entire body still recalling the pain. Dutchman helped her to stand, but from there she demanded to move on her own.

Maia's first steps were tentative, but when she discovered

that her body only ached and that the pain of the near-leap had vanished, she grew more confident. A few more steps and even the aching seemed mild. She gave her companion a triumphant smile and started for the nearest entrance to the Sears Tower.

There was a security guard, but under their influence, he paid no attention to the two intruders who opened locked doors, triggering no alarms in the process. Maia noted that Dutchman knew his way around the building, even pressing the button for the observation floor without looking.

"I have been here," he commented. "This is a line of focus."

She had no idea what he was talking about and since he appeared disinclined to explain, she decided not to press. Although the journey up was a relatively swift one considering how many floors they had to pass, Maia found herself highly anxious by the time the elevator doors opened. The area was only dimly lit, but neither of them needed extra illumination to see.

Dutchman led the way to a window that gave a view of the northwest. "Come see this, Maia."

Curious, the woman joined him and stared into the night. "I don't see anything."

He reached a hand out to her. Maia took it, her heart suddenly beating faster.

"Look again. With my help, you should be able to see it now."

She did . . . and this time was rewarded with a sight such as she had never seen. In the distance, an almost blinding glow surrounded the upper floors of another building. Even from where they stood, the illumination was enough to make her blink as her eyes sought to adjust.

"The Darkling," she muttered. "That's where they are." How could anyone fail to notice such painfully bright light? How could *she* have failed to notice?

"Do you know the building?"

She squinted. "It has to be the Hancock. I went there as a child . . . in this lifetime."

"Then that is where we must go." He paused. "How strange."

"What is?"

"The light . . . I am reminded of something, but I cannot remember what it is." Dutchman shook his head. "We must go."

Maia took a second look at the incredible glow, trying to identify it with anything out of her experience, but just as it started to come to her what the illumination most resembled, Dutchman turned away from the window and released her hand. The glow vanished and with it went the memory. She was tempted to ask him to let her study it longer, but he was already halfway to the elevator.

"We can't just rush over there," she called.

"Have you another suggestion?"

She did not. The best Maia could do was: "Let's get within a block or two of it. Then we'll have a better idea of what we're up against."

A smile briefly escaped him. It was a wondrous sight, considering the source. "I did not mean that we would enter the dark one's sanctum with swords raised and cannons firing, Maia de Fortunato. I would not risk your friend. I would certainly not risk you."

They were silent for the rest of the journey down. Another guard had joined the first, but he was equally oblivious to the intruders. As they walked past the two mortals, Dutchman looked them over. There was a growing sadness in his eyes.

"They have done nothing great, nothing history will recall," he commented quietly as they left the building. "They are only moments in an eternity . . . but they deserve their chance at full life as much as everyone who has died for me in worlds past."

"You never wanted to harm anyone. I know that. I can *feel* that."

He would not look at her. "That does not make it any
easier."

They appeared but two blocks from the John Hancock Center. Maia sensed nothing amiss and Dutchman confirmed her
observations with a shake of his head. If the Darkling's defenses stretched this far from his sanctum, then they were subtle defenses.

The Hancock was a more decorative structure than the
Sears Tower, its profile graceful. Most obvious even in the
darkness were the huge diagonal girders on the outside, which
crisscrossed to create a column of massive X's that rose all
the way to the top of the skyscraper. The dark framework also
made the edifice seem a most appropriate place to find the
Prince of Shadows. The many windows reminded Maia of a
legion of watchful eyes searching for her.

She shook off the sensation. The building had nothing to do
with what she felt; she was imagining things based on the
knowledge that the Darkling waited within, doing who knew
what to Gil and Philo.

"This is too open here. Follow me." She vaguely knew this
part of Chicago. Michigan Avenue ran north toward the Hancock and was fairly deserted. However, just a couple of
blocks to the west was what Maia was fairly certain was Rush
Street. If they took that, it would lead them a little farther
northwest and from there they could turn east again, coming
at the Hancock from a less conspicuous direction.

As they walked, they continued to watch for signs of the
Darkling's power, but only the skyscraper seemed infected by
his presence. They saw no outer defenses, but this did not
console them in the least.

Now and then, Maia had to ask Dutchman to enable her to
view the glow again just so that she could assure herself that
the Darkling was indeed in the Hancock. Each time the glow
was still there, as cold and as deadly as it had looked before.

A block and a half west of the Hancock, Dutchman stopped

so suddenly that Maia took two more steps ahead before she realized what had happened.

"What is it?"

"Something . . . nothing . . . I cannot say which." He surveyed the street. Unlit shops for the most part. Pigeons roosting. A car drove past them. A light breeze tossed a few bits of refuse around. The scene was one of nighttime peace.

What sounded like a bottle rolling in the gutter disturbed the peace. Pigeons awoke and burst from their roosts. A number of them fluttered into the faces of the two. Cursing, Maia tried to beat them off.

More pigeons flew near. They moved in a panic, but could not get very far from either Maia or Dutchman. It grew impossible to see much of anything other than wings, beaks, and claws. She had never thought of pigeons as overly aggressive, but already she suffered from several cuts.

A youthful laugh echoed over the street.

Dutchman raised a hand. The birds turned away, fluttering off in all directions.

"What's the matter, darling daughter? I thought you were looking for a bird."

Maia spun around. There stood August de Fortunato. He was still a youth, but only in form. The face, visible enough in the lights of the street, was too akin to that of the original monster with which she was so familiar.

"August."

"Call me 'daddy,' dear. I insist." The renegade slowly walked forward, each movement obviously calculated. August de Fortunato was ready for any suspicious movement on the part of his daughter or her companion.

"So has the Darkling let you off your leash?"

"No one has a leash on me, Maia. I am my own master . . . and yours, too, of course."

She remembered how he had tried to make her into the next generation of himself. He had wanted her to be exactly like him save in one respect . . . it was he who would have control and she who would have obeyed. Through her, August would have been able to extend his web of treachery and deceit beyond his own limits. Maia would simply have been a tool, a well-honed, deadly tool.

He had come too close to succeeding.

Acting on sheer reflex, the angry woman started toward him, but her path was abruptly blocked by Dutchman's sweeping arm.

"No, Maia. He will have you if you do that."

The dark humor vanished from de Fortunato's face. "You again. How dare you keep a loving father from his only offspring? Well, that will be rectified later, but for now"—he reached out an open hand to Maia—"I would have my daughter back."

To her horror, Maia began to walk to her father. Try as she might, she could neither turn nor slow down. August had never been *this* powerful, to be able to command her body against her will.

A strong hand grasped her arm. Her legs continued to try advancing her, but Dutchman was too strong. He dragged her back.

"I tried to be gentle," August de Fortunato mocked.

The window nearest to the pair exploded outward.

Dutchman and Maia ducked under the deadly rain. Maia used her skills as best she could to deflect the fragments, but a few struck her nonetheless. Most were harmless, but one grazed her temple, cutting along the skin. She felt the blood trickling down, grateful that she had suffered no worse.

Before they could recover, the pigeons were back, this time in greater numbers and far more savage. They pecked and clawed at Dutchman and her. The air was almost unbreathable due to the multitude of feathers flying loose around them.

Several of the birds concentrated on Maia's arm where Dutchman held her. She cried out as a beak dug deep into her flesh. However, despite the onslaught, the wanderer did not release her.

Rising, Dutchman waved a hand. Again the pigeons scattered. Maia coughed and, with his help, stood up.

Her father was nowhere to be seen.

Dutchman led her out into the center of the street, as far as possible from any more exploding windowpanes. "Be wary. There is still something strange going on here. Something that includes more than just your father, Maia."

"You were very simple to predict, my darling daughter." The voice came from everywhere. "So very simple. I expected better of you, but there's still time to correct your faults, to make you into what you were destined to be."

"I am not destined to be *anything* of yours, August!" The wise thing would have been to remain silent and calm, but each time her father spoke, it made her blood race.

He laughed from wherever it was he hid. She knew that the laughter was designed to unnerve her more, but even understanding that, Maia still fell prey to it.

Dutchman wrapped her in one arm. "You are strong. You are not an appendage of him, Maia. You are more than he will ever be. I know. She was like you, but you are even stronger than she was."

Mariya. He was speaking of the woman Maia so resembled. For some reason, hearing his words gave her back the determination that she had almost lost in the confrontation with her father.

"I'm not afraid of you, August!" she shouted.

"But you should be."

Behind the pair, a manhole cover flew into the air. Maia and Dutchman turned to face the new threat.

It took one moment too many. Out of the sewer burst the largest, most sinister Roschach that Maia had ever glimpsed. A glimpse was all she got of it, too, for, moving with incredible speed, it reached for her. She saw a long, fanged snout, tree-branch arms that were large enough to pick up a car, and, of course, the striped, so inhuman eyes.

It was impossible to react to something so swift. The Roschach snared her in its herculean grasp and pulled her toward the manhole. Maia had only enough time to gasp. Behind her, she heard Dutchman cry out her name. She also heard the renewed laughter of her father and what sounded like an explosion. It had to be an explosion, for the street shook even as the Roschach pulled her down into the hole and sealed it with some of its very essence.

The tunnel stank of old sewage and stagnant water. No light shone. All she could make out were the eyes of her captor. Maia struggled to free herself, but the Roschach struck her on the side of the head. An unnatural dizziness swept over her. *I've been stung. . . .*

The Roschach's features grew more distorted, more murky. She knew, however, that the distortion was due to her own lapsing consciousness. Her eyes closed despite her strongest efforts.

"Sleep, sleep, little one, and when you wake, my master will have won."

That was the last she heard.

He should have been able to detect the presence of a Roschach, but de Fortunato must have shielded it from his senses. Thrown off balance by the revelation, Dutchman reacted too late to stop the creature from taking Maia down into the sewer. He tried to follow, but then an explosion nearby sent him tumbling to the curb. When he was able to look up, he saw Maia's treacherous sire standing not more than two yards from him. The insidious youth was smiling again.

"Shall we talk? No one will disturb us, since I've kept this place shielded from the senses of others. As for Maia . . . the Roschach—one that I worked long and hard to control, by the way—will have her safely away by now. Her continued good health is in your hands from here on."

Never had Dutchman met such a foul man. Disgust rose within him that this August de Fortunato could treat his own daughter so. He rose, fully intent on making the youthful monster learn what it meant to harm those who did not deserve it.

De Fortunato hardly seemed worried, though. He watched Dutchman rise, smiling all the time. The wanderer's blood coursed faster. He wanted to strike the man across the face, to wipe away that taunting smile.

"Before you do something foolish, I would consider again what might happen to my dear, darling daughter if you try to harm me. The Roschach will do worse to her, I promise you that."

Dutchman paused. He believed everything the man said. August de Fortunato did not strike him as the type to make such threats idly. That made him all the more horrible. "What do you suggest?"

"I suggest nothing," the renegade said, his smile intact. "I demand. Maia remains unharmed as long as you cooperate with me. It's really a fair exchange, you see. You have something I want and I have something you want."

"I want . . . to tear you to pieces." The astonishing thing was, it was true. Dutchman really wanted to hurt him. The intensity of his feelings shocked him.

"I'm sure you do." August de Fortunato, on the other hand, took his counterpart's threat for granted. How many times had others said much the same? How evil could a man be? "You'll just have to restrain yourself, harbinger . . . or is it really Dutchman you prefer to be called?" When the cloaked figure did not respond, de Fortunato shrugged. "Dutchman is what the others call you, so that will do for now."

Mention of others reminded him of the reason that he and Maia had risked coming here in the first place. Philo and the jester were still prisoners and now he had also lost Maia. *No matter what I do, I fail. I can only bring forth death and destruction, never life and success.*

"I have a simple offer to make, Dutchman. Maia's life for your ship."

Still caught up in his thoughts, he did not at first understand what de Fortunato desired of him. "You want what?"

"Your ship, mariner. I want control of your ship. Take me to it, show me how it works, and when I'm satisfied that you've been forthcoming, I'll lead you to Maia."

Dutchman could not help but laugh. Of all the things for Maia's father to desire . . . he wanted the *Despair*.

"What the devil's so funny? My daughter won't find things so humorous if I let the Roschach have its way. It would like nothing more than to rip her apart. They live for that. Disgusting creatures, but for once I've found one useful. Now tell me what's so funny that you might risk lovely Maia's life?"

Dutchman sobered instantly. He stared intently at de Fortunato, but even his starlit eyes did not disconcert the renegade. "I cannot give you what I do not have. You ask the impossible, August de Fortunato."

Now the traitorous refugee grew angry. "What do you mean? It's your ship, mariner. You are its captain. Don't play games with me! The Roschach is an impatient sort. It'll start playing with her before very long unless I command it not to."

"The *Despair* is not mine to give. She is her own creature, de Fortunato. She does as she wills, even where I am concerned."

"That's not exactly the way the bird played it, but I didn't believe him, either." Nonetheless, the renegade paused to think.

Dutchman too was thinking. August de Fortunato had him where he wanted him and the wanderer had nothing to offer. If de Fortunato decided that he had nothing further to gain from either his daughter or her companions, what would the foul man do?

"I'm going to give you one chance, Dutchman. One chance and then my daughter plays with the Roschach. You will take me to the ship and you will show me how it works; and if you fail to do this . . ." he shrugged again, "she dies."

He had no choice. "Very well. I will take you to her, August de Fortunato."

De Fortunato looked beyond him, his gaze drifting up to the citadel of his ally. "Time is running short, Dutchman. You'd better not be stalling."

That was exactly what he was doing, but what alternative was there? Maia's insane father was too vicious and too powerful a creature for him to take on while she was a prisoner. Dutchman was strong, probably strong enough, and could not die by de Fortunato's hand . . . so he supposed . . . but any delay might mean Maia's death. He had his doubts that she would be reborn on the next variant. What de Fortunato threatened was *permanent*.

"The ship may be found this way." Dutchman pointed westward. He needed time to think. There had to be something that he could do to force Maia's release.

Stepping to one side, August de Fortunato indicated that Dutchman should pass him. "You will lead, of course."

"As you wish." He walked past the renegade, who, up close, definitely looked taller and older than he had the first time they had met. De Fortunato was nearly adult now. Aging was no improvement. If anything, the cruelty inherent in the man had grown more obvious, more defined, in his features.

"I trust this won't be a *long* walk, harbinger. I get tired easily and might accidentally forget to remind the inkblot not to touch my little girl. That *would* be a tragedy."

Dutchman could no longer help himself. He turned to his unwelcome partner and snapped, "It would also mean *your* death, August de Fortunato."

The youthful man frowned. "Get mov—"

His eyes widened as he looked past the wanderer. Dutchman followed his gaze.

A Roschach that had seemingly blossomed from the street blocked their path. Judging from de Fortunato's reaction, it was not the one he had turned. This creature obviously still obeyed the Darkling.

"It's all right!" shouted the renegade. "I have things in hand. You are not needed. You may return."

Not only did the creature ignore him, but a second joined it, rising from cracks in the street. The pair eyed the two men as if deciding which they would eat first. Some of de Fortunato's reserve suddenly faded. He clamped his mouth shut. Then, visibly steeling himself, he muttered to Dutchman, "Move on. Remember Maia. Kill them if you have to."

He could feel the renegade summoning up strength as they moved toward the Roschach. Dutchman knew that he would have to fight beside Maia's father, much as it disgusted him. He could do nothing yet for either Philo or Gilbrin, but as long as he cooperated with August de Fortunato, there was the hope that Maia could be rescued.

From the side of a building, another Roschach lowered itself. Unlike the others, this one took an active part in the situation. "Manling, manling, the master's abode is behind you, is behind you."

"Spare me news I already know, you idiot! This one has information that will be important to your master and I intend to procure it for him before this prisoner is turned over. Now move aside! We've got little time."

"Master should know, master should know."

De Fortunato looked ready to explode. He glanced at the tall figure at his side. "You seem to like hunting these things. I leave the two in front to you. I'll take the talker."

Dutchman had doubts concerning the renegade's decision. There was more to this situation than simply the three Roschach now visible. "You would do well to consider this longer, August de Fortunato. You would—"

"I don't need your advice, mariner, only your ship. Recall my daughter's precarious situation." He stiffened, preparing to attack. "The two are yours. You'll deal with them or else."

Dutchman slowly nodded, knowing that he had no choice.

"You are dismissed!" de Fortunato called out. "I'll bring the prisoner when I have—"

"That is all right, friend August," said a voice that came from all directions. "We shall have time to deal with the ship soon enough. There is no need to concern yourself with it at the moment."

The renegade swore under his breath. "Say nothing, harbinger, or she will die. Play along."

A brilliant light illuminated the street. Even with so much power shielding their presence from the eyes of the natives, Dutchman found it amazing that no passerby noticed the arrival of what had to be the Darkling.

The black form was outlined in a halo of blinding light. The shadows that surrounded his lower half danced as if with a life of their own. The only feature that Dutchman could make out on the newcomer's face was a single pale eye. This had to be the master of the Roschach, the bane of the Scattered Ones.

Only . . . Dutchman trembled inside . . . only he was also something else. There was a presence about the Darkling, a presence that seemed to scream, so powerful it was. The wanderer had felt it before, but long, long ago. A sense of horror crept over him, making his skin crawl. He wanted to back away.

"You have our gratitude, friend August," continued the Prince of Shadows, unaware of the emotions racing through his quarry. "So good of you to take the initiative and seek out our missing guest on your own. Be assured that you will be properly rewarded."

"I had a suspicion," replied de Fortunato, quickly grasping the proffered straw. "I'd hoped to present you with the complete package, though."

"He will be sufficient for now. Between him and the clockwork one, all I seek will at last be mine."

They continued to talk as if nothing were amiss, which Dutchman could not believe. Could de Fortunato not sense what surrounded the Darkling? Then again, he of all of them should have been most sensitive. Only now, only in the very presence of his captor, could Dutchman feel the horrible, alien force that was a very part of the Prince of Shadows.

It was the same force *he* had once unleashed upon his own world, the same force that had destroyed a thousand and more variants . . . and would soon destroy *this* world as well.

17. BETRAYALS

"You will come and join me in my humble home," the Prince of Shadows told Dutchman. "You will come and we will talk and you will tell me all that I wish to know."

Dutchman shook his head. "I will not. Not for you."

"Oh, dear." The Darkling floated earthward, but not within reach of either of the men. "You should really come. Your two friends will be most anxious to see you and their disappointment will only be outweighed by mine." His tone grew just slightly chill. "It is not good for me to be disappointed. Not for their sakes."

Next to him, August de Fortunato whispered, "Obey. I've got the girl. Remember that."

Maia. Caught up in the terrible discovery of the power surrounding the Darkling, the wanderer had forgotten her predicament. It would do no good to reveal de Fortunato's betrayal to the Darkling, for simply out of fury Maia's father would sacrifice her there and then. Dutchman's only hope for her safety lay in obeying the renegade, which in turn meant obeying the immediate dictates of the black figure hovering above them.

The question was, What could he possibly do to save any of them once he was the Darkling's prisoner?

"I will come with you," he finally announced.

The Darkling steepled his fingers and nodded. "Splendid! I

am so grateful that you could see your way to joining us." He looked beyond the pair to the waiting Roschach. "Bring him along. Be gentle, for he is a guest."

"Gentle Roschach," de Fortunato commented. "That would be a first."

"Accompany them, friend August," added the black figure, perhaps having heard the last comment. "See to it that all goes smoothly. I will go on ahead, the better to prepare a proper welcome for so grand a visitor as this."

"As you desire."

The Prince of Shadows chuckled. "Yes. Always."

The light around the Darkling flared, blinding both men and monsters. When Dutchman's vision recovered, it was to find that the sinister shadow man had vanished.

"Always with the damned entrances and exits." The renegade spat on the floor. "All right. Time to go." He saw the look on the other man's face. "Things haven't changed, harbinger."

The Roschach gathered around them. Dutchman noted that they still seemed as interested in de Fortunato as they were in him. De Fortunato also seemed aware of their interest, but he chose to ignore them, as if they were less than nothing. It was a wonder that his arrogance had not yet gotten him permanently killed.

"I hope you'll enjoy your stay."

Dutchman looked up at the bright light radiating from the top of the skyscraper. Knowing what it was made each step heavy despite the fact that any delay might cause one of the others to suffer. Nothing in his entire cursed existence had frightened him the way the discovery of the Darkling's power had. It brought back every terrible memory of his own tragedy, his own folly.

Yet, here he was now, walking into it, the lives of the others dependent on his decisions and inner fears.

Dutchman almost wished that the *Despair* would come and take him away.

* * *

Gilbrin would never have thought it possible to become bored in captivity, but he was. Never mind that he was the prisoner of a pair of monsters who would, at some point, decide he was no longer worth the trouble to keep alive; he was, quite simply, bored.

It also did not help that he was certain that his fellow prisoner could have freed both of them and did not, for reasons kept hidden in his clockwork head.

He tried his invisible bonds again. The one gave a little, but no more than it had earlier. Every muscle in his body was long past stiffness. Gilbrin wondered whether he would even be able to walk if he did manage to free himself.

Philo stood so still in his transparent cage that at times the Shifter wondered whether the animatron slept or, at the very least, had shut himself down. Their conversation had died not long after the animatron had revealed his shocking ability to break through the barrier. Since then, Philo had simply remained motionless, as if waiting for something to happen. Did he really expect the wanderer to rescue them? It seemed impossible, considering when last Gilbrin had seen Dutchman . . . and Maia. Yet, he could not see the animatron lying about his captain returning. What point would that have served?

Suddenly, the animatron stirred, his parrot head shifting from side to side. His entire demeanor changed, although, of course, his avian visage revealed nothing. Had Philo been a human being, Gilbrin would have sworn that he was tense.

At last Philo appeared to recall his presence. He looked up at Gilbrin. "The captain's come aboard."

Dutchman was here? The Shifter's spirits rose. Maia and the wanderer had come to rescue them after all. There was still hope. He opened his mouth to say something, but stopped when Philo shook his head. For a moment he stared at Philo in confusion . . . until finally the parrot's renewed silence made sense.

Philo's captain was not coming to rescue them. He was coming to join them as a fellow prisoner.

And what about Maia?

"Been waiting long, clown?"

From the light emerged August de Fortunato. There was something in his attitude that piqued Gilbrin's interest. August seemed quite put out about something . . . something very, very important. The renegade was trying to mask his dissatisfaction, but he was failing more with each passing moment. Possibly in order to relieve his tension, he had come to harass Gilbrin.

"Actually, I've been getting a little bored. Haven't got a book to read, have you, August?"

"It's time to stop being bored, buffoon. His highness has something in store for you and the bird here and when he's done, I suspect you won't be of any value to him anymore." De Fortunato walked up to him. Maia's father was older than when last they had talked. He almost looked like his old self . . . or rather, a Hispanic version of himself.

"Must be very stressful working as a toady for the Darkling, August. You're looking older by the minute."

"Your comments are tired and repetitive, just as you are, Gilbrin. Just so you know, we have a visitor. You especially might recognize him, parrot. He used to be your captain." When the animatron did not respond, de Fortunato frowned and turned his attention back to Gilbrin. "Do come along."

The bonds holding the Shifter ceased to be. He dropped to the floor, his face striking the hard surface. The pain almost caused him to black out. His nose throbbed madly and he sensed moisture around it, most likely blood.

"Oh, I'm sorry. I thought you were prepared."

"Damn you, August!" It was a tremendous struggle to rise, but he was not about to give Maia's father the benefit of watching him lie there any longer. As he stood, Gilbrin caught sight of red drops vanishing into the white floor. He gingerly touched his nose. It was not broken, but before long it would be quite swollen.

"You too, bird."

Philo tentatively stepped forward. Gilbrin knew that it was

a ploy. Whether the barrier still existed did not matter to the animatron, but there was no reason for August to know that. The Shifter still did not understand what Philo had in mind, but he liked to think that the animatron had no intention of letting him die.

The two of them stood before the renegade. Gilbrin pondered the chances of success should the pair of them jump de Fortunato, but beyond the traitorous renegade there now materialized five Roschach.

"Just in case you had any ideas," de Fortunato smirked.

With the Roschach flanking them, they followed him into the light. There was no sensation when they passed from one area to another. Gilbrin only knew that one moment they were in their place of confinement and the next they stood in what seemed a much vaster chamber, though it was impossible to see any walls or exits.

Several figures awaited them in the chamber. Most of them were Roschach. The two others were the Darkling himself, floating high above as usual, and, held by a pair of the larger protean monsters, the wanderer Dutchman. The exile was hatless and very worn. He was also very alone. Gilbrin saw no sign of Maia.

"Make no comment about my darling daughter," whispered de Fortunato. "For her sake, if not yours."

So August is playing some game and Maia is his pawn. He had a fair suspicion of what that game entailed. If August held his daughter a secret prisoner, it was because he expected her to be of some value to Dutchman and the others. If the renegade had also listened in when Philo had spoken about the ship, then it stood to reason that he, like the Darkling, would desire the ghostly craft. *Dangerous play, August. You could get yourself killed at last.* Still, it behooved Gilbrin to say nothing for now. De Fortunato could not harm Maia at the moment and if anyone knew how to escape her father, it was her.

"And now we are all here," announced the Prince of Shadows. The pale eye surveyed the group. "But I do not see one member of the group. Where is your daughter, friend August?"

"Evading for now. Don't you worry, I'll find her."

"Indeed." The Darkling floated down until he was no more than a yard off the level on which the others stood. The shadows danced almost merrily, an image that might have been humorous to Gilbrin if he had not understood why their master was so pleased. The Darkling had both Dutchman and Philo. That meant that the ghost ship would certainly be his before long.

What would they all do then?

"I had never thought you more than legend until recently, Dutchman. I am pleased and charmed that you are otherwise. You and I, we are similar in many ways, I think. This could be a long and profitable friendship if you are cooperative."

To Gilbrin, the Darkling had a tendency to sound as if he had stepped out of an old Flash Gordon serial, but he knew by now that the regal yet companionable tone thinly masked not threats but *promises* of what would happen to those who did not do what the Prince of Shadows desired. What was it like to be under the iron rule of the Darkling? Much, he supposed, like what they were experiencing now.

Dutchman did not respond to the shadow master, but he appeared slightly unnerved by him. That worried Gilbrin. If the legendary wanderer could not defeat the Darkling, then what hope was there?

"You have a ship, friend Dutchman, a ship that could resolve for me a problem that has made my existence precarious since I was forced to depart my own Earth. You have no idea the trials I have endured, ever seeking to flee the destruction behind." With one hand, the Darkling indicated Gilbrin. "I cannot foresee very clearly either the time of destruction or the window of opportunity. The first several times, it was more by chance than anything else that I survived. The ones like him, however . . ." again he indicated Gilbrin, "have given me a fairly accurate method by which I can know when to depart. Unfortunately, in the process of discovering the information I need, I have been forced to do things I would rather not in the name of my survival . . . and I will be forced to do them again if no other choice is left to me on this variant." Now he steepled his hands, perhaps attempting . . . and failing miserably in the Shifter's eyes . . . to look regretful. "With your guidance and your vessel, however, I see a way of putting to an end the terrible things I have done. No lives may be returned, but at least no more lives need be lost."

"I can give you nothing."

The short, simple statement did not sit well with the Darkling. The pale eye narrowed and he shook his head. "I think you fail to appreciate what occurs here. I will be forced to hurt or even kill others; and while you may not be able to die, I will be forced to teach you what I know of pain. Rest assured, I have had countless worlds on which to study thoroughly that subject."

Dutchman was equally adamant. "Whatever you do, I can give you nothing. It is beyond my power. You would not want her if you knew her, Prince of Shadows. She does not obey, she commands."

"All obey me in the end, friend Dutchman. Even you. Even the ship. Even friend August, if he desires to see his life extend beyond the next minute."

De Fortunato straightened. "What the devil's that supposed to mean?"

Before the Darkling could explain, Philo stepped forward. Everyone stared in surprise, most of all Dutchman. Gilbrin suspected what the animatron was about to do, but could think of no way to stop him.

"He tells the truth, Darkling Prince. The captain can't give you the ship. Only I can do that deed. She'll come to me and no one else."

"Philo—"

One parrot eye focused on the cloaked figure. "No, captain. I'll not see anyone harmed. If he'll give his word that we'll be let go, I'll see to it that he gets the ship."

"Of course I will give you my word, my clockwork friend. Give me the ship and nothing will become of you."

Philo acknowledged the words with a dip of his head. "Then you'll have it, my lord. You'll have everything that has long been due you."

Gilbrin's anxiety increased. *When's the rug to be pulled out from under him, Philo? When's the punch line of your joke?*

The animatron, however, did nothing to indicate that he was anything but earnest. He looked once more at Dutchman, then strode toward the Darkling. Even August de Fortunato was taken aback by his cooperation.

The Prince of Shadows was hardly naive, though. He eyed the approaching animatron with caution and when he evidently felt that Philo was near enough, he raised a hand, halting the bird man's trek. "That will do." The shadows swayed in the animatron's direction, a definite promise of what would happen if Philo did other than he had promised. "You have offered me much, avian. I have offered much in return. Now tell me how you hope to fulfill your end of the bargain.'

"Very simple, lord. I just have to call her. The lady'll come for me. We're one and the same in some ways."

Gilbrin's brow furrowed. Dutchman looked equally confused, not to mention still uneasy whenever the Darkling moved or spoke. The Shifter wondered again about that. Dutchman acted as if he recognized their captor, or at least something *about* him, and feared whatever it was he recognized.

"One and the same." The Darkling stroked his chin. His pale eye studied the animatron, then its captain. "One and the same, he says, friend Dutchman. What do you say?"

"You do not want her, Darkling, believe me. Even if he can call her . . ." here the wanderer stared again at his traitorous first mate, no doubt trying to understand, "she will not obey you. Believe me."

His words were having the opposite effect of what he wanted; even Gilbrin could see that.

"You will call your vessel," the Darkling commanded

Philo. "You will call your vessel and she had better come, else your human companions will have to suffer, I am afraid."

"She will come, lord."

"And when she does," the shadow master continued, as if Philo had not spoken, "you and your captain will show me how to control her. You will show me everything. Only then will I grant you and the rest my forgiveness."

He'll kill us is what he'll do. Gilbrin must have moved without realizing it, for the nearest Roschach struck him with one clawlike hand. It was enough to send him down on one knee.

"That will do," the Darkling called. "He must remain well, for now." To the animatron, he added, "You will commence."

Philo cocked his parrot head and looked around, his eye momentarily fixing on the rising, still sore Gilbrin. Then he looked away, but Gilbrin was again struck by the notion that there was more behind that eye than mere gearwork.

"One thing must be done first, lord. I must have open access to the sky. The sky is her sea, her domain. I can't reach the lady if I can't see the sky."

"It's a trick!" snarled August de Fortunato.

"Perhaps," the Prince of Shadows agreed. "You would know about tricks, would you not, friend August? I leave it to you to watch him closely, then. If there is a trick, you will see it, won't you?"

He knows about Maia. Gilbrin was certain of that. The Darkling was toying with the renegade.

De Fortunato quieted. The Darkling watched him a moment longer, than nodded to Philo. "You may begin."

"Philo!" Dutchman moved forward. The pair of Roschach holding him might as well have been made of wind, so futile was their attempt to keep him under control. "You cannot—"

"You are not being a civil guest, friend Dutchman. Remember the female. Her safety is your concern, isn't that correct . . . my friend August?" De Fortunato's jaw fell, but he did not have time to protest. The Darkling snapped his fingers.

A massive Roschach emerged from the light. In its arms was Maia, still unconscious. The Roschach bowed toward the black figure above, then offered up the woman to him.

"They are stupid but loyal, are they not, friend August?" The Prince of Shadows cocked his head as he eyed de Fortunato. Gilbrin had expected to enjoy watching the renegade's discomfort, but for some reason he did not.

"I was keeping her hidden in order to ensure the captain's cooperation."

"Of course you were. Just as you tried to turn one of my loyal Roschach from me for my own good."

In the creature's arms, Maia stirred. Gilbrin wanted to go to her and he saw that Dutchman wanted to do the same, but the monsters kept a wary watch on them.

August de Fortunato clearly had no other excuse to give the Darkling. He glanced from prisoner to prisoner, then back at the shadow master. "I was merely trying to make sure that the thing would follow my orders for once. Your insipid inkblots never obey completely; that's why it took so long to capture these others."

The Darkling drifted closer to the others, but his shadows were focused on the renegade. "There is something you should know about my Roschach, friend August. Something I am surprised you never understood." He looked around.

The others, Gilbrin included, followed his sweeping gaze. To the Shifter's mounting horror, they were surrounded by a legion of Roschach . . . more of the monsters than he imagined any Scattered One had ever seen. All shapes and sizes, of course, and each more gruesome than the next, as far as he was concerned.

"Tell him, my children. Tell him why you shall always be loyal to me."

As one the Roschach spoke, but this time the familiar, hissing voices were replaced by one equally familiar yet even more frightening in its own way, for it was the voice of their master, the Darkling. "We are extensions of our master. We are the Darkling. We are the Prince of Shadows. We will ever be loyal to ourselves, friend August."

De Fortunato's expression was not one of surprise or fear as Gilbrin would have expected. No, instead Maia's father was furious. "You've played me for a fool all this time with these things! If they're you, why can't they follow simple orders?"

"When I found them, they were ordinary creatures, destructive but simple. Living beyond what we laughingly refer to as reality. It was no difficult task to take them in, incorporate them into my shadows. They were granted a part of my great intellect, as much as they could handle. They were limited, but they know well what I desire and they do it or else I consign them back to the shadows forever." The pale eye did not seem so dead now. Rather, it looked more like the instrument of death for whomever it focused on. In this case, August de Fortunato. "Something, I might add, that also has applied to you, friend August."

The shadows darted out, snaring the renegade. De Fortunato cursed and tried to strike back, but little happened. Gilbrin sensed something about the shadows. They were not only keeping Maia's father at bay, they were also leeching him of his power.

"Release me, you damned freak! Let me go!"

Maia was awake now, but her Roschach captor held her tightly. The Roschach in general seemed to be enjoying the display, but Maia's expression was unreadable. Gilbrin sympathized with her. *What are you thinking about now, sweet? What are you thinking about now that your father may be getting his just desserts at last? Doesn't quite look like happiness after all.*

"I have been benevolent with you, friend August, granting much and expecting so little in return. Yet you never properly appreciated my gestures of goodwill." The shadows lifted the youthful traitor high, then dropped him. De Fortunato hit the floor hard. The Darkling nodded thoughtfully as Maia's father slowly picked himself up. "And now that goodwill, along with much else, is withdrawn."

"What . . . have you . . . done to . . . me?" August de Fortunato was able to stand, but just barely. He weaved back and forth, reminding Gilbrin of the pendulum of a clock.

"Punished you as I would any recalcitrant servant, friend August. Be grateful I have not done more."

Not only was the renegade now bereft of the power that all Scattered Ones had to some degree, but he was even older. His hair was gray and his build, while still strong, was much more worn in appearance. When he looked up, Maia gasped. It was the same August de Fortunato that both she and the Shifter had known during their first lives.

"You can't do this to me!" He would have flung himself at the Prince of Shadows if one of the Roschach had not seized him. De Fortunato looked into the inhuman visage of the creature, who smiled back hungrily.

"You would do well to mark all of this, avian. I was more than kind to friend August. I will not be so kind to you and yours if you attempt anything other than calling the ship."

"I'll summon it, lord. I know what your word means."

The Darkling nodded approval, evidently having ignored the hint of sarcasm in Philo's words that Gilbrin thought had been there. "Then I suggest that since there will be *no* further interruptions you begin again."

"The sky's still hidden, lord."

"Oh, yes. Do forgive me." Even as the Darkling apologized, a gap formed on one side of the chamber, a gap of darkness where only blinding light had been before. It spread, in seconds revealing a wide, tinted window and what was clearly part of an office. The window extended nearly from the floor to the ceiling and beyond it, outside, was the waning night.

Gilbrin carefully studied what he could of the original building. Did the window seem somewhat distorted, the walls slightly uneven? It was possible that it was his imagination, but neither shaking his head nor blinking dismissed the peculiar structural changes. It reminded him of Tarriqa's house during the distortion. That had been the result of a brief wave of instability, though, forerunner of this world's impending doom. This had to be the result of the Darkling's own destructive power.

For some reason, he could not ignore the similarities.

Philo walked toward the window, raising his arms as he went. He looked much like a supplicant calling to his god. Dutchman still struggled and Maia, too, looked more unnerved than she should have. *She acts like she knows something, too . . . but then, she's been on the cursed vessel and I haven't.*

That might change soon. If the Darkling gained access to the ship, it followed that he might want a few hostages aboard while he forced Dutchman to show him how to control the mysterious vessel.

There has to be something someone can do! Gilbrin tensed. With everyone's attention on the animatron, perhaps he could make use of some trick. Maybe he could at least try to get to the Darkling and . . . and do what?

It doesn't matter, Gilbrin old fool, have to do something to stop—

"Leave it, lad. Do nothing if you want this world to live."

"What?" Gilbrin blurted before realizing that the voice had echoed inside his head. The warning was not repeated, but he was fully aware of who had spoken. Philo. Philo had warned him not to attempt anything. *What by Carim's children are you, you salty bird? You're no toy pirate, if you ever were in the first place!*

He received no reply. That one warning was all Philo intended to give him. He had to trust the animatron, not an easy thing to do at the moment.

The parrot continued to silently implore the night. The Darkling's shadows shifted back and forth, from impatience or nervousness or both. The Roschach picked up on their master's emotions and also grew restless.

"It does not come, friend Philo," the Darkling finally blurted. "You were warned. . . ." The shadows moved, pointing at each of the prisoners . . . until they fixed on Gilbrin. "Bring that one."

"All you had to do was ask—" the Shifter gasped as he was tossed forward from one Roschach to another. The second monster dumped him unceremoniously before the floating figure. The Darkling's shadows seized Gilbrin before he could recover. *Why me? Why always me?*

The Prince of Shadows raised him so that the two were almost but not quite at eye level. Gilbrin's captor spread his hands in what resembled a gesture of regret. "He was warned, friend Gilbrin, was he not? I did indicate that there must be some suffering if he did not deliver unto me the ship."

"Maybe she's busy at the moment. Maybe she'll be on the way in a minute."

"I will miss your droll sense of humor, harlequin. I do apologize, but know that I *will* use you to further my own needs. I trust that will assuage some of your regrets concerning your violent demise."

And men call me *mad!* was all Gilbrin could think before the tendrils circled his throat and, despite their seeming insubstantiality, tightened enough to cut off his air.

"She comes!" Philo called out just as darkness began to seize Gilbrin.

Suddenly he could breathe again. The tendrils lowered him while the gasping refugee still sought to swallow enough air. A Roschach seized his arms, but Gilbrin paid the beast no mind. Air was all that mattered at the moment. Worlds and worlds of air.

"Astounding . . ." whispered the Darkling from somewhere beyond the Shifter's tear-filled vision. Somewhere else, Dutchman uttered words, but Gilbrin could not understand them.

The Shifter's vision cleared. He looked up at where all other eyes were now riveted.

Even though he had seen it briefly before, it was still terrifying.

The ship was more complete than Gilbrin recalled it having

been the last time. The sails billowed, full with a wind he doubted anything or anyone else felt. Dutchman's vessel did not exactly glow, but it was always visible, even when not outlined by the moon.

It was fast approaching the side of the building. If it kept at its present rate, it would crash through the window . . . and several floors . . . in only a few more minutes.

"Amazing . . ." the Darkling added.

"As promised, lord," Philo called. "She comes for you. She awaits you."

"Why, Philo?" Gilbrin heard Dutchman utter. "And why *him?*"

"Away," the Darkling commanded the animatron. When Philo had moved aside, the Prince of Shadows floated to the window, drinking in the sight of the eerie vessel coming closer and closer. "It is fantastic!"

A pair of Roschach had seized Philo the moment he had stepped away, but he seemed not to care. He looked at Gilbrin and, if the Shifter could believe his eyes, *winked.*

"I have been told it travels backward and forward through the time line of a variant," the shadow master called.

"Aye, lord, with ease."

The Darkling looked over his shoulder at the animatron. "I intend to bring you, your captain, and the rest aboard with us, avian. Recall what I have promised if you think to betray my trust."

"The ship will be yours. You will become her captain."

But the last captain couldn't command it to do anything. Dutchman had made that quite clear to Gilbrin and the others. It was the ship that commanded. Those aboard were simply helpless passengers.

Helpless passengers?

"The Darkling?" Gilbrin whispered. *Could it be?*

The Darkling watched with growing pleasure the coming of the great ship. The image of a sailing ship floating through the heavens was fantastic enough, but to know that the power behind it would soon be added to his own thrilled him as nothing had since before he had fled a world, a *universe,* that he himself had caused to die.

They would have had the nerve to try to bring me down, to topple me from the throne that I had rightfully seized! I build them a glorious empire over which I will rule and that is the gratitude I receive! He would build a new empire grander than the last . . . no, he could build a *thousand* empires! *How marvelous!* Even if it could not prevent this world from perishing, the ship would give him the ability to travel backward in time. He could go to the beginning of this variant, mold the rising human race to fit his vision, then rule over them until the End came. Then, with the harbinger's ship, the Darkling could journey on to the *next* variant and start anew.

I can craft empire after empire, each different, each magnificent in its own individual way! An eternity of glories! The wanderer had lived through countless universes himself. To the Darkling, that meant that one other thing the ship had to offer was an immortality of sorts. Thanks to his power and the field he had formed around him, his life span was already incredibly long. However, it was not necessarily infinite. What the ship offered would do quite well.

"Quite well . . ." he whispered.

Already the Prince of Shadows felt as if he and the ship were old, familiar friends. He would treat her well for what she would give him in return. *If you are everything I think you are, I'd make you my queen if you were a woman!* He chuckled at the image that conjured up.

The ship *did* seem familiar. The shadow master studied it carefully, his eye, which saw more than simply the surface, taking in every detail. He felt an aura around it. That was what was so familiar. It was similar in some ways to his own, but also different.

"Now what—?" he muttered. It annoyed him that some minute misgiving was disturbing an otherwise exquisite moment. The shadows moved in sudden agitation, disturbing him further, for they shifted of their own volition.

He focused the special eye on the ship again. Familiarity. What about the ship was so familiar? Certainly not the design. The aura was familiar, but that was only a part of it.

Then the Darkling noticed subtle differences. The ship looked rounder, a little more squat in the hull. Now it reminded him somewhat of a design more akin to his world. Now it—

His eyes narrowed. The Darkling had to remind himself that this was more than simply a craft. He concentrated, looking deeper, searching for the very core of the thing in much the way his devices searched for the core within each of the Scattered Ones.

Nothing at first. The ship was what it appeared to be. Perhaps he was just anxious. Yes, perhaps . . .

Then the secret was revealed. No . . . it was *given* to him . . . by the ship herself.

He backed away, feeling terror for the first time since he had fled from his dying empire. The shadows brought him swiftly away from the window, but the Darkling knew that the ship was still coming.

Turning madly to the right, he saw the clockwork man calmly standing there as if all was as it should have been. Not far from him was the wanderer, whose expression was anything but calm. They knew. They *had* to know. It had to have been a trick all this time. . . .

"Send it back!" he commanded the animatron. "Send it back!"

"But, lord—"

The creature was clearly stalling, but harming him might destroy the only method by which the ship could be turned. There were, however, other courses the Darkling could take. He studied the prisoners, finally choosing the one best suited for an example because he was the least important to the Darkling.

"That one," he said, choosing again the harlequin. The Roschach dragged him forward. To the clockwork man, the

Prince of Shadows commanded, "Send it back or I will be forced to permanently kill this little creature."

"She can't be turned once she's set on course, lord."

"Then he will die!" The animatron *had* to be lying. The Darkling looked over his shoulder at the ship. The ghostly vessel nearly filled the window.

Philo looked at the struggling little man. At first, the Prince of Shadows expected him to refuse again, but at last the avian replied, "Aye, lord, I will."

"Be quick about it."

Returning to the window, the animatron faced the approaching ship. The Darkling's gaze fixed on the horrific creation, a thing he had not thought could exist. *So they had sought a final vengeance, the fools. . . .*

Philo raised his arms, once more seeming to implore.

The ship began to slow. Within his black field, the Darkling smiled in more than a little relief. The crisis was averted.

"It's done." The animatron turned, bowed . . . and *leaped* for him. A powerful force swelled within the flying form. The same power that coursed through the ship now also coursed through the mechanical man. It had always been there, but the shadow master had not looked for it.

Only then did the Prince of Shadows realize that the avian had spoken the pure truth. The ship and its first mate were not simply linked together . . . they were one and the same creature.

And now that creature was nearly upon him.

18. RAMMING SPEED

Maia and the rest were stunned to see Philo falling upon the Darkling. Like the others, she had wondered about the animatron's betrayal and while it was a relief to know that he had been no traitor, she wondered whether Philo had any hope of defeating the Prince of Shadows.

Certainly it did not initially strike her so. The animatron landed atop his prey, but the Darkling's shadows, ever there for their master, seized Philo's limbs and torso. A few even wrapped themselves around his neck, possibly trying to remove his head.

But why doesn't Dutchman help him? The answer dawned on her the moment she looked at the wanderer. It was not so much the Roschach who held him back as it was himself. Even that was not the complete answer. The truth was, it was Maia who held him back. She could see it in his gaze when his starlit eyes met hers. Dutchman feared for her safety, even if in the end they would all likely die anyway, if the Prince of Shadows won.

Maia could think of no way to force the wanderer to act. She was held tight and her strength was not enough, not yet. The Roschach's sting still affected her.

Then the last voice she would have expected to hear echoed in her head.

You've but one chance, daughter dear. You must trust in me.

She glared at her father, who seemed as helpless as she was. Maia reminded him of that fact.

My power is gone, but my ability to link is not. I am the strongest will of us, Maia. Convince the others to link through you into me, if that makes you more comfortable. If you then focus their strength through me, we can deal with the Roschach and their treacherous master!

Deal with the devil? Maia thought. She wanted to tell her father what he could do with his plan, but what he offered was viable. He did have the will to utilize their combined power if they linked. If anyone was capable of succeeding, it was August de Fortunato.

Reluctantly, she quickly related the plan to Gilbrin, who was, of course, completely against it. When she demanded to know if he could do what August suggested, the Shifter finally acquiesced.

That left only Dutchman. Surprisingly, his only concern was whether it would harm her. When she assured him that August could do nothing to her if he hoped to accomplish his plan, he also agreed.

The world of thought was a swift one. The entire plan had been introduced, argued over, and agreed upon in only two or three heartbeats.

That was, however, almost all the time Philo had left. Surprising he might be, he was still not enough by himself to threaten the Darkling. The shadow master had him raised high over his head and the only thing that had kept him from being systematically dismantled was that the ship still floated beyond the window, demanding the black figure's attention. Maia wondered why the Darkling had not resealed the opening he had made in his sanctum.

Because he can't, came August's impatient voice in her head. *Either the ship or the bird is responsible. Now concentrate! Link! Think for your life, my precious child!*

His foul use of what should have been a term of endearment gave her the will she needed to make the link work. August was a thing of hatred, but he was a known monster. Not like the Darkling. They had first to deal with the Darkling . . . only then could she finally settle with her father, who no longer had the power with which to work his evil. When the time came, he would be the helpless one.

Maia looked forward to that.

But first the Darkling's creatures . . .

She forged the link with Gil, then Dutchman . . . and, at last, her father.

His pleasure touched each of the others, disgusting them all with its intensity. "We can begin."

The touch was obscene, evil. It so repelled Dutchman that he nearly broke the link. Only two things prevented him. The first was Maia, who wanted this of him. The second was the battle commencing just above them, a battle Philo was sure to lose.

He had never thought of the animatron as being so like a living creature. Oh, he had contemplated it, but in his mind any trace of humanity had been in his own imagination and nowhere else. Yet . . . now he knew that the mechanical man was as real as he was.

If not for his fear for Maia's life, he would have physically joined the fray. However, August de Fortunato's plan offered an opportunity to deal with their Roschach guards, especially the one holding the still-groggy Maia. It also promised certain death if the renegade's will proved inadequate. What de Fortunato planned was difficult; Dutchman wondered whether he himself would have had will enough.

Be ready! The words echoed in his head. Dutchman concentrated.

"I have been patient!" roared the Darkling to his adversary. "I have been forgiving! No more!"

He threw Philo against the window. Surprisingly, the window held. The animatron shook violently as the shadows drew him up again.

August struck.

As one, the Roschach hissed in pain. Many doubled over.

Dutchman felt the grips of his guards grow slack as they fought to survive. Their very forms shook madly, as if they were caught up in one of the distortions such as always preceded the End of the world.

"It's working!" Gilbrin called. Whether he spoke out loud or in Dutchman's head, the wanderer could not say.

"Silence!" returned de Fortunato. "Concentrate!"

The Roschach retreated, moving as if pulled by a single set of strings. With each passing breath, the inky monsters shook more violently. Some of the smaller ones appeared to be losing substance.

Dutchman began to understand. The Roschach were not creatures of reality. They should not have been able to survive and thrive as they did. It was the Darkling whose power granted them those abilities, but August de Fortunato, who knew them better than anyone except their master, must have realized that there were limits. That was why they dissolved on death. When the power imbued in them by the Darkling was disrupted or released, they could not maintain their existence. They literally ceased to be. It was something he should have realized long ago. He had certainly witnessed their demises often enough.

Then the Roschach that had held Maia struggled forward again, a murderous glare in its striped eyes. Maia, however, had her back turned to the creature.

Dutchman tried to warn her through the link, but the only mind that he sensed was that of August de Fortunato, who was intent on the task at hand. He tried again, but received only a swift warning from Maia's father to cease his efforts.

The Roschach was slow, de Fortunato's assault affecting it as much as it did the other monsters, but this one was larger and stronger. One massive, clawed hand reached forth for Maia, but came up short. The dark-haired woman, intent not only on aiding in the attack but also still recovering from her earlier captivity, did not even notice her narrow escape.

Above them, the Darkling again raised Philo high. With

even more force, he threw the animatron against the window a second time. The window shattered, sending a rain of glass down to the pavement far below. Dutchman feared for any locals who might have been below, but unfortunately, their deaths were something he could not prevent. They would die anyway and much more horribly when this variant passed. But there was still hope to save those closest to him.

Pulling Philo close, the Prince of Shadows eyed the damaged mechanism. The arms and one leg hung loose; the parrot head seemed frozen to one side.

"No more!" snapped the dark figure. "No more. You and she are one, are you, avian? Then she will feel your pain, your death, if she does not retreat. Send her away."

Philo said nothing. Perhaps he could no longer speak.

On Dutchman's other side, the Roschach still loomed over an unaware Maia. It had lost some mass and seemed in pain, but it continued to seek after its former charge.

Still August de Fortunato would not let Dutchman's warning filter through to his daughter. He cared for nothing but destroying the creatures of his onetime ally. He would likely succeed . . . but by then the Roschach would have Maia.

No longer able to stand and watch the horrible tableau, Dutchman broke his portion of the link and threw himself toward the woman and the beast, shouting a warning as he moved.

The Roschach paused as Maia slowly shook herself out of the link. Fortunately, the Roschach turned away from her, having recognized Dutchman as the greater threat.

He had fought the creatures in many forms, watched them die in many more. Under the circumstances of the past, the Roschach should have been little trouble for him, but this one was stronger than most and Dutchman himself was weaker. August de Fortunato, having lost his own power, had borrowed most liberally from his supposed allies. It would take Dutchman some time to recover and he did not have that time.

"Boatman, Boatman," hissed the monstrosity. Two new

limbs ending in pincers formed. "You should not interfere, you should not interfere."

A pincer and a clawed hand reached for Dutchman, catching one arm and leg. An electrical shock ran through the exile's form. He roared in pain. This was not a typical Roschach; Dutchman thought he felt de Fortunato's hand in this one. The renegade had said that he had turned one of the Darkling's monsters, but what he had failed to mention was that he had made some fiendish adaptations. Now those might come back to haunt them all if Dutchman could not defeat the creature.

"No!" From behind him burst Maia, who thrust a hand into the very visage of the Roschach. Startled by her audacity, it reacted too slowly. Her hand struck hard, outstretched fingers first. There was some power behind the blow, but most of the attack was physical. Such an assault would certainly have failed, though, if not for the target she had chosen.

One of the monster's eyes.

Her hand went through the striped orb with little resistance. The shock coursing through Dutchman's body ceased, but then his ears were assailed by a high-pitched squealing. The Roschach released its hold on him, all four appendages now turning back to deal with the woman who had so terribly wounded it.

Dutchman seized one of the limbs and twisted the creature back. If it wanted to maintain its ability to attack, it had to remain solid. The exile gritted his teeth and concentrated. What should have been easy now demanded heavily from his worn reserves, but this Roschach had tried to harm Maia and he could not stand for that.

What it had done to him, Dutchman returned a thousand times stronger.

The Roschach cried out again. Dutchman wanted to cover his ears, but could not if he wanted to complete his task. The murky creature struggled to shake him free, but his grip was tight. One of the pincers struck him in the leg, causing him to cry out. He could not bother with the wound, though. If his concentration slipped at all, the Roschach might recover.

It shook him again and again, trying to throw him off. Then, with a renewed squeal . . . it crumbled. The change was so sudden that Dutchman fell, striking the floor on his wound, which caused him to black out.

When he opened his eyes again, no more than a second or two later, all that remained of the Roschach was a quick decaying pile of black ash.

Maia was at his side. "Are you all right? Can you stand?"

"Inconsequential question," interjected a much too familiar voice. "His health . . . and yours . . . are no longer of importance."

Both of them were lifted off the floor as if they weighed nothing.

They were turned toward the Darkling, who no longer wore even a veneer of patience. To one side, his shadows still held the battered form of Philo. The animatron did not move, did not even twitch. One arm was barely still connected. A booted foot was missing. Some of the interior workings hung out from various points where the shell had been cracked open like an egg.

The gap left by the shattered window remained open, but it was much smaller than it had been prior to Philo's attack. Only half of the broken pane was still visible, but neither the ceiling nor the floor of the office could be seen. From where the Darkling held him, Dutchman could see that the gap was gradually shrinking. Their captor was regaining control.

"Your pitiful plan has all gone for nought, angel of death!" snapped the black figure. "I am immune to her within my domain! Did you think I would so readily give myself to her? All those years of hunting for me and in the end your tricks"—he brought Philo closer to Dutchman; one parrot eye stared uselessly at the wanderer—"including this thing, added up to nothing."

A pair of shadows snaked around Dutchman's throat. Two more did the same to Maia. One shadow reached out and explored the wound in his leg, causing the exile to twitch in agony.

"This ruin offends my eye." With a careless wave of his hand, the Darkling had his shadows toss down the broken form of the animatron. It crashed next to the still body of Gilbrin.

Dutchman glanced at Maia, but she had not seen the body of her former lover. It was impossible to say at this point whether the wiry young man was alive or dead; Dutchman did not have the concentration to find out. He did not know what had happened to the Shifter, but August de Fortunato was missing. The only others in sight were about a dozen weakened Roschach. At least that was some accomplishment, though the Darkling likely had access to more of the creatures when he needed them.

"Who are you, really?" the Prince of Shadows demanded of him. "Which one of them sent you? You would volunteer to follow me from eternity to eternity simply for your folly of revenge? Such dedication! Had you been so loyal to me, I would have rewarded you well."

"I don't understand a thing you say—" Dutchman would have protested more, but the shadows tightened, choking him. He struggled uselessly. The Darkling could spend the next hour strangling him, and even then he would not die. The same forces that prevented Dutchman from killing himself by slitting his wrists or leaping to his death also prevented him from drowning or suffocating. Deprived of air, he simply suffered until the pressure eased. Knowing this was no great comfort.

"I know what she is," the Darkling went on. "I know her." He indicated his sanctum with a grand sweep of one arm. "She is similar, very similar, to my little kingdom, but her purpose is more sinister. You have fashioned her to be a prison, have you not? You have fashioned her to be *my* prison, but she will remain empty."

Only a sliver remained of the broken window. The *Despair* was still there, however, seemingly trying to squeeze through what remained of the opening. For the first time, Dutchman felt a hunger emanating from the ghost ship that he had sailed with for so long, a hunger to reach a goal that had evaded her world after world, universe after universe.

She has always sought him . . . but then why me? Why choose me to be in his place?

The *Despair* did not answer him and he doubted that the Darkling could.

The last trace of the gap vanished. The brilliantly illuminated sanctum of the Prince of Shadows once more completely surrounded them. Yet, Dutchman sensed the ship still waiting outside, waiting with the patience of one who knows that her prey is trapped within.

Tendrils pulled him nearly face to face with the Darkling. The shadow master glared at him with the one visible eye. "Send her away or I will be forced to deal harshly with the woman."

"I cannot—"

"You are her captain! You are her master! You have to be!"

"I am her victim!" Dutchman snapped back, tired of hearing something over and over that he knew so well was untrue. "I am nothing to her!"

"We shall see. . . . " The shadow thrust the wanderer back against an invisible wall and kept him pinned there. The Darkling looked to one side. A pinpoint of black light pierced the brightness. Slowly it began to sweep toward Dutchman. "The device from which this beam originates is the one I utilize to ferret out the secrets of the Scattered Ones. It reads both the mind and . . . shall we call it the soul? . . . and translates the data into information for my instant perusal. I most often use it to discover when it is time to depart for the next world. A force builds within them, did you know that? It builds until it can no longer be contained and then it propels their essence on. Always just prior to Armageddon." The Darkling gestured at the oncoming beam. "The last to face the light was quite cooperative. A good, honest man. Rees was what he called himself. He sacrificed himself well for the greater good. Let his example guide you now."

Here truly is the face of madness, Dutchman thought. The black light continued toward him, only a few feet away at this point. Dutchman struggled against the tendrils, but the moment he did, the Prince of Shadows swung Maia into view. She was clearly having trouble breathing.

Dutchman ceased struggling.

The black light struck him squarely in the chest. Incredible pain coursed through him. He had no recourse this time but to scream.

"Show me who you are! Show me *what* you are! Reveal to me the truth and tell me how the cursed monster may be turned!"

Through the pain, Dutchman still managed to wonder how his insane captor expected him to answer questions at such a time, especially questions to which he did not know the answers.

Then, images started to flow through his mind. The pain actually encouraged their coming, creating an endless stream of memories and thoughts detailing the life of the man who would cause the deaths of world after world. He saw the story he had related to Maia, but with more detail. Memories long buried resurfaced, making him cry from something more than the agony caused by the Darkling's device. Once more his Maia was lost to him because of his impetuousness, his overconfidence. Once more his Maia died with the rest. . . .

Mariya . . . not Maia, one part of his mind corrected. It was odd, though. Each memory of his lost love had been replaced by the image of the woman who had sailed with him for a time on the *Despair* and had then journeyed beside him to the sanctum of the shadowy beast. Each time he tried to summon up the vision of Mariya, it was Maia who materialized.

Once more the arrogant voice of the Darkling broke through both pain and memory. "Incredible! You actually *are* nothing but a pawn! She used you as the only creature who bore some strong mark of my passing . . . I do not even recall your watery world . . . but I thank you for acting as a beacon for me, it seems. Sooner or later I would have broken through, but you made it so much easier."

Broken through? He did not understand. The pain was too great now. Even the memories were seared away one by one. . . .

Without warning, the pain suddenly eased. Dutchman opened his eyes, eyes he did not even recall closing, and found himself staring not at the darkened face of his captor, but at . . . at *what*?

It was and was not light. It moved, touching him here and there, then focusing on his head. Thoughts came unbidden, his thoughts but guided by another.

Again he relived his experiments. This time, however, new knowledge came to the forefront. The energy that had leaked into his world had not leaked at all; it had been driven forward, a wedge of sorts. The force behind that wedge was a malevolent intelligence that sought only to live on after its own universe had collapsed . . . by its own doing. It cared not what existed on the other side, only that the other side meant its continued life.

Dutchman saw now that his experiments had, in their own way, delayed as much as aided that intelligence. He had opened wider the path, true, but his manipulation of those first forces had drained them of their true strength. Had he worked longer with them, he might have actually weakened their master enough that the tear would have sealed completely, saving his Earth and ending a foul existence that had no right to demand new worlds to conquer.

The realization nearly overwhelmed Dutchman.

He had not caused the deaths. That had been the doing of another.

The malevolent intelligence, the thing that refused to die with the universe it had destroyed . . . was the Darkling.

Dutchman's had not been the first world to perish nor even the second. There had been others between his and that of the Prince of Shadows. The Darkling cared nothing about them save that they gave him a new point from which to search for the next route, the next escape. Life, the multiverse . . . nothing was sacred to him except himself. The forces he had gathered around him gave him great power, but they were destructive, contrary to the laws that held things together. The longer they infested a world, a universe, the more they caused instability in it. The Roschach were a part of that same force. The Darkling had drawn it from beyond the bounds of what was considered reality and brought it . . . and them . . . to where they did not belong.

The light that was not light retreated from Dutchman. The pain began to return. It could not release him from that, not yet, but he felt some sorrow, some regret for things that had been done. It had been commanded to fulfill a mission and it could not disobey those commands, however long ago given. The cost of failure had already been too great.

Just before the full intensity of the pain washed over Dutchman again, he knew that what had spoken to him was the *Despair*.

She was a prison, a prison sent by those who had sought to bring down a tyrant so foul that, even knowing their world was dying, they had sought to save others from his touch. However, she had been launched late, sent in desperation more than anything else. She had followed the trail knowing that she was incomplete, possibly insufficient for the task.

Tears of agony made his vision blurry, but he blinked them away. Dutchman still wanted to scream, but he would not give the Darkling the satisfaction.

The pale eye widened, then narrowed. The Darkling was clearly not satisfied with the results so far. "You still resist. Perhaps you are not truly a pawn and this was actually a trick! Well, pawn or not, you will still serve me, harbinger! I will have—"

The black light suddenly shifted direction.

Its new target was the Prince of Shadows.

The narrow but powerful beam caught the shadow master full in the chest just as it earlier had Dutchman. The Darkling howled and the tendrils shivered and weaved wildly as if no longer under his control. They swung Maia about without care. The ones holding Dutchman abruptly withdrew.

He fell to the ground, again aggravating his leg wound. Try as he might, Dutchman could not immediately rise. Instead, he could only watch as the Darkling continued to howl and the shadows dragged Maia back and forth.

"Finally I've done it!" roared a triumphant voice. "Finally after following you around like some whipped dog, I've turned things around! You're mine now, *friend* Darkling!"

August de Fortunato. He had been more or less forgotten by both Dutchman and the Darkling. Why not? The Darkling had drained the renegade of his power. Yet, loss had not affected the renegade's cunning and now it seemed he had some knowledge of the workings of the Darkling's sanctum. De Fortunato had probably been secretly studying his erstwhile ally's works since first they had joined forces.

"You've shown me your precious machine time and time again, always assuming it was beyond my control, but I am August de Fortunato! I've known how to use it for some time now, but you had too many other secrets I desired! Well, you've left me no choice now! Now *I* control the situation, your highness! Now your secrets and those of the ship will be mine!"

He still does not understand about the ship. Why would he? Maia's father had not been privy to the knowledge passed between Dutchman and their captor. It was doubtful that he would have believed even the truth.

Straining, the battered exile finally managed to raise himself. A moan from nearby informed Dutchman that Gilbrin had finally stirred. As for the Roschach, they seemed in a panic. Some of them scuttled off into the light, possibly with the intent of hunting down August de Fortunato, but Dutchman did not care. All that mattered was trying to rescue Maia.

He had barely taken a step when the Darkling's sanctum suddenly transformed into . . . if it was possible . . . greater madness.

It was yet the greatest instability this variant had suffered. The distortions were stronger, affecting everything and everyone. The Roschach became a variety of twisted, doughlike blots, truly more like the inkblots they were often called by de Fortunato and the others. Gilbrin struggled to rise on pin-thin legs, but his arms and torso had bloated up, making him resemble the Roschach.

Dutchman himself had suffered less of a transformation than he would have expected. His arms, legs, and torso had stretched out, but he was still fairly agile.

Maia was surprisingly untouched, but what held her now was an even greater horror. The Darkling and his shadows had become a sea of black tentacles thrashing in every direction, heedless of what they might encounter. One Roschach too close was assaulted by a pair of the tentacles and simply ceased to be. In the midst of the tangle of limbs, the Darkling, wide and squat, shivered uncontrollably, the black beam fixed on the center of his chest. He could not seem to escape and the only reason Dutchman could think of for that was that the Prince of Shadows still needed to keep his sanctum secure from the *Despair*. The shadowy prince was utilizing his power to its utmost to defend many different fronts.

To its utmost? It was the Darkling's power, though, that was responsible for the deterioration of whatever world he visited. This meant that the more that power was utilized, the swifter and greater was the deterioration. If pushed too much, it was possible that the death of the Darkling would fully unleash the devilish energy within . . . and end the life of this variant while the wanderer and his friends were still trapped in it.

Dutchman wondered if this time he and the Scattered Ones would survive. There were too many questions now, too many uncertainties. At least he had to save Maia.

The tendrils held her out of reach, though. Each time he managed to get near, they moved her away again. Maia was too entangled to be of any assistance and the power of the Darkling's shadows prevented her from using her own al-

ready weakened powers. As with Dutchman, de Fortunato had
drained her too much.

Gilbrin had finally managed to stand. He looked at Maia,
then at Dutchman, and finally turned around. The last Dutchman saw of the Shifter, he was racing in the direction some of
the Roschach had gone moments before . . . Roschach that
had probably been hunting August de Fortunato. Dutchman
was not disappointed that Gilbrin had not come to aid him;
stopping de Fortunato was more important. It was quickly becoming clear that the longer the Darkling remained a victim
of his own device, the shorter this Earth had, for in his pain
the black figure was releasing his power randomly.

If he could not rescue Maia directly, only one thing remained for Dutchman to do. He had to push the Darkling free
of the black light. A part of him rebelled at the thought, the
part that wanted the shadowy monster to suffer for all those
whose deaths he had caused.

He had only to look at Maia to make up his mind.

Dutchman braced himself, then jumped upward, trying to
seize hold of his former captor. A tendril moved, possibly
aware of his presence, and batted him away. He crashed to the
floor again, each ache tenfold worse.

The black light vanished.

The Darkling ceased screaming. His shadows drooped, but
the sinister figure was not dead. He was not even unconscious, although it was clear that he was very disoriented. The
Prince of Shadows sank lower.

Whether it was Gilbrin or the Roschach who had finally
stopped August de Fortunato, Dutchman did not care. Now at
last he could reach Maia. The Darkling was recovering
slowly. Maia had already taken advantage, freeing one arm
and at last removing the limp, nearly solid shadows from
around her throat.

She looked up in relief as he joined her, but said nothing.
Both of them knew that they stood a better chance of succeeding if they did not garner the Darkling's immediate attention. The ancient wanderer pulled free yet another tendril.

Their master might be free of his deadly device, but the distortions caused by his uncontrolled bursts of power still ran rampant. However, while this was certainly an advantage when it came to Maia's rescue, it was quite possible that the present wave would never end, instead continuing to build in intensity until the Earth collapsed.

They had all but Maia's arm free when the tendrils abruptly stiffened and moved with slow but renewed purpose. One seized Dutchman's leg, but he kicked at it and it retreated. Unfortunately, several more sought to take its place.

"I am at the end of my goodwill, harbinger!" snapped the Prince of Shadows. He leaned back, so far, in fact, that his own shadows had to support him. The black field that had surrounded all but the dead-white eye was now a dark gray near the center of the chest. The gray slowly turned black again, but while outwardly the Darkling seemed renewed, he was clearly still suffering the effects of the attack. This did not make him harmless, of course.

"Maia, stand as far back from me as you can!" Without waiting, Dutchman seized the one shadow still holding on to her. Summoning what will he could, he burned the shadow as he would have burned a Roschach. It should not have been as easy and would *not* have been if not for the distortion wave.

The shadow *did* burn and burned well. With a shout of anger, the Darkling retrieved the tendril, which crumbled to ash wherever Dutchman had touched it. The wanderer did not hesitate, throwing Maia farther back. Compared to the Darkling, any danger from the Roschach was almost negligible.

Shadows seized Dutchman again. The Darkling pulled him nearer.

"It is long past time that you were punished for your transgression, harbinger! You and yours have dared harm my personage! There is no greater crime!"

"Except perhaps causing the death of world after world!" countered the exile. He conserved his strength as much as he could. When the Darkling drew him near enough, Dutchman planned one last counterblow. If it was not effective, then all would finally be lost.

"That some must die to preserve my precious existence is a necessity!" The shadows gathered, every tendril focused on the black prince's adversary. "Your death . . . that will also be a much-delayed pleasure!"

At that moment, a violent crackle of energy caused the Prince of Shadows to whirl around.

The bow of a vast sailing ship emerged through the brilliance of his domain. Either because of the strain placed upon him or the distortions caused by that strain, the *Despair* had finally been able to pierce the Darkling's weakened barrier. Now, at last, she was coming for the one that she had truly hunted for so very long.

"No . . ." The dark figure's voice was little more than a whisper. "No . . ." Suddenly the fear was replaced by cold calculation. He turned to what remained of his legion and called, "To me, my children! Join as one! Let what I have granted return!"

The Roschach moved toward their master. The Darkling's shadows swelled. He raised Dutchman high into the air, but completely ignored Maia. The Roschach moved closer until the nearest of them stood just beyond the touch of their master's tendrils.

The shadows reached out and located each of the hunters. With each touch, a Roschach crumbled to ash, which in turn dissipated to nothing. In one breath, what had remained of the Roschach host ceased to be.

However, the Darkling's sacrifice of his minions had not been without reason, for, as he had done with August de Fortunato, the Prince of Shadows drew in their power to add to his own depleted reserves. Suddenly the ghost ship slowed, then came to a halt. The *Despair* paused only a few short yards from her prey. Dutchman could almost feel her frustration.

"Impudent creatures!" The Prince of Shadows lifted Dutchman high, more in control of his abilities now even despite the increasing distortion. "She wants a passenger, then she shall have her tried and familiar companion!"

He tried to throw the exile at the *Despair*, but Dutchman gripped tight the thickened tendrils. Without the distortion, his hands would have slipped clean through, but thanks to the chaos that the Darkling's own power caused, the shadows were still as solid as rubber.

A rope ladder dropped from the side of the spectral craft and quickly snaked forward, seeking, it seemed, the Darkling Prince. Dutchman watched it come, but there was nothing he could do to avoid it. If he released his adversary, the shadow master might also escape the *Despair*.

Someone shouted. Dutchman realized that it was Maia. He prayed that she would not try to help him. If she did, then this time she would surely share his fate.

The rope ladder touched the Darkling.

They're gone! Maia thought in disbelief. *They're both gone!*

Not only were Dutchman and the monstrous Prince of Shadows gone, but so, she saw, was the *Despair*. The ghost ship must have vanished the moment it had secured both men . . . but why would it have taken Dutchman when it was clear that it had actually wanted the shadow master? *It's not fair! He does not deserve to go on suffering like that! He deserves to be free at last!*

A tremor reminded her just what it meant to be free on this world. The distortions were increasing at an alarming rate.

Ahead of her, the gap made by the ship was still open. The broken window and the waning night beyond seemed to beckon to her. Maia rose and, fighting both the unstable floor and her own distorted form, wended her way to the window. Only as she neared it did she feel the wind, which nearly threatened to pull her out. Maia stumbled to the side of the pane and gazed outside. The city was beginning to stir . . . which meant that someone would be along soon enough to in-

vestigate the rain of glass . . . but otherwise the night was just
as it had been before the chaos. Maia looked up—

High above, barely within her range of sight, she saw the
ghost ship.

It rocked back and forth as if thrown about in a tempest.
She knew little about the mysterious vessel, but she suspected
that this was not normal. The *Despair* was struggling against
a powerful force, and that force had to be the Darkling. He
was not yet subdued. This meant that Dutchman was still in
danger.

She could do nothing to help him. She could do nothing but
watch.

A distorted reflection in the glass caught her attention.
Maia turned, relieved to have at least Gilbrin to turn to at this
time. Perhaps *he* would have a solution.

The slap caught her across the face with such force that she
might have fallen through the broken pane if her attacker had
not seized her arm and pulled her back into the collapsing
sanctum.

Maia looked up into the beaten features of her father. Blood
trickled down one side of his head.

"Didn't I teach you to pay attention to things, darling
daughter?" He slapped her again. "I've need of you now. You
obey or it'll be the worse for you."

Through the painful haze, she managed to remember that
August was without much of his power. However, power or
not, she suspected that her hated father was not bluffing now.

"You've got a choice, girl," de Fortunato continued, grab-
bing her by the hair. "You come with me and you might live.
You refuse or play any tricks and I feed you to them."

"Them" were two Roschach with pincers for hands, possibly the only Roschach remaining. They had to have been part
of the small group that had gone after her father. . . . How had
August, with no strength, not only kept them from killing
him, but turned them into his servants as well?

"The choice is yours, Maia, sweet." August de Fortunato
smiled. "Oh, yes. I should mention that your old lover was of-

fered the same choice. He chose the wrong way." Maia's father snapped his fingers.

A Roschach raised one claw. Part of Gilbrin's shirt hung from the point.

It was covered with blood.

19. FINAL CHOICES

Gilbrin dead and Dutchman lost.

Gilbrin dead and Dutchman lost . . .

"How dare you? How dare you!" Maia shouted. She slammed a fist into her father's chest, using anger to power her attack. August de Fortunato flew backward until a wall, an *office* wall, put a harsh end to his journey. The wall winked into existence where the renegade struck it, then out again as he slipped to the floor. Where he landed, the illumination of the Darkling's sanctum gave way to carpeting.

"Don't just stand there, you overgrown stains!" de Fortunato cried. "If you want your master back, she's the only way we can do it!"

The Roschach scuttled apart, trying to flank her. Anger still fueled Maia, though, anger focused more on the loss of the weather-worn, somber traveler than even on loyal Gilbrin. She did not try to reason out her emotions; all that mattered was that she could unleash her anger without regret.

"I have had all I can stand of you," Maia quietly told the Roschach. "You do not belong here; you never did."

One of the monsters thrust a claw toward her. Instead of ducking as it no doubt expected, she seized the claw and concentrated. The Roschach's appendage burst into flame.

Her pleasure at the triumph nearly cost her, for now the other Roschach attacked. The claws had vanished, the mon-

ster's appendages now tentacles that slithered around her feet
and pulled tight. Maia fell and the Roschach tried to leap upon
her.

"No!" She thrust both hands into the air, wanting only to
keep the horrific thing from enveloping her.

Miniature lightning played over the Roschach as her palms
touched it. The creature froze, quivering and hissing. The
lightning continued to play over it and the Roschach seemed
to burn away, growing smaller and smaller until at last nothing remained but a blot of black tar that slipped from her
hands onto the floor.

A heavy shoe caught her in the side. Maia grunted in pain.

"You're being a very disobedient girl, daughter! I don't like
that!" August looked to his side. "You're still functioning!
Shed that disgusting mess of an arm and pick her up!"

The other Roschach . . . I didn't kill it. . . . She tried to roll
to a sitting position, but the agony that flared in her side prevented her. Maia felt that she had once more failed to stand up
to her father. Somehow, he always escaped from the fate he
deserved.

The shadow of the Roschach draped over her. It was a wonder it could move, considering the chaos, but move it did. One
clawed appendage reached toward her.

An explosion shook the already unstable area. The
Roschach hissed as it was flung over Maia by the force of that
explosion. It went crashing through the shattered pane beyond
her. The hiss turned to a dwindling howl as the monster plummeted earthward.

"You're out of pawns, dear August!" a familiar voice
called. "Time to concede!"

"Gil?"

Suddenly de Fortunato's arm snaked around her throat. She
was pulled to her feet. Maia heard a clicking sound, then felt
cold metal just under her jaw.

"That'll be far enough, clown! In this lifetime, I learned to
handle a blade by the time I was nine and when I remembered
myself, I was able to add a few flourishes from past lives. I

could do some very interesting carving before you managed anything."

"What are you going to do, August? You've got little power left to you. It's really just a matter of time."

"Oh, you're right about that, clown, but not in the way you think. I know enough about this place to do more than reverse what his infernal majesty did to me."

"Are you blind?" Gilbrin looked incredulous. He extended one arm to indicate the collapsing domain of the Darkling. "His little kingdom is collapsing, August! This *whole world* is probably collapsing!"

"Not yet! Not yet!" Maia felt the blade scrape lightly against her throat as her father grew more upset. "It can't until I'm ready! I have to make sure that I can leap!"

The Darkling took more from him than just his power! It should have given her some satisfaction that he might die with this world, but the blade reminded her that there was much he could do before then.

"The End can't be far away," Gilbrin remarked almost good-naturedly. "Maybe just a few minutes. Maia and I can wait, August. We'll be going on. You probably won't. The Darkling's pretty thorough."

"I'll peel her skin off bit by bit if you don't obey me."

The Shifter shook his head. "Won't do, dear August. Maia would understand, wouldn't you, sweet? The suffering might be bad for a little bit, but then you'd be rid of him forever."

He did not try to link, possibly because her father still had the ability to do the same. She thought that she read him correctly, that he was bluffing. If it came to it, though, Maia prayed that she would be strong enough to outlast August's evil.

"I understand, Gil. It'll be worth it to see him finally die."

"Shut up!" She felt him quiver. The knife moved away slightly.

In her head, Maia heard Gil call out, *Now, sweet! You're his daughter, remember? He taught you, remember?*

She gave no response, simply acted. Maia counted not

only on her father's certainty that she could never be a true danger to him, but also on the fact that his concentration was shaky. She swung her elbow back as hard as she could, aiming for the area that August himself had taught her was the most vulnerable.

He gave a gasp of surprise and pain as her elbow dug into his groin. Maia seized his knife arm and twisted, causing her father to drop the blade. She then used both hands to pull with all her might, throwing him over her.

He landed on his back and she leaped on top of him, ready to throttle the life out of the man who had murdered her mother and betrayed so many others to the Darkling's terror. August looked up at her with surprise and perhaps even a little fear at last. He tried to throw her off, but she had him pinned well, another useful part of the very thorough training he had given her during her original life.

"No more deaths, August! No more lives lost to your insanity! Even if this world ends and we end with it, I'll have the satisfaction of knowing you finally suffered the way so many others did, . . . *father*."

"Maia! Easy!" Gilbrin started toward her.

She hesitated, hearing the fear and concern in his voice. She realized that Gilbrin was worried that she would act on her threat . . . and in the process truly become her father's child. Maia had always fought hard to retain her humanity, something August had lost long, long ago.

August de Fortunato used her hesitation to his advantage. He pushed hard, flipping her off of him before she could recover, then kicking her even farther back. He seized the blade again and leaned over his daughter.

Maia looked into her father's eyes and read her death in them. Images of her mother flashed in her mind.

She gritted her teeth, her fear gone. Using her power, Maia sent a tremendous jolt of energy through her father. He screamed and dropped the knife.

"Damn you!" August cried.

The moment he lost control of the knife, Maia slipped one

leg up and, once more utilizing his training, pushed him up and away. August fell backward. Maia tried to rise, but her efforts had left her momentarily drained.

She heard her father briefly cry out in anguish.

Gilbrin was there beside her, helping her to her feet. "Are you all right, Maia, sweet? I didn't dare do anything when you two were so entangled."

She could have asked him the same question. Only now did she see the bruises and the blood and that his shirtless torso was a legion of scars, some of which were still bleeding slightly. *No wonder August said he was dead.* "Are you all right, Gil?"

"As best as can be expected, the way I look and feel."

"August—"

"He's not going to hurt you or anyone else again." Gilbrin raised her up so that she could see.

De Forunato lay on his back some distance away, arms curled over his chest like a dead roach. His eyes stared at the ceiling. Blood pooled under his head and chest.

"What happened?"

"I think he fell on some shards of glass that dropped inside. Pierced his neck and maybe his back, too."

She studied the corpse, surprised to find that she felt some remorse for his death. Unbidden came a few memories of good times and caring. The gift of a small pet. A fatherly hug. Maia pushed them away, though, by recalling many, many more times when it had been shameful to be the daughter of August de Fortunato. The shame and horror vastly outweighed the regrets. "I don't see how the glass shards could have landed at such angles."

"Doesn't matter much at this point, does it, sweet? He's dead and that's that."

There was something in his tone that hinted that perhaps more than providence had been at work. Maia did not press. If Gilbrin had played a part in August's death, he had done so to save her from having to kill her father herself.

She took one last glance at August. How disappointed he

would have been, to know how he had died. Her father had always seen himself going out in a blaze of glory, no doubt a thousand dead enemies at his feet. *Sorry to let you down, August.*

The Darkling's sanctum was quickly fading away. Already there was more of the empty office visible than what remained of the brilliant illumination. The disturbances had not abated, though. There was still something terribly wrong with the world. The End was approaching fast.

The entire room shook and a crackle of energy raced through. Blue lightning sought each remaining fragment of the Darkling's luminous abode, absorbing all traces until nothing remained but a ravaged yet still very mundane office. That and August's crumpled form.

Even *Philo's* body was missing. . . .

"What the hell was that?" Gilbrin gasped.

They looked at each other, both trying hard to control their concern. Maia quietly replied, "The Darkling is still fighting back. He's gathering his power . . ." she shivered, but not out of fear for herself, ". . . and there's nothing we can do."

The *Despair* struggled in the sky. It was clear to Dutchman that she sought desperately to leave this variant, but some force held her back.

That force was the Prince of Shadows.

He stood on the deck, arms outstretched, still drawing in power from somewhere. The Darkling was clearly under strain, but he was by no means near defeat, unless Dutchman dared to interfere. Exhausted as he was, though, what could he do? Nothing seemed to slow the black figure for long . . . not even the *Despair*.

"I will not be imprisoned! I will bow to no power! Those who sent you are long dead and you shall find me your new master!"

The Darkling was speaking to the ship. More amazing, it seemed that the ship was responding, although Dutchman could hear nothing. Then images poured into his mind, images that he thought might be the same as the ones that the shadow master witnessed.

He saw a creature that ruled all with a fist of bloody iron. Entire lands, entire peoples, were swept away simply for trying to make life bearable for themselves. Dutchman witnessed the history of a man, a man whose face was ever shadow to him, who delved into any and all mysteries that might enhance his power, regardless of the cost.

It was the history of the Darkling Prince.

With more and more opposition rising despite his efforts to crush such, the Darkling finally came upon the ultimate force, a force so alien that by manipulating it he ended up ripping apart the fabric of his world. Yet that same force enabled him to do what no others could. He made a leap, a desperate one to be sure, into that very realm from which the power had come. From there he had been forced to wait until reality, seeking to heal itself, brought into being an entire new universe.

Whether there was a God or Gods was not clear. It was clear only that the universe insisted on remaking itself every time his entrance into it caused it to fall apart again.

Unknown to him, however, others had studied his work while he still played with it. They knew that there was no saving their variant, but they could not allow him to escape punishment. His crimes had been too great. So they had been more cautious, creating a thing that could, unlike the Darkling, manipulate itself to adjust to any new universe. They had not wanted their creation to destroy more worlds in the course of hunting down the monster who had ruled them. Unfortunately, that meant taking more time to design their hunter, time they had not had. Their creation, what Dutchman now knew as the *Despair*, had been forced to depart unfinished. Had the Darkling's foes been able to complete her as planned, he would have stood no chance of escape.

"Spare me your list of crimes, your condemnations!" the Darkling interrupted. "I am born to rule! You will obey, not command, where *this* captain is concerned!"

This was not the same creature who had once ruled so much, Dutchman now knew. There had been more sanity, if no less evil, in the mind of the Darkling who had commanded an empire. The constant journeys, the constant fleeing from what he himself had caused, had twisted the Prince of Shadows into something that lived far beyond the brink of madness.

A drawn-out groan made Dutchman look around. A different sort of madness was taking place. The ship suffered as if caught up in the coming collapse. Sails kept shrinking, then growing. The rails appeared to be trying to enclose the deck and the wood flashed brightly every other moment. The bow of the *Despair* was squat and practically pointed upward. It was as if the ghostly craft was trying to close in on itself with its pair of passengers caught in between.

Thunder rolled. Dutchman glanced up and saw that the clear sky had suddenly given way to storm clouds, massive black and purple giants, moving in from all sides. He had seen such before. They presaged the End of a world.

Exhaustion and some little fear had held him back, but he could hesitate no longer. More and more it appeared that the Prince of Shadows was not only defying the will of the *Despair*, but was actually coming near to breaking her. If the ship became his to control, no world, no reality, would ever be free of the Darkling's rule.

A worse fate he could not imagine.

Lightning illuminated the heavens as he raced toward the Darkling, who was still occupied with subduing the living prison. Dutchman prayed that the shadow master's attention would remain fixed long enough on his task to prevent him from noticing the new threat until it was too late.

The Darkling started to look in his direction, but then the ship took a fortunate lurch, not only upsetting the shadow master's footing, but also regaining his attention. Dutchman seized the Prince of Shadows, fully expecting to be attacked by the tendrils. The Darkling's tendrils were surprisingly slow, though, enabling him to get a good grip on their master.

"You will not give in to the inevitable, will you? I must dispose of you once and for all if I am to get anything else accomplished!" Now the shadows moved to pull him away, but Dutchman's desperate hold was strong. The Darkling could not dislodge him no matter how hard his tendrils pulled.

As they fought, the form of the *Despair* went through stunning changes. Sails shrank. The rail rose up on each side until it formed a huge skeletal cage. Now the ghost ship *did* glow . . . in much the same way as the Darkling's sanctum had.

The strain of fighting against both the shadows and their master began to prove too great. Dutchman felt his grip slipping. He was weak, but one notion occurred to him. How much force he could put behind the blow he did not know, but if any power was left to him, there was one spot on the Darkling that might prove vulnerable enough. It was only a hope, but at the moment he had little else with which to work.

He struck the Prince of Shadows in his single, pale eye, putting not only physical strength into it, but all the power he could muster.

The black figure shrieked and, more by accident than design, flung Dutchman away. The wanderer crashed into the door that led to the cabins, the force stunning him. His adversary paid him no mind. The Darkling continued to shriek, both hands covering the injured orb. His shadows darted madly, completely uncontrolled. The ship rocked back and forth and beyond its confines the storm clouds roared.

There's not much time left, captain.

It was the quiet voice of Philo . . . in his head. The mariner looked around, but there was no sign of the animatron. Then Dutchman recalled his destruction in the Darkling's sanctum. There was no more Philo. He was but one more ghost to add to those that haunted the exile's mind.

You must listen, captain, the voice said with more urgency. He could not recall Philo ever sounding so emotional. *I am the ship and she is me, captain. It's been that way since almost the time you brought me aboard. It's why you were allowed to drag a poor piece of salvage aboard, and why you even thought to do so. She felt bad, she did, captain. You were her only beacon, though. You had his touch on you, the taint of his power. That power calls to itself. She used you to track him, but he always escaped port before she could blow him out of the water. He never even knew she was there.*

The Darkling had ceased shrieking, but he appeared to be blinded, at least temporarily. His shadows snaked around, seizing everything they touched. Dutchman knew that they were hunting him.

This world hasn't much time, captain. He's coming. The Maelstrom. He's nearly here now and if he's allowed to stay long, it'll definitely be the end of this port of call. He's a part of it, too, the only way that she can make her way from place to place, but he was even quicker put together by the poor fools. Don't let him stay long if you care for this world and these folks. . . . There might not be another port after this. Our lady Despair *will do what she has to now that she's got this one almost in her grip, even if it means dangerous waters for all of us.*

"Philo . . ." Dutchman eyed the violent sky. "Philo . . . I don't think I can do anything more."

You've got mates, captain. Call 'em. The scurvy knave can't stand against you all—

The animatron's voice faded out as the Darkling suddenly rose. The Prince of Shadows slowly looked around, finally sighting his quarry. His eye was no longer dead white; it was a fiery, streaked red.

"You . . . *hurt* . . . me." The shadows rose like serpents about to strike. The lone eye narrowed. "You will be my way out of this."

Dutchman had no idea what the Darkling meant. He pushed open the door and hurried through. The shadow master would be close behind, but Dutchman knew the interior of the ship well. What he hoped to do below, the exile could not say. Stall the inevitable, he supposed. Dutchman kept thinking about what the voice . . . Philo's voice . . . had said, but his mind was still addled and things that no doubt should have made perfect sense made no sense at all.

He ran past the cabins, heading straight to the steps leading down to the hold. *To think I so often desired to embrace death and now I run from its personification.* Maia had done much to change his attitude.

A crashing sound from above warned him that he was closely pursued. "You cannot escape your just punishment!" echoed the voice of the Darkling.

Dutchman made his way into the depths of the ghost ship, marveling for the first time in ages that so much detail had gone into the shape she had worn for him all these years. The exile realized that his prison had tried to make him *comfortable* in her own way. She had taken on a form with which he was familiar. It was his own distraught, guilt-ridden mind that had caused subtle shifts in that form, creating a vessel that looked as if it had haunted, not sailed, the sea.

As he entered the deepest part of the hold, lights flickered on, the *Despair* illuminating his immediate path. Behind him, other flames were suddenly snuffed out.

Above him he heard more crashing as the Darkling evidently abused the ship in his search for Dutchman. *Why does she accept it? Why does she allow him to harm her so?* Did not all this damage weaken her further?

"This is a futile gesture," called the Darkling. "Come and take your punishment, friend Dutchman. I will be cruel but swift, I promise you."

Such promises Dutchman could do without, but he did agree with the Prince of Shadows on one thing. *Running is futile. I must do something.*

Dutchman leaned against the wall, trying to recoup his strength. To his surprise, a glow surrounded his hand. He pulled it away, then touched the wall again. The glow spread, rushing out from where his fingers and palm touched the wall to cover an area nearly as large as himself.

Dutchman felt strength rushing into him, strength and something more. He suddenly saw Maia standing in one of the cabins, her hand touching a wall that glowed as this one did. It immediately became clear to him that this was some actual event that had happened when she had been aboard earlier. The room around Maia had turned into a gleaming chamber and the woman had stared at it as if listening to someone. The *Despair* had been trying to communicate with her, but why tell him this information now?

His thoughts turned to Maia. She was still on the variant, far from him. . . .

And there's nothing we can do.

Once more he pulled his hand away. That voice had been Maia's. Why would the *Despair* . . . it *had* to have been her doing . . . force him to hear her voice when she was now lost to him?

What was it the voice of Philo suggested?

Almost it came to him . . . but, unfortunately, the Darkling came sooner.

Beams cracked. Boards shattered. Dim light filled the hold. From a gaping hole above, the shadows of the Darkling reached down to seize the trapped exile.

The Prince of Shadows only pulled him up. Then the pair rose higher, the tendrils smashing an opening for captor and captive. Still the *Despair* allowed the black figure to injure her further. She had to be conserving herself for something.

When they reached the deck, Dutchman saw that the cage-like structure had vanished. The ship had again reverted to what it had always looked like. This was not a hopeful sign. *The Darkling is overcoming her . . . and me.*

Even with her sacrifice of strength, he was not strong enough to overcome the Darkling. Perhaps with the aid of the others, he could have defeated the madman, but—

Others . . . Now he understood. First Philo's voice, then the *Despair* herself, had tried to tell him. Maia was the key. *Could it work?* He had not even considered it, so accustomed was he to having only himself to count on, but he and the Scattered Ones, especially Maia, could link their minds and power together. Even August de Fortunato had proved how effective such an act could be.

Dutchman concentrated. The ship had given him back some strength. Perhaps it would be enough. . . .

He was thrown onto the deck, tendrils curling around each limb and now his throat as well. His concentration broke.

"I will not waste effort, harbinger. I could crush you, snap your neck, or tear you apart. It would have been interesting to see how long you survived, since it appears your stamina is remarkable." The Prince of Shadows rubbed his chin. "However, one fascinating notion does come to mind." The storm clouds roared again. Lightning darted just beyond the bow of the *Despair*, but the Darkling seemed unimpressed by the fierce weather. "Yes, I think that this will allow me the smallest expenditure of energy while still supplying me with much satisfaction."

The shadows lifted Dutchman up and carried him toward the rail.

Dutchman knew he had little hope left. He had to reach Maia now.

The shadow master evidently took his action for fear. He laughed and added, "You should leave your eyes open on the way down. The view will be spectacular, I think."

For a breath, it appeared that he had failed. Then, he heard Maia respond, *Dutchman?*

He could almost see her. She stood in one of the elevators of the building. Gilbrin was with her, a fortuitous discovery. Dutchman immediately added the wiry young man to his summons. Both refugees quickly strengthened the link.

Where are you? asked the Shifter.

Maia! Gilbrin! Please listen! What we did with your father, Maia! Will you do it again now? The link! I need your strength! I need— His concentration shook as the Darkling raised him over the rail and held him over the city.

Carim! Maia cried. Through him, she saw what the Prince of Shadows intended. *Gil! My hand!*

Dutchman saw the two take hold of each other.

"No words?" queried the Darkling, seeming disappointed. "No urgent pleading for me to grant you clemency?" The shadows began to loosen. "Perhaps you will change your mind on the way down."

Dutchman! Open yourself completely to us! Gilbrin shouted in his head. The words resounded so much that the wanderer did not even notice when the Darkling released him.

The city of Chicago filled his view, growing larger and larger so quickly that he nearly forgot he was falling, so morbidly fascinating was the tableau. The buildings seemed to sprout upward, as if racing to meet him.

Dutchman wondered what it would be like to finally, permanently, die.

A herculean wind pulled him to the side, altering his direction so swiftly that at first he did not understand what was happening. Only when he began to *rise* again did Dutchman realize that the ship was retrieving him, just as it had whenever he had early on leaped from the rail in order to escape his cursed fate.

He rose over the rail, his momentum increasing. Peering over the other side was his foe. As he flew over the deck, Dutchman realized that his course could not be happenstance; it would send him directly into the back of the mad tyrant.

Maia and Gilbrin knew what he wanted the moment he thought of it. Both refugees were weary, their own struggle with de Fortunato having taken a great toll, but they gave what strength they had.

It was barely in time. Something made the Darkling turn from the rail, but perhaps because he did not expect the sight, Dutchman's soaring form did not register until it was too late. The two collided.

Only the shadows of the Darkling kept both men from falling over the rail . . . which would have served no purpose, for the *Despair* would certainly have brought them both back. Dutchman immediately seized both wrists of the shadow master and spread them apart. The tendrils themselves were a threat, but it was the Darkling that he had to deal with, regardless of any other danger.

Through him, Maia and Gilbrin also attacked.

"What . . . are . . . you?" was all that the Darkling could gasp. Then the combined power of the three, amplified perhaps by the ship's effort as well, coursed around both men, but mostly the black figure. However, Dutchman sought not to combat the forces enshrouding the Prince of Shadows, but rather to cut him off from any link to further power. For such strength as the Darkling wielded, he would have to be constantly replenishing from whatever source he used. No creature born of this world or any other should have been able to survive the containment of such forces. To Dutchman, that could only mean that the black field that surrounded him, the black field that included even the shadows as part of it, had to be what allowed his adversary to continue to stand when others would have fallen. It was the field that empowered the Darkling to create the destruction and terror he did.

Dutchman knew that he could not completely sever the monstrous creature from his power, but he was certain that if he could weaken the Darkling sufficiently, the ship could do the rest. Now the skeletal cage created from the connecting rails made sense. It had been the beginning of a sort of master containment field. The *Despair* had sought to do the same as Dutchman had, but the Darkling had been too powerful then. The ship needed Dutchman's aid.

"Release . . . me . . . and your . . . death . . . will be . . . nearly swift!"

"I . . . will . . . not." Dutchman strained against the strong counterforces the Prince of Shadows threw back at him. Only Maia's and Gilbrin's added might enabled him to withstand his adversary's assaults, but for how long? The Darkling was slowly weakening as Dutchman's efforts blocked much of his link to his foul power, but the pace was too slow.

Then a rumble shook the ship. The wind picked up to such

a fantastic rate that the exile nearly lost his grip. Despite the battle, he looked up, knowing what he would see.

A black and crimson chasm was opening in the stormy sky. Everything within immediate range of it was drawn toward it.

"The Maelstrom," he whispered . . . then screamed as his lapse in concentration allowed the Darkling to recover somewhat. The shadow master struck hard and it was only through sheer will that Dutchman did not lose control.

He felt Maia and Gilbrin weaken. His error had put the three of them on the defensive now. Philo's haunting words came back to him. The Maelstrom by itself was power enough to destroy this world. The longer it existed here, the worse the damage would become until finally reality itself collapsed . . . and the animatron had laid hints that this might be the last variant.

They needed to add strength. Had Hamman Tarriqa lived, he would have been a valuable ally, but the black man was dead and there was no one else . . . or was there?

It was a desperate gamble and meant opening the three of them to even greater assaults by the Darkling, but he believed that it was possibly the answer.

Maia, he called in his thoughts. *Maia, reach through me. Call all those you know and have them call all they know. Link with them through me as quickly as they can. Remember how you touched other minds, far away. The Scattered Ones must* all *link if we can hope to do this. You can do it. You are stronger than your father ever was. I know that. I have felt it.*

She understood what he wanted but was understandably doubtful of its realization. Nonetheless, the dark-haired woman did as he asked.

Sensing their growing weakness, the Darkling pushed forward. "You were . . . given . . . every chance to obey. I will kill you slowly now . . . and through . . . you . . . I will kill your companions."

Dutchman and Gilbrin did what they could, putting all their strength to defense rather than offense. They slowed the shadow master, but could not completely blunt his on-slaught. The conclusion to the battle was inevitable if Maia failed.

Sweat coursed down Dutchman's weathered visage. The roar of the storm had now given way to the roar of the Mael-strom, which continued to swell. What the humans below made of such a sight, Dutchman did not know. Soon such ponderings would not matter, for there would be no Earth at all.

Seconds passed and still only the faintest hint of Maia. No one else. Then her call suddenly grew stronger. It was not only her call, though, but the call of others, such as the male known as Mendessonn and a woman named Ursuline. Others joined and as each one did, their names, times, and very per-sonalities became known to Dutchman. There were warriors, artists, hunters, lovers, priests . . . the Scattered Ones encom-passed all shapes, colors, and lives.

Maia had reached the others through him, had told them who it was they faced. The word spread as only the Scattered Ones could spread it. Those who had never even heard of the Flying Dutchman still knew of the Prince of Shadows. To fi-nally be free of him was worth any sacrifice. Every one of the refugees had lost a friend or loved one when their world had perished and many had lost others to the sinister parasite since then.

Against such a suddenly raised but determined host, the Darkling struck a wall of steel. Dutchman sensed his abrupt confusion, then his growing uncertainty as the wanderer fo-cused the bitterness, the anger, and the demand for justice from each Scattered One against the field that served the Darkling.

The Darkling attempted one last great incursion against his revitalized foes. The shadows wrapped one after another around Dutchman's throat. If the Darkling could not strangle the exile, he evidently intended to tear off his adversary's head.

Dutchman was certain that the shadow master would succeed, too, but then one by one the shadows began to release him, *fading* as they did so. In rapid succession, each tendril dissipated. For the first time, Dutchman felt as if he fought only a man and not some supernatural creature.

However, the Darkling was not helpless. It was all Dutchman could do to keep a grip on his foe. Not only was the black figure strong, he was quick and agile. Twice he nearly escaped.

In the end, however, the Darkling could not fight the combined fury of the Scattered Ones. His power continued to dwindle. Dutchman's guess had been correct: Cut off from his foul source of energy by the forces focused through Dutchman, the Prince of Shadows . . . who was no longer master of any shadows . . . could make use only of his reserves. Those were nearly gone. With the power of the Scattered Ones, Dutchman had created a nearly impenetrable wall around the Darkling and his field. By itself, it could not forever prevent the dark tyrant from replenishing himself, but the *Despair* was already acting. The Darkling was doomed.

"You are done causing death, great prince," Dutchman declared with more satisfaction than he could have imagined. "No more worlds have to die for you just so you can live to kill. No more."

The ship was already transforming. This time the Darkling's might was not an impediment. The cage re-formed. A shimmering light spread across the deck, eliminating all traces of wood in the process. The light spread throughout the rest of the vessel, which now bore very little resemblance to a sailing ship.

"Release me! I command you!" snarled Dutchman's opponent.

The link that Dutchman had forged with Maia and the other refugees began to falter.

Maia grew faint. *Dutchman! You're fading away!*

It did not take him long to understand why. The same force

that the ship used to shield the Darkling from his source of power was cutting off the wanderer from his allies.

"You *fool!*" snapped the black figure. "You fool! Trap me and you trap yourself!"

Dutch—Maia's voice cut off. Coincidentally, the glow had finally encompassed the entire prison.

He *had* trapped himself . . . but then, once aboard the *Despair*, he had expected never to return to this variant. He and the ship had been together for so long that it could be no other way. She did not give up so easily what she considered hers.

The Maelstrom filled the sky before them, roaring in eternal hunger. The living prison turned so that she would enter the vast chasm dead center. Dutchman wanted her to move swiftly, both to prevent any chance of the Darkling escaping and to keep the Maelstrom from destroying this Earth, but he also suspected that when she departed the world this time, it would be never to return. There was no reason for her to ever bring the Darkling back . . . or Dutchman.

But Maia would be safe . . . Maia . . . Gilbrin . . . an entire world and more . . .

It was worth the cost to him.

He stared at the swelling Maelstrom. This time, the *Despair* did not hesitate but rather sped forward, eager finally to complete her age-old quest.

When he knew that it was safe to do so, Dutchman released the Darkling. The once-terrible tyrant now looked smaller. He was more than a hand's width shorter than the exile. Only the shadows had made him appear so very tall.

There was another change. The field that now covered most of the Darkling was not so dark. It was gray now, as if it was failing.

"There's *still* time! Together we can—"

"Together we can begin the journey of a lifetime." Dutchman walked toward the bow. The Maelstrom was a fantastic sight and for the first time in his existence, he could admire it properly. At this point, the Darkling was no more a concern.

It would likely be the last time that he ever saw the Maelstrom . . . or anything other than the ship and his fellow passenger . . . but Dutchman still managed to smile.

20. NEW WORLD

The world was safe. The distortions ceased and the moment the ship vanished through the awful chasm in the sky, the weather returned to normal. There was no way that the incidents of that night could be erased from the minds of the people, but no one would ever connect either Maia or Gilbrin to them.

This variant ... this world ... our world now ... is safe, Maia thought as she and Gil walked slowly through the brutally awakened city. The sun was just rising. Many people were on their way to work as if nothing had happened. Truly it took much to shake the majority from their routines. There would be those who would suffer some memory, especially those with some power of their own, but before long things would be more or less forgotten.

Even the Scattered Ones, now forced to one world and one life, would recover. There were those who had grumbled about their present lives, but each of them had lived many, many others. No one was that terribly put out, especially now that the Darkling was gone. That alone made any life worth living.

Maia, however, did not find the world so perfect.

The Darkling was gone ... but so was Dutchman. *It isn't fair. He of all of us deserved to be free. He of all of us was the greatest victim of the Darkling.*

"I'm sorry, sweet," Gilbrin whispered. Both were clad in outfits identical to what they had worn earlier. Gil had pointed out that it would not look good if they wandered about the city in the rags left over from the struggle and so he had taken it upon himself to replace them. "It wasn't very fair of the universe, taking him away like that, I mean."

"No, it wasn't. It shouldn't have happened." She had known Dutchman only a short time, less than she had known Hamman, but the exile had touched her in a different way. Maia would mourn the black man, but her sense of loss went deeper, for a variety of reasons, when she thought of the one-time scientist and mariner. She did not know what would have happened, but she would have liked to find out.

"Looks to be a beautiful day in the neighborhood," the Shifter commented with a musical touch in his tone. "Nice day for a drive . . . if I still had a car. I wonder where it is now?"

Despite herself, she could not help smiling briefly. Gil could always make her smile even at the worst of times. There was just something about him. That was why she had loved him for a time and still did now, although not the way she had long ago.

They were all in for some changes. Now they would begin to grow old, this time for the last time. Maia actually looked forward to that. Immortality, even as peculiar an immortality as they had acquired, had its points, but Maia wanted desperately to be mortal now. Most of the other refugees felt the same way. There was nothing she could do for the ones who did not. This was not the perfect world, but then, neither had any of the others been. She was fortunate, having been born in this time and place.

Fortunate . . . except that Dutchman was lost forever.

How long they had been walking, she could not say. Perhaps Gil knew, but to Maia the trek had been an emotional blur. She knew only that they were walking westward and now the Chicago River greeted them again. The weary woman paused before the bridge, for some reason almost afraid to cross. That was nonsense, though . . . there was no reason to fear the bridge or the river.

No reason to welcome it, either.

"Something the matter, Maia?"

Nothing that can ever be fixed. For Gil's sake, she shook her head. "No, nothing. Let's walk some more."

They started across the bridge. Midway, Maia had a sudden and uncontrollable urge to peer over the rail just as she had before meeting Philo. She stepped away from Gil and did exactly that, staring down at the green, murky water. The distorted shapes of many buildings wriggled below, but in the reflected heavens there floated no massive sailing ship.

Gilbrin's sandy-haired head appeared next to hers in the water. "Trying to find a fish in that murk?"

Both of them knew what she searched for. Maia finally sighed, then straightened. Her gaze returned to the path ahead.

A cloaked figure stood on the other side of the bridge, a bewildered look on his weathered face.

"I don't know what to—" her companion started, but then he too caught sight of the hatless figure. "Carim's blood! Miracles *do* happen. . . ."

If he said anything else, Maia did not hear him. She was already nearly to Dutchman, who stared at her as if finally recognizing who she was.

Maia embraced him, then, overwhelmed by his astonishing return, she kissed him. By the time she finished, Gilbrin had caught up.

"Maia . . ." Dutchman whispered. Then his gaze finally shifted to the other refugee. "Gilbrin."

"You're here!" She could not believe it. It had to be a dream. "You're here!"

"She let me go . . . she let me go. . . ." Dutchman himself seemed not to believe it. "We entered the Maelstrom, the chasm that you saw. Things grew chaotic. We were tossed about. I expected the ship to tear apart as she always did, but this time she did not. I was certain that there was no return, but then, as we fell into the depths of the giant, the ship exploded into blinding light." Dutchman blinked again. "That was all. One minute I could see nothing. It was brighter, more intense, than even the domain of the Darkling had been. The next moment . . . I found myself standing in a street with a compulsion to come to this place."

"And the Darkling?" Gilbrin asked before Maia could say anything.

"Gone . . . with her."

"She let you go. . . ." she finally whispered. "She actually let you go." *And sent him here. Here.*

"That's what he said, Maia, sweet." The Shifter took a few steps away from the couple. "That's what he said."

Maia could scarcely believe it still. "Then . . . you are free. You are *free*."

She felt a shiver run through him and for a moment she was frightened, but then she looked up into his weathered visage and watched as a childlike smile spread slowly across. *"Free . . ."* he whispered, as if understanding the word for the first time in his life. "I am free. . . ."

"And with a whole new world to explore," added Gil. "Places to go, people to get to know . . . well."

"Free . . ." Dutchman repeated yet again. He looked down at her. "Will you help me, Maia de Fortunato? I . . . I do not know if I remember what it's like to live free."

"Of course I'll help you." She had no intention of leaving his side, not now, not ever.

A car honked. The sidewalks had begun to fill with pedestrians. Dutchman's gaze strayed to their mundane doings and Maia was content to enjoy his fascination with his new world. They had time to take things slowly now, time to adapt. They had, in fact, a lifetime to deal with matters, just like every other human being.

It felt strange to realize that . . . strange, yet *wonderful*.

* * *

Dutchman was free. He was free. Maia was with him and now he had a future to look forward to, a future he hoped to share.

He was *free* . . . and that was that, as far as he was concerned.

The Darkling lifted himself up, then froze as he caught sight of his hand. It *was* his hand, pale, almost deathly. The black field that had become a second skin to him was no longer there. It no longer covered *any* portion of his body. Instead, a gray, form-fitting garment covered him from head to toe. It was, he belatedly realized, the same garment he had worn before creating the black field.

Slowly he became aware of his surroundings. A serviceable but otherwise inelegant cabin. There was a bed, which he now sat upon, and a closet. Little more decorated the room save a light by the cabin door. The closet drew his attention again. He tried to ignore it, but his gaze returned to it despite his best efforts. At last angered, the Darkling rose quickly, throwing open the closet with an urgency that bordered on compulsion. What he expected to find, he did not know, but what he did find filled him with loathing and horror.

The interior of the closet was reflective. He stared into a full-length mirror surface . . . to find staring back at him an ivory-haired, gaunt face with lines etched deep by worlds of destruction and the use of a power that only destroyed, never truly created. The flesh was more pale than the hair, washed out to the point where no color whatsoever remained save for one eye that burned red.

It was a face that the Darkling had thought never to see again and seeing it now made him throw closed the door. He stepped back, unable to accept its revelation.

Beyond the confines of the cabin, someone whistled a merry song that hinted of times on the sea.

The prince who no longer ruled shadows tore open the cabin door and rushed outside.

It was not the cage he had expected. He stood on the gleaming deck of a ship that might have been birthed in the heart of a crystal. The ship glittered no matter where he turned, disorienting him at first. The deck stretched long, so very long, but in width was barely twice his height. Sails stretched out from each side, creating the image of a huge bird in flight. A bird of prey.

The whistling, which had ceased the moment he had stepped out of the cabin, resumed from behind him. The Darkling turned, looking up to where a lone figure stood at the wheel of the ship, whistling the same song again . . . this despite having no lips with which to whistle.

The figure stopped, then slowly turned one huge, painted eye toward him. "Welcome aboard, captain. We've been looking forward to your arrival for some time."

"You!" The Darkling clambered up the steps to the wheel and tried to seize the animatron. However, barely a foot from his intended target, the former tyrant was stopped by an invisible wall. No matter how he battered at it, he could not reach the clockwork man. The power that he had wielded for so many lifetimes was no longer available to him. There was only his physical strength and it was sorely lacking. Exhausted at last, he who had ruled worlds and destroyed universes stepped back in defeat.

Philo calmly stared at him. "Orders, captain?"

"Orders?" The pale figure took a step forward again. "Orders? Turn this thing back! Return me to my rightful world! I command you to do so now!"

The animatron *tsk*ed. "Can't do that, captain. That was the last port of call. We've clear sailing ahead for the rest of the trip."

"Where . . . are we going?"

The animatron appeared to give this consideration, at last replying, "Now that really depends on her . . . the ship, you know, captain. She has a mind of her own. A very determined mind. I can tell you one thing, though. . . ."

He was not at all certain that he wanted to hear the rest of the answer, but something urged him to respond. "Tell . . . tell me."

Philo extended one arm to indicate the vast emptiness surrounding them. "It'll look exactly like this, captain. Exactly like this."

Exactly like . . . The Darkling refused to believe it. "But the next port of call—"

"That was the last one, captain. As I said, clear sailing ahead. . . ." For the first time, a hint of what might have been satisfaction intruded into the mechanical man's tone. "Make yourself at home. The ship's yours at last, just like you wanted, my lord Darkling. Yours forever."

As the conqueror of worlds and the destroyer of universes stared in growing horror, silent now that the full extent of his sentence lay revealed to him, Philo returned to the task of steering. Feeling especially cheerful, he began to whistle another tune.

It was a good day for sailing.

From here on, it always would be.

ABOUT THE AUTHOR

RICHARD A. KNAAK lives in Bartlett, Illinois. Besides the Dragonrealm novels, among which are the titles *Firedrake, Dragon Tome,* and *The Dragon Crown,* he has also been a longtime contributor to the Dragonlance® series, having penned several short stories and two novels including the *New York Times* bestseller *The Legend of Huma* and its sequel *Kaz the Minotaur.* His other works include the Chicago-based fantasies *The King of the Grey,* and *Frostwing.* His next novel, *The Horse King,* coming March 1997 from Warner Aspect, is a return to the Dragonworld. In the future, he plans more fantasy, science fiction, and also mystery. Those interested in finding out more about future projects may write the author care of Warner Books.

Fantasy Books by
Richard A. Knaak

CHILDREN OF THE DRAKE
☐ (0-446-36-153-4, $4.99, USA) ($5.99 Can.)
THE CRYSTAL DRAGON
☐ (0-446-36-432-0, $4.99, USA) ($5.99 Can.)
THE DRAGON CROWN
☐ (0-446-36-464-9, $5.50, USA) ($6.99 Can.)
DUTCHMAN
☐ (0-446-60-151-9, $5.99, USA) ($6.99 Can.)
FIREDRAKE
☐ (0-446-20-940-2, $4.99, USA) ($5.99 Can.)
FROSTWING
☐ (0-446-60-149-7, $5.99, USA) ($6.99 Can.)
ICE DRAGON
☐ (0-446-20-942-9, $5.50, USA) ($6.99 Can.)
THE JANUS MASK
☐ (0-446-60-150-0, $5.99, USA) ($6.99 Can.)
KING OF THE GREY
☐ (0-446-36-463-0, $5.50, USA) ($6.99 Can.)
SHADOW STEED
☐ (0-446-20-967-4, $4.99, USA) ($5.99 Can.)
WOLFHELM
☐ (0-446-20-966-6, $4.99, USA) ($5.99 Can.)

Available at a bookstore near you
from Warner Books.

420-C